EXTREME HEAT WARNING

The Shallow End Gals Trilogy

Book Two

TERESA DUNCAN

MARY HALE

VICKI GRAYBOSCH

LINDA MCGREGOR

KIMBERLY TROUTMAN

See Also
BOOK ONE: "ALCOHOL WAS NOT INVOLVED"

List of Characters at end of Book

A VERY SPECIAL THANKS TO:

SADIE CORBIN

BOB SMITH

MICHAEL SUTHERLAND

SUSAN WEAVER

EXTREME HEAT WARNING

The Shallow End Gals

Book Two

CHAPTER 1

Jeremiah Dumaine was seventy-four years old, a fourth generation swamp man with a tuft of long gray hair, and one blind eye. He had seen a lot in his years of living in the haunting bayous. His cypress clad home had been his grandfathers, and he had helped his own father carve the belly of this boat. These were dark waters tonight... silent...as if life itself was holding its breath. He stood, his bent frame nudging through the thick muggy air, and slowly glided his craft to Mambo's den on the other side of Honey Island.

His eyes moved to the half dead woman in the corner of his boat. Almost didn't see her curled on that cypress root in the swamp. Lucky a gator didn't find her. Mambo would know what to do. He stooped as the draping moss tickled across his boney shoulders, and he listened for the whispers of the marsh. The occasional soft splash of his paddle and the subtle ripples on the water were the only hints he was there. His skin twitched with fear tonight. This was the second woman he had found in his swamp.

Jeremiah secured his boat to a large cypress root at the edge of the swamp near Mambo's den. The dirt path into the marshland was well worn from many visitors. Tiny animal skulls and colorful clumps of feathers tied with thin leather straps adorned the low branches of shrub trees. Where the path met the green iridescent crust that cloaked the black water edge, the swamp gasses bubbled and occasionally released tiny spurts of blue flame.

Scientists had explained the phenomenon as decomposing organic material mixing with the stagnant swamp waters, creating methane that would ignite and create a pop like sound. That didn't explain the concentrated pockets of activity. In spite of the efforts of numerous research teams, this mystery of the swamp remained impossible to duplicate in a lab. The scientists were left with unproven theories.

Nights like tonight, the blue haze from the gasses made the wings on flying insects appear florescent and the huge webs of the cypress spiders glow blue. Jeremiah didn't care what the scientists' thought. He knew that in all his years in the swamp, the most flames were at Mambo's. The eerie blue glow surrounding her hut could be seen for miles at night. Any fool could see the Spirits lived here.

Jeremiah had come to Mambo last month when he had found the first woman in the swamp.

Mambo had taken her in and brought her back to health. Instead of leaving, the woman had stayed to help the aging Mambo in her daily chores. Mambo had named her Heeshia, meaning 'chosen one.'

The path to reach Mambo was narrow and overgrown. If you didn't know where her hut was, you would never see it. Her hut had been built in the center of a large clump of gnarled cypress trees. Decades ago moss and wetland shrubs had enveloped the entire structure except for a small chimney opening in the roof. The cypress clad door was covered in moss, and piles of offerings were scattered at the threshold.

Believers brought staples and gifts for the gods in exchange for potions and amulets. They wanted Mambo's blessings and protection and believed in her abilities to summon the Saints. Mambo was the recognized Voodoo Queen of the faithful.

Jeremiah helped the woman he had just found out of his boat, and he wondered what Mambo would say. He didn't know what else to do.

Heeshia met him at the door and helped him walk the woman over to a cot in the corner of the large main room. Mambo was sitting on the floor in front of a small open fire pit throwing pinches of powder into the flames and chanting softly. The powder would briefly ignite and shoot colorful flashes of light that danced around the walls casting shadows from unseen sources. Her large dark eyes followed them across the room, and then she slowly stood. "Heeshia, bring our guests food." Mambo sat on the edge of the cot and put the woman's hands inside her own, "You are protected here."

The young woman burst into tears and Mambo stroked her hair, "You have seen evil and survived. We will build from that." Mambo slowly walked back to her place in the center of the room and lowered her crippled body to the floor. She had her arms held up over her head and was chanting loudly. Then she closed her eyes and began swaying to a softer chant. She slowly lowered her arms, crossed herself, and began a slow rocking motion. She looked so frail. No one really knew how old she was. She had always been described as an old woman, even when Jeremiah was a boy.

Jeremiah went outside and cut firewood for Mambo's stack. He filled a water bucket from the rain cistern and carried supplies he had purchased to Mambo's little porch. Heeshia stepped outside to speak to him. Her long black hair was pulled loosely back from her face, and she was wearing clothes that probably had once belonged to a man. Her boots were worn, and she had made a belt of rope. Even in the middle of the swamp she was a striking beauty.

"I need to leave here now. Mambo will need to help the new one. Did you find her, like you found me?" Jeremiah nodded. Heeshia said, "Dangerous men are bringing women to this swamp, to die. I am strong enough now to stop them. Can you take me to the city tomorrow?"

Jeremiah looked at her lean body and wondered how she could stop the evil that had come to his swamp. He started to speak, then saw something in her lavender blue eyes that was very powerful, almost hypnotic. It was as if her eyes had tiny pulsating points of light behind them. Jeremiah was instantly reminded of a story his grandfather had told him. A band of Polish warriors came to Haiti on the orders of Napoleon, but they soon changed affections and helped the Haitian people win their revolution against the French Army. A few descendants of these folk legends could still be found in rare blue-eyed Haitians.

Almost exclusively women, Voodoo lore professed them to have special warrior skills. They were believed to be cherished by the Saints, *messengers* of Erzulie Dantor, sometimes called 'Black Madonna'. A female warrior spirit and fierce protector of women and children. Jeremiah was quite certain Heeshia was a blue-eyed Haitian. Mambo named her the chosen one. Jeremiah would not question the wisdom of the Spirits.

He nodded respectfully to Heeshia, and slowly walked back to where his boat was tied to the shore. He pushed his long paddle against the tall swamp grasses and quietly steered his craft into the open black water towards home. Heeshia stood at the swamp's edge and watched his boat slowly glide away. He could see her form fading in the blue haze, yet he could still see those eyes.

Jeremiah had a plan. He had a large stash of mink furs and alligator skins he would take to the city tonight to get money for Heeshia and buy more supplies for Mambo. He would also purchase ammunition for his guns. Jeremiah didn't like guns, but evil had come to his swamp.

A single frigid breeze whipped around his shoulders and vanished. Jeremiah shuddered as the icy sensation trickled down his spine. He looked around for some source of the sudden chill. It was unseasonal, unexplained. The moon peeked from behind the dark clouds and offered a brief display of diamonds sparkling on the black water. Sounds of wildlife rose from the marsh like an orchestra warming for a performance. The long grasses rustled and began to dance near the shore from invisible trespassers. The swamp was coming alive again.

With traffic, Supervisory Special Agent Roger Dance had an hour drive from the Indianapolis courthouse to the Indianapolis FBI Center. Memories of the last year blasted through his mind. The hunt to catch Devon and Patterson had taken its toll. A full year for the case to come to trial. Just last evening there had been an "After Party" at the PUB celebrating Devon's first day of trial. Everyone involved in the case was back in the area as witnesses for the prosecution.

Roger's mood turned even more somber. This new development with the Devon/Patterson case meant Paul and he would be thrown into that hell again. He entered the FBI Headquarters in Indianapolis and asked to meet with SSA Dan Thor, Senior Agent for the Operation Center. Agent Thor appeared, greeted Roger, and walked him to his office. Once inside, Thor sat heavily in his chair and exhaled, "Damn bad luck there, Roger. How bad is it?"

Roger relayed what he knew about Devon's escape and what he thought had probably happened. He ended with, "Paul is on his way to the prison now with two agents to interview prison staff and secure film."

Thor rubbed the back of his neck and shook his head, "You are one of the few people who will understand when I say, I just want this done." Thor stood and ran his fingers through his dark blonde hair and massaged his temples. He turned to Roger, "I am spent. I have been a year dealing with the families of these victims, and to find out we only have half a case now...'til we catch Devon again. You know what they call us here? The Death Squad." Thor returned to his seat and dropped his hands on the file covered desk. His expression was etched with despair. He was empty.

Roger was taken aback by Thor's confession. This case had broken him. Thor had a well-earned nasty reputation at the bureau, and few friends. Roger assumed Thor counted him as a friend, or he would not have said what he did. He thought for a minute and asked, "How much help have you had from that young Agent Nelson out of

St. Joseph, Michigan? I had him make the Patterson arrest. I assumed the bureau would let you keep him until this thing was over."

Agent Thor threw his hands up, "That's another damn thing. Good kid! Damn bureau thinks he doesn't have enough experience, and they haven't let him stay on the case! I think it's because he's good, and St. Joe didn't want to lose him. Now it sounds like we have lost Devon? It's going to make the Patterson side of this a lot harder to hold together."

Roger was nodding. He knew Thor wasn't getting the whole picture yet. "You know that Patterson is probably gone too?" Roger leaned back in his chair and waited for the eruption.

Thor answered, "Nahhh! I heard they were testing his DNA to be sure, but…" Thor didn't like the expression on Roger's face, he leaned forward with a menacing scowl, "you think he's gone too?"

Roger nodded, "Seven months gone. Look Dan, I believe this was a well-orchestrated plan they had in place long before we caught them. They paid for some very good help to pull this off. I think we have two impersonators, and Devon and Patterson have been gone for seven months."

Thor couldn't even speak. A moment passed. Roger knew that look. Thor couldn't do it. Roger said, "Why don't I call the Director and see if I can't pull in a few favors to get Nelson back on this. I still have Paul, and maybe you could take a backseat role for the kid. Keep some of the bullshit off him." Roger saw the first glimmer of hope in Thor's eyes.

"I would owe you forever," Thor said. Roger held the highest designation an agent could obtain and had been offered a position as Deputy Director and refused. He liked field work and abhorred the politics of law enforcement. Dan Thor was sure Roger could arrange anything he wanted.

Roger asked, "Regardless of how Patterson shakes out, I need a place to work, probably room for at least five agents on and off. We have to open this Devon/Patterson case again. Can you house me?"

"I got everything ready the minute I heard what happened in court this morning. I'll walk you to your wing."

As they walked down the hall, Roger asked, "Do you remember my cat...the black cat?"

Thor laughed, "I don't care if you want a mountain lion here if it helps you get the job done!" Roger smiled, he was hoping to have his cat back.

Kim had heard the news about the trial and was pacing across her living room. Every channel on the television flashed 'Breaking News'. This can't be happening. She was worried about Roger and Paul. They will have to catch Devon all over again. Just then her phone rang with "Help me Rhonda", her mom's ring tone. "Mom? Hi! I haven't talked to you in a long time." Kim plopped on her recliner smiling.

I answered, "We have been in some serious crazy training. I think Ellen is trying to kill us off! *Again.* Right now we are at a biker convention in Nevada, of all things."

Kim laughed, "How are Linda, Mary and Teresa doing?"

I answered, "Other than having to dance with drunken bikers and learn how to move mortals against their will, fine." It was wonderful to hear her laugh again. "Ellen asked if you would call Roger and see if he wants our help again."

Kim was serious now and said, "I'm worried about Roger and Paul, Mom."

"I know. I am too."

✻ ✻ ✻

Roger smiled at his caller ID, "I have been sitting here hoping you would call."

Kim laughed, "Because you missed my lovely voice or because you hoped that mom was asking about you?"

Roger chuckled, "Both actually."

Kim said, "I enjoyed last night at the PUB. I'm sorry it went from a celebration to *this*!"

Roger was nervously clicking his pen and said, "No shit! Has your mom called?" He was holding his breath for the right answer.

Kim laughed, he was so transparent. "You could at least pretend to want to talk to me! Yes, she called and asked if you wanted their help. They are training at a biker convention. She says they should be ready soon. Ellen can help you right away."

Roger was laughing, "Did you say a biker convention?"

Kim answered, "Yup. Don't see it, do you?" Roger realized the only time he seemed happy was when he was talking to Kim. So it was set. He would have his gals again. Maybe there was hope after all. They talked a few minutes, and Roger asked Kim to let Ellen know he really needed her and the gals.

Roger dialed the Director of the FBI. This would be one of the most important calls of his career. He hadn't spoken to anyone at the Bureau since the news broke at trial, just two hours ago. Roger had been very careful to keep the Director involved in this case since it started. It was always a high profile case and now the media feeding frenzy was at full force. The Director listened carefully to him, asked a few questions, and asked Roger for his gut feeling on where the case would go. Roger confessed he was worried. He felt this time would be even nastier. It was apparent Devon and Patterson had some very influential friends helping them.

The Director had just finished the paperwork for Roger and Paul's commendations on their work last year on the Devon / Patterson case. It wasn't their fault these guys escaped, but right now the whole system looked bad. The Director needed Roger to have every advantage possible if this was going to turn around.

Roger hung up and just stared at the phone for a minute. The Director had just made him lead, nationally, on this case. It was the most powerful designation that could be bestowed on an agent, and could only be issued by the Director. It also meant that Roger could utilize any resources of the FBI without prior approval. Roger only knew of one other time an agent had National Authority. The Director said he would issue the bulletin immediately.

Roger walked down to Thor's office to tell him he could have Agent Todd Nelson. Thor was staring at his computer screen. He turned around to look at Roger. "Holy shit! The only time I ever heard of them doing this was Dillinger!"

Roger smiled, "I was thinking that too. The release is already out?"

"Yeah, do I get my boy?"

Roger smiled, "Call him. Whatever else you want, make a list. You think about what role you want in this and just let me know. I don't need any explanations, and I don't want to interfere with the demands of this office."

SSA Dan Thor thanked Roger and watched him leave his office. They had both been serving the agency over twenty years. Both had started in their early twenties. Thor felt a great deal of respect for Roger. He knew that Roger was taking on the world right now, and needed all the help he could get. Yet he was willing to let him bow out for free. Roger was the kind of agent Thor had hoped to become. "Class act," Thor said as he lifted the phone to call district and get Special Agent Nelson.

CHAPTER 2

James Devon was having a really good day. He felt almost giddy. He was getting ready to leave for a late lunch with William. He checked his image in the mirror. New nose, a little more chin, actually good looking. A hell of a lot better than it used to be. I should have done this years ago. He moved his face closer to the bathroom mirror. You could barely see the fine scars from his surgeries.

His mom's voice was in his head, "You understand you are an ugly boy, right? You will never have a pretty girl. Such an ugly, ugly boy." People had said she was the most beautiful woman in town. At her funeral, many were surprised she had a son, especially an ugly son. The thought she had spawned the likes of him was her life's greatest curse. She hid him in boarding schools and summer camps.

When he killed her, he made sure there was no skin left on that pretty face. He began his private chant of "Pretty Mommy, Ugly Boy!" as he walked toward the front door to leave. He put on his special surgical gloves. Ordered them by the hundreds. He told people he had severe skin allergies on his hands. The FBI had his prints and DNA now. He needed to be careful. His mother had been wrong. He could have all the 'Pretty Girls' he wanted. He took them and used them up. They never looked so pretty when they realized they were about to die. He laughed out loud at those precious memories. He guessed that by now his murder count had to be nearing fifty.

He established a second identity about five years ago, primarily to hide himself and his money in the event law enforcement got near him. His new name was Attorney Michael Parker, a semi-retired, licensed lawyer. This state didn't fingerprint attorneys. He still based his clientele on the elderly, mostly because it was so easy. He had respect in the neighborhood, the French Quarter in New Orleans.

After all of the trouble in Indiana last year he was lucky he and William had contracted a professional to plan their escapes. It had been expensive but worth it. Now he could do whatever he wanted, to whomever he wanted, and it seldom even made the newspapers. The crime in New Orleans was so bad, the citizens were calling for the National Guard to be brought in; *Murder Capital of the United*

States. He smiled in the foyer mirror as he curled his lips and checked his teeth. He blended in so well.

* * *

SSA Paul Casey was interviewing the guards who had been assigned to Devon from December, when he was arrested, to February 15th. According to Devon's defense attorney, he had first met Daniel Warren, thinking it was Devon, at the prison on February 15th. The attorney had been commissioned by a Florida firm to represent Devon. He had received large monthly payments for doing so. He claimed the first he knew his client wasn't James Devon was in the courtroom today.

Paul had called in two other agents to help him, Supervisory Special Agent Simon Frost, a veteran of about fifteen years and Special Agent Pablo Manigat, a relatively new agent transferred from New York. All three agents were present and taking notes for each of the guard interviews. According to the Warden, two guards were within sight of Devon at all times.

During the interviews, the agents discovered the guards became convinced Devon was a very passive, solitary personality. He seldom even spoke. They assumed Devon had just accepted his fate or was totally detached from reality. He spent all day, every day, in the law library researching his defense, presumably looking for some miraculous loophole. The guards eventually took to reading while they watched him. They all stated that now, in hindsight, Devon had played them. He had bored them into a relaxed security environment.

Devon had not had any contact with the other prisoners and only began receiving visitors when he decided to retain council in February. According to prison records, there had been two visits by attorneys to Devon between February 13th and 15th. Both visits were within the view of security cameras.

Paul called the DA's office to see if they had agreed to do the deal with Daniel Warren, the Devon double. The District Attorney couldn't take his call, was in a meeting, and would call Paul later. Paul expected this to be the difficult part, dealing with the personalities. Everyone would be in overdrive to cover their collective asses. Paul decided to call Roger about the DA deal. When he reached him, he found out about Roger's new classification. "Whoa, I am impressed! Do I have to bow to his highness now?"

Roger made a faint chuckle sound, "Yeah, right."

Paul started, "Well, maybe *you* can do something about getting us this Warren guy. No one is taking my calls."

Roger said he would call the Director. He was still unsure about how far his boundaries really went. The Director made it clear Roger would have anything he wanted. Within minutes the State Attorney General contacted Roger and assured him the deal with Daniel Warren would be signed, and Warren would be made available to the FBI immediately. Roger thanked him and requested Warren be transported to the Indy office.

Roger called Paul, "Daniel Warren is going to be prepared for immediate delivery to our office here."

Paul laughed, "I'll go back to the courthouse and supervise the transport."

Roger added, "And Paul, we are going to have the gals soon."

Paul exhaled loudly, "Praise the Lord!"

Mathew Core was what they called a 'Fixer'. Ex-military, his business started as a private contractor with the Department of Defense and the CIA functioning as an Independent Information and Action Source. What that really meant was he provided the government with plausible deniability, a highly valued asset, for all kinds of nasty jobs. One of Mathew's key contacts was Jason Sims, who had been the top CIA computer forensic genius. He had actually been one of the key designers of what the CIA lovingly referred to as super-frame. The heart of the CIA computer system.

Jason had been injured in an auto accident and had convinced the CIA to allow him an early disability retirement. He had claimed his memory just wasn't there anymore. In reality, Jason and Mathew had devised a plan for Mathew to continue to work with the government and also begin a very lucrative business with Jason. This allowed them undetected access to the government's computers, and thanks to Jason, access to the highest level of sensitive information.

When Carl called with the assignment to do the job for William Patterson and James Devon, Mathew's initial reaction was to decline. He wasn't really interested in helping some murderer and a pervert escape federal prison. He preferred assignments that were a little more international. Carl's assignments always meant big money, so Jason verified William Patterson and James Devon were worth hundreds of millions between them. Suddenly the job seemed more attractive.

Jason and Mathew had established second identities for Devon and Patterson and had established both domestic and offshore banking accounts for them. The bulk of monies belonging to Devon and Patterson were safely concealed from any government searches. Jason had established a clearing account that laundered any transactions from those accounts. Jason had hard programmed snoopers that could follow any transaction that cleared the Federal Reserve, including offshore wires.

Carl notified Mathew that William Patterson was worried he and Devon would be arrested soon. Mathew put the first part of the escape plan into effect. He had used the facial recognition software of the Department of Corrections and Military data bases to locate eight candidates each as potential doubles for Devon and Patterson. Next, he profiled the eight candidates until he had narrowed it down to three each. Those six were presented with the initial proposal, twenty thousand dollars good faith money, and the promise of a million dollars each when they got out of jail. Of course there was the threat that if they spoke of the plan to anyone, they would be killed.

Mathew had the homes, cars, and cell phones of each of the candidates bugged. He assigned his men to stay close. Four of the six broke the rules and were killed, along with the people they told. Those gruesome photos solidified the commitment of the remaining two to the project. Daniel Warren would replace James Devon in prison within two months of his arrest and Guy Johnson would replace William Patterson. That part of the plan went perfectly.

The second part of the plan was to kill the imposters, Warren and Johnson, once the trials began and their true identities were discovered. Mathew estimated confirming the true identities of Warren and Johnson would take at least a couple of days after the initial trial exposure. He had a man at the courthouse already. A neat and clean end to the job. With the impersonators dead, there was no link back to Mathew's organization.

Mathew Core's phone rang, "I got Johnson. Warren's gone. Already in transport to the Indy FBI Building. What do you want me to do?" Mathew hesitated. How did they move so fast? It had only been hours. He needed a minute to think. Mark killed Patterson's double already and Devon's double was in transport. Mathew didn't know how so much red tape had been cut so fast, but it didn't matter. This could be a suicide mission and Mark Mills, his sniper, was one of his best men. Mathew had been careful that Warren and Johnson knew little about him and his operation, but there was only one way to be *sure.*

"Get a spot at the south garage door at the Indy FBI Center. That's where they bring in transport. They probably won't be expecting anything. Jason will block their communications temporarily. You may have time. Mark, be careful. If you can't leave clean, don't do it."

Ellen manifested herself into a black cat and went looking for Roger's office. She found Roger in a hall talking to some other agents. He saw her, picked her up and said, "There's my girl! Where have you been?" Ellen winked at him, and he knew to get to a phone. Roger excused himself, went to his office, and put Ellen on his desk. "Do you want me to call Kim?" Ellen winked and turned on the TV in Roger's office. He was dialing and watching the TV at the same time. The screen showed a black SUV weaving through traffic at a greater speed than the surrounding cars. He glanced at Ellen, this probably wasn't good.

Kim answered on the first ring, "Roger? Oh my Gosh! Ellen just called, there's a sniper heading toward your office that is going to shoot some guy named Daniel Warren!"

Roger's eyes got big as he looked at the TV and then to Ellen. "Is that the sniper?" Ellen winked. Roger said, "Thanks Kim," and hung up.

He dialed Paul, "Casey."

Roger told him about Ellen's tip and that he was watching the sniper on his TV. Roger asked Paul, "Where are you?"

Paul answered, "In the transport van with Warren about ten minutes away." Roger could tell that the black SUV was about to enter the downtown district. Roger told Paul he would call back.

Roger knew he couldn't let anyone else see what he was watching on the TV, but he needed Thor's help getting manpower to catch the sniper. He looked at Ellen and said, "Can I buy a little time?" Ellen winked and the Black SUV started pulling hard in traffic and veered to the shoulder. It had blown a tire. The man in the SUV was moving like a NASCAR pit man changing the tire. "Thanks Ellen." Roger called Paul, "Get here fast.

He has a blown tire. That will buy us maybe seven minutes. Come in the main garage. Not the transport. I'll have security waiting for you." He looked up. The TV was blank, and Ellen was gone.

He buzzed Agent Dan Thor's office, "I just had a reliable tip that a sniper is on his way here to kill Warren, Devon's imposter. We have *minutes* at best. Paul is in the transport van with him and will be using the main garage. I want to catch this guy." Thor was shocked but dialed his tactical team to meet in the conference room stat. Roger beat Thor there.

The captain of the tactical team was showing Roger the map of the transport area and a map of the surrounding buildings. "Depending on how good this guy is, there are several spots we have identified as most likely places he will set up."

Roger asked, "If you were new to the area and pressed for time how would you do it?"

The captain rubbed his chin, "No doubt, from a car."

Roger looked at the captain, "I want him alive." They decided to put every available man at street level and in the parking lot. They chose a secured frequency and arranged for a dummy transport van to take the place of Paul. All eyes were waiting for someone to pull into the immediate area.

*"Black SUV...facing North...just parked on Capital Ave...one guy....Got it....our feet on sidewalk....*Roger was listening to communications with Thor, inside the garage bay.... *Eye on transport van....moving*

toward Garage…SUV has rifle…. Back door of transport van opening …some muffled noises….we have a gun to the back of his head….his hands are up…subject in custody."

SSA Dan Thor stared at Roger with one eyebrow raised, "That was some damn tip."

Just then Roger's phone rang, "Dance."

The voice on the other end said, "I don't know if you got my earlier message or not. I have been trying to reach you. Patterson's trial double, stand-in, whatever you want to call him, Guy Johnson, was just killed by a sniper when we were preparing for transport."

Roger said, "Exactly how long ago?"

The voice answered, "It's been about thirty minutes now. I'm sorry Sir, but our communication lines had been compromised. The sniper is gone."

Roger snapped his phone shut and looked at Thor, "That was confirmation Patterson's double died from a sniper shooting thirty minutes ago preparing his transport from here to Virginia."

Thor said, "Oh. Shit." Roger realized he had come very close to having an unexplainable knowledge about events. He was reminded why Kim and Ellen were so careful. This was tricky. Thor scowled, "You haven't been here two hours!" He was shaking his head walking back to his office.

Roger called Paul and told him to put the sniper in interrogation room one and keep Daniel Warren, the imposter, in holding for now.

CHAPTER 3

William Patterson, now known as Bernard Jacobs, was sitting in his drawing room. He was contemplating if he wanted to go through with his lunch meeting with Devon or not. William didn't have the stomach for Devon's killings. Actually didn't have the stomach for Devon, but he knew Devon provided the necessary mindset to keep them free. William also knew Devon had a lot more money than he admitted to. That was okay. He didn't mind kicking in more than his half. After all, it was Devon's insistence for a plan that had gotten them out of jail eight months ago. He still couldn't believe how flawless it had been. William would never live long enough to spend all the money he had anyway. Over thirty years of stealing from trust accounts. What a joke. The government never did find his real money.

After Katrina, William had purchased a beautiful two story home on Burgundy Street only three blocks from the police station. Real estate costs inside the Quarter were outrageous, but it was the only island of safety in the city. Devon had talked him into establishing a second identity in case William's life style choices landed him in trouble. He had completely renovated the house for his eventual retirement home. The title to the property had been in question after Katrina. Many of the records had been lost or had not been prepared well in the first place. It wasn't very hard to get the new title corrected to his alias Bernard Jacobs. Just took a few well-placed dollars.

Establishing a second identity for future use was also easier than he thought. Actually that was how he met Carl. No questions and the job was done. When he began to worry about getting caught in Indiana, it was Carl who took over the details. Having a plan in place for their escape seemed expensive and extreme at the time. It proved to be the best money he ever spent. Now he lived only three blocks from Bourbon Street, the heart of the tourist district, and Royal Street where the wonderful art galleries and antique shops were located. Life was good.

William's thoughts went back to Devon. He decided he might as well go. He had to eat after all, and he had a job for Devon to do. It was just a little pub called Mickey's, a few blocks down the street, nobody he had to impress there. He decided to walk and soak up some of the flavors of the city.

The air hung heavy and smelled of an underlying stench of sour mash, topped with spices and sweets. The sounds of the city pulsated with the yelps of people looking to party. The syncopated rhythms of street music streamed from every dark corner and alley. Like some strange symphony absent a conductor, the cobbled sidewalks pulled the subconscious into the bluesy score that defines New Orleans.

Devon was already sitting in his favorite booth in the back watching the news. The bartender always brought him a remote for the TV when he brought his bourbon. Even though Devon never tipped, he knew William would probably join him and he tipped very well. William walked in and noticed he didn't know anyone there except the staff. He had taken to using a walking cane, that he now used to tip 'hello' to Scotty, his favorite bartender. He didn't need the cane, but he thought it made him look more prestigious. It was also a handy weapon. Today's cane had cost him thirty thousand dollars. Hand carved by some now famous "Tramp Artist" from Louisiana. Very fitting, he thought.

He hung his cane on a hook at the side of the booth and nodded to Devon as he squeezed his big frame into the tight space. "Why don't you sit at a normal table like normal people do?" he asked Devon.

"Maybe I'm not normal?" Devon answered with a sneer. "You'll want to hear this." He pointed the remote at the television and turned the volume up just enough for William to hear.

The news anchor was in Indianapolis, "The sniper shot and killed a Mr. Guy Johnson who authorities have identified as an impersonator of the famous William Patterson. Patterson, facing multiple murder charges was scheduled for his own trial in just a few weeks. He was the first witness for the prosecution in the trial of James Devon, alleged serial killer. Authorities had discovered the true identity of Mr. Guy Johnson after today's stunning announcement in the James Devon trial. The imposter for Patterson, Guy Johnson, claimed the man in the defendant's seat was not James Devon. Authorities said Mr. Johnson was being moved to a secure site for questioning when the sniper attacked."

William was stunned. Devon cracked up at the look on his face. "Oh get over it. You just saved one million dollars."

William whispered, "*Was this the plan all along?*"

Devon smiled, "Of course you fool. Why keep them?"

The bartender brought William his scotch and took their food order. After a moment William asked, "What about your guy?" William noticed a brief look of annoyance on Devon's face.

Devon answered, "I haven't heard anything on that yet."

After their food came William looked at Devon and said, "I have a small favor to ask of you." Devon kept chewing and just raised an eyebrow. William continued, "It seems one of my little friends from a couple of months ago wants to negotiate a settlement. More his parents, I should think. I certainly don't want a child molestation charge right now." Devon just kept chewing. "I want this to go away." William snapped his napkin open and laid it on his lap as he made his announcement.

Devon swallowed and asked. "Permanent go away? Or financial go away?" Then he took another bite of food as he looked at William's face. Weakness, that's what he saw, weakness. He knew William found killing distasteful, and he loved forcing him into it. As sick as it was, William was the closest thing Devon had to a friend, and he was still useful.

William sputtered, "Oh God No! *Financial* go away, of course. Jesus *D....*" he had almost said Devon's last name. *Rule #1.* Don't.

Devon asked, "How financial can this get?"

William thought a moment and said, "Well, you just said I saved a mil, make it a mil?"

Devon thought a moment and said, "Why don't we give the kid half, and I keep half for a retainer. You need to get me five mil for that," as he pointed to the TV.

"Five million dollars? Are you *crazy?*" William hissed. He was sick of Devon's greed.

Devon wiped his chin and said, "The cost of freedom, you know?" He got up, patted William on the shoulder, and said, "Get that family's contact info to me in the morning, and I'll get this done. Wire the money to my account today. All of it." And he left.

William started eating again. Devon wasn't even gentleman enough to wait until they were both finished before he left. *And* he stiffed him for the whole tab. The TV anchor was still talking about the sniper and the belief Patterson and Devon had escaped seven months ago. They were running pictures of them. With Devon's new face and William thirty pounds lighter with some facial hair, it didn't even look like them. The bartender startled William when he asked, "Would you like another scotch Mr. J?" He was still getting used to people calling him by his alias, Bernard Jacobs. William watched the people out on the sidewalk. He also had an eye on a handsome young man who was sitting at the bar.

"Yes, I think that would be nice, Scotty. Get one for my new friend at the bar too." William had noticed the nice looking young man looking his way and lifted his glass as a "Hello."

We were on some hillside looking at shapes the clouds were making. Ellen had told us to entertain ourselves until she finished with some sniper thing. That didn't sound good to me.

Ellen showed up and stretched out on the grass with us, "I have a dilemma." We were all sitting up now looking at her. "Roger and Paul have prisoners at the FBI Center. These prisoners have thoughts that would help Roger figure out how this organization pulled off Devon and Patterson's escapes. I don't have mortal thoughts like you gals do. I am having trouble figuring out how we can get the information to Roger quickly enough. I think *timing* is becoming *crucial.* I could use a little mortal devious thinking here." Everyone pointed to me! I knew I would come in handy.

I wanted to re-state the problem to make sure I understood it right. "Somehow Roger and Paul need to find out what is in these guys' minds. Angel rules say Ellen can't talk to Roger, and there isn't any way to get Kim here fast." I put my finger up in the air to signal I had an idea. "Mortals have these little baby phone thingy's that someone can wear in their ear. What if you tell Kim everything these guys are thinking and she tells Roger, during the interrogations? Kind of like real- time- almost- mind-reading?"

Ellen sat up, "It is like letting Roger read their minds, but technically it is still going through Kim. Sneaky! I like it!" I was so proud I couldn't quit smiling. "We need to get special permission from Granny to go that way." Ellen stood and said "Be right back". She was hardly gone a minute and then she was back. "It's a go! What we need to do now is prep Kim and Roger. Well, do you feel *ready* for this?"

Teresa said, "We're ready!" A *sniper* dude? I am so not ready.

Idea. I offered to go see Kim and make sure she was available and explain what we wanted to do. Ellen said, "Look at the underside of your watch." We all flipped our watches to peek at the under-sides. "Do you see that thing that looks like a clasp bar?" We were all nodding. If you slide that to the left, you automatically record mortal thoughts. Everything Kim is hearing will be recorded. Thoughts are going to come at her fast, and we want to actually 'catch' them. This will work for all of you."

Ellen looked at Mary and Linda, "I need you guys to go to the cell where they are holding Daniel Warren. He was the Devon imposter. Record his thoughts." *Note to self*, much rather visit Kim than go to a prison cell. "When you get there, slide that bar on your watches, and we won't have to worry about missing anything. Teresa, why don't you get a head start with the sniper. Use the bar on your watch, and I will join you when I'm done with Roger."

Teresa said, "Okay," but she looked at us like *Yikes.* I don't think Teresa realizes it yet, but she is definitely our Ninja Angel. Ellen didn't pick her by mistake to be the one listening to the sniper.

CHAPTER 4

Kim was putting on makeup and had her nose about six inches away from her makeup mirror. I wanted to try something, but I had to wait until she finished putting on her eyeliner. As soon as she started with her lipstick I got inside her mirror and said, "Hi!" Kim screamed and her top row of teeth were now colored 'baby pink'. Oops! That didn't go as planned.

Kim screamed, "Get *out* of there! What's *wrong* with you?" I hear that question often enough I should know the answer.

I hopped over to the edge of her bed, and petted her cat Johnny while she finished at her dressing table. Kim looked at me, "I could have poked an eye out!"

I showed the appropriate amount of shock on my face and said, "I waited until you started your lipstick on purpose, so that wouldn't happen."

She was frowning at me, "When did you learn to do that kind of stuff? Just show up inside of *things*?"

I thought about it, "I don't know. This was the first time I tried it. Pretty cool, huh?"

Kim was shaking her head, "I suppose now I am going to have to look at everything I touch."

I had a funny thought, "Yeah, you better look at that Twinkie before you take a bite!"

Kim turned around fast and pointed her finger at me, "Stay out of the food!" Then we both started laughing.

I told her what we were trying to do with Roger. Kim looked thoughtful, "I think I better call work and tell them I might be a little late. It's too bad you have to go through me and can't just let Roger listen to their thoughts directly. I don't mind helping, I just hope I don't translate something wrong." I agreed that would be easier, and I showed her the slide bar on the watch that would catch the thoughts too.

Kim and I made her bed up with fresh sheets and fed the cats while we waited for Ellen to contact us. Kim said, "I can't imagine how hard this would be if I couldn't still see and hear you."

I looked at her and said, "I think that all of the time. It has been a long time since my last visit. How are you adjusting?"

Kim looked at me, her chin quivering. "Some days not so good Mom, but it is getting a little better." I gave her a big hug, and we turned on the TV to some comedy show. My answer to everything was humor.

Ellen was at the FBI Center and had transformed herself back into a black cat. She was sitting in the middle of the wide marble floored hall refusing to budge. People walked around her, and she knew eventually the word would get to Roger that his cat was looking for him. Some people stopped, patted her head, and said, "Nice kitty." She hated that.

Paul and Roger turned a corner when they saw Ellen. Paul asked, "Does this bring back memories or what? Look who wants you," and pointed.

"I might need you there too." They got near Ellen, and she turned and walked them into Roger's office.

Paul whispered, "I feel like I am being led to the principal's office." Ellen looked back at him.

When they were inside, Roger closed the door and Ellen jumped onto his desk and put her paw on his phone. "You want me to call Kim?" Roger asked, and Ellen winked at him.

Paul pushed his chin forward in his nervous twitch, leaned back in his chair, and said, "And here we go."

Roger dialed Kim, and she picked up on the first ring. "Hi there! You are going to love this! Ellen has a plan."

Roger looked at Ellen, "Ellen has a plan, huh?"

Kim said, "Yes, and I think Paul should hear too." Roger told her to wait a minute, while he put the phone on speaker. He did, and Kim continued. "Ellen says she can read the minds of your imposter and your sniper and relay what they are thinking to me. Then through an earpiece, I can tell you what Ellen says they are thinking, while you are doing the interrogations. I guess it would be like tele-mind-reading."

Roger looked at Paul, "You think we can actually do this? I would be hearing what they are thinking?"

Kim said, "Ellen says yes! Isn't that cool? But I have been thinking, wouldn't their thoughts change your questions? Wouldn't other people listening wonder why you were asking certain questions? This could get tricky for you."

Paul said to Roger, "You and I could go in the room together. I would be your witness to the interview, and we could do it in a secured room with no recording devises."

Roger looked at Paul, "I think it would raise too many questions if we asked for a secure room. I almost got into trouble with Thor over this sniper thing already. I think we should just wing it normal, and pray I don't mess up. I know Thor will want to listen in. If I do say something questionable, you'll just have to cover me." Paul nodded.

Kim said, "Ellen is transmitting the thoughts of these guys already to some watch Mom is wearing, and Mom says the sniper guy is planning on suicide by cop as one option. He thinks he's dead now anyway." Roger and Paul looked at each other. This was going to be really tricky.

Paul asked, "How do we get this special earpiece hooked up to you?" He no sooner said it than an earpiece appeared in front of Roger. "Okay, earpiece done." Paul was shaking his head.

Kim said, "In addition to what you hear, somehow I am going to transmit every single word this guy thinks to you, according to Mom, so you will have it for a reference later. How should I get it to you?" Roger and Paul looked at each other and shrugged. Ellen was tapping the computer.

Roger said, "I guess Ellen plans on sending that to my computer. It sounds like I need to do the sniper interview pretty soon?"

Kim answered, "Yes, and Ellen is thinking the sniper knows a lot more than the other one. Can we test that earpiece before you hang up?"

Roger put the earpiece in and asked Kim if she could hear him. "Yes. Loud and clear. Can you hear me?"

Roger answered yes and looked at Ellen, "Should we do this now?" Ellen winked. Roger said, "I guess we're going in Kim."

Roger looked at Paul. "I think I am going to stop at Thor's office first and tell him I am going to use a behavioral specialist for assistance during the interview, to explain this," he was pointing to the earpiece.

Paul said, "Good idea. Should we go in without weapons? "

Roger said, "Why don't you keep your gun and just sit at the far side of the room. We may need it."

Ellen went to the interview to be with Teresa. The sniper in the interrogation room was hand-cuffed and had a vest on that was chained to a large metal ring on the wall. There was maybe five feet of chain from the wall to where he was sitting. He looked a little like Paul, kind of a young Robert Redford look to him. He was extremely muscular with a very intent look on his face and a military posture. Roger looked through the small window in the door. The agent inside the room guarding him was armed and only standing about four feet from him. Way too close. Roger didn't want him to move closer to the sniper when they came in. Roger asked the guard outside the door, "Is there a speaker that goes to this room?"

The guard told him, "Yes." It was in the adja-cent room. Paul went into that room, activated the speaker, told the guard inside the room to move as far as possible from the suspect and then to leave. Roger saw the prisoner's mouth twitch and a hint of disappointment on his face when the guard moved away. They had probably arrived just in time.

Roger and Paul went in, and Paul sat as far from the table as he could. He was armed, but Roger wasn't. Even chained, they knew this guy was trouble. They had run his prints through the military data base and obtained a name of Mark Mills. Roger had a file on his lap, but left it unopened as he laid it on the table. Roger started, "So tell me Mark, how does a decorated marine end up an assassin?"

Mark Mills looked Roger over and thought, *It's the money stupid,* but he said, "I want an attorney."

Roger said "You're not getting an attorney. You were pointing a rifle at federal agents. This is probably linked to terrorists. I think you may be the next visitor at GITMO. What do you think, Paul?" Paul was nodding his head.

Mills: *No attorney…doesn't matter…I'm dead now no matter what.*

Roger said, "Not necessarily."

Mills looked at him, "What?"

Roger said, "You're not necessarily dead now anyway. If you give us information, we can protect you."

Mills: *It will take more than the FBI to protect me from Mathew.*

Roger decided to let that go. "We know you did the assassination on Patterson's double, and we also know the communications of the FBI was compromised."

Mills was laughing on the inside. *Damn right FBI communications were compromised. Jason has the whole* **system** *compromised. You assholes will never catch Jason. He is too good! His computer programs can bring down the Pentagon if he wants to.* Mills said, "I don't know anything about that."

Roger looked at him, "How do you see this ending Mark? We just send you to some prison where you are killed by your friends? Or you escape, and try to *hide* from your friends?"

Mark Mills looked at Roger, *I know how it ends for me. There isn't a damn thing anyone can do.*

Roger said, looking at Paul, "Don't we have some information about Mathew and Jason in here?"

Mills looked like he had been shot with a stun gun! *How do they know about Mathew and Jason? If they really know, the whole thing could come down. Maybe I can get out of this. That explains how they knew I would be here.* Mark Mills laughed, "You'll never get Mathew. He's too smart, and you're bluffing."

Roger leaned toward Mark, "Am I?" Paul was busy taking notes of the conversation and outlining the phrases he thought they would have to "*Explain*". This was a big one, who the hell *were* Mathew and Jason?

Roger said, "I have you. I'm guessing that you should have called Mathew by now to tell him the job was done or had to be compromised. Correct?" Mills didn't say anything. Roger continued, "I can have it all over the news that Daniel Webber in there was killed by a sniper. Take a minute to think about it Mark. You can help us finish up Mathew and Jason and the rest of them. And you live. Your call." Roger signaled to Paul, and they left the room.

Thor was waiting in the observation room. He met Roger and Paul in the hall. Roger quickly excused himself to make a phone call from his office, and Paul stayed to talk to Thor. Roger thought he would get more information from Mark Mill's thoughts by leaving the room for a while.

Thor asked, "Did you guys get some Intel I didn't get? Who the hell are Jason and Mathew?"

Paul was expecting Thor to have that question, "I know Roger has been getting calls all morning, you know, this new designation of his. A lot of people are contacting him that I don't know. I guess he will catch us up when he gets a minute."

Paul shrugged and Thor said, "Sounds like he hit a ball though. That guy is thinkin' about turning. I bet you." Paul laughed to himself. Any lie would make more sense than the truth of how they got the names Jason and Mathew.

Roger was in his office, and Kim was still sending him Mark Mill's thoughts. Roger was taking notes. So far he had learned Jason was in Virginia somewhere, and Jason had once worked for the CIA. Mathew's last name was Core, and he was the leader. Mark was afraid of him and his teammates. Mathew was very careful, and Mark didn't think they could catch him. Mark knew a phone number to reach Jason and had a burn cell for Mathew. The number would expire later today. Jason was also in charge of moving the money, somehow. Mark was trying to think of a story for Mathew that might work. He was considering flipping to the FBI.

Roger was wildly writing down everything Kim was telling him. He needed this information now, and he didn't want to wait for it to appear on his computer. Kim said Ellen got a *visual* of where Mathew might be from Mark Mill's memories and was going to check it out. Roger shook his head, this is amazing. Kim told Roger she was exhausted from talking so fast. He told her he was exhausted from listening and taking notes. Kim took a breath and mentioned that surely they could plan better dates in the future. Roger laughed as he hurriedly kept writing.

When Paul got to Roger's office, Roger started shoving the pages of notes to Paul as Kim dictated them. Paul looked like he was reading a crime novel, flipping each page, his hand out for the new one before Roger could even finish writing. The mood was tense and surreal. They were reading someone's thoughts which was bizarre and felt sneaky.

Suddenly, Ellen was sending Kim Mathew Core's thoughts. She had found him in New Orleans. He was in a building in the French Quarter. Kim gave Roger the address. Mathew was upset Mark hadn't called. Mathew hadn't heard anything yet. He needed to call Jason and warn him. Ellen implanted an information tag from Mathew's computer line to Jason's line. She got a visual and an address on Jason for Roger.

Ellen also implanted a data window for Ray to be able to infiltrate Jason's computers. A special Ellen code. Ellen said Mathew feared Mark had been caught by the FBI, and there wasn't any safe way to get to him. Mathew was sending a data message to Jason they might need to prepare to go underground with operations. Roger told Kim to let info go to the transmitter for a few minutes. He had to go back to Mark Mills. Roger ran down the hall and went into the room where Mills was sitting. He had a handful of papers from Kim's notes and looked intently at Mark. Roger whispered, "Say these two *addresses* out loud, tell me *what* they are, and I will do my best to guarantee your safety."

Mark Mills looked at the addresses, stunned, and looked back at Roger. Mills knew the FBI *had* them. He was shocked. There were so many layers of security built into their operation; he had begun to believe that it could not be penetrated. After all, they had been conducting business in the States for almost ten years and never had a single problem. Mathew Core was very careful, but the FBI knew his name and address! Mark knew he was a dead man if the FBI didn't finish Mathew. He figured he might as well switch to the winning team. At least it might buy him some time.

Mark Mills raised his voice and repeated the addresses as Roger pretended to write them down. Then Mills said, "The New Orleans address is the home base for Mathew Core, and the Virginia address is our computer-money man, Jason Sims."

Roger thanked Mark and left the room. He met Thor in the hall. "How the hell did you get him to give you those addresses?"

Roger just said, "Not *now* Dan. I'll talk to you later." Roger ran back to his office. He called the Director, advised him of the development, and informed him he was ordering full assault teams for both addresses immediately. Then Roger personally put in the call to Special Agent Ray Davis, the FBI computer specialist, instructing him to go immediately to the Virginia address, and wait for the assault team. He was going to be needed on those computers at the moment of transition. Roger didn't want to risk Jason would have one second to send a warning message to Mathew. He also didn't want any gaps in Mathew Core's ability to reach Jason. He needed Mathew to think Jason was safe.

Roger told Thor to arrange the seizure of the Virginia computer lab and the arrest of Jason Sims and tell the assault team to wait for Ray. Agent Simon Frost was given the task of contacting the FBI Center in New Orleans, having Mathew Core's operation seized, and arresting Mathew Core. Then Roger went back to the earpiece. "Kim, I'm back. I'm going to have a heart attack here, but I have covered the two addresses. Are you still hearing from Ellen?"

Kim answered, "Yes, Ellen says Mathew Core is on the phone with someone, right now. He is being warned you are coming! It looks like he plans to leave the building soon." Roger looked at his watch. Kim said, "Ellen also said she was going to do some kind of computer thing to Jason's firewalls, so he can't destroy information. I'm not hearing any more from Ellen right now."

Roger said, "Okay". He relayed some information to Ray, looked at Paul, and said, "I think I covered us knowing these addresses. Mills repeated them for me in exchange for promising him protection."

Paul said, "That might be quite a job, especially if we don't get these other guys."

The wait was excruciating. It was an hour before the teams had been put together and briefed. One team in Virginia to get Jason, and one in New Orleans for Mathew Core. Roger and Paul sorted the notes from Kim and stared at the phone. Paul began to pace. Roger's phone rang. They both jumped. "Dance........Good .... Secure him. Is Ray Davis from IT there now?...Okay. He is the new Jason. We should be getting a lot of good information coming in if Jason didn't have a chance to block it." He looked at Paul, "We got Jason."

They knew Mathew Core would be the real test. The task leader in New Orleans called Roger from location when they were in place. Roger told them to use extreme care; this guy was ex- military and good. Twenty minutes later the task team leader called Roger back. They found escape passages through the basements of the adjoining two buildings. Core's building was secure, but Mathew Core was gone.

* * *

Mathew Core didn't have to go far, so he just waited for them. He had seen them positioning themselves from his security cameras. He laughed. The Feds were so predictable. His motion and weight sensors were carefully placed where only deliberate threats would likely register the alarm lights. He noticed the exit sign on the neighboring building blinking. That meant there was someone on the roof of his building who weighed at least 120 lbs. Also, the bar sign on his building had turned red, meaning someone was in the gated alley to his side door. The cameras showed several dark figures pressed against the brick wall, armed and wearing vests that said FBI. Mathew smiled. It was not hard to disappear in New Orleans, and within ten minutes he was in another safe place. He wasn't worried about getting caught. He logged into his laptop to warn Jason. Ellen made sure Mathew's computer messaged "Temporary Internet Connection Issues" until she was ready.

An hour later, Ellen was still listening to Mathew's thoughts. She had followed him through the basement escape doors and was now with him in a beautiful old Mansion type home on St. Charles Street. Mathew was still worried the FBI would compromise Jason. That data was the heart of his operation. Mathew had grabbed his book of codes and was using a laptop he had stored at this house for future use. Ellen was communicating Mathew's keystrokes and thoughts to Kim who was passing them on to Roger. Roger had Ray on the other line at Jason's desk.

Ray didn't know how Roger was getting his info, but it seemed to be working. Ray was communicating with Mathew, getting instructions for transferring money and sending alerts to the rest of Core's team. He hoped to hell he could figure this out and carry out Core's instructions, or the whole cover would be blown. When Mathew hung up, Ray stayed on the line with Roger. "Holy Shit! Do you realize what I am going to have to do to figure out these things?" Roger said a prayer that Ellen could help somehow. She was on her way.

Mathew Core was grateful Jason was secure. At least he didn't have to worry about that. He still had two guys in the field he could use if needed. He knew Mark had turned. How else did the FBI get his address? At least Mark didn't know much about Jason. Right now Mathew had to make sure things kept running as usual.

Linda and Mary were in with Daniel Warren in the interrogation room, floating near the ceiling. Ellen had asked them to stay with Daniel and record his thoughts, so they could be passed on to Kim and then Roger.

Daniel, it turned out, really didn't have a lot of thoughts. He was actually happy! In his mind the plan had been flawless from the beginning. The

DA accepted Daniel's deal and right now he was in an FBI center instead of prison. The lunch they had brought him had tasted better than the prison food. When he got out, he would be a millionaire! Sweet.

Linda and Mary looked at each other and shook their heads. This guy was clueless. They decided to play cards until Ellen showed up. Not much going on in this mortal mind.

After talking to Kim, Roger and Paul sat staring at their notes. Paul looked over at Roger, "We still have Daniel Warren." Roger knew Kim had to leave for work, so he wanted to get what was available on Warren before she left. He called Kim to see if she was ready for round two.

"I'm ready," she answered.

Paul and Roger stood outside the room where Daniel Warren was being held. Paul noticed Daniel looked smug, as if he had pulled off some kind of Oscar win. He was smoothing down the sides of his hair and checking his reflection in the observation window. Paul couldn't help but think that Daniel might even be uglier than Devon.

Linda and Mary watched Roger and Paul enter the room and take seats across from Daniel. Linda started sending Daniel's thoughts to Kim.

Roger looked at Daniel, "You are going to tell me everything about the plan to get Devon out of jail."

Daniel looked at Roger, "I don't really remember that much. It was a long time ago man."

Roger slammed his fist on the desk. Mary and Linda jumped farther into the corner. "I don't have time for bullshit!" Roger had his face within inches of Daniel's. "Your buddy that impersonated Patterson? He's dead. Killed by a sniper this morning, right after he testified. I have that sniper in the next room! He was here to shoot you! Do you know why? You aren't worth shit to them anymore." Roger pushed his chair away from the table, He shrugged and looked first at Paul and then Daniel. "You are a liability to them alive. How long do you think you are going to last in that prison after I send you back? If you think they are going to pay you any money, you are a fool. You are not a fool are you Daniel? So you are going to remember, a lot, and I am going to decide if what you do remember is worth the hassle to protect you."

Mary and Linda thought Roger made a very convincing argument. Evidently Daniel Warren thought so too. Daniel told Roger he had been recruited because his military picture looked like Devon. They had shown him pictures of all of the dead people who had not followed the plan. A lot of dead people. Daniel said he was made to practice changing clothes from a suit and into a prison uniform until he could do it in less than four minutes. He said it took days. Then he spent days leaning how to walk and talk like an attorney. They wouldn't let him leave the facility, and they drove him to the prison for the exchange.

Daniel assumed they gave Devon a ride from the prison to the airport. They had their own pilot and jet. He said they had told him as soon as his true identity was discovered, probably at trial, he would only have to do a couple of years in jail, and they would pay him one million dollars. Daniel kept talking, and talking, and talking. Linda and Mary were shocked at what they were hearing. Roger was beginning to get a picture of Mathew Core's organization, and he didn't like it.

CHAPTER 5

Carl had been told to get to the duck pond at Lincoln Park, off Capital SE, in D.C.. It was close to the Capitol Building, making it convenient for Thomas, not for him. He wondered what was so damn urgent. He didn't appreciate being summoned, and he didn't like being seen anywhere near Thomas. He looked at his watch again and adjusted his large frame on the wooden park bench.

He was annoyed at everything today. Even the sunshine pissed him off. He needed to get away. There had been a time when all of the political manipulation was exciting and fun. He had believed what he was doing was important, actually made a difference. He knew now that his youthful enthusiasm and arrogance had just fit their plan. Recruits were in training to take his place at any time. There wasn't anything special about him. He just knew how to play the game.

He saw Thomas walking toward him on the path. He was walking quickly and with purpose. Capitol Hill was playing on Thomas too. You could see it in his furrowed brow. Thomas sat down next to Carl. "We need a new fixer, and I need this address to disappear within the hour. You still have someone inside CIA?" The intensity of Thomas's stare pierced Carl's train of thought.

Carl slowly answered, "Yes, I have someone. A *'new' fixer*? What's wrong with…"

Thomas cut him off, "Just do it!" He handed the paper with the address over to Carl.

Thomas stood and cracked his neck. "Find out what they know. Now. I put a temporary number on there for you to report to me." He turned and walked back to the waiting BMW.

Carl looked at the address on the paper and started walking quickly toward his car. Shit. *Virginia*. Core's computer lab. *Why?* He was close enough he would make a few calls and just drive there himself, verify it was done. All *hell* was getting ready to break loose.

Ellen called a meeting at Kim's house. Kim had finally finished with Roger and left for work. I was watching "The Jerry Springer Show" on Kim's TV. Now *there* are some mortals who need help. Ellen, Mary, Linda, and Teresa got there and all assumed various positions of fatigue on the furniture. It was the picture of exhaustion.

"I guess I don't have to ask how your morning has gone." Boy, did I feel guilty. I had been playing with the cats while Kim talked to Roger. I painted an oil painting of a tropical beach for her to hang in her bathroom, just kind of chilled.

Linda pointed, "Look at that! She painted an entire painting while we were working." Shit. Leave it to me to create evidence I've just been messing around.

Ellen said, "There is a mountain of information the FBI is getting right now from the computers at that Virginia lab of Mathew Core's. We have to find clues about Devon and Patterson in that mess. Anyone have any thoughts?"

Linda said, "Mortals always say to follow the money. Patterson and Devon both must have money, and surely they had to pay *big* money to Mathew Core to get this done." I was thinking we needed to read Jason's and Mathew's minds some more.

Ellen looked at me and said, "I agree. Vicki thinks we need to read Jason's and Mathew's minds for more info. Teresa, you and Vicki come with me to visit Mathew in New Orleans. Linda and Mary can go listen to Jason in jail. We need something specific Roger and Paul can use to catch Devon and Patterson."

Ha ha. I got out of going to jail, again!

Linda and Mary found Jason Sims in the FBI building in Quantico, Virginia in a large cell with an observation window and two guards outside. In the room were a table, three chairs, a small cot, a sink, and toilet in the corner. Mary and Linda put their seats up at the ceiling as far from the toilet as they could. "Yuck," Mary said.

Linda was already adjusting her watch bar to start her memory transmission for Kim and Roger. She looked at Mary and said, "Who do you think invents all of these gadgets we use?"

Mary thought about it and said, "Maybe there's another class where they invent this stuff? That would be a good place to stick Vicki!" They both laughed.

From the cot they could hear some of Jason's thoughts coming. *Mathew has no idea how screwed he is right now. We are supposed to get that five million dollar payment today! It still has to get moved to a safe account. The Feds might not see it if the Global Corp. firewalls have not been compromised. Maybe they will try to stiff Mathew and not pay since we hit a snag. That would be a mistake. Maybe the Feds already have Mathew. If I could just get a computer for five minutes.*

Linda and Mary looked at each other. "Five million dollars? That's a lot of money!"

Mary was frowning. "I think it might be payment for killing the two stand-ins. He said they might not pay it because of the snag. What do you think?"

Linda said, "I am going to tell Ellen."

Linda had a look of concentration on her face as she pushed the small blue button on her watch, and said, "There. I think I did it."

Mary was looking at her, "How will we know?"

Linda shrugged. Her watch started glowing blue. They both stared at it, and Linda tried to take it off. "These things don't come off!" The blue was getting intense and started pulsating large blue rings of color that filled the entire room.

Jason was looking around, "What the..?"

Mary looked at Linda and yelled, "Stop it!" Linda was starting to fly in figure eights around the ceiling. She was getting faster and faster.

"I *can't* stop it! I'm stressing here!"

Mary felt herself getting caught up in Linda's little flight pattern. Soon they were both flying in figure eights around the ceiling at rapid speed. Mary was screaming and swatting at Linda as they passed each other, "*Stop it!*"

Ellen was with Teresa and me in New Orleans watching Mathew. All of a sudden the room we were in started pulsating a blue color. Teresa and I were swooped to the ceiling and began flying in figure eights at high speed. Teresa was lapping me at every corner.

I was screaming, "I'm turning left here! Not liking this! What is happening?" Mathew looked out his windows and looked at the ceiling trying to determine the source of the pulsating blue color.

Ellen frowned and said, "You guys, I will be right back!" She just left us flying in circles.

Ellen popped into the cell with Mary, Linda, and Jason and grabbed Linda's arm as she circled overhead. She touched Linda's blue button and the room immediately became clear of the blue color. Mary stopped flying.

"Oh my GOSH! I thought the blue button was to send you a message," Linda was weaving a little.

Ellen was laughing. "It is. I think your watch just had a malfunction of some sort. Here is a new one." Linda's watch popped off and disappeared. A new one was on her wrist.

Linda was looking at it. "How do I know *this* one works?"

Ellen said, "Touch the blue button and send me your thoughts now." Linda touched the blue button, and the blue color started pulsating again. She and Mary resumed their flight pattern on the ceiling. Ellen grabbed Linda's arm again. She touched the blue button. They were once again in a normal colored room and had stopped flying. Jason's eyes darted around the room. He figured it was some sort of FBI mind trick, some new torture technique.

Ellen started laughing, "Oops. I told you the wrong button."

Linda said, "Oops?"

Mary was laughing, "It is so nice to see some-one else make a mistake for once!"

Ellen was really laughing now. "Oh, how ironic. I'll tell you about it later. Yeah, the button I should have told you to push is that little silver one on the very top, see?" Linda and Mary were nodding. Ellen asked, "So what is it you were trying to tell me?" Linda and Mary told her about the five mil-lion dollar payment Jason said was supposed to come today to Mathew. Maybe Roger could use that transfer to find out more about Devon and Patterson. Linda and Mary thought it was payment for the sniper hits.

Ellen agreed it was very important and told them to keep listening. Ellen started laughing, "You gals should see your hair!" Then she was gone.

CHAPTER 6

Agent Todd Nelson had been the arresting officer of William Patterson last year. SSA Dan Thor had called the district office to get him re-assigned to the case again. Thor had been impressed with the young agent's attitude and energy. Thor found out Nelson was actually in Indianapolis already on other business. Nelson finally arrived at the Indy office of the FBI. SSA Paul Casey had invited Nelson to assist in reviewing the prison tapes from Devon's escape. Thor headed for Paul's office to welcome Nelson back on the team.

Thor found Frost, Nelson, and Paul reviewing the tapes from the prison. Paul said, "Look at where Devon places books when he's finished with them. *Now watch.* Here a week later, he has added a full foot to the height of an entire wall with that extra row."

Nelson was nodding, "Flash forward to February 15th. You're right, look! He is entirely hidden now when he goes behind that row of books, and the guard isn't even watching him."

They forwarded the video until they saw Devon stand up from the table and shake his attorney's hand. They appeared to speak for a couple of minutes then both went behind the row of books. Four minutes later a man in Devon's orange prison uniform came from around the corner and sat at the table. Two more minutes and the attorney came from around the corner and sat across from him. Evidently Warren had forgotten to give Devon his watch behind the books. They watched as the man in the orange prison garb removed a wrist watch and passed it across the table. The man in the suit put it on. They zoomed in. Devon was in the suit!

"Right there! Right there is where they switched! That was smooth. That had been rehearsed." SSA Frost was standing now, pacing in the small office. Then he said, "By them asserting their right to represent themselves at trial, they have free reign of the library. They are allowed to meet with second position council, in the library."

Todd looked at Paul, "We are actually lucky this has not happened before!" Paul switched video tapes and found the frames where Devon signed out from the building. The guard in charge barely gave him a nod. Thor moaned, he knew what was coming next. He left for his office.

Paul turned his chair around to face Todd Nelson. "Well, now we know how they did it. I bet when you get Patterson's tapes it will be the same. Agent Dance has arranged for you to take lead on the Patterson side of this. Agent Thor is your supervisor. However, I am thinking that it may serve us best to work this as a combined case. These guys may still be in contact now, wherever they are."

Ellen found Roger in Thor's office and decided to wait outside in the hall. Agent Todd Nelson walked up to the open door, knocked, and said, "Do you have your cat here Agent Dance? There is a black cat in the hall. You know ever since we worked together in South Bend I think of you whenever I see a black cat!"

Roger smiled and answered, "Yeah, that is my black cat friend, and you can call me Roger. I assume you need to meet with Agent Thor and get briefed." Roger stood and gestured for Agent Nelson to take the seat he had just vacated, "I think I'll see if Paul wants to get a bite of lunch somewhere." Roger looked at Thor, "Any recommendations?"

Agent Thor scratched out a simple map to a bar just a few blocks around the corner, and said, "Good burgers."

Roger followed Ellen down the hall and into the office he was using. Paul was in the office next door. Roger poked his head in, "You feel like lunch?"

Paul said, "Yeah, just give me a couple of minutes."

Roger sat at his desk, and Ellen jumped onto his lap and touched the computer screen. Roger saw an e-mail from Kim. He opened it and saw where Mathew Core and Jason Sims were expecting a five million dollar payment today from somewhere, probably for killing Guy Johnson and Daniel Warren. Roger called Agent Ray Davis who was pretending to be Jason and passed on the tip.

Paul appeared at the door, looked at Ellen, and asked, "Do we dare leave?" Ellen winked and disappeared.

Paul filled in Roger about the video tapes from the prison as they walked to the bar. Roger was impressed at how simple the plan had been. It was beautiful. Prisons were designed to keep people from leaving, not from voluntarily coming in to be incarcerated. Warren only had to sign in and flash an attorney's license to have access to Devon in a lightly monitored environment.

"Beautiful!" Roger said out loud.

They found the bar easily enough and sat in stools at the far end, so they could watch the door. An old habit. After ordering, Roger filled Paul in on what Daniel Warren had said about Mathew Core's recruitment method for the scam. The killings, his training, and the money he had been paid and promised.

Paul looked excited, "You know this five mil payment if it *does* come in today, may tell us where Devon and Patterson are hiding now. Depending on what Ray can chase down, we may even get the aliases."

Roger was nodding, "I guess it is like Christmas at Core's lab. According to the Director they have already connected the dots on several open cases. Seems for such a sophisticated operation, a whole bunch of their security software has malfunctioned."

Paul choked while taking a gulp of his soda and said, "What a coincidence. Just when Ellen got involved," and smiled. "You know, we are going to forget how to do this the hard way."

Roger laughed, "I have had that thought." Roger's facial expression got serious, "Tell me about the agents who were with you at the prison, our new guys. I know they have been in briefing since you got here. What's your feel for them?"

Paul pushed his chin forward, his thought-ful tick, and said, "SSA Simon Frost. Been with the Agency fifteen years, was in Fraud Division for ten of those. Comes from big money, has big money. Very smart, doesn't talk a lot. Jacket says he is exceptional weapons expert. Ivy League edu-cated, qualified for forensic accounting years ago. Divorced, still friendly with ex, has a daughter in law school. He spent two years breaking the art fraud case in New York last spring."

Roger nodded, "That was him? He is *very* good."

Paul said, "Yeah, that's where he met Agent Pablo Manigat. They worked well together, and Frost asked for Manigat to be assigned here for this. I get the feeling he is trying to mentor Manigat up the ladder."

Roger asked, "Manigat. What is that?"

Paul answered, "Haitian. Family came to the States in the early 1800's and settled in Louisiana. Parents were in the music industry in New Orleans. Mother was a fairly well known blues singer, made a couple of records, got hooked on heroin. Died last year. Father left when kids were young. His file says he is Catholic, but a practicing Voodoo."

"What?"

Paul laughed at Roger's expression, "I swear, I couldn't make this up! When we were waiting to interview the guards, I asked him about it. He gave me a little history lesson. Said his family was all devout Catholics and like so many of the true Voodoo believers worshiped many of the same Saints. He said a large percentage of true Voodoo believers are descendants of Haitian refugees and slaves. They went underground in the early 1900's and were replaced by a commercialized sect, once Hollywood began to exploit the religion for tourists and profit. Pablo said about fifteen percent of the population in New Orleans are practicing Voodoo, and the grave of one Voodoo Queen, Marie Laveau, gets more visitors yearly than the grave of Elvis Presley."

Paul and Roger looked at each other. Roger asked, "I wonder how the gals deal with Voodoo?"

CHAPTER 7

Devon logged into his laptop and saw the confirmation notice that Patterson's money had been received by his bank. He was tempted to only send half of the money on to the fixer. He only had confirmation that half the job was done. But he didn't want to piss that guy off! It wasn't his money anyway. He hit a few keystrokes and sent five million dollars to the wire instructions he had been given and looked at the remaining one million in his account. He had told Patterson he was keeping half a mil for the hassle of getting Patterson's private life cleaned up, again. He decided to move two hundred thousand to his stash account and leave the rest in the office account. He was going to meet with the family today. Maybe he could get them to settle for even less.

He looked out the large picture window in the drawing room past the huge wrap around porch guarded by ornate iron fencing. From the street the house had a very attractive look, two story, very French. The main level of the house was actually elevated and through the back alley you could drive into an underground garage that opened into his private room. It was in this room that he entertained his girls. He had Patterson pick them up when he was through. He used to strangle them, but frankly they were just too heavy to transport that way. Patterson had devised a way to make a little money off his live scraps and take care of the bodies for him. A perfect arrangement.

He used to pump Patterson for the details of their demise but soon grew tired of the unimaginative stories. They were gone, that was all that mattered. After his appointment today, he wanted to go shopping for a new guest. It had been a whole month, and he was feeling frisky. He might kill this one himself. He kind of missed the thrill.

Agent Pablo Manigat took a deep breath, and knocked on the open door to SSA Roger Dance's office. Roger invited him in, noticed the troubled look on Pablo's face, and asked, "Is there something wrong?" Pablo asked if he could speak to him for a couple of minutes. Roger said, "Of course," closed the door and directed him to a seat.

Pablo took a moment and then said, "I just received a call from my sister in New Orleans. She moved there a year ago to take care of our mother who has since passed away." Roger was twirling his pen and listening closely. Roger was an FBI Behavioral Specialist and as such was one of their top profilers. Pablo's eyes were red rimmed, dilated, and filled with a fierce anger. Roger knew he was looking at raw rage. Pablo continued, "Jeanne was abducted about six weeks ago, held captive, raped, then sent into a swamp to perish." Pablo straightened in his chair, looked at the ceiling, and crossed himself. He looked back at Roger and exhaled heavily. He was practicing deep breathing to control his anger and rubbing an amulet he had retrieved from within his shirt. Roger was stunned at what he was hearing but remained silent.

Pablo continued, "Jeanne was saved by an old swamp man who took her to a Mambo who lives at Honey Island. A Mambo is a Voodoo Queen. She stayed with Mambo until this morning when the swamp man brought her back to the mainland. He had found another woman in the swamp who he also delivered to Mambo."

Roger asked, "Is your sister *safe* now?"

Pablo answered, "She told me the man who made her walk into the swamp told her if she survived the alligators and snakes, to keep going and never come back. Or he would find her, kill her, and kill all of her family." Roger noted that Pablo had not answered his question.

Pablo looked intently at Roger, "My sister took a family medical leave to help our mother. Jeanne is also an agent with the FBI, Computer Division. She is sure the man who abducted her is James Devon and the man who took her to the swamp is William Patterson. She thought it all along but had convinced herself she was hallucinating or something. She says that Devon kept her heavily drugged. She knew we had them in prison. Then this morning she saw on the news that they had escaped. She *knew* it was them! Agent Dance, Jeanne says she followed that case closely. She is *sure*. Devon and Patterson are in New Orleans."

Roger was startled at what Pablo had just said, but it fit with the information they had obtained from Core's thoughts. "Tell me what you want Pablo."

Pablo took a deep breath and said, "I know that protocol does not condone this request, but my sister wants to work this case with us. I want to stay in it, and I want our team to go to New Orleans." Pablo had articulated what he wanted with precision.

Roger knew this was going to be an important decision. The standard agency answer would be no. Jeanne would need extensive debriefing and treatment for her experience. Pablo would be emotionally involved with the case, which was a risk to everyone. Roger felt the intensity of Pablo's stare. He sensed that Pablo would quit the agency and work the case anyway.

Roger asked, "Would you agree to me meeting with your sister before I give you a final decision?"

"You are willing to give us consideration?"

Roger answered, "I am." When Pablo had left, Roger pulled up the agency information on both Pablo and Jeanne. He was impressed with both of their records and noticed Jeanne had joined the agency two years before Pablo. She was an over-achiever. Every Supervisor had used the word *driven* in her evaluation reviews. Pablo had been New York City Homicide and left to join the FBI. His supervisors had commented that while he was proving to be an exceptional agent, highly skilled, there were concerns about his temperament.

Roger had told Pablo to get travel information for the team from the FBI pilot in Indy, speak to his sister, and then get back to him. There was little debate that the team was heading to New Orleans. It seemed likely that Mathew Core, James Devon, and William Patterson were all there.

Paul was bringing Thor up to date on the case, and Roger's decision to work the Devon and Patterson cases together. Thor said, "I'd like to know where Dance gets all his information." Thor waited for Paul to make a comment. When he didn't, Thor just shrugged, "This is his call. If he thinks this will go better combining the cases, I don't care." Paul made the offhanded comment that Roger always had good instincts. He hoped that would satisfy Thor's curiosity.

Paul came into Roger's office and said, "Thor is curious about where you keep getting such good information." He saw the look on Roger's face and asked, "Now what?"

Roger told him about his conversation with Agent Manigat. Paul was rubbing his chin and shaking his head, "This could go sideways. We have Mathew Core in New Orleans too. Devon knows what you and I look like. He knows what Jeanne looks like. Patterson knows what Agent Nelson looks like, he arrested him last year. The only one of us who knows what they look like now is Jeanne, assuming they altered their appearances." Paul was up pacing, "You and I can't be hands off on this. We only *have* Pablo and Frost that are up to speed on the case that Devon and Patterson could get close to. I don't like this."

Roger took a deep breath, "We need more information on Mathew Core and Jason Sims."

Just then Thor knocked on Roger's office door and walked in, "Got a minute?"

Roger smiled, "What do you need Dan?"

Thor looked at Paul and then Roger, "I think I want to be more involved in this case. I appreciate you took what I said before to heart, but I think I had a *change* of heart. These young guys have no clue how bad this could blow up, or what Devon and Patterson are capable of. I guess I'm worried. I've been there, so to speak."

Roger smiled and said, "Well, you couldn't have had a change of heart at a better time. How well do you like Cajun food?" Thor raised an eyebrow, and Roger proceeded to tell him about his conversation with Pablo.

Thor was standing; his neck was beet red, "What a *friggin'* case! I hate this case! What kind of **hell** are we in?" He was yelling at the ceiling at no one in particular.

Roger chuckled. He was starting to recognize Thor had a very dry sense of humor, "You know Dan, we have to deal with what we are dealt. I'm still thinking this out myself."

Thor looked at Paul, "How can you spend so much time with this guy?" Thor started pacing as he yelled. "He's *killing* me here! And it's still his first –day- in- Indy." Thor was holding up fingers as he continued his soliloquy. "I have a dead imposter, a live imposter in holding, a sniper in holding, and now an abducted woman witness. A seizure in Virginia of an entire computer lab, a computer geek arrested, some piece of shit named Mathew Core that escaped **us** in New Orleans, *and* we already know where Devon and Patterson probably are? Are you on drugs or something? How do you keep this straight?" He looked so stressed out they all just started laughing, even Thor.

Roger just shrugged and said, "*And* it's only three o'clock in the afternoon. Well, are you going to New Orleans or not?"

Thor stopped laughing, "Yeah, I'm goin'." He shook his head and walked out of the office.

Ellen appeared on Roger's desk. Paul reached over and shoved the office door closed. Roger looked at Ellen, "Did you hear all of this?" Ellen winked. Roger said, "I think we are heading to the Big Easy, you in?" Ellen winked and vanished.

Paul stood, stretched his back, looked at Roger, and said, "I'm having one of those *feelings*. This could get ugly."

"It is already ugly. What do you know about law enforcement in New Orleans?"

Paul answered, "I know there is a lot of doubt surrounding the local PD. Their crime numbers are the worst in the country. They are actually under a joint federal mandate with the State Attorney General's office to restructure the entire department because of corruption convictions. NOPD pays less than shit, and there is virtually no training in place."

"I want a secure place to work from." Roger paused, "The only secure place I've heard of in New Orleans is the building Mathew Core was in. Our guys said the whole place was top notch professional security. It's in the Quarter, so we shouldn't be bothered with day to day crime. Call our agents there, and start setting up for our people. Have someone contact Ray, and set up whatever computer needs they will have. I think we've just seized Mathew Core's home base for us."

Paul was surprised, "Are you serious?"

"I trust Mathew thought out that location carefully. Yes, I want it. Core is going to know we are in town anyway if he's still around. He won't be using that building now that we know about it."

Paul stated he wanted to follow up on some of the information from Ellen's computer transmission from the interviews. He wanted to make sure they were not missing anything important before they left. Roger gave him a couple of specific things to double check.

After Paul left the office Roger closed the door and placed a call to Ray, "Did you get the phone record I asked for?"

Ray answered, "I have *something...*" After they spoke Roger put the phone down and walked over to the window. Thanks to Ellen, Roger knew the exact time Mathew Core received a call warning him they were coming. Now he knew where that call had come from.

CHAPTER 8

Ellen had us meet her at the Indianapolis Office of the FBI. We followed her from office to office, so we could see what each agent looked like who was now on the team. We started in Supervisory Special Agent Dan Thor's office where he was cradling a phone on his shoulder and asking someone to take care of his house for a week or so. He had two large bottles of Tums on his desk. He also had a stack of papers with a paperweight that said "Later" on it, another smaller stack had a paperweight that said "Now", and a huge stack with a paperweight that said "Too Late." I couldn't help but laugh. I could have used those when I was mortal. Actually, I had a similar drawer system. Agent Thor got off the phone and sent an inquiry on his computer to the shooting range to see if they had an opening for him to take an hour or so for practice. They did. He checked his gun and left the office for the basement range.

Teresa asked Ellen, "What is the difference between their titles? I'm getting confused."

Ellen answered, "People start at the FBI as agents if they meet the educational and physical requirements for the Agency. They become Special Agents if they obtain certain levels of competency in additional areas of study. A *Supervisory* Special Agent is at the top of the Agent ladder and has a higher pay grade, level of responsibility, and standing within the agency."

Mary asked, "This team has four SSA agents then. Roger, Paul, Dan and Simon, right?"

Ellen answered, "Right. Roger has actually been offered a Deputy Director position and turned it down. He likes being a field agent."

Next they went to an office where SSA Simon Frost and Agent Pablo Manigat were talking about New Orleans. Agent Manigat had light brown skin and piercing black eyes, a lock of his black hair was hanging slightly over one of his eyes as he told Simon about his sister's encounter with Devon and Patterson.

Simon frowned, "You should not be involved in this anymore! You are way too close!"

Pablo stood and said, "I can handle this. I've talked to Jeanne, and she is okay. I want to catch these guys. Agent Dance is giving us consideration."

Simon loosened his tie, looked at Pablo, and said, "This is what I predict. Your sister is out, other than identification, and you will be on a leash so short you will need Roger's permission to crap! That is the best you can hope for my friend. And that is *more* than fair." Simon was not happy about this development. The risk factor had ratcheted up about six notches for all of them.

Pablo was packing a briefcase. "We'll see," he said as he zipped it closed and turned to go out the door. Frost knew Roger didn't need this. None of them did.

Mary said to Linda, "These guys don't look real happy about going to New Orleans."

Ellen said, "I think they are all worried about how dangerous this assignment might become. All mortals have fears. What do you guys think Simon is afraid of?" We all looked at each other. He didn't look like he was afraid of *anything* to me.

Teresa said, "Not catching a bad guy?"

Ellen answered, "Simon is afraid of growing old alone. The job has cost him his family for now. He's hoping to fix that later." Ellen said, "Your ability to locate people will be enhanced if you try to hone in on all aspects of a mortal's character. You will get better at it as time goes on. Really try to read their thoughts as often as you can."

Next, Ellen took us to a mess hall type room where Agent Todd Nelson was standing in a short line. Thor had passed him in the basement hallway and told him they were going to New Orleans. Todd had decided he better get a bite to eat and then call his girlfriend to let her know he was going to be out of town for a while. He was pretty sure this would be the last straw. She was already unhappy with him. As he looked at what the kitchen had called a club sandwich, he tried to remember the last time he'd had good food. New Orleans wouldn't be all bad.

Teresa had stood behind Todd in line and came back to us and said, "Todd is afraid of not being a perfect agent. He comes from a family of agents and doesn't want to let them down."

Ellen beamed, "That is perfect! Exactly how you need to do that!"

Ellen motioned us to gather around, and she asked, "In your mortal lives have any of you visited New Orleans?" I looked around and then raised my hand.

Linda said, "Can you believe it? The only one of us that has been there is Vicki?"

Teresa looked at Ellen, "It had to be twenty years ago! She never goes anywhere."

I spoke up, "Hello? I'm still here. Ellen, wouldn't you say that even after Katrina, New Orleans is a city that doesn't change much over time?"

Ellen was nodding, "She's right, that city doesn't change from decade to decade, other than now there is more suffering from an extraordinary amount of crime."

Mary said, "Didn't Ellen DeGeneres come from New Orleans?"

Ellen smiled, "Yes she did! Well, this is what I am thinking. It may take a while before the guys get there. You need to practice 'locating' mortals. This is how you do it. Mortals emit auras we can track with our spiritual minds. We can find their auras by concentrating on what we know about them and requesting our spiritual mind to locate them. Does this make sense?" Teresa, Mary, and Linda were nodding.

I was confused. "Just think about someone, and you will know where they are?"

Ellen looked at me, "Basically, yes." I was thinking this would have been helpful when Kim was a teenager.

Ellen asked Mary, "Tell me where your baby sister is right now."

Mary closed her eyes and said, "I think she is at the Kroger store on Chapel Street in the frozen food section."

Ellen said, "Right!"

Teresa said, "Give me someone to do!"

Ellen said, "What is your sister Sheila doing right now?"

Teresa closed her eyes and said, "She is in my mom's basement art room painting a picture with my mom!"

Ellen said, "Right." Ellen looked at Linda, "Tell me where Agent Paul Casey is right now."

Linda closed her eyes and said, "He is on his computer in his office."

Ellen said, "Read me what is on his computer screen."

Linda said, "He is sending an e-mail to Ashley telling her they think they know where Devon is, and he will keep her posted. Wow! Could we do this all along?"

Ellen answered, "No, we just upgraded your watches to include mortal locating this morning. Now you just need to learn how to use them. Vicki why don't you try one, what do you know about Mathew Core?"

"I know he is a bad guy, and I know his name. He is connected to Devon and Patterson because he helped them escape. He kills people! You found him in New Orleans. He has military background. Is that enough?"

Ellen said, "Maybe not, you need a sense of his soul, but just try." I closed my eyes and saw a blurred vision of an alley, fire escape stairs, and a blurred street sign.

I told them what I saw and Ellen said, "Me too. There is something about Mathew Core's soul that is blurring his aura. Which means, you gals can locate most mortals now with just a small amount of information. Good job!"

"Well here is what I want you to do between now and when the FBI team gets to New Orleans. Locate Jeremiah Dumaine, Jeanne Manigat, and Mambo. Just spend a little time with them. The more you see into their souls, the easier they are going to be to locate. DO NOT try to locate Devon and Patterson, I need to be with you for them. The rest of the time just have fun. Mix among the mortals!"

Mix with mortals! I heard *mess* with mortals. Hee hee.

Ellen was looking at me, "Not *too* much!"

I asked, "When can we go?"

Ellen answered, "Pretty soon," with a big smile.

I had a question, "I am really tired of being in the same clothes."

Ellen started laughing, "You are the only ones who can see what you look like! Just imagine what you would like to be wearing, and it will happen!"

I looked over at Teresa, and she was in full combat gear! *Shit*! Teresa said "Ninja Angel!" Okay. Mary had a soft tropical print tourist dress on that came to her ankles, sandals and about twenty long strings of beads. Linda had a big hat on with flowers all over it, a very smart short set, and a big handbag that said "BIG EASY" on it. Hmmmm. I decided on a pair of white gauze pants with a matching over shirt and a bright coral tank top. Sweet. This feels so much better! I looked at Ellen, "Is all of this new too?"

Ellen said, "Yep, kind of a bonus skill we developed just for your little group. The rest of us really don't care about such things."

I said, "When I was at Kim's house, I discovered I could get inside things, and she could still see me."

Ellen laughed, "Yeah, I saw that. It was pretty funny. The only mortal that can hear and see you is still Kim." Ellen started waving at us, "Bye now. Have a good trip. Send a card. See ya later."

Teresa said, "I think she wants us to leave."

We took off for New Orleans, and Ellen returned to Roger.

CHAPTER 9

Jeremiah had arrived at Mambo's den at dawn and had brought with him some supplies. The woman Mambo called Heeshia was waiting at the swamps edge for him, "Jeremiah, are you taking me with you this morning?"

Jeremiah answered, "Yes," as he tied his small craft to the cypress root and began unloading the supplies. Heeshia helped him, and he was surprised at how strong she was.

Heeshia said, "Let me get these while you visit with Mambo." Jeremiah continued to move boxes. He did not believe in a woman doing man's work.

They worked together until the craft was empty and the supplies were all on Mambo's porch. Mambo had prepared a large basin of heated water and soap for the woman she was calling Kyeeta, meaning quiet one. Jeremiah and Heeshia sat on small rugs in the center of the room and waited for Mambo to join them. When Mambo was seated, Jeremiah gave her a small cloth purse that contained money, and he also passed her a pistol and a box of ammunition.

Mambo looked at the gun, pushed it all back, and said, "I am protected by the Saints. I have no use for this weapon, or your money, but thank you." Then she looked at Jeremiah and said, "Heeshia says she is leaving with you today. She is strong now. The Spirits will protect you both." Mambo reached in a small bag made of flour cloth and pulled out a small amulet hanging from a thin leather strap. She motioned Heeshia to lean forward. She placed the amulet around her neck. With her hands on the top of Heeshia's head, she began chanting. Mambo crossed herself and gave a bow to Heeshia. Then she motioned for them to go.

The woman Mambo called Kyeeta was watching them. Heeshia went to her. They held hands and whispered. Heeshia returned to the center of the room, nodded to Mambo, and told Jeremiah she was ready to leave.

The early morning air was already thick and humid as Jeremiah slowly pushed the boat from the shore and into the more open waters of the swamp. Jeremiah looked at Heeshia and said, "I have a truck to take you where you want to go, and I have some money you may have." He had a patch over his bad eye this morning, and he looked tired from the day's labors already.

"My name is Jeanne Manigat, Jeremiah. I have enough money for my needs, but I may need a favor when we get to your home. Can you draw me a map of the swamp where you found me?"

Jeremiah looked at her and answered, "Yes, and I think I know where you entered the swamp too. I've been doin' a little snoopin' for ya." He smiled at her.

Jeanne said, "If I wasn't afraid I'd tip your boat, I would run over there and give you a big hug!" Jeremiah flinched and smiled.

Jeanne could see various sized alligators sunning along the shoreline. She also caught a glimpse of a large snake sliding through the tall marsh grass along the water's edge. Jeremiah said, "They will let that snake get about two more feet from them, then watch." He no sooner said it than two large alligators slid from the shore and surfaced in a frenzy tearing the snake in half. Jeanne had never witnessed such a stealthy kill. Jeremiah was chuckling, "Most days a human would be their *last* choice for dinner. Most days."

He looked very serious now, "I found bones near where you had been. Human bones. A lot of them." His voice had gotten soft and sober, "I have started looking at night. Something evil has come to this swamp."

Jeanne nodded, "Yes it has."

They arrived at Jeremiah's home, tied the boat securely, and walked into the humble building. Jeanne noticed how clean it was and how purposefully every item had been placed. There was a large slab of wood Jeremiah used as a table with two handmade chairs. He must get company occasionally. There were flour sack curtains on the windows and a stack of rifles against the back of the door. He had made a large cupboard that held his pantry supplies, and there were several small shacks scattered around the grounds. Each one was in full view of a window. She saw a hinge on the floor peeking out from under a worn rug and guessed it was his storm shelter and root cellar.

Jeremiah saw her looking, "You have to be careful living in the swamps. Some of the varmints have two legs." He was smiling.

Jeanne said, "Jeremiah, I don't know how to thank you for all you have done for me. My pride requires I return a favor to you, I know you understand."

Jeremiah was looking at her, "There is nothing I need Ms. Jeanne. Exceptin' when you get feeling better maybe you could help me fix my tunnel. I'm afraid these old bones aren't much good anymore."

Jeanne pointed to the floor, "Is that your tunnel?"

Jeremiah nodded, "Goes clear over to that shack there." He was pointing out the window. Jeanne was stunned. It had to be 200 feet away.

"You are kidding me, right? How can you have a tunnel in swamp land?"

Jeremiah laugh, "My grandfather knew these parts like *nobody* else. There is a vein of rock bed and a vein of good soil that runs about two miles only on this side of the swamp, right here. He made this tunnel to help the slaves escape to the

North through the swamp and all the way to the Mississippi River. My father put the shed over that end there, used to be a couple of bushes, and a board. You know, this property was very important at that time in history 'cause nobody expected a tunnel in the swamp lands."

Jeremiah got a lantern for himself and one for Jeanne, lifted the trap door, and they descended down the narrow steps into darkness.

When they reached the bottom of the stairs, Jeanne was amazed. The tunnel was about seven feet high and four feet wide with lanterns hanging about every twenty feet. It had stone floors and cypress walls. Jeremiah led the way, lighting lanterns as they walked. They came to an area about 200 feet from where they had started. Jeanne noticed the boards along the sidewalls were showing signs of dry rot. About ten feet farther into the tunnel she could see where the ceiling had collapsed.

Jeanne studied the situation and asked, "How far are we from the other staircase?"

Jeremiah answered, "This should be just about where the staircase starts, fell in last summer." He looked about to cry.

Jeanne said, "Let's go back and look at this from the other end." They did, and Jeanne had a plan. "You and I can fix this! We have to go by my house in the city. I need to clean up, get some of my money, and my car. After you take me home, I want you to follow me to the supply shop. We'll need your truck. Then I want you to just let me work on this from the shed side for a couple of days. I'm waiting for my brother to come to town and need something to do. Deal?"

Jeremiah choked back a sob and said, "Deal."

James Devon, or as the sign on the door said, Attorney Michael Parker, had just met with the parents of William's latest child molestation victim. He had encouraged them to take the settlement of two hundred thousand dollars and be grateful that someone didn't report them to authorities for negligence and child endangerment. After all, what were they thinking letting their son go to a museum with a total stranger? Besides, they only had the word of a seven year old child against that of a highly regarded citizen of the city. The only reason they were being offered anything was to show compassion for an obviously troubled family. It had worked. By the time they left, Devon was mad he hadn't offered less.

He flipped the sign to closed on his front door and grabbed today's copy of the Times- Picayune to see the crime stories and the obituaries. The crime stories were like reading the comics for him. Murder here. Murder there. Police had no leads. Police charged with corruption in fire murder. Convicted defendant walks out of courtroom at sentencing, still missing. You couldn't make this stuff up! He flipped to the obituaries. He was looking for a funeral with a large family. Those were always the most fun, and good for business. Both businesses.

He found one that looked promising, two o'clock this afternoon. Not too far out of his way. He decided to pick up a few supplies in town and then go home to make ready. September in New Orleans was just *God Damn hot*. He could smell his own body odor as he got in his car. He took off his suit jacket and grabbed the half empty bottle of water near his console. The water was hot, but at least it was wet. Funeral home had better have good air conditioning.

He stepped into his bank and transferred to his personal account the remaining three hundred thousand William thought he had paid the kid's family. He took out a thousand in cash to have some emergency money at home. The teller at the bank was actually flirting with him. He was pretty sure. His new face had created some new experiences. Pretty girls had *never* flirted with him. Now they were. The idea that he could have them without kidnapping them had never entered his mind. He thought about it for a minute and decided a real girlfriend would be too much work. He would have to kill them eventually anyway. He couldn't risk anyone knowing too much about him. Besides, he would miss that look of terror as he raped them.

He had learned from his previous abductions in Indiana that it was best to keep a secure room, with a bathroom, so his visitors could take care of themselves. The room was absolutely sound proof and escape proof. He had camera surveillance, so he could watch from upstairs. Other than the fact the room had no windows, at first glance it looked like any guest room in any house. He even had his cleaning lady keep it tidy when it wasn't occupied. There were hydraulic bolts that locked the door on three sides when activated. He had seen that at the prison. Very effective.

Today he was arranging a lightweight shatter-proof vase with fresh flowers for next to the bed. He had a bag of groceries to stock the small bar frig. He checked the dressing table and replaced the brush, comb, and perfume bottles. He checked the bathroom and left a new toothbrush and toiletries. He smiled. As rapists go, he was a first class host.

Agent Ray Davis looked at the two CIA Agents standing at either side of the door to his office and placed a call to Roger. "Agent Dance? This is Agent Davis from IT, in Virginia." Roger was alert. There was no reason for Ray to be so formal with him.

Roger said, "Yes, Ray?"

Agent Davis continued, "I have two agents from the CIA in this office demanding that I vacate the premises to them."

Roger wasn't totally surprised, "Put *one* on the phone." Roger spoke with an Agent Harrison who stated they were given orders to be on standby to take over. Roger told him he would get the advice of his Director, and in the mean time they were to continue to wait. Roger called the Director who said he had been in phone conversations for the last hour with the CIA who felt the computer operation should go to them in light of some of the international data being found. The Director had just finalized a compromise. Ray would have a couple of playmates for a while.

Roger called Ray back and told him he was to play nice and be sure no one did anything accidently to destroy data. He also asked him if the five million dollar payment was showing anywhere yet. Ray was already sending over information regarding the payment and the tracking results. He also sent an account history of all banking activity for the last three months on all of the accounts associated with the wire. Ray stated he was also getting the personal identification information on all of the accounts, but it was going to take a while. Some of the transactions were sourced in offshore accounts and might be extremely difficult to trace.

Roger thanked him and then asked, "Do you remember when we got Devon's cell phone from Sandy when we first found her? Where can I find the forensics on the calls that had been made? Also, I want to review the calls made from Sandy's phone that Devon was using at the time of the arrest. Can you get those too?" Ray answered he had kept a lot of that information in a file and would send it over as soon as possible.

Ray had been making copies of the hard drives since he had arrived and decided he would slip them into his car just in case the CIA took over the entire operation. He had also downloaded the complete hard drives to a cloud data storage file for later retrieval by his own computers. Ellen had made sure the cloud transmission had left no trace. She also left Ray a special door for entry to the cloud. He sent a couple of entries to Roger and told the two CIA agents he was going to drive down the street a ways to pick up a sandwich at the Sub Shop. The CIA agents gave Ray orders for themselves and continued copying files and viewing codes. They were waiting to receive more specific orders from their operations.

CHAPTER 10

William Patterson and his new friend had enjoyed a leisurely breakfast on William's veranda and were sharing the morning newspaper, the Times-Picayune. George was reading the crime section and said, "I don't understand why New Orleans can't police this city. We have over 1200 officers, and they are on the crime pages as much as the criminals!" William just grunted. He was beginning to tire of George's company already. He knew George was just hanging around to get paid, so he reached into his robe, pulled out a small roll of hundred dollar bills, and counted off six.

George looked pleased and said, "Would you like some company tonight after I close the Gallery? Say for dinner and drinks?"

William looked at him, "I probably will George, but I dare say it won't be with you. Nothing personal."

"How is that not *personal?*" George was pouting, and William realized he had a drama queen on his hands.

"You are too old George. Nothing personal. Show yourself out." William snapped his paper open and hid behind the print. George got up. He was so angry he had started crying,

"Don't even *tell* me you are one of those sick bastards who wants *kids*! Sick *bastard*!" William didn't bother to answer. George left the veranda, and moments later William heard the door slam.

William walked into his drawing room and sat on his favorite chair. On the table was a stack of travel brochures. He was trying to decide where he wanted to spend the winter. As he flipped through them he realized it was time for a manicure. His house maid would be reporting this morning to clean, so he decided to get dressed and spend the morning at the manicurist and the travel agency. His phone rang. It was Devon. William answered. Devon told him the boy's family had accepted payment and had signed a confidentiality contract.

William was pleased. "I am making plans to winter somewhere. Maybe Belize, I haven't decided yet. Are you staying here?" Devon answered he had no intention of leaving, and William should keep him up to date on where he was in case he was needed.

A police car screamed past. William sighed. He needed a break from all of the crime in the city. He didn't consider himself a criminal.

Agent Manigat buzzed Roger to tell him he had travel information available. Roger told him to assemble the team in about one hour in the conference room, and they would map out their initial plan. Roger called Paul, "Do you have a few minutes to help me review the information Ray just sent over?"

Paul answered, "Yeah, just give me about ten minutes to finish up here." Paul was reviewing the information that had been transmitted from Ellen. Some of the thoughts of Mark Mills and Jason Sims Roger had not seen yet. It was amazing to Paul they were actually reading the *thoughts* of these guys. Roger was right. Very tricky stuff.

Paul found Roger bent over his desk, a colored marker in his mouth, with small stacks of paper he was sorting. Ray had sent a handwritten diagram with account numbers to try to help Roger follow the transactions. It looked like a two month job, *at least*. Ray had made some notes on things that jumped out at him, and Roger was comparing that page to others in the piles. He had decided to use colored highlighters to keep things straight, and had a pile of markers lying on the desk. Paul looked at the stack of markers and said, "Art class? Oh goody."

Roger looked up, "Can you believe this? I know I am looking at a gold mine here, but it looks to be covered in mud. I need new eyes on this."

Paul got closer to the desk and winced, "Oh brother! I hope Ray is available for us to call. I have some notes for you on Ellen's transmission when you get a minute." Paul was holding up a thick stack of paper.

Roger moaned and said, "Pablo is organizing a briefing in about forty-five minutes from now. Maybe we can look at your notes first and then get back into this?" Paul thought Roger probably needed a break from the wire records, so he laid out the highlights of what he had found on a large credenza against the wall.

Paul started, "Right here are the thoughts from Jason BEFORE his raid when Ellen had first found him through a phone call from Mathew Core. HERE are the thoughts of Mathew Core during that phone call. HERE are the thoughts of Mathew Core just BEFORE his raid, HERE are the thoughts of Mathew Core AFTER his raid, and HERE are the thoughts of Jason AFTER his raid. This whole pile are the thoughts of Mark Mills, the sniper." Paul had his eyebrows raised and was giving a questioning look to Roger. The unspoken truth was that there was no way the two of them could even hope to finish these documents in forty five minutes!

Roger was shocked at the volume of printouts Paul had sorted, "Have you read *all* of those?"

Paul answered, "I don't think I am ready for a pop quiz, but yeah. There are a few things here that don't make much sense to me yet. I was reading through pretty fast, just looking for a nugget of gold, as *you* would say."

Roger answered, "You and I are the only ones who can see this stuff." Roger was holding up the papers from Ellen. "Why don't we have Simon work with us on the money transfers from Ray? He was in fraud, and maybe Ray will have some more by the time our travel meeting is over."

Paul said, "Then you and I don't have much time to go through this stuff." They each grabbed a pile and started reading and taking notes. Paul stopped reading and looked at Roger, "Jason was thinking after the raid he and Mathew had plenty of Intel to just trade for their freedom. He thinks he has good dirt on the CIA and FBI. Listen to this. He says he works for the FBI and CIA...he does dirty jobs. He's thinking about hits. He was thinking about recent governor pardons, paid for. He was also making a mental list of corruption cases he could prove in New Orleans and some plan to block the federal reorganization of police there. **This is some big stuff**! He is even thinking about the past mayor, and something about missing court records during Katrina. Illegal city contracts." Paul turned his palms up and said, "I can't think of anything this doesn't cover!"

Roger was engrossed in his papers from Ellen, "Mathew was pretty cocky before his raid, not so much after. He thinks our having the computer Intel is enough, and we wouldn't need him or Jason. He doesn't think they have any bargaining power if the computer lab is found. He thinks if Jason gets caught, he has to leave the country. He's done, retired." Roger looked at Paul," If we want to catch Mathew Core, he can't know we have the computer lab. And another thing, Ray confirmed for me that Mathew Core got a *warning* call from the FBI field office in New Orleans before the raid."

Paul looked at Roger, "No shit? We can keep this team from mentioning the computer lab. Who else knows?"

Roger shook his head, "I have no idea. This is another reason I want to work out of Core's old office as much as we can. We obviously have some problem of our own in New Orleans that we haven't identified yet."

Paul pushed his chin forward, he was reading from the Ellen notes. "I wonder if this means anything. This is Jason after the raid. He wants to contact some guy named Carl. Says Mathew has an insurance plan in place in case this happened. Jason is wondering if he can tap some old friends at the CIA. He doesn't think we can get to a lot of the computer information because of protection programs." Paul looked at Roger, "He doesn't know about the Ellen factor."

Roger was reading the print out from Mathew after the raid. "He was debating shutting everything down. Calling someone named Carl. He is thinking he has enough money to live well for the rest of his life. This is the first mistake he thinks they have made...*but it is a big one since the FBI has Mark Mills and knows he is connected to him.* Screw him." Roger looked at Paul, "Doesn't sound like our sniper Mr. Mills has much to bargain with does it?"

Paul said, "Jason doesn't have much either. He thinks he does, but I don't think so. How do you think CIA got in this so fast?"

Roger said, "I wondered that at first, but Ellen took down protection programs. I imagine they started getting all kinds of warnings about data being compromised from that location. Then they found out we were there."

Paul laughed, "That had to piss them off."

Roger looked at his watch, said they had better put the Ellen papers in a secure file, and go to the travel briefing. Paul collected them, secured the stack, and wrote on the top Profile Notes. Hopefully, if anyone got hold of the papers they would just think Paul and Roger were playing with profile scenarios. Then he put them into his brief case and looked at the pile of computer records from Ray. "I can't wait to see Frost's face when he sees this pile." They both left for the meeting.

* * *

Jeanne and Jeremiah had returned from the supply store with a truck full of material and tools. Jeremiah had assured her his generator was fine, but she picked up a new generator for him anyway. He had insisted on helping her unload the truck near the shack. He only went inside when Jeanne complained the groceries would all be wasted if he didn't get them refrigerated. She told him to take a nap for a while, so she could plan. She actually was worried he was getting too tired.

She spent the majority of the afternoon rigging a pulley system to remove the dirt from the collapsed wall and ceiling and making a temporary support. The physical labor felt good. Jeanne was drenched with sweat by the time she decided to take a break. The work was coming along well. Jeremiah would have his tunnel back in no time. She needed to get something to eat and went to the house to find Jeremiah plating the table with some kind of stew and the bag of large rolls they had purchased.

Jeanne said, "This smells wonderful! I am starving!"

Jeremiah smiled and poured her a big glass of milk. It was quite a luxury to have both bread and milk at one meal. She had probably spent more in this one trip to town than he did in a year. Jeremiah waited for her to taste his stew. She closed her eyes and moaned that it was delicious. He smiled, "Do you want to know what's in it?"

Jeanne looked at her spoon. "No," they both laughed.

Jeanne told him she planned on working another couple of hours building new side walls in the tunnel, and then she was going to get some groceries for Mambo. She asked if he would take her later, and he agreed. Jeremiah said, "We will be in the swamp at night. I will show you where I think the women are being brought into the marsh if you want." Jeanne thought about that awful night. She felt herself shudder, but she needed to see what Jeremiah had found. She slowly nodded.

Ray had lost his parking spot in front of the building to an old vintage Ford truck. He drove to the end of the street and turned around to park on the other side. A Fed Ex truck pulled away from being double parked in front of the building next door, and a man on a bicycle peddled into the alley. Ray watched the window washer across the street stop working, move his pail and long handled squeegee to the back of a van. He wiped his brow with a red rag from his trouser pocket and waved at a passing motorcycle. Ray thought of Norman Rockwell. He would have loved this street scene.

Ray slowed down to look at the cookie stand the Girl Scouts had set up in the middle of the block. He had a real soft spot for Thin Mints. He decided he would park and walk back to buy a few boxes. Ray's radio started playing Dr. John sign-ing, "Right place, wrong time." The closest Ray would ever come to being a *bad boy* was lovin' their songs. He turned it up and started singing along, slapping his palms on the steering wheel to assist the drummer.

The ground rumbled and then exploded with a series of thunderous baritone booms. It was defi-nitely a bomb. A block ahead of him the pressure blast sent cars and people flying through the air like toys. Bricks and glass projectiles whistled from the sky mixed with fiery molten debris. Large chunks of concrete slammed into everything below. The dust cloud made it impossible to see. His wind-shield exploded, and he felt a searing pain in his shoulder and across his chest. Everything went silent.

Ray started to hear muffled sounds. Sirens. Screaming. His eyes wouldn't open at first. He sensed that someone was leaning in his car from the passenger side. His eyes opened for a brief moment. There was a man taking things from his briefcase. Ray tried to speak and everything went dark again.

CHAPTER 11

Agents Manigat, Frost, Nelson and Thor met in the conference room with Paul and Roger to discuss travel arrangements for New Orleans. Roger felt they all should go as soon as possible based on Pablo's conversation with his sister Jeanne. Roger said, "I made arrangements with the field office to prepare Mathew Core's building for our use." He noted the surprised looks at the table and continued, "I understand there are sleeping accommodations for five or six at this site, and I hear it's pretty nice. I'm thinking Dan, Todd, Simon and Pablo can stay there. I've asked that things be made ready and that someone stock the place with some food. September in New Orleans is hot and humid. Give some thought to your clothing choices and how to conceal your weapons. It would help if we could blend in."

Roger continued, "Our tech man, Ray, sent instructions for our computer needs and those should be ready by this time tomorrow. Paul and I can get rooms at the Marriott on Canal Street. Our back yards will practically be touching. The Marriott has a privileged parking garage, and I will make arrangements for extra spaces. You are not going to get street parking in the French Quarter. There are neighborhoods you can't get a car through, period. Paul and I will be concentrating on Mathew Core and his crew and the rest of you on Devon and Patterson."

Agent Dan Thor spoke. "Devon and Patterson know what Nelson and I look like. I think I should get sketches from Pablo's sister right away?"

Paul answered, "Definitely, and Dan if you could interview her and do an assessment, that would be great too. Have Frost be your lead investigator on Devon and Patterson for now." Pablo was quiet. He knew the decision had not been made yet about what role he could have in the investigation if any.

Thor said, "Nelson and I could work with the local office to see what help might be there."

Roger's phone rang with the Director's caller ID. He excused himself to the other side of the room and faced the wall as he took the call. Paul could tell from Roger's body language that something was *very* wrong. After about five minutes of conversation, Roger turned to face the group. He was pale.

"Someone bombed that Virginia computer lab we seized. Less than an hour ago. Two CIA Agents are dead, and Ray Davis is in the hospital. You guys arrange the earliest flight to New Orleans, and Paul and I will meet up with you. I do not want that computer lab mentioned outside of this room. We have a problem in the New Orleans field office. Mathew Core was warned we were coming."

Thor's jaw dropped, "How do you know that?" The room was silent. Paul's mind was racing. What could Roger say now?

Roger answered, "Ray was able to run a trace back on Core's phone. Some special program from the computer lab. The call originated at our New Orleans field office."

Agent Simon Frost spoke, "I think we have a much bigger problem here. That lab. It takes some serious weight to locate and destroy a location *we* have only had a few hours." The room was silent, the implication of Simon's statement ominous. All eyes turned back to Roger.

Roger answered, "Yes it does."

Agent Pablo Manigat said, "There is one FBI jet that could leave Indy airport in about an hour."

Paul said, "Make the arrangements, and let us know when you get settled. Try to rush them. Also get whatever you need from the field office down there. We are going to be using Mathew Core's building as our operation center. It is in the heart of the French Quarter. Remember, try to blend in until we have a strategy in place for finding these guys. You need to look like locals or tourists." Everyone was actually still in shock. Roger called the meeting to a close and wished them a safe trip.

Thor walked with Roger and Paul back to Roger's office. Roger asked him, "Are you worried about Manigat when you get there?"

Thor looking thoughtful answered, "I'm willing to give him the benefit of the doubt. I am not sure I could control myself in his position, and he is young. I plan to keep him on a very short leash."

Roger said, "I'm putting quite a bit on you Dan. I have *no* question you can handle it. Are you sure you *want* this?"

Thor looked at Roger, "I'm sure. These people just tried to kill one of ours, and *did* kill two CIA Agents. I might want this *too* much now." Roger understood. This case had land mines everywhere he looked. Something had to diffuse the stress. Agent Thor sensed Roger and Paul wanted to talk in private, so he said goodbye and told them he would see them in the Big Easy.

Roger closed the door to his office. He sat in the desk chair, and Paul could see the strain on his face. Roger said, "I want to go to the hospital and see Ray for myself. Do you know I don't even know what he looks like? I could be standing next to him at Starbucks and not know it. That guy has been my information life blood for six years! I can't imagine functioning without him! I consider him a friend, and I don't know what he looks like?" Roger was about to lose it.

Paul said, "We all have people like that in this job. I'm sure he thinks of you as a friend too."

Roger said, "He wouldn't have been there today if I hadn't sent him."

Paul said, "Let's call the hospital and get an update on his condition. We can take one of our jets from the Indy airport and be there in an hour." Roger was nodding his head but looking out the window. Paul said, "Paul, why don't you call the hospital for me? Okay, I say to myself."

Roger turned around and smiled, "I would appreciate that."

Paul placed the call to the nurse's station at the hospital. The head nurse told Paul Ray was listed in good condition and was making noise he wanted to leave. Roger actually laughed. Paul had told them that under no circumstances could Ray be discharged before he and Roger arrived. Then Paul called and ordered the jet. He looked at Roger, "Get your coat. We don't want to miss our flight. I'll take our paperwork, and we can just buy clothes when we get to New Orleans."

Roger laughed, "Actually, I never got a chance to check in anywhere here. My stuff is in the car."

Paul said, "Mine is too." Roger nodded and like a dutiful child, stood, put his coat on, and started packing files into his briefcase. The world felt so heavy.

* * *

Devon had arrived at the funeral home as the service was starting. He had missed the reception period which was his favorite part when you can find the vulnerable ones. He noticed a petite blonde woman sitting in the back of the room, and he went to sit a few seats from her. She smiled at him when he sat down, and he whispered, "Are you a family member?" She answered, "Actually I work for Hospice and have been Mr. William's nurse this last month." Good so far. No wedding ring, no husband to miss her for a few days.

Devon had his Taser in his inside jacket pocket. He only needed to get her near his car when the service ended. He also had an injection of his favorite drug ready in the console.

He noticed she had bare legs that were very shapely, and her toes were painted a bright pink. That was his favorite! She had on strappy heels, and with her legs crossed he could see a little of her thigh. Her cotton dress had a sundress look to it, and he could imagine her walking along a beach carrying her shoes.

A baritone voice interrupted his daydream. "I'm sorry I'm late." A tall man sat next to her on the other side. He kissed her cheek! Bastard! Devon got up and left the service. Bastard! In his car he took off his jacket and turned the air conditioning on high while he sat in the parking lot trying to decide where to go. Bitch! Bastard!

He wasn't going to let them spoil his plans for a fun evening. Devon pulled out of the parking lot of the funeral home and headed toward the Quarter. There were always pretty girls to find. Tourists who needed directions to somewhere. As he came close to Canal Street, he noticed the teller from his bank standing on the corner waiting to cross traffic. He stalled to get the red light and yelled to her from his now open window, "You need a ride?"

At first he didn't think she recognized him, and then she smiled that big southern smile, "Why I most certainly *could* use a ride Attorney Parker!" He yelled for her to hop in while he hid the Taser gun in his console. She rushed into the car, and the light turned green. Perfect timing! Devon asked, "I didn't think you knew who I was for a second there, Rebecca." She looked at him, "Oh, I just thought it was some handsome guy flirting at first!" She giggled. Handsome? Did she call him handsome? That had never happened before. He liked it.

"Where are you off to on this hot afternoon?" he wondered why she wasn't at the bank.

Rebecca answered, "I took the afternoon off to do some shopping, but it is just too hot to walk around! I was going to catch a cab and go home."

Devon found himself asking, "Why don't I drive you over to the mall? We can shop for a little while, get a bite to eat, and then I'll drive you home."

She was absolutely giddy. She reached over and rubbed his arm, "Oh, I would just love that! I can't believe you stopped for me! You know the girls at the bank tease me about you."

Devon was cautious when he asked, "And what do they tease you about me for?"

Rebecca smoothed her skirt and winked at him. "They know I get all excited when you come into the bank. I probably shouldn't have said that, but I have been flirting with you for months now. You had to have known."

Now Devon was the giddy one. A woman that actually *wanted* to be with him, and she was pretty. Very pretty. This was a new twist.

George Fetter had left Bernard's house furious and sickened. A *pedophile.* He needed to open the Gallery in three hours. He knew nothing would come from it, but he was going to report that sick son of a bitch to the police. Not that the New Orleans police would ever do anything, but he had to do it for his own conscience. Maybe at least they would start a file on the sicko, or add to an existing one. He arrived at the police station less than twenty minutes after having left Bernard's home. He was greeted in the common hall by a desk sergeant who asked, "What do you need?"

George straightened his posture and said, "I would like to file a complaint."

The desk sergeant didn't even ask him what kind of complaint. He passed a clipboard to him, pointed to a seat under the window along the wall, and said, "Fill this out."

George took the clipboard and used a hand wipe to swipe the top layer of filth from the chair seat. He filled out the report the best he could until he got to the space that asked for a description of the complaint. How do I say this? He wrote that Bernard Jacobs had admitted to him that he liked children in a sexual way. There. That says it all. He took the clipboard to the desk and the sergeant read the complaint and looked at him. "*The* Bernard Jacobs?"

"What do you mean, *THE* Bernard Jacobs?" George had his hand on his hip and felt his blood pressure rising.

The sergeant pointed to a far wall covered in photos and plaques. "Over there, this months 'Special Citizen'." George walked over to the wall. There was a picture of Bernard handing an over-sized check for one hundred thousand dollars to the police commissioner.

George looked back at the sergeant, "Yeah, *The* Bernard Jacobs." *Holy Mother of God.* "Well, I can *guess* where this complaint is going."

The desk sergeant gave a low chuckle, "We'll process this like any other complaint, and someone will get in touch with you." When he said that, he raised his eyebrows a couple of times and kept smiling. George shook his head and left. Damn cops.

George hailed a cab, got in, and told the driver to drop him at the corner of Royal and Canal. It was only seven blocks away, but it was too hot to walk. He entered the Marriott and sat on a stool at the sidewalk bar. Julie was bartending, saw him, and poured him a coffee. "Why the long face, *sugah?*"

George took a sip and answered, "Tried to do something decent and got shot down by the cops. Big time." He rolled his eyes and asked, "Think things will ever get better here?"

Julie threw the bar rag over her shoulder and said, "Some things only get better when we all make a decision to make a difference. You know, the man in the mirror thing."

George stared at her, "That was actually profound." Julie nodded and walked to the other end of the bar. He took another sip of his coffee, left a ten on top of the cup, and left. He figured it was about time he made a difference.

He left the comfort of the air conditioning and walked out onto the sidewalk. The gold trim of the Marriott made it look like the building was on fire. The sunlight blasted off every reflective surface and blinded him. He had on an expensive cotton suit and pulled his sunglasses from the top of his head. This decision may require recruiting a partner that has ears to the street. He headed toward Bourbon Street looking for Tourey.

George found Tourey sitting cross-legged on the sidewalk in front of Mickey's Bar. A wide brimmed hat was pulled low over his face, and his saxophone was lying across his lap. A stocking hat sitting next to him was being used as a money receptacle. Looked like it had about twenty bucks in it. George stopped, dropped a fifty into the hat, and waited. Tourey slowly raised his chin, tipped his hat back, and said, "Georgie Porgy Pumpkin *PIE!*"

George laughed, "Pretty damn hot to be sitting on the sidewalk isn't it?"

Tourey slowly rose and looked George in the eye, "A man has to make a livin', but you be right. Let's catch us a cold one in heeah." They went inside Mickey's and found two bar stools at the far end of the long room. It was still early in the day and the place was empty. The tourists would start to party about ten tonight and the locals would filter in beginning about two in the morning. Give the lightweights time to leave.

Tourey looked George over, shook his head, and said, "You are one fine lookin' dude. You just slummin' or lookin' for me in particular?" Tourey was a local, about forty years old, college graduate, in physics. Very smart. He liked to keep that a secret from most people. He had made some serious money from a couple of inventions and decided to retire early. George knew Tourey had a modest home, well kept, a cleaning lady, and a guest bedroom that had been converted into a library. Tourey claimed he was doing research on human behavior these days. Planned to write a book. Besides, he enjoyed the rumblings of sidewalk life. George knew Tourey could be trusted.

The bartender brought them a couple of beers and then disappeared. The jukebox was playing Ray Charles, "You Don't Know Me". The place was dark. The reed shades were all down to keep the blasting morning light from coming in. George turned to Tourey and whispered,

"I have made a decision. I know of a pedophile, and I want him to get caught." George waited for Tourey's reaction.

Tourey said, "Got your feelings hurt did ya? Told you that you're too old?" Tourey raised his eyebrows and had a smirk on his face.

George frowned and stammered, "That doesn't change the fact that he should be stopped!"

Tourey took a long slug of his beer, "No, should be stopped all right. I take issue with you saying you made a decision. You're just pissed is all. Means nothin'. Look me up in three days. We'll see what kind of decision you want to make then."

George was pissed. "Why are you assuming I will just change my mind?"

Tourey pushed his bar stool out a little, looked at George, and in a very measured voice asked, "Just what do you think you can do? You think you can catch him? You think you can get close to him again? Without him wondering what you're up to?" Tourey ordered another beer, "You're in *Nawlens* boy! How much time you think the cops got for this?"

George saw Tourey's point. George ordered another beer too. "It doesn't help that he just gave the cops a hundred grand either!"

George took a big slug of his beer, and Tourey leaned forward and whispered, "What's this dude's name?"

George whispered, "Bernard Jacobs."

Tourey put his hand on George's sleeve, "I'll look into it. I'll stop by the gallery in a few days.

You still the boss man there?" George nodded and got up to leave.

George laid a ten on the counter and said, "This isn't a passing thing for me. Scum like that needs to be put away." George's eyes were glistening.

Tourey watched George go through the door and back to the street. Moments later a striking young woman walked in. She was wearing blue jeans, boots, and a cropped knit top that showed off her ample bosom. Tourey thought she might be the most beautiful woman he had ever seen. She kept walking toward him. Her eyes were a piercing blue against her light brown skin. Her long jet back hair was tied loosely at her neck. She sat on the stool next to him, looked straight ahead, and ordered a beer.

Tourey saw she was wearing an amulet on a leather strap, was probably native. She looked athletic and smelled of soap. Her thick pouty lips rested on a squarely set jaw. She was all business. He knew she was there for him. There was no one else in the bar, and she had walked past twenty stools to sit next to him. "What brings a pretty lady such as you out this early in the day?" Tourey smiled. She didn't.

She looked at him, "You been playing sax long?"

"Mos' my life."

She leaned out and looked around him to the bar stool the saxophone was resting on. "Henry Selmer Paris, Alto, extended bell, low "A" key. Circa 1969?"

Tourey's guard went up, "You *know* your musical instruments. 1968."

She saw the rough outline of a knife in his sock and saw that his arms were fairly muscular under his shirt. He had on a light over-shirt that easily could conceal a gun. She looked him in the eyes. She was very aware of the hypnotic affect her piercing blue eyes could have. "Pity. You have no embouchure marks on your lips. You have the wrong mouthpiece and no reed." She raised an eyebrow one split second before she slammed his head on the bar, pressed her forearm against the side of his face, and twisted his arm up high behind his back. She whispered in his ear, "FBI. Do not move." He let her frisk him, take his knife, and then she sat back on the stool next to him. She flipped open the wallet she had retrieved from his pants and looked at his driver's license. She closed it, pushed it back to him, and asked, "Tell me what you were really doing on that sidewalk for three hours, Mr. Tourey Waknem."

Tourey smiled and whispered, "CIA."

Jeanne smiled, lowering her thick black lashes to half mast, "Prove it."

CHAPTER 12

Roger and Paul arrived at the hospital room of Agent Ray Davis. His shoulder and chest were wrapped in bandages, and he was hooked up to IV's and monitoring equipment. He rolled his head their direction when he heard their voices coming down the hall. He knew Roger's voice anywhere. They stood in the doorway of the room, and Ray asked, "Which one of you is the asshole that made me go to that goddamn place?"

Roger smiled, "That would be me, Ray. How are you?" They walked over, and the three men shook hands and exchanged introductions that should have taken place years ago. At this point they had grown to trust their lives to the familiar voice on the other end of a telephone line. Roger and Paul took seats next to the hospital bed.

Ray nodded his head slowly, "Other than a splitting headache and a gash in my chest I'm fine." Roger had noticed that the FBI had a security guard posted. Good. He should have thought of that.

Roger spoke, "I am so sorry about this…"

Ray held up his hand to stop him and said, "We have a bigger problem." He proceeded to tell Roger and Paul about the explosion and the man who removed the flash drives from his briefcase.

Roger put his hand up for Ray to stop speaking. Roger had noticed flowers on the bed stand and motioned to Paul. Paul removed the card that simply said, "Get well, the team." He handed it to Roger. Paul's eyebrows went up, and he pushed his chin out, his nervous twitch. He looked to the hall where the guard had been standing. Roger had not ordered flowers and didn't know anyone who had. He felt through the arrangement and found a listening devise. Roger started making some small talk while he was writing on a piece of paper from the bed stand. He wrote, "*Check out guard.*" Paul was up and out the door in three steps. Roger drew his gun and followed after closing Ray's door, and yelled, "FBI. GET DOWN!" The nurses at the nurses' station dove for cover. The guard was gone.

Roger yelled for Paul to stay with Ray. He told the nurses to have security lock down the hospital, and he took off looking for anyplace the guard could have gone. Local PD had been called in, and after an hour Roger returned to Ray's room. Roger looked at Ray and said, "I think some pretty powerful people are worried about what you might know."

Ray looked pale, "I'm not a field agent. I'm a geek. I'm not into this rough stuff! That bug can be boosted over cell phones." He looked at the blank faces of Paul and Roger as he held up a small wire, "I disabled it. Not cheap equipment! They could be anywhere that has cell phone towers and listen. They don't need to be close. I think I want to be wherever you two are."

Roger got Ray's personal information and called the local field office to send people to Ray's home and check things out. About thirty minutes later they received a call that Ray had definitely had company and most of his computers were gone. Roger relayed the information to Ray. "Damn. *Damn!* I've got years' worth of special programs on those computers!" Ray was sitting on the edge of the bed. "They went to my house? Now what?" Roger felt like he needed time to think. He asked two state police troopers to watch Ray. Paul and Roger found their way to the hospital cafeteria.

Paul got himself two cups of coffee and a small roll. Roger got a carton of milk. They sat at a brightly lit table, next to a window, far from the rest of the cafeteria crowd. They watched as security and local cops passed the doorway and crawled through the parking lot. The whole place was on high alert. Paul took a bite of his roll, swallowed, and said, "I think *Thor* has a point!"

Roger took a swig of his milk, "What's that?"

Paul smiled, "How do I spend so much time around you?" Roger and Paul both chuckled. Paul knew seeing Ray relatively healthy went a long way toward restoring Roger's momentum.

Roger's phone rang. It was the Director. Roger had called the Director earlier and told him about the bug and the unknown guard. Now he listened for a while, said "Thank you, Sir", and then snapped his phone shut. He looked at Paul and said, "Our guard was a spook. After the bombing he stayed with Ray to protect him. Left when he saw us arrive. No info on the flowers, and none of the nurses could remember when they were placed in there. The Director says they are currently negotiating which agency gets the bug. Everybody wants these guys."

Roger asked, "What do you think of taking Ray with us? If the doctor says he can travel."

"I was thinking about how strange it sounds, but *New Orleans* may be the safest place for him."

Roger was nodding, "I think so too."

Earlier in the day Ellen had told us to locate Mambo, Jeremiah, and Jeanne and get to know them to increase our ability to locate them by aura. We decided to find Jeanne first. She knew both Jeremiah and Mambo, and we could get information from her that might help us with them. We found Jeanne standing in a bookstore by the front window. She was pretending to look at books but watching a man who was sitting across the street, on the sidewalk in front of Mickey's Bar. He had a saxophone across his lap, and he looked like he was sleeping.

Mary said, "I am trying to read her thoughts, but I am just getting mumbles." Teresa leaned in closer to Jeanne, I accidently knocked a couple of books from a shelf. The loud bang made Jeanne jump.

Linda looked at me, "Why don't you just sit down somewhere?" Fine. I summoned a chair and sat above them.

Teresa said, "She is wondering what that guy is really doing across the street. Mathew Core's building that our guys are going to use is right next door to this bookstore. She thinks that guy is spying on what is happening over there."

Just then we saw a very good looking man stop and talk to the saxophone man, and they both went into the bar. Teresa said, "She doesn't like this. She wants to know who that is." They waited about ten minutes, and the good looking man came out of the bar.

Jeanne put the book back on the shelf and walked across the street. Mary asked, "Are we going in?"

Linda looked at her, "Yeah, why?"

"I just think I'm going to change clothes is all." I thought Mary looked fine, but the short set she put on was really cute. She had a visor hat that said Mickey's Bar.

"How cute!" I said, and made a hat for myself too! It really helped with the glaring sun. I elbowed Mary, "You should have been a fashion designer instead of an elementary teacher! That short set really rocks!"

Mary answered, "You know, I thought seriously about that at one time. My mom…"

Linda interrupted us, "Can we do 'This is your life' after we check out what is happening in here?" Geesh.

We went in just as Jeanne was smashing the guy's head into the bar. *Okay*, this chick isn't messin' around. We all flew in and made a protective circle around her. Teresa was ready for action, but Jeanne had everything under control.

We hung around for a while and found out the guy was named Tourey. He was a CIA undercover agent who actually lived in New Orleans. He was watching the building to see if anyone else appeared to be watching the building. He knew the FBI was moving in. He had watched the raid earlier. Jeanne didn't give him any information. She got an address for him, a contact phone number, and asked if they could call him if needed. She apologized for roughing him up and left.

Linda captured his address and phone number on her memory card, and we followed Jeanne to her car. We all got in her back seat, so we could listen to her thoughts for a while and try to get a stronger handle on her aura.

She drove around some of the most beautiful neighborhoods, very slowly. She went down a few alleys, and we heard her think, "I know his house is around here somewhere. I remember an alley and a wrought iron fence. She laughed at herself, "That describes half the houses in New Orleans." she drove a while longer and then started out of town toward the swamps. We could tell from the Swamp Tour signs we were very close. Jeanne pulled into a dirt drive that curled around for some distance before opening up to a small shack of a house with several out-buildings. An old red pickup was parked by the shack, and a large flat bottom boat was tied to a log at the edge of the swamp.

An old man walked from around the corner of the far shed. He raised his hand in greeting, and Jeanne smiled. She liked this man. Teresa shouted, "That's Jeremiah!" Cool, now we don't have to find him. We watched them walk toward the boat and sit on two stumps near the swamp edge. Jeremiah was skinning minks.

"Ugh!" We all said at the same time.

"How gross!" Mary said as she put a hankie to her nose. Matched her outfit. *How cute!*

Jeanne pulled a knife from her boot and started helping him skin. They made small talk for a while, but we were all more interested in the swamp. I kept looking into the water between the marsh grasses looking for snakes and alligators. Teresa yelled at us from about thirty feet into the swamp, "You guys! Come here!" We all flew over to see a whole family of alligators sunning along the bank. Even a couple of itty-bitty ones.

We all said "Awwww." The mommy rose up, opened her mouth, and made a terrible noise. She slammed her tail a couple of times on the ground and was looking right at us! Shit!

"She can see us!" I screamed as I flew back to Jeanne and Jeremiah.

Linda yelled at me, "Come back and talk to them."

What? I flew back and looked at Linda, "Do what?"

She answered, "See if you can talk to alligators."

"You talk to the alligators."

Mary said, "Let me try. Hello, we think your children are adorable." Nothing.

Then the big alligator said, "What are you?" We all figured he was the dad.

Mary swallowed and said, "We are angels. We won't hurt you."

The other large alligator said, "Go away." Don't have to tell me twice.

We all flew back to Jeanne and Jeremiah. "They just aren't real sociable," Teresa said. "Now we know we can talk to them."

Jeremiah looked at Jeanne and said, "Are you ready to go see Mambo?"

Jeanne answered, "Yeah, and I want you to show me where you think I was sent into the swamp."

We all looked at each other. Teresa said, "An adventure!" Oh goody goody.

I was starting to feel hot and buggy, "I think I'm sweating. Do we sweat? I didn't like to sweat when I was alive, and I'm not real happy now."

I no sooner said that than Mary squealed, "Al! Oh My Gosh, it's Al!" We all turned around. Al Roker was standing behind Jeremiah and Jeanne as they were loading the boat.

"Hi Gals! Did I hear someone request a refreshing breeze?" His big smile appeared and a cool breeze started blowing over us….awahhhh….Mary was a huge fan of Al Roker. She couldn't stop giggling.

Al said, "You know this is hurricane season. I'm trying to decide if we are going to need one to help you gals, or maybe *stop* one to help you gals. Who knows? I think we can at least lower the temperature some and have a small storm threat while we sort this out." He looked at me, "And a little breeze." I said thank you, and he disappeared.

Mary was beside herself! "Oh *my*! I can't believe it!"

This unbelievable stuff was happening with a fair amount of regularity lately. I was starting to wonder what would truly surprise me when a large knife slashed through my chest. Jeanne had thrown it right through me at a large snake crawling down a tree branch right behind Jeremiah. Jeremiah looked behind him. "Thanks, that one was poisonous," and kept loading the boat.

I looked at Teresa, *"Did you see that?"* Teresa nodded. Jeanne went over and yanked her knife out of the tree. The snake was about four feet long and fell to the ground motionless, in halves. Okeey Dokeey.

Jeremiah picked it up and threw it into the swamp. "Snack time for the gators. We ready to go yet, or you wan' to kill somethin' else?" Jeanne chuckled and joined him in the boat.

"I work for the FBI, Jeremiah. I don't want you to worry about me."

Jeremiah chuckled, "I figure you be somethin'. And it be a lot more 'en FBI. I'd be more worried about the other guy after watchin' you with that blade. You shoot too?"

Jeanne answered, "Yes."

Jeremiah adjusted the patch on his bad eye, shook his head, and said, "My daddy would never have believed this. You just give me fair warnin' if'n I ever piss you off. I only got one good eye you know."

CHAPTER 13

Devon and Rebecca had gone to a couple of stores in the mall and were walking towards the exit. Devon had actually enjoyed his time with Rebecca. He saw a jewelry store and said, "Why don't we pick out some earrings for you as a memory of our shopping trip?"

Rebecca squealed and leaned in to kiss his cheek. "How wonderful! Thank you!" She ran ahead of him and was looking through the case. The merchant was pulling out a display for her to look at closer. Devon noticed she had picked out the smallest stones in the store.

He smiled to himself, "Why don't we look at these?" he said to the merchant who readily moved down the case. They were now in front of the nicer earrings.

Devon let her pick out a pair and told her to wear them. He paid the merchant and put the box and receipt into his pocket. He would need them in a few days when he returned them. She wouldn't need them after she was dead.

Thor, Nelson, Manigat, and Frost all boarded the FBI jet for New Orleans. When they were settled, Thor asked Frost, "Are those the transactions Roger wanted you to review?"

Simon Frost was sorting a huge pile of papers and answered, "Yeah, there's a ton. Want some?"

Thor looked out the window of the plane and said, "Bring a couple over here and show me what you look for." Then he looked at Nelson and Manigat, "You guys might as well learn something too. I have a feeling Roger will need all of us to get through the data in this case."

The center of the jet had a table that folded down, and they all sat around it. Frost handed them each a stack of papers and said, "Ray Davis, the IT guy that got bombed this morning, sent this cheat sheet to Roger as being account numbers of particular importance. We should look for patterns between accounts. Here are the codes you use for the international transfers. I have numbered the tops of these pages. There are three hundred and forty seven of them. I suggest you write your findings on a separate piece of paper. These may be the only copies we ever see of these transactions." They all looked at each other.

Thor said, "Something in here is important enough to kill federal agents. This is probably the map to a lot of dirty secrets." They all quickly became engrossed in their work.

Thor looked at the stack in front of him. This morning he would have cried if someone asked him to do this. Now he felt a fire in him that had been gone for some time. He looked at the other agents concentrating on their task. This was a damn good team. Roger had put him in charge. Roger had faith in him even after…Thor's phone rang. It was Roger. "Yeah," Thor listened a while, shut his phone, and noticed the team was looking at him with anxiety. This must be what Roger experiences about twenty times a day Thor thought. "Actually good news, Ray is in good enough condition to travel, and Paul and Roger are bringing him down here. Someone searched his home, took his computers, and planted a listening devise in his hospital room."

Frost said, "The good news must have been he's in good enough condition to travel. The rest of that sounded pretty bad."

Thor nodded, "You deal with what you're dealt." He laughed to himself. Roger had just said that to him an hour ago.

* * *

Ellen had summoned a pet carrier for herself and was waiting in the FBI jet when Roger, Paul, and Ray boarded. Roger had been wondering how he was going to manage without Ellen. He looked at the carrier and said, "Hey, you beat me here! Did they treat you okay? Do you want out?" Ellen just curled up with her back to the carrier opening. It was all just for show, for Ray, to explain how she got to New Orleans, so she decided to take a nap.

Ray, who was obviously surprised asked, "That's your *cat*? You take it on field assignments?"

Roger put his finger to his lips, "Shhhhh. She doesn't think she's a cat."

Ray looked at Paul who just shrugged. Ray shook his head and looked for a recliner type of seat. There was one in the back, and he asked Roger if it would be okay to rest his eyes a while. Roger said, "Please, you probably should still be in the hospital." Ray waved him off, and they heard him snoring within ten minutes.

Paul whispered to Roger, "You know, this is how those rumors start about crazy bosses." Roger held his hands up like "What can I do?"

Paul had lowered a table and had brought out the notes from Ellen's conversations with Kim. Ellen appeared next to them on the table. Roger and Paul both looked back to Ray who was sound asleep. An earpiece appeared, and Roger put it on. He looked at Ellen, "I suppose I should call Kim?" Ellen winked.

Roger called Kim, "Hi, I'm at the casino. Ellen called and said Paul needs to hear Ashley's thoughts." Roger said, "Are you sure?" Ellen winked. "Okay, I'm giving Paul the earpiece."

Paul's eyes got big, "Me?" Then he said, "Kim?"

Kim answered, "Ellen wants you to hear Ashley's thoughts."

"Okay." Paul looked at Roger who just shrugged. Ellen was gone.

Paul heard Kim say, "She is worried she made a mistake. She doesn't want to get into trouble. She has a friend, a guy named John Barry who she sent to New Orleans to find and kill Devon. He has already arrived there. She doesn't know how to reach him to stop him. The number she had for him has been disconnected. I think that's all."

Paul said "Thanks," took the earpiece off, and looked at Roger.

"Ashley hired a hit man for Devon. Now she wants to stop him, but she doesn't know how to reach him. His name is John Barry. She thinks he's already down there."

Roger rubbed the side of his face, "That's all we need. John Barry is a retired spook." Roger looked at Paul, "Call Ashley. See if she won't just confess to you. Maybe she can remember something that will help us stop him before he ruins his life, hers, and our case!"

Paul noticed the earpiece had disappeared, and Ellen was back in her carrier. He dialed Ashley, "Paul? I have been thinking about calling you. Are you all right?"

Paul said, "Yes. How are you holding up?"

There was a pause, "Paul, I think I made a terrible mistake, and I don't know how to fix it."

Paul sighed with relief. Ashley was going to tell him, "And what mistake is that?"

A nice looking man in his fifties sat on a stool in the sidewalk bar at the Marriott on Canal Street, watching the people walk by. The bartender, Julie, asked him if he wanted bourbon. He answered no, and asked her how far he was from the police station. She drew him a little map and told him to cab there. It was too hot to walk, and he didn't want to walk through some of those neighborhoods. He thanked her, went outside, and hailed a cab.

The cabby dropped him off and said, "You want me to wait? Not that easy getting a cab to come here."

He chuckled, "Seems like it would be pretty safe in front of the police station."

The cabby said, "Not the fares you pick up! Deliveries are fine." He told the cab to wait. He walked up the wide staircase and marveled at the beautiful architecture of the building.

He approached the desk sergeant and asked, "Where is your homicide department?"

The desk sergeant frowned at him, "Who wants to know?"

He answered, "Retired CIA, John Barry."

The desk sergeant buzzed someone, talked for a minute, and told John to take the elevators to the third floor, and turn left. John thanked him, found his way to the office, and opened the door. It was utter chaos. John could tell in a glance they were woefully understaffed.

A New Orleans police detective rose from behind a desk and invited him to have a seat. The detective's badge said Johnson. John said, "Detective Johnson, I am retired CIA , John Barry, doing a favor for a friend. It requires locating an escaped murderer from Indiana we believe is now located in New Orleans. Probably been here since February. Have you noticed any new activity?"

The detective threw his head back and laughed, "Oh shit that is good! Did you not do your home-work? Look around! This is the murder capital of the US. All we have is new activity!"

John Barry smiled. He knew things were bad. He pushed a card to Detective Johnson, "I plan on being here a while, and I am willing to volunteer my services in exchange for access to records. Could you take this to your supervisor for me and have him call."

Detective Johnson looked at the card. "You're kidding right? You are retired and willing to jump into this shit again? For free?"

John Barry answered, "Like I said, a favor for a friend."

✳ ✳ ✳

William Patterson had finished his manicure and decided to go to the library. Their story hour would start in twenty minutes, and if no volunteer showed up, he could read to the kids. When he arrived, the librarian recognized him and said, "I was hoping you might visit today. Our volunteer didn't show up yet for the reading hour, and I am short staffed. If you are busy, we can cancel with the children." William clasped her hand and said, "My dear, I would be delighted to read today. Just point me toward the children."

"Mr. Jacobs? I sent the videos of the children presenting their art entries over to the gallery for the contest. We had fifty entries this year! Will it be like last year with newspaper coverage and everything?"

William smiled, "Of course! The committee has increased the prize amount for this year too! I think the winning child and their school each get a check for a thousand dollars. Isn't it grand?"

The librarian was beaming. "I feel so privileged to work with your group Mr. Jacobs. What wonderful people." She pointed to a room at the end of the hall. "The children are waiting in the reading room." Her sensible shoes made a clopping noise as she returned to her desk. William couldn't stop smiling. The club could watch the videos any day now.

Tourey had decided to go purchase a proper mouthpiece for his saxophone and a couple of reeds. He had cracked his regular mouthpiece on the bridge of some punk's nose last week and hadn't replaced it yet. How amateur she must think he was. He decided that was what bothered him. She had gotten the best of him, and he had deserved it. About the only thing the encounter had confirmed for him was that the FBI had a serious interest in New Orleans, and it involved the building across from Mickey's Bar. He had witnessed the raid and had noticed the building was being stocked with supplies. He had never really noticed any activity there before. He'd always assumed it was residential apartments. He had decided to watch for anyone else who might be keeping an eye on it. After his shopping he was going to do a little snooping to find out more about the building's owner. Yeah, she had made him look pretty bad. Tourey smiled.

After leaving the music store he stopped in to see Spicey. Real name, Sadie Corbin.

A self-proclaimed medium with a Voodoo shop covered in signs offering fortune telling, potions, amulets, and the rest of the tourist trap goodies. It was a corner shop and had an entrance door on each street. He knew Spicey actually was a true voodoo believer and really only pushed enough tourist trade to support herself and give a little to the church. She had helped him before, and he knew she would help again. There were shelves upon shelves of trinkets, beads, bottles, and dolls. The place smelled of incense and clove. A brightly colored blanket hung over a doorway tied back with a large red velvet rope like you would see in a bank lobby.

The tinkling of the bells from the door opening brought Sasha from behind the counter. "Tourey! My MAN!" Sasha was Spicey's friend who helped run the store.

Tourey smiled, "How you doing gal? Looking beautiful as usual." They exchanged cheek kisses. Tourey asked, "Where's the boss lady?"

Sasha pointed behind her, "She has a client in there. Should be done shortly. You want to wait, or have her call ya?"

"Have her call. I'll walk the block a little."

"Shore thing hun." The bells dangled again as he left. It was getting later in the afternoon, and the tourists were starting to venture out. Sightseeing before dinner.

He walked down to Jackson Square and watched a portrait artist work the tourists. Good likeness of the little girl and her mom. After they paid and left, Tourey sat down. "Why don't you do one for me I can send my mom?"

The artist scowled, "Every time I see you, I end up in trouble. Go away."

Tourey laughed, "Got a five bill question, Dusty. Will take a little diggin' and needs to be on the quiet side"

The skinny man started drawing and asked, "Five hundred bucks, huh?" Dusty was a college graduate but discovered most employers expected more motivation than he was willing to produce. He managed to squeeze out an existence with his art and now only claimed New Orleans as his home. The saddest thing he could think of was havin' to say he was from anywhere else.

Tourey answered, "I want to know who used that building across from Mickey's Bar, up until yesterday. Be careful, the feds have it now." He handed Dusty his card.

Dusty tore off a sheet of paper and handed it to Tourey, "Here's your free portrait. I'll call you if I get something." Tourey said thanks and looked at the picture. It was a cartoon penis with Tourey's face on it. Good likeness.

Tourey's phone rang. It was Spicey. "Sasha said a handsome man come callin' for me?" Tourey asked if she had a few minutes. She answered to come in the back way. She would be in her apartment for a spell. He arrived about fifteen minutes later, knocked, and went in when Spicey yelled, "If you be handsome, come in." Tourey gave her a hug, grabbed a beer from the fridge, and sat across from her on a big overstuffed chair. He looked at her beautiful light brown skin. She was half white, half Haitian. She had large brown eyes and thick, short dark hair. Her body was voluptuous and draped in bright colored silk and cotton prints. She was a very attractive woman and knew it.

"Spicey, I need information, but I need you to be real careful. I don't know what level of 'bad' I'm lookin' at." He took a slug of the beer and studied Spicey's face. She was nodding her head. Her strands of beads and amulets rested in her cleavage and her arms had bracelets up to her elbows. He counted eight rings on her fingers and one long one on her ear.

She winked at him and asked, "Who we looking at?"

Tourey answered, "The name is Bernard Jacobs. He has money, likes kids. He bought a house over on Burgundy Street. He didn't exist before five years ago when he bought that house. He just moved to the city, full time, in February. I think the house has been vacant the rest of that time. He had some remodeling done. He gave the cops a hundred grand this month. A citizen donation." Tourey said, "That means there was probably another hundred that went into someone's pocket."

Spicey rolled her eyes and said, "Whewwww! That's one *bad* conscience now ain't it? Likes kids huh? I know some people who could find stuff out if he has a dark side. His aura will be easy to trail." Tourey knew that Spicey believed in Spirits and auras. She also knew everyone in the Quarter. More importantly, she knew what most of them were doing. She could organize a research team so efficient most of them wouldn't even know they were involved. She was a very smart lady.

Tourey said, "I appreciate it. Here's a little seed money to get you started."

She looked at the roll and raised her eyebrow as her cleavage devoured the money. "That was about a thousand, I would guess. You must want this soon?"

Tourey stood, kissed her cheek, and said, "Yesterday."

Spicey frowned and said, "Wait. You sit back down." She started flipping Tarot cards on the coffee table. She looked at him, "There is a dark Spirit looking for you. You are in danger. Go see Mambo." Tourey only half believed in the powers of the Voodoo Queen, and he certainly didn't feel like going into the swamp. Spicey frowned at him, "You will go. Mambo is expecting you."

Carl called the number on the paper Thomas had given him.

Thomas answered, "Well?" Carl told him the job was done, but his insider was still verifying how much information had been transmitted and the potential damage. Thomas was silent for a moment and then said, "I understand there was a survivor?" Carl explained all the information the survivor had was confiscated.

"Stay on it. I want to know our exposure." He hung up. Thomas Fenley was the Washington insider. The most powerful men in the world worked to keep him happy. In fact, if you weren't extremely important, you probably had never heard of him. Thomas wasn't happy right now. Carl looked at his silent phone, snapped it shut, and headed for his office at FBI Headquarters.

We had all taken seats on Jeremiah's boat and were marveling at the wildlife of the swamp. Jeanne and Jeremiah had loaded some supplies onto the boat, and Linda was sitting on a cooler filled with ice. Jeremiah had decided to give Mambo his old generator since Jeanne had bought him a new one, and they had two barrels of fuel aboard to set it up. Jeremiah looked at Jeanne, "You sure you know how to set up this generator? I think blowing up Mambo would not sit well with the Spirits."

Jeanne laughed. "Today we will set it up and run wire for two outlets. Tomorrow we will bring her a small refrigerator and a space heater/fan. The Spirits are going to love you!"

Jeremiah laughed, "Yeah."

When we got there, Jeanne and Jeremiah unloaded the boat load of supplies, the generator and then went inside. We all followed and saw Mambo sitting in the middle of the room chanting with a young woman. Mambo motioned for Jeanne and Jeremiah to sit, and for the young woman to move to the cot. Then she looked directly at *us*. Oh shit.

We had all summoned chairs and were sitting up near the ceiling. Mambo's big black eyes narrowed then grew very wide. She closed her eyes, raised her frail body, and began a slow dance. She was chanting, and every so often she would throw some kind of powder at us. She kept glancing sideways at us through the narrow slits of her eyes. She kept tossing handfuls of powder on us. Mary was coughing.

Linda said "She's killing me here, my migraines!"

Teresa rubbed her eyes and said, "She can see us! I think she wants us to leave!"

The powder wasn't bothering me, but then Mambo stopped, picked up some kind of stubby club, and started shaking it at me. The club made a weird clunking noise and it looked like a cave man rattle for a huge kid! Mambo's chanting was now louder and sounded like she was blending it with strange hiccups. She kept getting closer and closer shaking that rattle at me. I was leaning back in my chair hanging onto Mary. I started waving my hands in front of me to keep Mambo from getting too close. *What the heck?*

Ellen appeared and began dancing with Mambo. Suddenly they both stopped and sat on the floor again. Ellen put her hand on Mambo's forehead. Mambo was silent. This lasted for over ten minutes. Mambo glanced at us a couple of times. Hmmmm.

Jeanne whispered to Jeremiah, "Is she alright?" Jeremiah shrugged.

Ellen came over to us and said, "I am actually on a plane with Roger, Ray, and Paul right now, so I have to leave. Mambo knows you are here, she can see you. She wasn't sure what kind of Spirits you were at first. Ellen giggled. She said you weren't right. I explained you are all special. Ellen giggled again. I have told her about our assignment, and she will help if she can. She thinks you need to talk to Kyeeta, that young woman. She knows something."

Teresa asked, "How can we talk to her? She can't see or hear us?"

Ellen said, "You can read her mind. If no one is looking, you can write her a message." Ellen handed Mary a tablet of sticky notes and a pencil. "The notes will disappear minutes after writing them. Do not lose that pencil! It is invisible, like the notes, until they touch each other. Remember your notes can only last minutes, and you only have so many of them. Good Luck." Ellen vanished.

Mary was holding the sticky notes and pencil, "You're kidding right? Why am I holding these?"

Teresa said, "You're the teacher of the group. I think it makes perfect sense Ellen put you in charge of the notes."

Mary sat up straight, "She did no such thing! I am not in charge of anything. She just had me hold them!"

I looked at Mary, "I'm with Teresa on this. I think she put you in charge." I couldn't stop smiling. Mary was adorable when she was mad.

Linda said to Mary, "I think it is quite a compliment that Teresa and Vicki both think it is okay to have you in charge of every single note we have. That way we have to *ask* you for a note before we write one..." Teresa and I looked at each other. Maybe that wasn't so smart. Linda was laughing.

Mary said, "I think I had better be in charge now that you put it that way. As soon as Jeremiah and Jeanne go outside to work on the generator, we can give Kyeeta a note." Linda just giggled.

CHAPTER 14

Mathew Core had watched the black haired beauty in the bookstore watch the man on the sidewalk. Core's building seemed to be drawing a lot of attention. He was upstairs in the jewelry store apartment. He knew the occupants would be at work, so he had let himself in. He watched Jeanne walk into the bar and return after about ten minutes.

He had followed her to Jeremiah's driveway in his borrowed orange city utility truck and had watched them skin minks. He saw her blade that snake and nearly laughed out loud at Jeremiah's expression. He almost gave away his hiding spot in the thick brush near the boat dock. He watched them push into the swamp and had heard them mention Mambo.

After they left he walked around the property, looked into the sheds, and found the entrance to

Jeremiah's tunnel. He went down the stairs from the shed and followed the tunnel into Jeremiah's kitchen. He was impressed. He walked out the front door, made his way down the road to the truck, and headed back to the city. Now he wanted to find saxophone man.

Agents Thor, Nelson, Frost, and Manigat arrived at New Orleans Airport at six-thirty. It was Tuesday night and the airport was lined with cabby's grabbing tourists. They decided to have a van cab take all of them to Mathew Core's building. On the flight Thor had cautioned everyone that Roger had requested a low profile. Twice. Roger felt it was important they blend into the community if they were to be successful in locating Devon and Patterson.

In the van, Agent Nelson asked the cabby where he would recommend they have their first dinner in the French Quarter. The cabby looked at them in the rear view mirror and said, "That depends, you goin' as Feds or common folk?" They all looked at each other. They thought they had dressed down pretty well.

Agent Nelson asked, "You made us as Feds that fast? We want to blend in. What did we do wrong?"

The cabby laughed, "I've always wanted to do this. Are you serious? I can tell you what is wrong?"

Agent Frost spoke, "We want to look like tourists or locals."

The cabby pulled the van to the side of the highway, put his flashers on, and turned around to face them. "Okay, first off, none of you will ever pass for locals. Besides, you don't *talk* right. If you want to just blend in, pretty boy here only has to get rid of the gun. He looks gay, and he could wear anything and fit in." He had pointed to Pablo. "And you," he was looking at Simon, "you might be able to pass as his sugahh, but you need some nice cotton suits and a lot of silk. And dump those shoes, all of ya. When we get close to town, I'll give you a short fashion tour, for free, so you can see for yourself!"

He cleared his throat and then looked at Thor, "You might have to stay the way you are. Just get tennis shoes and lose the obvious gun. You could fit as a tourist, mid-life crisis type. Everyone laughed at Thor. The cabby looked at Nelson, "You could go gay or druggie. Gay, buy some nice clothes and that snot they wear in their hair. Druggy, go to the Goodwill store and buy a bunch of shit that's too big for ya."

Thor looked at them all and said, "I think if Albert here is willing, we need him to take us shopping before we even get to town. Vote?" And so it was decided that Albert was off the clock as a cabby and was now a fashion consultant. They went to a Goodwill store, changed in the store, and repacked their suitcases when they got back in the van. Thor gave Albert two hundred dollars for his trouble which pleased Albert immensely. He dropped them off individually about two blocks from their destination, and watched them walk away.

Albert laughed all the way back to the airport. It was so much fun messin' with the Feds. They would stand out like a Nun on Bourbon Street. He wiped his eyes so he could see. It was just so friggin' funny! The way the pretty one kept lookin' in the mirror, askin' if he looked gay enough. Albert slapped his knee, and they paid him two hundred bucks! The guys at the garage were not going to believe this!

Devon asked Rebecca if he could swing by his office and check his messages before they went to dinner. Rebecca batted her lashes as she said, "Of course, Attorney Parker."

Devon looked at her, "I think we know each other well enough. You can call me Mike."

She giggled, "Thank you, Mike."

Devon was actually driving her towards his house. He stopped the car and said, "Hold still. Don't move. There is a big spider behind your head." She froze as he slipped the needle from under his cuff and injected her neck.

She squealed, "OOHH, I think it bit me." Then she fell against the door.

He pulled down the alley and opened his garage door. Once inside he unlocked his guest suite door and dragged her in. He took her cell phone, left her on the floor, shut the door, and triggered the hydraulic lock. She would be too druggy to be any fun for an hour or so. He would go pick up some groceries for dinner and come back.

He drove to a small grocery store and was ready to check out when he heard a voice behind him, "Attorney Parker! Are you done with your date already?"

He turned around. It was another teller from the bank. "Excuse me?" he asked, genuinely puzzled.

"You probably don't remember me from the bank. Amy? Rebecca sent me a text this afternoon that you guys were shopping at the mall and then going to dinner! I think that is so cute!"

Devon had to think quick. That bitch just got her friend killed. "I suppose the whole bank knows now, huh?" Devon was smiling, but there was murder in his heart.

Amy answered, "Oh, you probably want this kind of quiet. I get it. I don't think she told anyone else. She isn't really friends with anyone but me at the bank. I took this afternoon off too for shopping, and we had talked about meeting up. When I texted her, she answered she couldn't because she was with you!"

Devon smiled, he had an idea. "Why don't you leave your car here and come join us for a BBQ? I have plenty of food for all of us!"

Amy looked like she was considering, "No, I think I should just go home and get some work done. I wasted most of today shopping."

Devon said "Okay." His mind was racing. He could follow her to her car, but it was so public and daylight. He could follow her home.

Then Amy said, "I hate to ask, but I don't have a car. It would help if you could drop me home. I think I may have spent my cab fare money here." She looked sheepish and ashamed she had asked.

Devon sprung on it, "Don't be silly. My car is right out front."

She hadn't even buckled her seat belt, before he shot her with the stun gun. He loaded the needle with more dope and shot her in the arm. This was too easy. Rebecca will have a playmate. How sweet.

Roger, Paul, and Ray's plane landed, and they took a cab directly to Core's building. Roger and Paul decided to check into the hotel after dinner and after meeting with everyone. They reached the door and buzzed for entry. Agent Simon Frost's voice came over the intercom, "We actually saw you coming. Alarm lights are going off everywhere. This place is cool!"

Roger asked, "Are you going to let us in?"

Frost answered, "Oh yeah."

When they heard the door unlock, they entered the vestibule and climbed up a flight of stairs to the main living area. Roger sat Ellen's carrier down and opened the door of it for her. Ellen stepped out, looked around, and went back in. Thor pulled his head back and asked, "You brought your *cat*?"

Paul and Roger just started laughing when they saw them.

Ray looked around like he wondered what he had walked into. "Those were some damn good drugs they gave me."

Paul choked out, "What the hell are you guys dressed up for?"

Thor scowled, "Roger said to blend in!" Thor told them about the helpful cabby who took them shopping. How he had paid him two hundred dollars, and how Pablo and Nelson were gay, Frost was a "sugahh", and he was a mid-life crisis dude.

Paul's jaw dropped as he looked at Roger.

Roger was stunned. His whole team had gone mad. "Haven't any of you been here before?"

Pablo spoke up, "I haven't been back since high school." The rest of them just shook their heads.

Roger walked over to the front window and looked down at the street. He watched several groups of people walk by and turned to ask them, "Have any of you looked outside since you got here?"

They all looked at each other. Thor said, "We haven't been here that long. We turned the TV on and just waited for you; checked out the building. Why?" Thor was walking towards the window.

Paul had moved over by the window, looked out, and just started laughing. "You guys have been *played*! Nobody dresses like that!"

Pablo ran over to the window and just started pulling his clothes off screaming, "That **bastard**!"

Thor and Frost started cracking up.

Nelson looked disappointed and said, "I kind of like how I look."

Ray sat down on the couch and looked at Roger. "I don't feel safe anymore."

Roger told the team to watch the street crowd and relax while he and Paul checked into their hotel. When they wanted to go to dinner, they could call. Roger knew of a crab shack that was essentially a cop bar, so it didn't matter if they got made or not. He knew Devon and Patterson wouldn't go there. Roger told Ray he would be bunking here with the guys.

Ray looked around and said, "I want my own room." Thor gave him the finger.

Roger and Paul made their way to the Marriott and checked in. Roger had to do some serious talking to get Ellen approved, and they insisted he take the staff elevator to his floor. Ellen thought Roger's pleas for her staying were sweet and sounded very genuine.

After leaving Ellen and their things in their rooms, Roger and Paul met in the lobby and decided to sit in the sidewalk bar until the other guys called. As soon as they walked in, Roger walked straight to the back bar stool and said something to a man at the end of the bar.

Paul walked over and Roger said, "Paul, I would like you to meet John Barry." Paul's eyebrows went up. John stood up, shook Paul's hand, and they all sat down.

John looked at Paul, "Roger says I need to call Ashley. I want you guys to know I was not going to do anything Ashley or I would regret. I did think I needed to follow up for her. I didn't want her calling anyone else. I have already been to the police station, gave them my name and number, and offered to volunteer for them in exchange for access to records. I wouldn't have done that if my motives were other than what I said."

Roger wasn't convinced but felt some better. "How did you know to come to New Orleans?"

John answered, "Ashley said Paul told her you thought Devon might be here."

Roger glanced at Paul who shrugged his shoulders.

Paul pushed his phone over, "Do you mind calling her now and giving her a new contact number?" John said sure and dialed Ashley.

John talked for a minute and looked at Paul, "She wants you." Paul took the phone and walked away. He was in the lobby talking for a while. John looked at Roger, "You may not know this, but Ashley's mother and my father married when I was new to the Company, and Ashley was a baby. She is my little half-sis. I did not believe for a minute she was committed to this. She just felt helpless and scared."

Roger took a long silent moment, "As far as I'm concerned none of this happened. You just have the bad luck of vacationing in New Orleans when all hell is going to cut loose."

John nodded, "Do you need help?"

Roger said, "I honestly don't know John. What is your relationship to the Company now?"

John looked serious, "Officially I am retired. I garden."

Roger nodded, "And unofficially?"

John said, "I trust you Roger, I saw what the Director did for you." Roger was impressed. John just let Roger know that he had access to top level FBI internal bulletins. John took a swig of his bourbon and said, "We have a problem in the Company." Roger nodded. John's glance became piercing, "You wouldn't say anything if you knew, but you have a problem at the Bureau too. I'm OSI now."

Roger was a little surprised, "I thought Office of Special Investigations was primarily Homeland Security related cases."

John nodded and said, "That's what the brochure says." He smiled.

Paul came back and sat down. He looked at John and said, "I appreciate what you are doing for Ashley. I understand a little what she can be like."

John laughed, "Oh yes! Did she tell you we have the same parents?"

Paul nodded, "She did." Just then Roger's phone rang. It was the rest of the guys ready for dinner. Roger asked John to join them. He could meet the group and get a feel for their case. John said he would like that. He paid the bartender for all of them, and they hailed a cab. Paul told John what the cabby had done to the guys. John said that was the best laugh he'd had in years. He asked them not to let the guys know he knew.

CHAPTER 15

oger, Paul, and John arrived at the Crab Shack a few minutes before the rest of the guys. Roger told the waiter they wanted a table for eight, maybe towards the back. When everyone arrived and the introductions were made, the conversation turned to maps, brochures, and cryptic discussions about the case. John stated he had actually lived in New Orleans before Katrina, and it appeared not many things had changed in the Quarter.

Roger had always felt one way to build a team was to allow them ample time to socialize with each other when on a field case. Often that meant combining update meetings with meals. Some of these guys were meeting each other for the first time, and Roger wanted to see how they interacted with each other.

Halfway through a feast of crawfish and crab legs a big guy came to the table and looked at John. John wiped his hands, got up, and introduced everyone to Detective Johnson, Homicide from the local PD. Detective Johnson said, "I gave your contact information to our supervisor, and he seemed to be pretty anxious for your help. He will probably call you tomorrow. He was meeting with the mayor most of the afternoon."

John said, "Thanks." The detective walked to the other side of the room to sit with three other officers.

John addressed the table, "I have followed this case in the news, and I know some of the people involved. I offered free homicide help in exchange for access to records. Being I am retired CIA, I think they will let me look at the data. Maybe. Anything I can do to help you guys just let me know." Roger noticed Thor looked a little skeptical. That was good. Pablo kept looking at the bartender.

Roger asked, "Pablo, something bothering you?"

"No, I just thought that bartender was reading lips. I'm probably wrong. Just ignore me."

Frost looked at him, "How in the hell can you tell if someone is doing that or not?"

Pablo said, "I do it. You have to concentrate, and it helps to block out some noise. Eyelids lower, you don't blink, sometimes you cover one ear. He was watching us and kept covering his ear with the bar rag. Usually, you don't even realize you're doing it." Roger looked over. The bartender was gone.

He looked at Paul.

Paul rose from his chair, "I am going to refresh my drink."

He walked over to the bar and a short little gal popped up from rinsing glasses. "What can I get ya?"

Paul asked, "Where is the bartender that was here a minute ago?"

"I'm the only bartender here."

Paul became anxious, "There was a guy standing behind the bar one minute ago."

The gal answered, "Oh, he was fixin' the drain or something. Do you need a beer?"

Paul left his beer on the bar and sprinted out the front door in time to see an orange utility truck pull out of the parking lot and quickly turn the corner. He couldn't catch the plate number. He ran back in and asked the gal behind the bar if her manager was there. She pointed toward a door at the end of the hall. Paul simultaneously knocked and pushed open the door to see a waitress straddling an ugly fat man on a chair. They both jumped up.

Paul held up his badge and yelled, "**FBI**. Did you call for a plumbing repair? There was a man behind your bar. Do you know who that was?" The waitress screamed and slipped out of the room straightening her skirt.

The ugly man stammered, "I didn't call no plumber. Was I supposed to?"

Paul slammed the door and went back to the table. He told the guys what had happened and Thor raised his beer mug to John, "We almost made it through a friggin' meal. Welcome to hangin' around that guy!" as he pointed at Roger. Roger asked Pablo if he could describe the guy to a sketch artist. Pablo said yes. Roger also told everyone to write down the conversations they were having to the best of their memory. This guy might have 'heard' it all.

They decided after dinner they would stop by the field office, introduce themselves, and have Pablo sit with the artist. Pablo asked, "Can I call Jeanne and have her come over when we get done?"

Roger said, "Actually she needs to meet with the artist too. Try not to talk about the case until Thor has a chance to interview her."

Thor looked at Roger, "I might as well do that tonight." Roger could tell Thor was back on his game.

They paid their tab and were outside waiting for cabs. Ray looked beat. Roger said, "I think you need to rest. We won't bother you tomorrow either if you need to take it easy." Ray just nodded.

Frost was going to step off the curb to hail a cab, and John jumped in front of him. "Let me get that, *Sugahh.*"

Frost gave him a pretend slug to the arm and said, "That is now classified."

Spicey and Sasha decided to go for a little walk. They turned the store signs over to say "CLOSED" and checked they had their pistols. The locals who knew them nodded or waved. The tourists marveled at how colorful their dresses were. Sasha said, "What we doing hun?" She knew it took an Act of God for Spicey to want to take a walk as far as Burgundy Street, especially in this heat. She knew it probably had something to do with Tourey.

Spicey answered her, "Tourey wants some dirt on a dude who lives down here. I think he owes Tourey some money, and Tourey gunna squeeze 'em."

Sasha said, "We best be sneaky so not to look involved."

Spicey said, "Yes, girlfriend." They walked up to the wrought iron gate in front of the house. Spicey opened it and started walking to the door.

Sasha grabbed the back of her skirt and asked, "What you gunna say?"

Spicey turned around, "You just watch and try to look stupid."

Spicey grabbed the big brass knocker on the front door and slammed it four times against the metal plate. The sound was deafening. Sasha was moaning, "*Dang, dang.*"

In a minute flat, a skinny little woman answered the door and said, "We don't want none!" She started to close the door on them.

Spicey yelled, "Wait, *wait*! I was sent here for *you*!"

The little woman looked at Spicey and all the amulets around her neck and asked, "Who sent you?"

Spicey smiled and crossed herself, "You must first confirm your name to the Spirits. This is too important."

The skinny woman answered slowly, "I be called Wilma Abrams."

Spicey reached into her cleavage, thumbed off two hundred dollar bills, and cupped them in her hand. With her other hand she had been making motions over Wilma's head and chanting. Wilma was spellbound. Spicey dropped her arm and said, "The Spirits sent me to answer some of your prayers Wilma. Look in your pocket there."

Wilma didn't take her eyes off Spicey, but she lowered her hand into her apron pocket and felt the money. She quickly pulled it out and started screaming, "Praise the Lord. Oh my Heavenly Father. Praise the LORD!" She hugged Sasha and Spicey. "I have been prayin' for a miracle. You brought me my miracle!"

Spicey said, "Can we sit inside for a minute? I am pretty warm out here, and I have more to tell you."

Wilma looked up and down the street. "Come on in. I think we have a quick minute or two here." They stepped into the cool air of the front parlor. There was a slight spicy aroma in the air, and the marble floors reflected like mirrors.

Sasha noticed the quality of the furnishings and remarked, "Wilma, you certainly have good taste."

Wilma chuckled, "Oh dear me, this is not my house. I'm just the cleaning lady for Mr. Jacobs."

Spicey said, "I was told if I found you, to tell you to go immediately to your church and pray. There would be more miracles in your life, soon."

Sasha asked Wilma, "Where is your church?" Wilma said, "Oh my, it's about four blocks away, but I haven't finished cleanin'. Mr. Jacobs is very particular. I'm afraid I can't leave." Wilma looked flustered.

Spicey said, "Sasha couldn't you walk with Wilma to her church? I'll stay and watch the house for Wilma in case Mr. Jacobs comes home. That way he will know Wilma didn't just leave her job."

Wilma looked at Sasha, "Would you do that? Would you go with me?"

Sasha said, "Sure," and gave Spicey a dirty look.

Then Sasha said to Spicey, "Why don't you finish Wilma's cleaning for her?"

Spicey gave Sasha a big smile Sasha knew wasn't real, "What a grand idea! Then Wilma won't even have to come back here tonight. She can pray as long as she wants!" Sasha gave Spicey a dirty look again.

Wilma said, "You just lock up when you're done. Finish wiping this glassware and dust that room over there. But do NOT go upstairs. I finished all that, and no one is allowed in Mr. Jacob's office up there." She grabbed Sasha's hand and pulled her out the door. Sasha looked over her shoulder and stuck her tongue out.

As soon as Sasha and Wilma were through the gate, Spicey locked the front door and quickly walked straight to the back of the house. She found the back door, unlocked it, and saw it was directly across from the servant's narrow stairwell to the upstairs. Good escape route if she got caught. Out the back door was a tall stone wall courtyard. Shit. She walked outside and found a side gate. It was locked. She studied it. Even fearing for her life she couldn't straddle those iron spokes on the top. She went back in and found a small ring of keys on a hook by the back door. She tried them all and found the gate key, unlocked it, and went back in. She knew there was no substitute for proper exit planning.

Once she was upstairs she found a locked door she assumed was his office. She squatted on the floor, opened her bag, and brought out a soft leather case she zipped open. Inside were her professional lock picks. She was in the office in less than two minutes. She placed her large handbag on the desk, pulled out a wireless scanner, and began scanning his rolodex. Then she picked the desk drawer and found several small address books, and one little black book with just a few names. She scanned all of them. She relocked the drawer, a much more difficult task, than opening one. Then she started scanning his day planner and a bank statement.

Spicey knew she was running out of time, so she quickly scanned a few old phone bills and left the office. She was relocking the office door when she heard a voice from below.

"Wilma?"

Spicey froze. Then she heard the male voice again from farther away.

"Wilma?"

She quickly made her way down the servant's stairwell only to hear heavy footsteps going up the main stairwell. She froze mid-step and estimated that if the wall wasn't there, they would be looking at each other about now. She held her breath. The slightest sound could give her away. His steps continued up. She slipped out the back door, the side gate, and ran down the alley behind the house.

She leaned against an old dumpster to catch her breath. She was still panting when a young man jumped from around the dumpster with a knife and said, "Give me yo money Bitch!"

Spicey looked him in the eye as she lowered her hand into her purse, found her pistol and shot through her purse to the ground next to his feet. When he jumped, she tackled him, took his knife, and held the gun to his temple. He froze. She pawed around in his pants until she found his roll of cash. She let him watch as she peeled off two bills from his roll with only her thumb. Spicey yanked him to his feet, shoved the rest of his money roll down the front of his pants, and said, "You owe me a new purse. I want your momma's name." He mumbled something and Spicey shot again next to his shoe. "You don't hear so good boy! Momma's name!"

He answered "Donna Blew."

Spicey said, "How old is she, and who's her daddy?"

The boy frowned at her. "I don't know how old she is. Her daddy named Daryl."

Spicey frowned, reached into the front of the kid's pants, and retrieved the roll of cash. She thumbed off another bill and stuck the roll back in. "Now. Tell me your momma's name."

The kid was terrified. "My momma's name is Adele Brown. She's been missin' a couple weeks now. I ain't lying', lady. I just tryin' to get by 'til she gets home."

Spicey sensed that was the truth. She looked at the kid, "What's your name?" He answered Jerome. Spicey motioned with her head, "You're coming back to my place, and we are going to talk. I just might be able to find your momma." She glared at Jerome, "You try something cute…"

Jerome interrupted, "I know, you'll shoot me."

"Damn right."

Mark Mills, the sniper, was being transported from the Indy Federal Building to a special prison in Richmond. The transport van had an FBI driver in a caged front seat and an armed FBI agent in the back with Mark. Mark waited until they were in heavy traffic and began making very slow half circle rocking motions with his chin. The agent just stared at Mark's face. Mark was a trained hypnotist. He hoped eventually the agent would focus on his nose and enter a hypnotic state. The agent glazed over in ten minutes. The driver was consumed with traffic. Mark moved to the agent's side, took his keys, unlocked his cuffs, and the back door of the van. Mark also took the agent's gun. Mark quickly moved back and said, "When I count to three, you are going to tell the driver you have to piss. You want him pull to over to the shoulder, and come back here. You will not notice your gun is missing. One. Two. Three."

Mark was back on his side of the van. The agent looked around some and grabbed the radio hanging on the side of the van. "Hey, pull over somewhere I can take a piss. Hurry. You come back here and watch this guy." Mark chuckled. The agent looked at him, "Maybe I should just piss on you?"

Mark said, "Whatever makes you feel important."

The driver pulled over on a large grassy shoulder between two highway exits. He put the flashers on and killed the engine. He walked around to the back of the van, opened the door, and stepped in. Mark shot them both. He took the clothes off the driver and put them on. He also took their money, phones, badges, and keys. He stepped out of the van, locked the back door, and slid into the driver's seat. He knew the van was on GPS tracking, and he continued his way to Richmond. The whole thing took minutes. Once he arrived downtown he parked, took a cab to the airport, and got on a private jet to New Orleans with a pilot he and Mathew used fairly often.

Once in flight he called Mathew's burn number, it was only good for another hour. Mathew answered, "Mark?"

Mark said, "Yeah. Wanted to let you know the Feds got me, I escaped in transport, and I'm headed to you now. I didn't talk Mathew. They knew your name and address and Jason's. I think they got the lab."

Mathew was silent, "They could have got all of that from you."

Mark said, "All I ever knew about Jason was that he was in Virginia. I never knew his address. You believe me or not. I'm not running from you. This is your call, and I am telling you straight. Where do you want to meet?"

Mathew gave Mark another number to call when he arrived and hung up.

✳ ✳ ✳

Jeanne and Jeremiah finished the work on the generator and were preparing to leave. Mary asked, "Okay, what do we write on our note?"

Teresa said, "Let me write it. I have tiny handwriting. We can get more on one note."

Linda asked, "What do we ask?"

I said, "Write that there are Spirits in the room who can read her mind and to think of anything that will help us catch the man who did this to her."

Linda said, "Good. Also ask her name.'

Mary frowned, "You guys, it's a sticky note. Not a manuscript!"

Teresa said, "Before you start writing we have to get her attention. That note is only going to last a minute or so."

I went over to the couch and held a blanket over me. She could see the blanket moving and screamed for Mambo. Mambo told her, "The Spirits want to tell you something." She shrugged and returned to her spot on the floor. At least I got her attention. Teresa was writing like crazy and put the note on Kyeeta's nose. She peeled it off and read it. It disappeared in her hand. She looked at Mambo.

We heard her thoughts. "If you can hear my thoughts, I am afraid for my son. The man threatened to kill him if I came back. I don't know his name, but there are two of them! The one who raped me lives near the Quarter somewhere. He has a prison room in his house. Wears plastic gloves all the time. My son, Jerome Brown, needs me." That was all we got. She just kept thinking the same thing over and over.

Mambo pointed to the outside. It looked like Jeanne and Jeremiah were leaving. Mary started waving goodbye to Mambo, and Mambo made a motion like she was swatting a fly. Okay then. We rushed out to the boat, and Jeremiah was telling

Jeanne they were heading toward where he had found her.

The swamp was beautiful and scary at the same time. Jeremiah let Jeanne guide the boat for a while. He pointed to where he had found her. There was a small island type area that had a few huge cypress trees all knotted together. Jeremiah told Jeanne she had been curled up on the cypress roots. He almost hadn't seen her.

He had her paddle a ways farther and pointed to a marshy clearing. "Look through those trees there, you see it? That narrow dirt area there. I think he drove you there and made you walk into the swamp. You made it quite a ways." Jeanne's skin was crawling. It looked *very* familiar, even though she knew she had been drugged. She remembered.

Jeanne look at Jeremiah, "When we get back, I want you to show me where that is from the road." Jeremiah nodded.

Teresa was watching several alligators swimming around the boat. Mary said, "How did she get over there from here without being eaten alive?"

Linda shuddered, "Can you imagine how much worse this is at night?"

Jeremiah took over the paddle and said, "We best get you back so you can go see your brother. I think Mambo is pretty puzzled what that generator is supposed to do for her. I don't think she has ever had electricity. This may get the Spirits jumpin'." He laughed. It sounded like a bunch of swamp birds started laughing too.

Some pretty creepy noises were in the swamp. Jeanne couldn't help but think you would need Spirits nowadays to live without electricity. She asked Jeremiah why no one had thought to bring Mambo a generator before. Jeremiah answered, "I think folks believe she is above all that. They don't think of her as having human needs like you and me. You saw what she did when we tried to give her a gun. Livin' in the swamp all alone and still wanted no part of it. Plus, I hear tell that most things you give her she gives away."

* * *

Tourey walked to his house after visiting Spicey. He couldn't stop thinking about what she said about Mambo. Maybe he would go tomorrow. When he got to his door, there was a business card stuck in the trim by the handle. He pulled it out and turned it over. John Barry, a cell number, and a hand scratched note: Meet me at eight.

Tourey put the card in his pocket and slowly walked through his entire house. John Barry. Possibility he was on the wrong radar. What was it that Spicey said about a dark spirit looking for him? If there was, John Barry would know.

Tourey assumed they were meeting in their favorite spot, the Law Library at Loyola University. He decided to take a nap. He had almost two hours, and it was too hot to do anything.

CHAPTER 16

Dusty was trying to think of the guy's name that used to hang out at Mickey's bar all the time. Seems like he came from that building across the street every now and then. If Tourey was willing to pay him five hundred dollars, he wanted to get it. His income from portraits was still only half what it had been before Katrina, and it seemed his bills kept going up. Swear to God, if Tourey got him in trouble again, it would be the last time! He decided just to stop in at Mickey's, do a couple of portraits, get a feel for the place. You couldn't really ask any questions without puttin' on suspicion. Not in *Nawlens*. In Nawlens, you put yourself somewhere, and the information comes to you.

He walked into Mickey's about eight o'clock. Quite a few tourists were having sandwiches and beer. The bar stools were all occupied but one at the far end. Dusty took that stool and laid his drawing pad next to him. The bartender came over and asked, "What you havin'?"

Dusty really didn't want a drink, but he had to justify being there, "Man I hate to ask, but I think one of those girly drinks that tastes all fruity sounds good. I've been out in the sun all day."

The bartender laughed, "Why don't I fix you an ice cream grasshopper and put it in a coffee mug, so no one knows it."

That actually sounded good. "You do that, and I'll do a free picture for ya." Dusty turned his pad over and started sketching. He wanted it to look flattering, so the bartender would promote him to the locals.

By the time the bartender came back Dusty was done. He tore the picture off the pad and handed it to him. "Damn, that looks just like me! Thanks man!" The bartender walked past everyone on the stools holding up the picture and pointing down at Dusty. Then he taped the picture to the mirrored wall behind the cash register. The drink tasted great. No wonder the chicks liked this stuff. Dusty gulped it and pushed the mug to the edge for another. The bartender came down and said, "They may taste harmless, but they're not. I'll get you another, but at least give the ice cream a chance to melt." He grinned and left with the mug.

A couple in their thirties walked down to the end of the bar and asked if he would sketch them. He had them sit at a small table behind him, turned his stool around and did the sketch without leaving his spot.

They liked it so well, they gave him a hundred dollar bill. Dusty turned around and asked the bartender to break the bill into twenties. When he came back, Dusty gave him one and said, "Your commission."

"Thanks," put his hand out and said, "Name's Scotty."

"Dusty." He raised his mug and said, "To my new best friend," and smiled.

Scotty smiled and asked, "You want another?"

Dusty shook his head, "Nah, time I took a nap. I might see ya later after the tourists crap out. You work the late shift?"

Scotty answered, "All but Wednesdays. I pull the good tip nights." He held up the twenty Dusty had just handed him, "Like tonight!"

Dusty's cell phone rang. The caller ID said, "Govt." Ah shit! He laughed that his guilty conscious was getting the better of him. He answered, "Yeah?"

It was Agent Frank Mass from the local FBI field office. Agent Mass asked, "Hey, Dusty, I know it's late, but our artist is out sick. I need a couple of portraits done here if you've got the time. I'm willing to pay double for the short notice."

Dusty said, "Sure, I got time. Be there shortly." He hung up his phone and thought about all this sudden extra money. He might just go down and pay off the whole light bill this month. At one time!

* * *

Thor and Pablo headed over to the field office so Pablo could meet with the artist, and Thor could get a feel for the staff there. The plan was to have Jeanne meet with the artist, and then come back and interview with Thor at Core's building. Now nicknamed Star Ship because of the level of technology in the structure.

Agent Nelson and Agent Frost decided they wanted to visit the local police and just drive around the area. They had rented a car and were armed with several maps of the area as well as a local newspaper, the Times-Picayune.

Roger and Paul had gone back to the Marriott to look over some papers. John Barry had stated he wanted to hook up with an old friend and do a little bar hopping. Ray decided since it had only been eight hours since he was blown up, he was going to bed.

Roger invited Paul to come to his room to go over the Ellen papers. Paul came into the room, saw the empty carrier, and looked around. He asked Roger, "How do we explain Ellen popping in and out of places? Cats don't do that do they?"

Roger said, "I don't know what we are supposed to do. I guess I have just expected she will know what she can get away with." Just then

Roger's phone rang, he looked at the ID and mouthed "Director" to Paul. Paul sat down. He watched Roger's expression deteriorate quickly. Then Roger asked, "Are they both dead?" Then, "I'm sure he's headed here. I'll keep you posted."

Roger closed the phone and said, "Mark Mills escaped. Killed two transport guards. He has their badges and weapons."

Paul couldn't believe it. "What is the problem? Everybody is just escaping us? We have four dead Feds in one day? You think he's coming here?"

Roger answered, "I would. He has to convince Mathew he can still be trusted, or he is dead. Oh shit. He knows we got the lab." Roger was pacing, "There is an APB out for a private pilot who left Richmond for New Orleans two hours ago. Mills is probably already here. I have to call Thor."

Paul rolled his eyes and said, "Thor's hanging by a thread now!"

Roger said, "I know."

"While we are talking about threads, I think it is a thin one that Barry chose to stay at the Marriott and sit in the lobby bar. Kind of like he was expecting us."

Roger nodded, "He was. He knows I stay here. The Marriott is Fed friendly. I don't know exactly what we have with Barry either, but he did tell me he is OSI. Keep that one to yourself." Paul had a lot of questions he needed to ask if this roller coaster ever stopped. Roger dialed Thor. Paul could hear his reaction from across the room. Roger was holding the phone away from his ear and shaking his head. It was a good five minutes before Roger was able to tell Thor that he would talk to him in about an hour.

Paul stated that the Ellen papers may have saved their asses. Roger nodded agreement, while he called room service to order a few cartons of milk for Ellen. He had actually seen her drink it before. Paul laughed, "We need to pick up a litter box even though she doesn't use them. I'm sure the hotel staff will wonder about a cat that doesn't shit!" Roger laughed.

Paul sat at the small table with both his hands on the pile of Ellen papers and said, "This has been quite a day even for us. I'm starting to question everything and everybody, and you haven't even decided about Manigat yet!"

Roger nodded, "If we ever close this case for good, it is definitely going to make the Bureaus top ten case files. We may be famous!" Roger smiled.

Paul laughed, "I'm already famous just being able to hang with you! I heard Thor call us Bat Man and Robin to Pablo."

Roger laughed and said, "He's just pissed that cabby got him."

Paul was now wiping his eyes he was laughing so hard, "I will never get that vision out of my head! They think this case is nuts, and they don't even know about the gals and Ellen! The more I think about it the more it blows my mind!"

"I doubt either one of us passes the Bureau shrink this year."

* * *

Mathew Core had some decisions to make. He was sitting on his veranda sucking on a straw shoved into a sweet tea. It was either all over now, assuming they had the lab and Jason, or he had to take the whole game. He decided to call Carl.

Carl spat, "I'm going to have to ask you not to call this number…"

Mathew interrupted him, "Listen to what I have to say first. About five years ago, I decided that my personal business needed some insurance. I have paid a premium on that insurance policy from each transaction you assigned me. Five percent to you and five percent to Thomas. Offshore accounts, your names, and a few scattered transactions to prove you were aware. Plus you guys gave each other money from time to time. You are a very rich man now Carl, but you have a problem. Jason and his little programs were not the only system I have in place. Failure of certain transactions to be ordered by me will cause a lot of data to be sent to places and people you don't want seeing your real business. Now, were you about to say you had a different number for me to call?"

Carl was silent.

Mathew asked, "You still there Carl?"

Carl answered, "How do I know you're not bluffing?"

Mathew said, "You got a piece of paper? Let me give you an account number and a code you can use to see some of your money." Mathew dictated the information and hung up. He took a long draw on the straw in his sweet tea and wondered what he was going to do about Mark.

William Patterson finished reading to the kids at the library story hour and walked over to Mabel Cummings, the Head Librarian. She quickly looked up and smiled. More than once Mr. Jacobs had saved her from an embarrassing announcement that Reading Hour had to be cancelled. William smiled and handed her a glossy brochure with pictures of Disney on the cover. She glanced at the brochure and gave him a questioning look. William smiled and said, "A non-profit group I support, funds trips like this for under-privileged children a few times a year. As a supporter, I am able to recommend children to the selection committee. I would like the library's support by allowing me to host another art competition, with the prize being this trip."

Mabel was beside herself, "What a lovely idea! You just bring in whatever promotional materials you want to, and I will present it to the Board." William thanked her and left smiling. The president of the Library Board was one of his club members. He would get the posters ready tomorrow. By his count they still needed at least four more boys and a couple of girls.

* * *

Tourey walked up the wide marble staircase to the Loyola Law Library only to hear John as he walked through the doorway, "Let's take a walk instead." Tourey turned his head and saw his old friend leaning against the end cap of a long row of books.

Tourey shook his hand and said, "Retirement becomes you John." They both turned and made small talk until they were well into the common park area. John pointed to a secluded bench, and they both sat down.

John asked, "What are you working on right now?"

Tourey kind of shrugged and answered, "A world of loose ends."

"The Company gave me permission to borrow you."

Tourey looked at him, "For gardening?"

John laughed, "I see you checked out my cover. I'm OSI now."

Tourey just stared at him. Then Tourey started shaking his head, "I remember the last time you borrowed me, I got shot. Twice. And run over by a friggin' truck!" They both started laughing.

John said, "You set me up with a diseased hooker and told me twenty minutes too late!"

Tourey sat up straight, "I didn't know!" They both started laughing again.

John looked away, "Too bad we can't call them the good ol' days, can we?"

Tourey looked serious, "No we can't." Tourey looked at John, "Isn't OSI mostly Homeland? I *never* leave New Orleans, part of my deal with the Company."

John answered in a hushed voice, "I can't tell you everything, or I would. Office of Special Investigations is exactly that. Who do you think investigates the Company and the Bureau now?"

Tourey shrugged and asked, "Aren't I part of the problem then?"

John laughed, "You have been so deep, so long, half of your own guys don't know you exist. I'm not worried you are part of this problem. I trust you, and I'm sure I need you. What are you working on if I can ask?"

Tourey answered, "Officially, we have a primeval soup of international nasty that seems to swirl around Nawlens these days. There isn't any effective law enforcement. I can't keep up. We are even drawing international criminals because of it.

Assassins, gun runners, drugs, human trafficking, you name it. Who would have thought there would be a place in the States to do all of this and not get caught? It works out great for the bad guys, not so much for me these last three years. Unofficially, I just started checking on a pedophile for a friend, and I have been looking to find out something about the building across from Mickey's in the Quarter."

John spent twenty minutes bringing Tourey up to date on his involvement. How it started with a request from Ashley to find Devon. That led to him finding out from the FBI that Devon and Patterson, a pedophile, were in the French Quarter, and their escape had been masterminded by Mathew Core. That led to the FBI discovering a Virginia computer lab that both the FBI and the CIA had seized this morning. So you know there were some serious security breaches both domestic and foreign. Then they had a bombing of that location three hours later, with two CIA operatives killed and an FBI Agent wounded. Then they had the bugging of the survivor's hospital room, the escape of the sniper Mark Mills, and the killing of two FBI transport agents.

Tourey listened with the facial expressions of a kid being told a horror story. Tourey exclaimed, "Jesus Christ! That has all happened today?"

John nodded, then he said, "We may have had an encounter here at the Crab Shack at dinner tonight. Watch out for orange utility trucks." John chuckled and slipped Tourey his card, "Put me on speed dial, and I think you should introduce yourself to Roger Dance. You don't want him thinking you are on the wrong side of any of this."

John told Tourey he was sure Mathew Core was in New Orleans. The FBI team that had just arrived was going to turn the town into the Wild West if they had to.

Tourey didn't like the sound of any of it. He whispered, "I've heard Dance and Casey border on spooky. They figure things out in hours that should take months."

John was nodding, "That's not a rumor. That's true. They have not asked for my help, and may not. Roger is a very cautious man. Did you know the Director of the FBI designated him *National Lead* on the Devon- Patterson case?"

Tourey whistled. "Another Dillinger? I guess I have to study up on this case. I didn't realize it was so God damn important. I knew the FBI was moving into that building, I didn't know why." Tourey rolled his neck, "I met one of them."

"It's really not just Devon and Patterson. It's who they know and how they pulled this off. We end up back at Mathew Core, and I doubt if Mathew bombed his own computer lab. Who do you know that could have pulled that off in hours?"

Tourey shook his head, "Nobody."

John nodded, "Which leads me to believe this is going to end up OSI anyway. You in?"

Tourey said, "*Ah shit.* You know, a psychic told me this afternoon a dark spirit was looking for me. Is it you?"

John smiled, "It's probably Mathew Core."

CHAPTER 17

Thor had Pablo call his sister Jeanne to meet them at the N.O. FBI field office to work with an artist. Pablo waited by the main door for her arrival, and Thor introduced himself to the agents there. Pablo was going to describe the man at the Crab Shack who may have been lip reading. Roger suspected it might have been Core or one of his men. Jeanne was going to describe Devon and Patterson. It was always a light crew in the evenings, but the field office Senior SSA Frank Mass had stayed to meet them. Thor kept remembering Roger said there was a problem in this office. In spite of his questionable personality, he was trying very hard to appear cordial and make a good impression. He didn't want to contribute to Roger's stress. He couldn't stop thinking about everything that had happened in just one day! He felt like he was in a movie.

Just this morning at breakfast he had told his favorite waitress in Indy he might be close to being able to take a long deserved vacation. Was that only this morning? It seemed a week ago! *Then that damn trial!* His thoughts were interrupted by squeals of joy from the lobby. He looked over, and Pablo was hugging the most beautiful woman he had ever seen.

HOLY>>>> The closer she got, the harder it was to *breathe*. Damn. She could be a weapon!

Jeanne reached her hand out to Thor and said, "SSA Thor, I think I can provide the artist enough information on both Devon and Patterson to help catch these bastards, sir." Her demeanor was that of a trained warrior. When she stared at Thor, her piercing blue eyes almost made him want to turn away. **Holy crap, you didn't want this chick mad at you**! He couldn't imagine how Devon had overpowered her. As if she read his mind she said, "He kept me heavily drugged."

Thor partially composed himself and pointed her to where the artist was waiting. When she left, Thor looked at Pablo. Pablo said, "We're twins."

Thor threw his head back and laughed, "You might be pretty, but you got the short stick!" Pablo laughed. He knew for Thor that was actually a high compliment. Roger had asked Thor to get some more information on Pablo. Thor pointed towards a small office where he and Pablo could talk while they waited his turn with the artist.

✱ ✱ ✱

Special Agent Nelson and SSA Frost had gone to the local New Orleans Police Department to let them know they were in town and to offer their services. FBI seldom gets involved in local policing unless asked, and can only participate if it doesn't jeopardize a case they are working on. When they walked in, they asked the desk sergeant if they could speak to the officer in charge. He told them to make themselves comfortable, and he would page him.

Nelson and Frost walked around the reception lobby and ended at the Wall of Fame. They looked at the picture of Bernard Jacobs giving the Police Commissioner a one hundred thousand dollar check and whistled. Todd kept looking at Bernard's face and said, "This damn case has me suspecting everybody. That guy right there looks like a skinny Patterson with a beard."

Frost laughed, "I know what you mean, and I have only been on this case one day!"

Todd looked at him, "That's right, you and Manigat just started this... *hang on!*"

A moment later a fortyish officer came around the corner and greeted them. "Do you guys mind if we talk in here?" he was pointing to a small conference room off the lobby.

Frost said, "No problem." The officer's badge read Demiere. Frost said, "Officer Demiere, we are FBI, and we have a few other agents with us. We are in the city because a very nasty case of ours has led us here. We want you aware we have agents staying at the Marriott on Canal and in a building across from Mickey's Bar in the Quarter."

Officer Demiere had been taking notes and said, "What are you guys looking for specifically?"

Frost answered, "My senior agent has not given us permission to talk about the case yet. I may be back here tomorrow. We just wanted to make a courtesy call and offer our services if you want them." Both Frost and Nelson passed him their cards.

Officer Demiere asked, "I'm sure you both are aware of the struggle this department has had with both crime and corruption. Are you looking at us? "

Frost chuckled, "I think you are the only ones we aren't looking at!" Officer Demiere laughed.

Nelson said, "We have a couple of maps and just want to get a quick feel for the city tonight. Any places in particular you think we should stay away from?"

Just then the door burst open and the desk sergeant said, "We have an officer down and two more pinned over on Desiree. I have one unit responding. It sounds like quite a shootout."

Officer Demiere quickly rose and said, "Sorry, I have to go to that. We're short tonight, and we have a nasty gang trying to horn into that hood."

Frost and Nelson looked at each other, "You want company?"

Agent Frost drove, and they followed Officer Demiere through what they thought were some very bad neighborhoods. Both of their cars screeched to a stop in what could only be called Hell. They saw an officer pinned behind a dumpster taking fire and one on a porch taking fire.

A patrol car was parked on the lawn, one officer was on the ground leaning against the car and another shooting from behind the passenger door. Two cars circled them with shooters, and three shooters were running on foot. Officer Demiere parked next to the wounded officer's car and was taking fire trying to reach him.

Todd looked at Frost, "Remind you of a training exercise?"

Frost said, "Yep. I'll drop you in thirty feet." Todd prepared to exit the rapidly accelerating car. He threw his door open, rolled to a clump of trees, and began shooting. Frost took the corner on two wheels and jumped out seconds before hitting one of the cars head on. He rolled about five feet, leaped behind a dog house, and started shooting. He hit two tires on the second car and the passenger shooter in the center of the forehead. The back seat shooter's head exploded in red from a round from the other direction. The passengers of the vehicle Frost rammed were shot as they ran from the wreckage. Frost counted. All ground shooters were down, and one of the second auto's passengers had his hands up. It was over. Three more police units pulled up sirens blaring. Frost went looking for Nelson.

Agent Nelson was helping Officer Demiere prepare the injured patrolman for the ambulance. Todd had blood streaming down his white shirt sleeve. Simon asked, "You okay?"

Nelson answered, "Just nicked me." The other officers came over to introduce themselves. Frost and Nelson knew the local officers were under-paid, certainly not appreciated and often under-trained. New Orleans had a long way to go, and it was getting worse.

One young officer was shaking his head and said, "We have four shooters in each car and three on foot. All dead but one guy in the last car there. I have only seen that kind of shit in the movies! Jesus! You guys can shoot! And move! Hell that guy rolls faster than I can run!" He was pointing at Nelson. Frost saw the ambulance pull around the corner and motioned for everyone to get out of the way.

A minute later the coroner's wagon showed up. The driver got out and asked, "How many?"

Nelson answered, "Ten."

The driver got on his radio, "Need another wagon or two."

Officer Demiere offered to give them a lift to the hospital to have Nelson's wound dressed. They gladly accepted. Thor wasn't going to be happy. They had totaled a rental car less than an hour after pick up. In the car on the way to the hospital Officer Demiere said, "Back at the station you asked me which neighborhoods to stay out of?" They all started laughing.

While Frost was waiting for Nelson to finish with the nurses, they all thought he looked like Brad Pitt, he called Thor and told him what had happened. Thor told him when they were done to get back to the Star Ship and try not to destroy anything or kill anyone on the way.

* * *

Spicey and Jerome had walked back to Spicey's place and were sitting at the small dinette table in Spicey's kitchen. Colorful beads covered the one small window instead of curtains, and the small counter was lined with colorful jars of spices and bowls of ripe fruit. Spicy had watched Jerome devour a poor boy sandwich and two bowls of cereal. He had said grace and thanked Spicey when he finished. He had been raised by a momma that wanted him to do good. Spicey looked at him, "I need you to tell me nothing but the truth here if you want me to help you find your Momma. You got that?" Jerome nodded. "Tell me about her."

Jerome took a deep breath and wiped a tear. He told Spicey about his momma raisin' him alone, how she had a tailor shop in the Quarter with an apartment like Spicey's. He came home from school two weeks ago, and his momma was gone. His voice broke when he said she hadn't come home since. Spicey's heart was breaking for him. Adele sure didn't sound like the type of woman to do that to her kid. Spicey asked, "What did the police tell you?"

Jerome stood up, "The police? I didn't go to no police! Momma told me you can't trust the police in Nawlens!"

Spicey motioned for him to sit down. She looked at him and said, "For the most part what your momma told you about the police is true. There are a lot of good people trying to change that. A lot of those good people are police. They work for very little money and risk their lives every day. Why you think the good ones do that?" Jerome just shrugged. Spicey continued, "They have hope they can make a difference, and eventually Nawlens will be back to the city we all loved. What do you suppose happens if the good citizens decide not to go to the police anymore?" Jerome shrugged. Spicey yelled at him, "I want to hear an answer! Think it out! What happens if there is no police anymore?"

Jerome said, "I guess there would be nothing to stop the bad people, and the good people move away."

Spicey nodded and smiled, "That was the right answer! They aren't perfect, but they're what we got! We have to go to them when we need them to give them a chance to prove they can do it! You and me are going together in the mornin' to the police station. Then you are going to go to school, and I am going to call in some very special favors owed me in this town. We are *gonna* find your momma!"

Jerome came over and hugged her. He wouldn't let go. Spicey could tell he was cryin' and didn't want her to see. She almost started crying herself when Sasha stormed through the door.

"I've had 'nuff *Church* to do me 'til next year! I finally told Wilma the *Spirits* needed a nap! Lordy." Then Sasha saw Jerome and said, "Hi," real quiet. She looked at Spicey with one eyebrow up.

Spicey said, "This is Jerome. His momma is missin', and we are going to find her startin' tomorrow morning."

Sasha ran over to Jerome, "How long your momma been gone, hun?"

Jerome said, "Couple of weeks."

Sasha was shaking her head making tsk, tsk sounds. Then she said, "Your momma a friend of Spicey?"

Jerome said, "No."

Sasha said, "You a friend of Spicey?"

Jerome said, "No. She robbed me. And shot at me." Jerome looked towards Spicey with a little grin on his face.

Sasha looked shocked and turned to Spicey who was waving a dish rag at Jerome, "You tell her who robbed who first!"

* * *

Dusty had finished the sketches and had been told by Jeanne and Pablo that they looked just like the people they were describing. Dusty asked about the sketch of Mathew Core, "Just what did this guy do?"

Thor asked, "Why? You know that guy?" Dusty wasn't sure. Hate to get someone in trouble for nothin'.

He answered, "Just looks kind of familiar is all."

Thor answered, "If you think of something, you call me. That guy is bad news if he is who we think he is." He gave Dusty his card. Dusty slipped the card into his shirt pocket. Shit, shit, shit. That was the guy he'd been tryin' to find for Tourey.

Thor looked at Pablo and Jeanne. He cleared his throat, "I know it's late, but do you mind going to the Star Ship? I'll catch up with you shortly. We can get these interviews done tonight. Tomorrow may be as much fun as today."

Pablo rolled his eyes, and Jeanne put her hand out to Thor. "Thank you SSA Thor," and she turned to leave. Thor went looking for Frank Mass. He had already left. So much for hospitality. Thor asked another agent what reports Frost needed to complete for them in regards to their shooting tonight. The agent explained Frost could just fill out the computer form for Incidents, and their office would do the rest. Thor thought it was good news for them, but probably not for the field office. More than likely there would be more incidents to follow.

CHAPTER 18

Teresa, Mary, Linda, and I were sitting on Jeremiah's boat watching alligators. Every now and then Mary would point her finger at one of the alligators and say, "Don't even think about it." Jeremiah had gone into his house and Jeanne had left for town.

Teresa looked at Linda and said, "Well, we found Jeanne, Jeremiah and Mambo. Do you think we should try to find Adele's son, Jerome?"

Linda looked at Mary and me and shrugged, "I don't know why not. Ellen took off to be with Roger and Paul and didn't really tell us what to do."

Mary asked, "If we each try to do that aura thing, we might end up in different places. Can we do this as a group?"

I said, "Adele's voice is what I remember. You could hear the motherly love in it. Maybe if we all try to remember her voice and concentrate on Jerome's name, it will work."

Linda said it was worth a try. We all concentrated and held hands so we wouldn't lose each other. Suddenly, we were standing on a corner looking into a Voodoo shop. Mary said, "This probably isn't right." Just then a lady exited the store with two poodles on leashes. One was bright pink and one was neon blue.

Linda said, "Can you believe what they do to their pets?" I looked out to the street. It was filled with people all dressed as clowns. It must be a *parade*! A guy went past us on a unicycle with monkeys hanging all over him. There were jugglers, people with flaming swords, and clowns holding big hoops that pink tigers were jumping through and…."

Teresa jumped in front of me. "STOP IT!"

She startled me so much I lost my train of thought and all of a sudden the people on the street looked normal. Sort of.

Mary said, "I kind of liked Vicki's version better."

Teresa said, "How are we supposed to accomplish anything if we can't tell what's real?"

I didn't want to seem argumentative, but we weren't real.

Linda looked at me and frowned.

Teresa said, "Let's go in and look around a little. Maybe Jerome is close to here or something." That sounded good to me. Besides I've always wanted to look in a Voodoo shop. We were no sooner through the door than Ellen popped in. "Good work! I am so proud, and I didn't even have to ask you to do this! You gals will be ready to do this stuff on your own in no time!"

I wanted to stop that thinking in its tracks. "Oh NO you don't! You can't **ever** leave us on our own!"

Ellen started laughing, "Just messin' with ya! Follow me. Jerome is in the back here."

We all tiptoed to a small room that had a bright red blanket for a door. Ellen pulled back the blanket, and we saw Jerome sleeping. He was dreaming his mom had come home, and they were happy. Ellen dropped the blanket back down and pointed to Spicey who was sitting on a large chair, eating popcorn, and watching TV. Ellen said, "I am going to give you guys an extra five sticky notes just for this assignment. Spicey was at Patterson's house today. She just doesn't know it. She scanned a bunch of documents she is going to give to Tourey. Do you remember him from Mickey's bar?" We all nodded. Ellen continued, "These are very important documents for Roger. Tourey isn't going to think much of them for a while. He doesn't know who Bernard Jacobs really is."

Teresa said, "You want us to steal the scanner?"

Ellen shook her head, "We don't steal."

Mary said, "Vicki stole that guy's mail that one time!" Oh get over it! That was last year! I can't believe she brought that up. Mary was smiling at me. She is getting good at mind reading too. I'm doomed.

Ellen said, "We all make mistakes when we are new at something. She won't ever steal again."

I was making little circles with my right toe on the carpet. Pretty rug.

Linda said, "New topic." Whew.

Ellen said, "You guys try to convince her to scan those documents to this e-mail address. It's Roger's. She thinks she has powers, so you might be able to use that. I need to go check on something else that is happening so have fun!"

Spicey was on her couch watching a movie and eating popcorn. We decided to take a popcorn break too and sniffed our wrists where our aroma sensors were. We watched the movie until it was over, and then tried to figure out how we were going to get her to scan to Roger's e-mail.

Spicey shut the television off, stretched, and walked over to peek in on Jerome. Mary said, "Why don't we tell her to go to her crystal ball?"

Linda was clapping, "OOOh this is fun!" Mary wrote a sticky note and put it on Spicey's nose. Spicey looked at it cross-eyed and started making a quiet chanting sound. She started backing away from Jerome's room, turned to go into her kitchen, still cross eyed, and the note disappeared. She swiped her nose, looked all around the floor, and sat at her dinette. Her eyes were darting around the room, and she was still chanting very softly.

Teresa said, "Well, there went one note. She didn't even read it!"

Linda told Mary, "Do it again. She is sitting down now!" Mary scratched off another note and stuck it on her nose again. Spicey yelped and started slapping her face. The note dropped to the floor. Teresa flew in to grab it and stick it on her again and it disappeared in her hand on the way back to Spicey's nose. Spicey had watched it flutter to the floor, spring back up towards her face, and poof into thin air.

Well, that started quite a memorable moment. Spicey's muu muu had these huge sleeves. She started running in circles flapping her arms and chanting. She was being quiet. We heard her thinking she didn't want Jerome to wake up. All of a sudden she ran into another little room and sat down at a small table with a crystal ball in the center. Perfect. It wasn't exactly how we planned to get her there, but she was there.

She had her face up real close to the ball, and Mary wrote a note that said 'scan info to rdance @ govt.com.' Mary stuck the note on the ball, and we all watched her read it. Then it disappeared. She just sat there. And sat. And stared. Hello? That was our third note. Teresa said, "I'm just going to find her scanner and bring it to her." Good idea.

Spicey sat at the table and watched the drawers open and shut all over her shop. Then the items on the shelves moved and finally her purse floated from the kitchen to the little table where she was. The purse flap opened, her scanner came out and rested in front of her. Teresa said, "Let's try this again."

Mary said, "Get a pen and paper out of the purse for her to write down this e-mail." Linda went digging in the purse, but she couldn't find a pen. Finally, she just dumped the whole purse upside down on the table. No pen. She went out into the store front, came back with a tablet and pen, and laid them next to the scanner. Spicey's expression had not changed through any of this. I was beginning to think she might have had a heart attack and was just sitting there with her eyes open, dead. Mary heard me and said, "Don't even think that!" Okay.

Mary said, "This is our fourth note. What if I say, "The Spirits want you to e-mail the scanner info to rdance@ govt.com?"

Teresa said, "I better write that, a lot of words for a sticky note. I write tiny." We all agreed this was a job for Teresa. She wrote fast and stuck the note on the ball. Spicey leaned in real close to read the tiny print. Linda stuck the pen in her hand, and Mary waved the notebook in front of her.

Spicey moaned and fainted. Her face fell straight down on the notebook and her head hit the crystal ball sending it rolling into the store-front. "Oh for pity's sake!" I screamed as I ran to chase down the ball. "We only have one note left! How hard is it?" Linda was sitting at the table with Spicey.

Linda's head was in her hands. "This isn't work-ing." I had an idea. I picked up Spicey's pen, put it in her hand, and clenched her fingers around it. Then I yelled to Teresa, "Help me make her write!" Teresa grabbed her wrist and tried to force her to write. You couldn't read anything, it just looked like scribbles.

Mary said, "That is just scribbles. SCRIBBLES? *SCRABBLES* ... Look for a Scrabble game! They have letters!" We started tearing the place apart, neatly, looking for a Scrabble game. Who doesn't have a scrabble game? Right. Spicey doesn't have a scrabble game. Geesh.

Linda shouted from the store front. "I found a Ouija Board!" Eeeks.

I said, "I can't do it because that stuff creeps me out."

Teresa looked at me, "You're kidding right?" I don't think you kid about stuff like that!

"No, I am not kidding. Those things are creepy. Besides, I can't spell very well."

Linda was laughing, "We aren't exactly going to use big words, but how do we make the @ sign?"

Mary said, " Just spell 'at'. A.t." Teresa grabbed the board and placed it in front of Spicey who had by now raised her head, but her eyes were still shut.

I said, "Should I put a sheet over Mary and just let her do it?"

Mary looked at me, "You are not right." What? I thought it was a good idea, and faster than waiting for Spicey to get this on her own.

Teresa agreed with me, "I think she might be right. We need her to think the Spirits want this, so if one of us puts a sheet on, we can still let her work the board."

Linda yelled, "I'll do it! I always wanted to play ghost when I was a kid."

Teresa said, "Just sit at the table with your sheet on. We don't want to scare her." Yeah, she won't think anything of that.

Linda got a sheet from the closet, held it up over her head and walked into the room. I thought we lost Spicey for good. Her eyes practically bugged out of her head, and she was waving at Linda like she was shooing her away. Linda started making all kinds of spooky sounds, and we started cracking up. Teresa snickered, "She can't hear you, and that is very distracting."

Linda stopped. Her sheet moved a little when she said "You guys aren't any fun." It took a very long time of Spicey barely touching the Ouija and Teresa pushing it, but she finally had the whole message written out. Now she was staring at the message and staring at her scanner. She picked up the scanner, walked over to her lap top computer in the corner, plugged the scanner into the computer, and sent the email.

I looked at Teresa, "You know what? I think *we* could have done *that* ourselves." She just stared at me. Then she picked up the scanner and sent the e-mail again. What do you know?

Mary said, "I bet Ellen will be proud to hear we figured out how to do that ourselves."

I said, "I bet she knew all along and was just waiting to see how much we would do before we figured it out!" Suddenly we all felt a little foolish.

Linda said, "We still have one note left. What kind of message can we give her?"

Teresa said, "How about, Jerome will have his mom soon." We all agreed that was the best way to use the last note. Mary wrote it and stuck it on the crystal ball. Spicey read it and fainted again. I chased down the ball again, and we hung around long enough to make sure she was okay. She went to bed with a fistful of amulets and a Bible.

Back outside the store a guy dressed in bright blue feathers and a leotard rode a unicycle around the corner. Teresa frowned at me. "He's real! I didn't do that!"

Roger and Paul decided to meet in the hotel lobby at nine and walk over to the building, which by now even they were calling Star Ship. Roger had to tell everyone about Mark Mills escaping, and he wanted to see how Ray was feeling. He found Paul in the lobby talking to John Barry. John shook Roger's hand and repeated what he had told Paul. John explained who Tourey was, and that he was as up to date on everything as John was. Tourey could be trusted and would be useful. John said, "Tourey won't risk being seen around you guys. He has been under for a long time and won't risk that. He did agree to introduce himself to you both, so you know who he is."

John told Roger he planned to start tomorrow at the police station going over missing person reports. His initial focus was to find Devon and go from there. He felt he owed that to Ashley, and unfortunately, the rest of the case was probably going to take a long time. Roger made a decision. "John, I am pretty sure the Bureau will question my judgment on this, but we have a whole basement floor at the Star Ship. If you need a secure place to work out of. The hotel here is going to create privacy issues for all of us."

John looked at Paul, "Are you okay with that too?" Paul nodded. John said to Paul, "I am assuming Roger told you, I am OSI. I don't think OSI would approve of this arrangement either, but I am willing to bet we will get this done quicker together. Roger has been given some leeway with the Bureau, and I have some with OSI. I say let them scream when it's done." Paul appreciated John telling him about OSI. It displayed a level of trust in Paul that Paul deserved.

They reached the door of the Star Ship and showed John how to use the code for entry. Roger told him that once Ray was feeling better he was going to have him change the code daily. They went upstairs to find Ray, with a cup of tea, sitting on a chair, looking out the window facing the street. Roger made the introductions and asked Ray how he was doing. Ray answered, "I'm still feeling kind of drugged, but I really don't hurt like I thought I would. I'll probably sleep well tonight." He smiled.

John asked Paul to give him a tour. When they had left, Roger asked Ray if he had the computer equipment he needed. Ray answered, "Not really. They sent some stuff I didn't ask for and left off a lot that I really need if we are going to go full blast." Roger said to expect full blast. Ray laughed, "I probably should pick a different way of saying that, I've been blasted once too often today as it is." They were still laughing when Thor, Pablo and Jeanne came in. Paul and John had returned from the downstairs rooms, and Paul introduced Ray and Jeanne to John as retired CIA. Trusted, and free.

Jeanne looked at Ray and asked, "Are you THE Ray Davis?" Ray answered a long slow yes. Jeanne said, "I'm Magic Jeannie!"

Ray lit up like a Christmas tree! "You are kidding me, right? My God we have been talking for years! Oh cool! Look what they did to me!" They both went over to the computers and started exchanging complaints about the equipment. Roger looked at Paul and just shrugged.

Thor said, "Must be some geek thing." He kept staring at Jeanne, and then noticed Roger had caught him.

Pablo didn't miss any of it and said, "If you look at her official jacket, she is also sniper trained, martial arts, and holds the Bureau title in blades."

Thor straightened up, "*Knives?* Huh." He was thinking, I knew you didn't want to piss her off.

Pablo said, "She never did play with dolls."

This was the first time Roger and Paul had seen Jeanne in person and her agency photo didn't begin to reflect how stunning she was. They looked at each other. They had worked together long enough they could almost read each other's minds. They both started shaking their heads. Another troublesome twist.

Ray asked the room, "Does anyone have a bug scanner? I want to test the links on two of these security programs now that I have Jeanne to run the protocol on the other computer. I know Core wouldn't bug himself, but you said he had warning. I want to be sure our software is working right now."

Nobody knew what he was talking about, but John produced a cell phone size devise. "This is the latest model being used by the Company." He turned it on, and it started beeping and flashing. John held up his hands and motioned for a search. They were not alone.

Everyone started searching. Roger thought he caught a glimpse of Ellen going into the room Ray had chosen as his. Just to be sure, he got up and walked into that room. Ellen was standing in front of the closet. Roger was afraid the rest of the guys would see her, but she walked through the closet door. He opened the door, and she was standing inside the closet. He couldn't figure out what she wanted. He did have a question for her. He whispered, "Can I trust John?" she winked. Good. Then she walked through the back wall of the closet. How was he supposed to follow her there? Then she reappeared and walked back through it again. She came back, tilted her head at him, and walked through again.

Roger heard Thor's voice boom behind him, "You find anything here?" Roger decided to follow Ellen's lead, and he pushed on the back wall. It slowly started to turn on a pivot.

Thor yelled, "Holy SHIT! How the hell did you know that would happen?"

Roger answered, "Lucky guess."

They were now in the bookstore storage closet. The bookstore was closed when they entered the main structure. They closed the closet door behind them, and looked at it from the bookstore side. It was all deep grooved paneling. The outline of the door was absolutely invisible. Roger noticed a small pine knothole and pushed on it. That was the pressure point. This had been a very thoughtful design. There was fine wiring all around the door casing, and lock mechanisms through the framing studs. They knew there was an alarm hooked to it somewhere that had been disabled. Core probably disabled it after he was warned they were coming, so he could come back.

They met the other guys back in the main room to see what else had been found. Frost and Nelson had just arrived. Thor went around every wall, pushing, prodding and shaking his head. He eventually came back to the main room, looked at Roger, and said, "That was the only one. I watched you just walk in that closet and push the back wall open. That was a damn lucky guess!"

Roger looked at him, "What do you think Thor? That I've been here before? Or maybe Core called me and told me where to look?"

Thor shook his head, "Noooo. I think you are spooky and don't know it!" Paul lost it. He laughed so hard, he knocked over a small table where they found another listening device.

Ray had been sitting in his computer chair listening to all of them and finally spoke, "Do I have this right? All evening I have been here alone, drugged out, and there was a secret passage door in my closet?" Nobody bothered to answer him. Ray threw his arms up into the air and went back to his computer.

Pablo noticed Nelson's shirt had blood on it. "What happened to you?"

Frost answered for him, "Todd and I helped the local PD at a shootout. Ten dead, two wounded." He pointed at Todd, "He's one of the wounded."

Roger said, "WHAT?" Frost explained to Roger what had happened. When they got to the part about the rental car being totaled, Roger looked at Thor who said, "You deal with what you're dealt."

Roger chuckled, "Yes you do. Dan already knows this, but speaking of bad news…" and he told them about Mark Mills escaping, killing the two FBI transport agents, and taking their badges. He finished by saying it was a pretty sure bet that Mark Mills was already in town.

Frost was up and pacing. He shouted, "Nothing holds these guys! How can they keep escaping from us? Those two with badges is bad."

Ray spoke again, "I know this isn't the biggest problem we have, but someone may still be listening. We haven't found the source pad." They all stopped talking and continued the search. They found it built into the microwave.

After an hour long meeting, the team decided whoever wanted to have breakfast at the Marriott at 7:30 was welcome, and then at 9:00 have a briefing at Star Ship. Pablo asked Roger for permission to stay with Jeanne at her house. It was about six blocks away. Roger thought it was a good idea. There was still plenty of room at the Star Ship, three floors of space, but he didn't want Jeanne alone. Roger told Jeanne he wanted to meet with her directly after the next morning's meeting.

Paul, Roger, and John were walking back to the hotel when John said, "I appreciate you bringing me in the loop with your team."

Roger said, "I know I can trust you John."

John started laughing. Paul and Roger stopped walking and just looked at him. John seemed to have a case of giggles he couldn't control. Finally he held his hand up and said, "I am sorry. I appreciate you said that Roger. You can trust me. Absolutely, but most people in your position wouldn't at this stage of the game. Which is why I can't stop laughing..." he started all over again, stopped himself and said, "It's like you know you can trust me. Tourey told me today he heard you and Paul were spooky, and Thor just said..." then they all lost it. They were all so tired they were just slap happy. Paul was hanging onto the side of the building laughing, as a couple walked by and gave them thumbs up. He was sure they thought the three of them were drunk or high.

CHAPTER 19

Suddenly Mathew Core was looking at a blank screen. They had found the source pad. He wished he had gotten home sooner, so he could have watched more of the feed. As it was, he had only seen a few of them discussing finding the passage to the bookstore. He chuckled to himself. None of them would sleep well tonight. He had gone jogging and his body smelled of sweat and New Orleans. He went into the kitchen, grabbed an apple from a bowl of fruit on the counter, and yelled for Lisa. He heard her mumbled answer come from the basement family room. He went downstairs to see what she was doing.

Lisa had yards of bright pink fabric lying on the floor and his daughter Jamie had her body spread out holding a fold of fabric. Lisa had a row of pins sticking out of her mouth and waved her elbow at him as he came down the stairs. Mathew rubbed Jamie's head and said, "What are you and Mommy making tonight?"

Jamie's eyes got big and she said, "Dad, you can see we have an unbelievable amount of work to do. I can't talk right now." Lisa rolled her eyes. They joked that their daughter had been born an adult. Her vocabulary for a six year old was fantastic. The school said she was one of the brightest children they had ever seen.

Lisa removed the pins from her mouth, "Jamie and I are putting some finishing touches on the school play costumes she volunteered me to make." Lisa rolled her eyes again.

Mathew bent down and kissed her cheek. "I'm going to take a shower and then about a two hour nap. I need to meet a guy tonight I haven't seen for a while. Is that okay?" He was smiling.

Lisa smiled, "Like I ever know where you are?"

She raised her chin for him to kiss her again, and Jamie moaned, "YEWWW….we are never going to finish if you don't stop that. There is a proper time and place. Daddy you stink."

Mathew rubbed her head as he passed by her, "Daddy knows."

After his shower he went out to the veranda and placed a call to Carl. He answered immediately, "What now?" Mathew asked if Carl had spoken to Thomas. Carl answered yes.

Mathew was pleased, "I am assuming we are back to business as usual?"

Carl paused, "That might be an issue. I have two dead CIA agents."

Mathew answered, "You did that, not me. I didn't order that lab bombed. You and Thomas, that's on you. And I want Jason back."

Carl hissed, "Jason! There is no way Jason is getting out of this! How would I explain that?"

Mathew said, "You'll think of something. I want him released tomorrow at the latest. And Carl? I had to take a little money from your account to replace my lab, I know you understand."

Carl spit the words, "I'll see what I can do." Mathew chuckled as he placed the phone in his pocket. He rolled his neck and decided to take that nap. He was meeting Mark at midnight.

* * *

Jeanne and Pablo decided to walk back to the house. A strong breeze blew and the air smelled of storms coming. They walked the first four blocks in silence. Finally Pablo asked, "How are you?"

Jeanne looked at him, "Better than I thought I would be. It actually helped a lot that I stayed at Mambo's. She helped me get my center back."

Pablo stopped walking and touched her arm, "You know Roger may not want you involved in this anymore." Jeanne looked at him and started walking ahead. Pablo caught up with her and asked, "Can you stay out of it if he asks you to?" Jeanne wouldn't answer him.

They reached the house, and Pablo was struck at how familiar it all still seemed. It had been almost twenty years since he had stood on that porch. He had been seventeen. He saw the lines on the door jamb that they used as a growth chart and chuckled, "Look how short we were!" Jeanne laughed. Most of the time their mom was too 'sick' to be much of a mom. It wasn't until they were much older they realized it was her 'medicine' that made her sick. She still had managed to live into her fifties. Pablo and Jeanne split her bills, and that was pretty much the extent of their relationship with their mother after high school. A few phone calls, Jeanne visited once. It was all very depressing.

Jeanne turned on a light next to the couch and turned the TV on. Pablo thought the house looked much better than he had remembered. Jeanne noticed Pablo's expression and said, "I had a friend remodel one room at a time as Christmas gifts from us."

Pablo said, "Why didn't you tell me? I must owe you a lot of money."

Jeanne smiled, "Just don't worry about it. I think I might live here a while and then we can sell it. I have money in the bank and this suits my needs right now."

Pablo gave himself a tour and came back into the living room with a beer for Jeanne and one for himself. He noticed a large post at the end of the living room that obviously didn't belong. "Looks like you have some big termites down here." The wood was shredded from floor to ceiling. He knew what it really was. Jeanne stood, turned her back to the post, and in one stealth motion, pulled a knife from her pants, spun around and threw the knife squarely in the center of the post. She had speed and precision. Pablo was impressed. He went over to yank the knife from the post and return it to her.

He raised an eyebrow and asked, "How did he get you?"

Jeanne took a big gulp of her beer, looked at Pablo and said, "I was feeling sorry for myself, just buried Mom, no boyfriend…I was getting ready to go back to work, thinking about the grind of it all. New York City in the winter." Pablo noticed Jeanne had begun twirling a thin strand of her hair. She used to do that when she was young. Only back then, she would twirl it tight and pull it out. He had found twisted strands of her hair all over the house. Jeanne continued, "I talked to him. At a bar. He is fairly good looking now, but I remember he wore surgical gloves. Said he had skin allergies. I think I felt sorry for him." Pablo was shaking his head. Jeanne continued, "He must have drugged my drink. I remember feeling drugged, leaving the bar. He told me he was driving me home. Then he injected me."

Pablo was up pacing, his heart was on fire and temples were pounding. Jeanne kept talking, "It was days of being so drugged, I barely realized what was happening. I finally stopped eating and drinking the water, and I became stronger. I fought him, almost had him. Then he shot me with a stun gun and injected me again. That's when Patterson came and took me. He drove me to the edge of the swamp and told me if I could get to the other side alive to just keep going. His friend wanted me dead. He was giving me a chance. I was so drugged and sick....I couldn't even move for two days." Pablo was sick to his stomach. He went to the bathroom and puked. When he returned to the living room and sat down, Jeanne asked him, "Can you stay out of it if Roger asks you to?" Pablo wouldn't answer her.

We were giving ourselves a tour of Bourbon Street. Mary had turned into quite the fashion diva. Every time I looked at her she was wearing a different outfit. She said she was getting inspired by the people we were passing. The problem was that we kept losing her! I must have tapped the shoulders of twenty women thinking they were Mary.

We came upon a bar that was having an Impersonator Show and decided to go in. **It was fabulous!** They had Cher, Diana Ross, Bette Midler and Gladys Knight! When Gladys Knight began to sing, we all decided to become Pips. We got on the stage with her. This came naturally for Mary and Linda because they were famous for breaking into song whenever the conversation moved them!

Teresa did a mean *Whoo Whoo* for the train sounds in "Midnight Train to Georgia", and I just tried to keep up with the fancy footwork of Linda and Mary. It is really too bad that no one could see us. I think we stole the show!

We stayed to watch one more show. People kept sitting on us, and there really wasn't enough room to practice our new routine. We figured we should move on, so we went back out to the sidewalk.

Suddenly, a guy dressed as a pirate jumped in front of us and said "Boo!"

Mary yelled, "He can see us!" I think I screamed. Linda said, "Hi Ellen."

Then Ellen said, "Time to get to work. You gals follow me. We are going to Devon's house." Uh oh. We followed Ellen and ended up in Devon's bedroom where he was sleeping. It sure didn't look like Devon. That new face must have cost a fortune! Ellen said, "See that glass of water next to his bed there?" We all nodded. Ellen said, "That bottle on his night stand is the drug he keeps giving these women. We are going to put some of that in his water. We need him to stay here at least all night tonight and some of tomorrow morning."

We watched Ellen dump about an ounce of the clear drug into his water. Teresa said, "You sure that's enough? Why don't we double up and make sure?"

Ellen frowned, "We can't really harm him, remember? We are angels. Now look over there at that screen." We all looked and Ellen turned on a picture of two women in a room. They were on a bed, crying. Ellen said, "We are going to go see them now and see if we can find out anything to help Roger. First we are going to turn off the air conditioning in this room, so Devon gets hot and drinks all of that water!" As we left the room Ellen said, "Nighty-night," to Devon.

We found the room in the basement and listened to Amy and Rebecca talk. They both sounded really drugged. We could tell from what they were saying that Devon had already raped them at least once. The girl named Rebecca was especially upset. She blamed herself for Amy being there. Amy said as soon as she felt better she was going to study the lock. Her dad was a locksmith, and she used to go with him on jobs. Ellen told Mary, "Write a sticky note for them not to eat or drink, it's drugged. They are so druggy I don't think they will remember the note." Mary quickly wrote out the note and put it on Amy's nose.

Amy peeled it off and tried to read, ""Don't eat or drink ..*wha*t?" and the note disappeared in her hand.

Mary wrote a second note and put it on Amy's nose, "You're being drugged." Amy's eyes got big and the note disappeared in her hand again.

She reached over and swatted the bottle of water from Rebecca's hand before she drank any. "We are being drugged! Don't drink or eat anything!"

Rebecca was weaving a little and mumbled, "How do you know that?"

Amy lay down on the bed, "I don't know. Let me think."

It was very hard to read their thoughts because of the drugs. Between their clear memories and Ellen's help, we were able to piece together the story. Now we had to figure out how to get Roger to discover the information.

"Amy and Rebecca had some text messages that refer to Devon, so we want Roger to find their phones, somehow." Ellen looked at Teresa, "You and Linda go back upstairs and see if you can find out where he buys those plastic gloves. Also see if Amy's groceries are in Devon's car. If they are, the receipt may be in one of the bags. Oooh! Devon bought Rebecca earrings at the Mall....see if you can find out which store and how he paid for them." Ellen looked at Mary and said, "You know, we could probably use one of Devon's phone bills too…might be able to get Patterson's number from there. We need to connect the dots for Roger. This isn't going to be easy."

Once we had all the information we could find, we went to the basement of the Star Ship. It was evening and I couldn't believe I could see in the dark. As a mortal I had night blindness and never went anywhere. Ellen said it would be safe to work in the basement because no one was down there to see us moving papers. When we arrived, we sat around a huge table, and Ellen grabbed a notebook from a shelf and started writing. " Okay, I found out both Amy and Rebecca work at the French Quarter Bank branch on the corner of

221

Royal and Bienville Ave. They both took yesterday afternoon off to shop and of course neither one of them will report to work in the morning. I don't know if the bank manager is going to be alarmed enough to do anything. We need to get Roger to that bank."

Ellen also had us review all of the information scanned from Spicey's scanner to Roger's e-mail. Ellen kept shaking her head and saying, "We have a lot of work to do." None of Spicey's information made sense to any of us and every time Ellen said something like "We have a lot of work to do", we all freaked out. I am pretty sure our mortal is getting in the way of some of this.

Mary asked, "Can't you give us a hint what is coming up? You know, so we can prepare our mortal a little?"

Ellen answered, "I wish I could, but I think your mortal has to be given this stuff a little at a time. Remember Roger and Paul have to discover all of this stuff in an explainable way. It can't just all be dumped on them at once." The meeting went on and on. Ellen finally announced we could go sightseeing for a while, and she would call us.

Most of the streets were empty. It was six o'clock in the morning, in the French Quarter. At least Mary wasn't changing clothes every five minutes. Linda saw a black cat sitting in an alley, and she touched Teresa's sleeve, "Is that Ellen? Is she following us?"

Teresa laughed, "I think it is just a black cat." We walked down another street looking in the windows of the shops and a black cat was sitting on the sidewalk ahead of us. Teresa looked at Linda, "Maybe it is Ellen." Teresa yelled, "Is that you Ellen?"

Just then a big truck came around the corner and blasted us with water. The force of the spray was so strong it blew us all against the brick wall and held us there until it passed. Every morning in the summer the city sprays down the streets and sidewalks in the Quarter with sudsy lemon scented disinfectant water to clean the streets.

Like some strange sea monster it spit water on everything in its path and turned the corner. We were all soaked. The air smelled like lemon puke. Geesh! I looked at Linda's facial expression and started laughing so hard I tripped myself and sat on the sidewalk. The black cat walked up and sat on my lap.

Mary said, "Even that stupid cat knew to get out of the way of that truck!"

I looked down and put the cats head between my hands and rubbed its nose with mine saying, "You aren't a stupid cat are you? You are a pretty kitty." Then poof, it was Ellen's face in my hands. FREAKED me OUT! Ellen was rolling on the sidewalk laughing.

Ellen said, "I actually let that happen to test how your mortal is dealing with mass. We still have some work to do. If you had thought about that wall being mass you could have just gone through it, and not felt the force of the water. Your mind will determine if a mass is solid or not. It will be whatever you want it to be." That actually made sense to me. Huh. Why am I afraid to fly? My mind can make everything in my way disappear. This might work.

Ellen continued, "I think we can best help Roger by starting to collect information that identifies William Patterson's associates. Roger has the information from Spicey in his computer, but I think it will be a while before he gets a chance to review it. I am thinking that the names in the little black book are going to be the important people to investigate." Ellen smiled at us, "Okay, touch the face dial of your watches."

We did and each of our watches projected a hologram screen in front of us. Cool! I wonder if we can watch movies? Ellen glanced at me, "I don't think you have time for a movie right now. Now think pages from Patterson's little black book." Ellen was still smiling as she watched each of our screens fill with data from Patterson's book.

Teresa asked, "I see a name. How do I locate without knowing any aura information?"

Ellen said, "Request locator map on your screen and follow the little yellow dots. See them?"

Mary yelled, "Oh how cute! A little smiley face that leads us where we need to go."

This looks like Pac Man. I wonder if heaven is aware of patent rights. Ellen frowned at me. Just sayin'.

Ellen rolled her eyes and continued, "Each of you pick a name, locate them, and study their thoughts to determine an aura and whether or not we have to tell Roger about them. You can locate each other just by thought and compare notes. When you are finished, just let me know. I need to wake up Roger. This is going to be another one of those days that mortals remember for a long time."

That didn't sound very good.

CHAPTER 20

Roger woke to Ellen sitting on his chest softly slapping him. He said, "Good morning", and looked at the clock. It was 7:00 am. He had overslept. He jumped up and went to the shower; Ellen curled up on his warm pillow. When he was done with his shower and dressed, he noticed Ellen was sitting on the small table next to his laptop. There was a printer/fax machine there. Roger asked Ellen, "Did you get the printer?" She winked and touched the lap top. Roger went over, opened the laptop and saw he had an e-mail from "Spicey's House of Voodoo". He was thinking this was a strange start to the day. He hit print and was trying to read the pages as they came off the printer. Ellen started tapping Roger's phone. "You want me to call Kim? It's pretty early. You're going to get me in trouble." Ellen closed both her eyes.

Roger took that as an, "Oh well," and he dialed Kim.

Kim answered, "Good Morning." She sounded cheerful but sleepy. "There are times I don't like being the only human Mom and Ellen can talk to. Ellen has a lot of information she dictated to me, and I put it in an e-mail to you. She told me not to send it until you called, so here it comes." Roger pulled the e-mail up, hit print, and started reading. Kim was still on the line.

Roger said, "Okay, I think I understand this. Talk to you later." He hung up. He had a bad habit of forgetting to say goodbye. He shrugged his shoulders when he realized he had hung up on Kim, again. He knew she would understand. He placed a call to Paul, "You still in your room or in the restaurant?"

Paul answered, "I'm already in the restaurant having coffee. What's up?" Roger told him he would see him in a minute. Roger took the stairs down four flights to save time, found Paul in the restaurant, and gave him the printout of Kim's e-mail. "Read fast." Paul read while Roger watched the door in case some of the other guys decided to join them.

Paul's eyes opened wide as he read. He returned the page to Roger and said, "We have to find excuses to make these dots connect. It's like a scavenger hunt list of hints to find Devon."

Roger was nodding. "I can make up an excuse to go to that bank, but I can't ask Ray to trace those cell numbers without a reason. Also, how do we explain going to that drug store and asking about plastic gloves?"

Paul was nodding, "We can't show anyone that phone bill to check the numbers because we don't have the phone bill, right? Or the grocery or jewelry receipts."

"Right. I also have an e-mail from "Spicey's House of Voodoo" with a lot of information on a Bernard Jacobs. I don't know what that is all about, or who, but Ellen says Spicey thinks the Spirits made her email the information to me. Spicey had gathered it for Tourey."

Paul asked, "John Barry's guy? I wonder what his interest is in Jacobs?"

Roger answered, "Remember Jeanne told Pablo the swamp man had brought another woman to Mambo?" Paul was nodding, Roger continued, "Ellen told Kim her name is Adele Brown, and Adele's son is with this Spicey-Voodoo woman. They are going to go report Adele missing this morning at the police department. I think John was planning on being at the PD this morning."

Paul looked past Roger, smiled, and said "Well, good morning Dan." Paul was smiling, and hoped his facial expression looked normal. He felt anything but normal.

Agent Dan Thor nodded and sat next to Paul at the large table, "Frost, Nelson, and the Manigat twins are joining us. Ray has been hooking up computer stuff and cussing at someone on the phone since six this morning. We already had one delivery of computer junk, and he sent a bunch back. I don't know how he got someone this early in the day! You can't walk in that basement anymore. I don't know about John Barry."

Paul said, "I see John now." He waved him over. Roger's mind was racing. How could he structure this so Paul and he could discover what they already knew? John sat down, and Pablo and Jeanne walked up to the table. Jeanne sat next to Thor. Roger could see him tense up. Jeanne was stunning, even in old blue jeans and boots. Pablo asked if everyone slept ok and was met with a round of laughter.

Thor scowled, "Can't wait to get this day started. It's already a hundred friggin' degrees."

Paul lowered his head and glanced at Roger. Roger looked at the group, "I'm glad you have all joined Paul and me for breakfast. Hopefully this will be a productive day. We can get some of our planning done now. The paper says it is supposed to get well over a hundred degrees today with high humidity." Everyone moaned.

Thor asked, "Does anyone know what they spray on the streets? It smells like lemon puke out there!"

Jeanne looked at him, "Lovely table talk." Thor shut up. Pablo smiled. They ate breakfast and exchanged stories of the bayous they had read in the paper.

Roger placed his credit card in his wallet after paying the waitress and gathered Ray's to-go order.

He noticed two uniformed officers heading for their table. Paul glanced up, "I don't like this."

The tall officer introduced himself and said, "I am looking for SSA Roger Dance?"

Everyone looked at Roger who said, "I'm Dance."

The officer said, "The field office said you were staying here. I have a dead body behind Mickey's Bar that has a note addressed to you pinned on the chest."

Thor cracked a smile, and said, "Well, at least we finished breakfast."

* * *

Amy had crawled over to the door. She could tell it was a hydraulic lock. Her dad always said that meant there had to be an emergency release. She wouldn't put it past this damn guy to have it rigged without one though. She was on the floor looking up at the underside of the handle. Sure enough there was a small hole which could be the emergency release. She needed to find something with a long pointed end on it, small enough to go in that hole. She began searching everything. Rebecca was passed out again, and Amy was so drowsy she wasn't seeing clearly.

Finally she sat on the bed and tried to wake Rebecca. "Becca, Wake up! Becca!" Rebecca moaned a little, and Amy felt herself going under again.

Devon tossed in his bed. His head was killing him, and he was hot. He reached over and grabbed the glass of water and gulped it all. He figured he must have caught a virus. He clicked on the camera screen and saw the girls sleeping on the bed. He smiled. They would be there when he felt better. He put his head back on his pillow and fell asleep.

Jeremiah woke early, drove over to his nephew Alan's place in Slidell, and convinced him to help take the small refrigerator and heater/fan to Mambo's. His nephew was an electrician, and Jeremiah wasn't sure Jeanne knew what she was doing on that generator. Jeanne had told him she worked for the FBI which made him feel better. He had wondered why she carried a gun. He had also watched her practicing with her knife. He was sure whatever monster had harmed her was going to be very sorry.

Jeremiah and Alan carried the small refrigerator and heater onto the boat, and Alan said, "You know, the only time I ever saw Mambo was when you took me there as a kid after I stole old lady Nelson's truck." Jeremiah laughed as he positioned himself to push off into the swamp. Alan continued, "That was an important lesson for me that day. She scared the crap out of me! I still have that amulet. Shit, I think I'm scared to go back! How old is she anyway? She was an old woman back then." He dug around his neck and pulled a long thin leather strap from under his shirt. "I've never broken a law since, and I believe this helped."

Jeremiah laughed and said, "What would you say if I told you she was an old woman sixty-five years ago when my dad took me?"

Alan looked shocked, "How can that be? She'd have to be over a hundred years old!"

Jeremiah was nodding his head, "My dad got took there too by his dad. Makes ya think, don't it?"

Alan spit out, "Now I really don't want to go!"

Jeremiah lifted a snake with his paddle and placed it farther from the boat, "We got us a storm coming." His nostrils flared as he smelled the air. "Best we get this done as fast as we can." Alan sat on the rail of the boat and watched the wildlife scrutinize their presence. Small flocks of swamp sparrows followed them. Occasionally landed on a cypress tree and watched until they passed, only to fly ahead again and wait.

Alan asked, "Wasn't that a water moccasin, cotton mouth, whatever?"

Jeremiah answered, "Yup."

Alan moved in toward the center of the boat, "Those are poisonous!"

Jeremiah looked up, "Yup, got one on that tree branch there, too."

Alan looked over his left shoulder and yelped. "How do you live out here?"

Jeremiah laughed, "You don't mess with nature, and you do just fine. Its city folks got no respect for the livin'." Jeremiah slowly lifted his paddle to move another approaching snake.

Ellen told us to meet her on the roof of Mickey's Bar. Okay. We arrived just as Roger and the team walked around the building to the back. Already two agents from the local FBI office and two New Orleans officers on horseback were in the lot. The body of a man was lying in the center of the concrete. We sat along the edge of the roof and watched. We could hear what they were saying and some of what they were thinking. There were so many people now, it was confusing whose thinking we were hearing.

Roger and Paul reached the body first and looked at each other. Thor walked up and asked,

"Isn't that Mark Mills, the sniper?" Mark Mills, eyes open, had a small red circle directly in the center of his forehead. There wasn't even any blood showing on his face.

Roger was putting on plastic gloves and answered, "Yes it is." Roger crouched down and removed the pin holding the note to Mark Mill's shirt. He handed the pin to Paul who had put gloves on also and was opening a small evidence bag. Roger held the folded note. The face of the note simply said, SSA Roger Dance. Roger opened it, being careful to only touch the edges. Inside, the note said, "Check pocket."

Roger reached into the pants pocket and brought out the two badges of the FBI agents Mills had killed. He clenched them in his hand. Roger's heart was stirring. He had not had much time to think about the loss of them yesterday. As he clenched the badges they felt as if they were burning. Roger had not even read the report yet. He didn't know if they had families, he didn't even know their names. He only knew they had been murdered to give Mark Mills a few more hours of life.

SSA Frank Mass had not been briefed on yesterday's events, and his current case had kept him out of the office almost all day yesterday. Last night he had managed to introduce himself to Thor, briefly, but he had needed to leave the center again. He had no idea what Roger's team was there for, or what was happening now. He walked over to Roger and introduced himself; Frank was the Senior Agent for the New Orleans Center.

Agent Mass said, "Whatever you need from us, just let me know." He waved his hand toward the body of Mark Mills, "I'll have this taken to the medical examiner."

Roger said thanks and asked if they could make an appointment to meet later today. Agent Mass gave Roger a card and told him to just call when he was ready. Roger asked him, "Do you know anything about this guy? Ever seen him?"

Mass said, "Nope. How bad was he?"

Roger held out the two badges and answered, "This bad."

Roger told the team he wanted a brief meeting across the street to get the day started. Roger and Paul stayed behind the group a few steps.

Paul asked, "What do you think the purpose of the note was?"

Roger answered, "To let us know he doesn't need the badges, he's got something better."

Paul thought about it a minute and said, "If he has serious connections, John Barry is eventually going to come in his cross hairs too."

Roger nodded, "Exactly what I was thinking."

Roger asked Paul, "How should we split everyone up today? I'm hoping I can get some tips from Jeanne that will connect a couple of our 'dots.' Go from there. While I'm with Jeanne, can you see how close Ray is to being up and running? And find out what Thor thinks about Pablo. Then we will hand out assignments."

Paul asked, "You going to let Jeanne and Pablo stay in this?"

Roger shrugged, "I think we need them both. I don't know. What's your thinking?"

Paul shrugged, "She seems pretty solid, what I've seen. Pablo may have more issues than she does on this. I think they would work it on their own if you told them to back off, and I think Pablo could be a problem." Roger nodded.

Inside the Star Ship Roger could hear Ray and Jeanne talking geek talk. He asked Jeanne if she could give him a few minutes. Roger had shut the door to the kitchen area so they could have some privacy. Jeanne told him about her experience with Devon and Patterson. She mentioned that Devon always wore plastic gloves. She told him about staying at Mambo's, Jeremiah, and the woman Jeremiah found after her. She asked Roger if she could stay on the case. She could help Ray. She understood she could not compromise the task force.

Roger told her if she helped Ray, any information they discovered could not be acted on by her. Under the circumstances, if they were to go to trial again on Devon and Patterson, her involvement could not influence evidence or results. Jeanne said she understood. Roger said he wanted Jeanne to go with Thor to get the woman at Mambo's and bring her back. Roger thought Jeanne could solicit the help of Jeremiah and make the woman feel more comfortable. She agreed. Roger told her he was going to talk to Ray a few minutes and would give assignments shortly if she wanted to join the others.

Roger was shocked when he reached the basement and saw what Ray had set up with the computers. It was very impressive and had two main computer stations. Roger smiled to himself as he waited for Ray to get off the phone. Ray was planning on having Jeanne at that second computer station. Ray turned around and said, "I have a software program that is being downloaded from the Securities and Exchange that will help us sort these bank transactions a lot quicker. Guess what I remembered in my sleep? I moved everything to a cloud!"

Roger was worried that Ray was still feeling the drugs, "What?"

Ray laughed at Roger's expression.

"Before the bomb! I had moved everything to a data cloud… storage….never mind, but we have all the information that was at the Virginia lab. And nobody knows! It's secret! The data cloud has been encrypted, and I have the only password."

Roger thought fast, "And very dangerous. Can you keep it secret, and still use it?"

Ray looked thoughtful, "Depends. Who do I have to keep it secret *from*?"

Roger took a leap of faith in Ray, "The FBI and the CIA."

Ray looked pale again, "Shit! Let me work on that."

Roger turned around before he went upstairs, "Are you sure you are ready for this?"

Ray smiled, "I know I'm going to regret this, but, bring it on!"

Roger said, "Okay, first assignment. That five mil transaction yesterday, one of those accounts has to belong to either Devon or Patterson. I need aliases."

Ray said, "Got it boss."

Roger talked to Thor for a while about Pablo. Thor felt the same way Roger did. Pablo would go off on his own. Might as well keep an eye on him. Roger asked Thor to take Jeanne and go get the woman at Mambo's.

Thor rolled his eyes and scowled, "You know you will have a memorable day when it starts with a Voodoo Queen. I thought you were starting to like me." Roger smiled.

When Roger entered the main room, he asked Todd and Pablo if they would go to the local FBI center and work the computers there to find out anything they could about Mathew Core, the history of this building, and any other real estate Core might be involved in. He reminded them there was still an unidentified problem at the center. Roger told them if he and Paul came upon any leads they would be calling.

Thor interjected, "Expect a few calls."

Then Roger looked at Agent Simon Frost and asked if he would look over the results of the Security and Exchange program Ray was running. Roger really needed to tie up the money on this case, and Simon's forte was following the money. John Barry offered he was going to the local police station to review missing person reports, but if anyone needed him to just call. Roger and Paul looked at each other. The unspoken signal was, "We've covered it so far."

CHAPTER 21

We had all been listening to the assignments everyone had been given. Ellen said, "I think two of you should go with Thor and Jeanne to Mambo's, and two of you should go with Roger and Paul. I'm going to try and help John Barry at the police station, and help Nelson and Pablo at the FBI center. We all looked at each other. None of us wanted to go to the swamp again. Ellen frowned, "Fine. You all go to the swamp, and I will call if I need you." She actually stuck her tongue out at us and disappeared. Really?

Teresa said, "Guess we are going to the swamp."

* * *

William Patterson saw rays of morning light flickering through his lashes. It seemed too early to wake up. He thought he might still be dreaming because he felt something surreal about his room. When he opened his eyes, there was a man sitting on the chair in the corner, sipping on something in a mug, staring at him. William bolted upright and said, "Who are *you?*"

The man in the chair answered, "Well, like they say in the movies, I can be your best friend or your worst enemy. I made myself a cup of tea. Hope it's okay."

William had pulled his blanket up under his chin. His voice was trembling, "What do you want?"

Mathew Core answered, "Most of your money. I know how much you have, everywhere. I helped you hide it."

William felt an icy chill spread throughout his body. He now had a pretty good idea who this guy was. *Shit.* William's voice was barely a whisper, "I don't understand."

Mathew set the cup down and leaned forward, "An FBI team arrived in town yesterday. They're looking for you and Devon. They will find you. Maybe in hours, weeks, or months, but they will find you. I want half of all your money now, and another twenty-five percent after you are located somewhere safe with another new identity."

William was stunned but said, "How do I know this is true?"

Mathew stood up and showed William a photo of a group of officers standing over a body. "This was taken an hour ago. Six blocks from here."

William counted at least ten officers in the crowd. "Who is the dead guy? Is it Devon?"

Mathew simply said, "Not Devon. Yet."

William's mind was spinning, "I can't leave! I have a new life now, I have plans…"

Mathew chuckled, "How many of your plans can you do dead?" Mathew tossed a card and the photo on William's bed and said, "I wouldn't wait too long to make a decision. Even I need a little time to prepare." He smiled and walked out of the room. William never heard the door open or shut when he left. The guy was a ghost.

William dialed Devon. No answer. He was shouting at the phone, "Pick up you asshole!" He threw his phone across the room and began pacing. He didn't want to leave! He didn't want to get caught. Damn! How did they find out he was in New Orleans anyway? It had to be Devon. He did something! William went over and picked up his phone and dialed Devon again. Still no answer!

* * *

Amy was shaking Rebecca's shoulders and hissing, "Wake up!" Rebecca moaned and then her eyes opened wide.

She started crying, "Amy, Amy, what is going to happen to us?"

Amy said, "We are going to get out of here! Do you have anything long and pointed?"

Rebecca's brow furrowed, "What?"

Amy said, "I think I can pick the lock, I need something long and pointed."

Rebecca started patting her chest, "Where's my bra?"

Amy was shaking her head, "Becca, you have to listen to me! Don't worry about your bra. Do you have anything long and pointed?"

Rebecca frowned and said, "In my bra, those support things under the cup."

Amy jumped up and started searching the room. "Where is it?" she was frantic. She found the bra in the bathroom and tore it apart removing one of the long support wires. She held it up, "This is too fat! Take off your bracelet!"

Rebecca gave Amy her bracelet, tried to stand and fell down, "There's something wrong with my legs!"

Amy said, "We've been drugged. Start trying to move around, it will help."

Rebecca started crying, "Where is he? Is he coming back?"

Amy went over and gave her a hug. "Look, I am doing a little better than you are right now. I am going to try to pick that stupid lock, and we are going to escape. Just concentrate on that. Get yourself dressed." Amy was wildly untwisting the braided wire on Rebecca's bracelet. She finally had a strand that looked long enough to use.

Amy crawled over to the door. It was still hard for her to walk more than a few steps at a time. Her muscles felt like Jell-O, and she was fighting the urge to lie down and sleep. She looked over at Rebecca who was asleep on the floor. Amy positioned herself next to the door and looked up at the underside of the door handle. She had to make several tries, but she finally got the wire into the hole and pushed up. She heard a hissing sound and knew the hydraulic pressure was being released from the lock. She tried the handle. It moved part way and hit resistance. Her arm felt like concrete, and it was hard to keep a grip on the thin wire.

Amy inserted the wire again and heard the pressure release again. Then she heard a click. She pulled down on the handle. The door opened. She could hear a phone ringing in the background. It sounded like it was coming from upstairs. He must be home if his phone is here. Amy started to crawl back to Rebecca. She told herself she had to save them. It was now or never. When she reached Rebecca, she slapped her, hard. Rebecca's eyes flew open, and Amy whispered, "The door is open! You have to stand up. This is your life Becca. Help me save you."

Rebecca grabbed the side of the bed and began pulling herself up. She was hanging on to Amy, and they both fell to the floor. Amy said, "Fine, then we're crawling out of here."

245

Roger had arranged for cars to be delivered to them from the field office. One car for Thor and Jeanne, one for Nelson and Pablo, and one for Paul and him. If all went right, they would have Devon yet today. Roger and Paul got in their car. "Put the light on the dash. I think we are going to need it to get through these streets and park where we want. Let's get these gloves. Jeanne told me about him wearing them. I count that as dot number one."

Paul laughed, "Hey, I'll take any dots you can muster." Paul turned on the dash light, and they drove straight to the pharmacy listed on the receipt.

It turned out to be located across from the French Quarter Bank branch Ellen said Amy and Rebecca worked at. Paul pointed, "Dot number two. We left the Bank, I had a headache, we came here for aspirin, and we asked about gloves."

Roger said, "Works for me."

They walked into the pharmacy and asked to speak to the manager. The pharmacist came over and asked if he could help them. Roger showed him both the receipt and his badge and asked if he could identify the purchaser. The pharmacist was rubbing his chin and said, "I can describe the guy, but I don't know his name."

Roger had noticed the receipt was for cash and asked, "Has he ever filled a prescription here?"

The pharmacist answered, "Yeah, let me think. He got some pain scripts after some nose surgery. Gosh, when was that?" Paul was going out of his mind waiting for an answer. Roger realized he was rubbing the handle of his gun and stopped. It was making the pharmacist nervous.

Roger asked, "How does he know when his glove order is in? Has he left a phone number or anything?"

The pharmacist was shaking his head, "Nooooooo, I don't think so, he just stops in. Huh, I remember having to go in the back and look for him once. He was pretty insistent they should be here, and he was running low. You know I think he took a phone call that day while he was here, and it sounded like he was a lawyer or something." Paul was ready to scream. Then the pharmacist said, "I remember now, he had a nose job the same day my wife did. Same doctor. Let me check my records." He went behind the counter and produced a copy of a prescription. The Pharmacist scrunched his mouth as he hung on to the paper, "Can I give this to you? Don't you need a warrant or something?"

Roger said, "This is a very important case. I can have a Federal Warrant issued and delivered here. In the meantime, I am not leaving. My car stays out front with the light on." The pharmacist handed the copy of the script to Roger. The script was written to Michael Parker. They had a name.

Roger and Paul thanked the pharmacist and walked across the street to the French Quarter Bank branch. Paul said, "Jesus! Could that guy think any slower?"

Roger said, "I know, but we have a name! Let's see what we can get in here." Roger called Ray as they entered the bank building, "Start looking for any Michael Parker in New Orleans."

Ray answered, "I was just going to call you. Just tied one of the accounts you gave me on the five million dollar transfer to a Michael Parker. The account is at French Quarter Bank, I have the number for you."

Roger wrote it down, looked at Paul, and said, "We have Parker's account number here."

They walked up to a teller station and asked if the manager was there. They were told he was on the phone and would be a minute. The teller walked very slowly toward a back office to deliver the note that he was needed up front.

Paul looked at Roger and said, "I am getting the impression nobody moves very fast in this town."

Eventually the branch manager came to the teller window and said, "May I help you gentlemen?" He had on a light blue cotton suit and a pink dress shirt with a blue tie. Paul thought he looked like he had been shopping with the cabby.

Roger flashed his badge and said "FBI. Is there somewhere we can talk?"

The manager started fanning himself with some papers he was holding and said, "I just don't know how much more I can take this morning." Paul and Roger looked at each other.

Roger noticed there were only two tellers working and the lines in the lobby were beginning to reach the door. When they got into the office, Roger asked, "Are you short help? It looks pretty busy out there."

The manager sat heavily in his chair and gestured for them to sit down. "I have two girls decided not to show up today, a customer who showed up and insisted on making a cash withdrawal of practically everything we had available, and now you."

Roger said, "I am hoping you will cooperate with me and not force me to seize this branch until a warrant can be drawn up."

The managers eyes grew huge, "Seize the branch? For what?"

Roger continued, "This is what I want. I want the names of the two tellers who didn't show this morning and their phone numbers. We suspect foul play. I also want any information you can give me on this account and the account holder."

The branch manager was stunned, "You sure got here fast! Amy and Rebecca didn't have to start work until 10:00, and it's only 10:30." He looked at Roger and Paul, "You can get your warrant whenever you want. Or not. We don't cotton to formalities here in Nawlens. Give me that account number."

Roger passed it over to him, and he began typing into his computer with two fingers, very slowly. Paul was rolling his neck and fidgeting in his seat.

Finally Paul stood up and said, "Can I look at your personnel files while you are doing that. Maybe one of the tellers can pull Amy and Rebecca's files for me?"

The manager nodded his head and said, "Shoot. You got me so nervous I have to start again." He was pressing the delete button one press per second.

Roger looked pleadingly at Paul. Paul had to race from the room to keep from laughing. He knew Roger was ready to *shoot* the guy.

Paul walked behind the tellers and announced, "FBI. Everyone be patient, I need the services of one of these tellers, for a minute or so, and then you can get back to what you were doing." Everyone gasped and the tellers looked at each other like they were in shock. Paul pointed at the closest one to him and asked, "Do you know where the personnel files are kept?" She nodded, slowly. Paul tilted his head, "Let's go. Now."

Paul had made the copies of the files himself since he didn't want to wait for the teller to do it. Roger left the bank manager's office with a few sheets of paper in his hand and gestured to Paul that he was ready. They practically ran back to the car and burst out laughing as soon as they closed the door. Paul finally said, "Oh my God! I couldn't live here. I would shoot everybody!"

Roger laughed, "Let's see what we have." In the personnel files they had cell numbers for both girls. Roger called Ray and asked him to see if they were on.

Ray answered, "Do you know who services them? Of course you don't. I will find them if they are on, ping them, and send you the location."

Roger smiled, "It's so nice having you back."

Ray answered. "Yeah."

Paul asked, "Do we have anything that says this Mike Parker might be Devon?"

Roger said, "No. We don't even have an address. He opted for internet banking and doesn't have a street address for statements. The bank must have an address for him somewhere. Signature card?" Roger looked at Paul, "I'm going back in. Call Nelson and Manigat to look up all three of these names. Amy, Rebecca, and Parker. Find any real estate tied to any of them, especially Parker." After about twenty minutes Roger came back to the car. "I cannot believe there is no address of record for Mike Parker. He even has State of Louisiana listed as his beneficiary."

Paul said, "Wasn't there an address on the phone bill?"

Roger said, "Shit, I forgot all about that!" Roger dug through his briefcase and produced the phone bill. No street address, but we have a mailbox service. Roger called Ray back to get the address of the nearest office of Mailbox Service, Inc..

CHAPTER 22

Jeremiah and Alan had returned from Mambo's and were tying the boat to the cypress log when they noticed a car pull onto the property. Jeanne and a man got out and walked over to them. Jeanne hugged Jeremiah, and he introduced her to Alan. Jeanne introduced SSA Dan Thor to both of them. Alan looked surprised, straightened his posture, and asked, "Did you say *FBI?*"

He looked at Jeremiah who pointed at Jeanne and said, "She's one of 'em too." Jeremiah looked at Jeanne. "Alan and I just hooked up that fridge for Mambo. You should've seen her face. She's not giving *that* away! I took her some popsicles and put 'em in the freezer part." Jeremiah had a huge smile on his face.

Jeanne could tell Jeremiah was already tired, and he was wearing his patch which meant his eye was bothering him. "Jeremiah, we have to go to Mambo's and get that woman. Can Alan take us?"

Alan said, "I got time, I'm just not sure I remember how to get there."

Jeremiah said, "If none of you had a big breakfast, we could probably do it. That be five people which is about two too many." Thor and Jeanne looked at each other. Then Jeremiah said, "Hell, Jeanne there don't count as a whole person. Neither does that lady at Mambo's. Alan, you steer, and I'll tell you where to go."

Thor did not like the fact they had to debate whether or not the boat could handle the weight of them all. The last thing he wanted this morning, other than meeting *Mambo*, was to sink in a swamp. They all piled in, carefully distributing their weight. Only about six inches of clearance was between the deck of the boat and the water line.

About fifty feet from where they pushed off, Jeremiah looked at Jeanne and asked, "You bring your gun?" Jeanne pulled it out, and Jeremiah pointed to a rapidly approaching large water moccasin. Jeanne shot it just as Thor saw it. Thor drew his weapon, and Jeremiah pointed to the other side of the boat at one for him. Thor missed his first two shots and had to shoot again. A wiggling snake, underwater, accelerating, was not the easiest target. Jeremiah said, "We sittin' so low they can flop right on the deck. Best you guys keep your eyes open. Don't be shootin' the bottom of this boat! We got us a storm coming, and they're lookin' to eat their fill. Always bad when a storm comin'."

Thor looked at Jeanne who was smiling at him. Thor frowned, "You are one *sick* broad if you are enjoying this!" Just then Thor saw a huge alligator slink from the shore into the water.

Jeremiah turned to him, "You leave them alone."

Jeremiah and Jeanne said at the same time, "You are the last thing he wants for dinner." They laughed. Thor was convinced Roger had sent him to hell.

Alan looked at Thor, "I'm with you man. This is not fun." As soon as Alan said that a large snake plopped onto the boat right by Alan's ankle. Jeanne threw her knife and killed it just as it started to coil to spring. She inched over trying not to tip the boat, yanked her knife back, and kicked the snake into the water.

Jeremiah said, "That was probably a nest we went through. It might not be bad 'til we get to Mambo's. She got some big ones over that side. Mind the trees, they like trees." Thor's head spun around as he scrutinized every branch above them.

Jeanne had been looking at the boat, and she asked Jeremiah, "What is in that box on the front there? Right in front of Alan?" She was thinking that it might be something they could leave at Mambo's to reduce their weight load.

Jeremiah answered, "Most in there are them bones I told you about. Must be about four or five people in there."

Alan lost it, "*People* **bones?** Uncle Jeremiah, what in the hell is going on?"

Thor started walking toward the front of the boat to look, and they started taking on water. Everyone yelled at him to go back and sit down. Thor looked at Jeanne, "Bones?"

Jeanne nodded. "Yup. Jeremiah found them where he found me."

Thor decided he had to call Roger. When Roger answered, Thor asked, "Is Paul with you? Put this on speaker." A moment later Roger told Thor he was on speaker, and they had pulled over to hear him. Roger told Thor they might have Devon's alias already. Thor said, "Of course you do. You'll probably catch the bastard before lunch! I'm on a sinkin' swamp boat with Annie Oakley here, with a *box* of **five dead people** on the boat! I can't look at the bones because we have to keep shooting snakes! But *not* the Alligators….nooooo…they're our *friends*. And if I move my fat ass one *inch* on this boat, we are going to *sink*. Just thought you two would want to know what *happened* to us!" Roger and Paul were trying not to make any noise, but their laughter kept breaking through in little bursts. Paul had to leave the car. Roger told Thor to keep him posted. After he hung up he realized how cold and unsupportive that sounded, but that was all his brain could bring him to say. He struggled to get those words out.

Paul got back in the car and could barely speak, "What did you tell him?"

Roger spit out, "I told him to keep me posted."

"He told you he was in a sinking swamp boat, calls you for help, and you told him to keep you posted? At what point does he 'post' you again? When he's underwater? You are going to hear about this." Roger looked at the card Special Agent Frank Mass had given him and called to request help.

When Agent Mass answered, Roger asked him if he had access to a swamp boat that could go to Mambo's behind Honey Island. Frank answered the boats he could get were too big to get that far down the swamp. You need a special flat bottom boat. Frank didn't think any of his guys would go to Mambo's.

Paul could hear Frank asking Roger, "What the hell are you guys doin' out there?"

Roger was shaking his head. He finally answered, "It's a long story, Frank. I need you to think of something and call me. I have a situation out there. I could use some help, fast. Also put together a forensic team, we've got human bones."

About five minutes later Mass called Roger back, "I found a guy with a boat who is willing to go to Mambo's. Should I send him?"

Roger asked, "Send my guys with him. Do you know this guy?"

Agent Mass answered, "Got a couple of busts for poaching and weed is all."

Roger said, "Okay. I guess I don't have a choice. Tell my guys to bring extra ammo, the snakes are bad today."

Roger called Thor and told him a second boat with Nelson and Manigat would meet them at Mambo's. Thor said, "Thanks," and hung up.

Agents Nelson and Manigat were riding with one of the local agents to get some guy's boat and go to Mambo's. They had barely started working on the computers at the center, looking for data on Mathew Core, when Roger had called. The local agent asked them, "What kind of case are you guys on anyway?"

Todd and Pablo looked at each other, and Todd said, "We're looking for an escaped serial killer."

The young New Orleans agent driving asked, *"At Mambo's?"*

✳ ✳ ✳

Funny thing happened on the way to the swamp. Ellen told us to take a short cut through the Federal Bureau of Investigation's Headquarters in D.C. and visit the Director's office for exactly twenty minutes. We would record everything that happened in that office, then get to the Virginia federal prison where Jason Sims, the computer lab guy, was being held, and record what happened there for exactly ten minutes. Then get to the swamp as fast as we could.

By no stretch of the imagination was going to Washington D.C. a short cut to a Louisiana swamp. We also discovered the only thing our watches didn't do was keep time! Mary did the one-Mississippi, two-Mississippi thing for both visits. She was actually hoarse. When we were ready to leave, Linda noticed a desk clock near a computer and turned it around. No sense getting Mary mad. By the time we actually made it to the swamp we were all exhausted.

Amy was crawling behind Rebecca and pushing her butt forward every other step. Rebecca kept collapsing, and Amy was cheering her forward. "Keep going Becca. I can see the edge of the alley. Hurry! Try harder!" Amy was sure Devon was going to notice them gone any minute. He was definitely home. His SUV was in the garage, and she had heard the phone ringing. It was morning, but the air was already thick with humidity. There was a very strong breeze, and Amy could tell there was a bad storm coming. All she wanted to do was get to some street where someone could pick them up and take them to the police station.

They had made it to the edge of the alley. Amy pulled herself up and was leaning against the side of a utility pole. Rebecca was trying to stand with her. Amy saw an SUV pull into the Alley. "Becca! STAND UP! A car's coming!" Rebecca pulled from strength she didn't know she had and was standing, hugging the utility pole as Amy stumbled straight into the path of the SUV.

Thank God it stopped! A man got out and shouted, "My God what is wrong with you girls?" He put his arm around Amy and helped her stand. Rebecca slid down the pole and collapsed in a heap on the ground.

Amy grabbed the man's arm and pleaded, "Help us, please. We were kidnapped by the man in that house! We need to get to the police." Amy heard the man tell her he would take them to the police, and he helped her into the back seat of his SUV. He told her to try and slide over he was going to get her friend. Minutes later Rebecca was sitting next to her.

The air conditioning felt wonderful and the last thing Amy remembered was the man saying, "You poor, poor girls. Oh my God. You just rest a minute."

William Patterson looked into the rear view mirror of his SUV at the two drugged out girls. *WHAT THE HELL?* Devon is going to get us both killed! Where the hell is he? Now he has women escaping in broad daylight? William had driven past Devon's office and his favorite breakfast café looking for him. He had decided to check out Devon's house. Now this? He drove to a main intersection and turned the SUV to head out of town.

Amy mumbled from the back seat, "I think you missed your turn." Then she fell asleep again.

* * *

Spicey and Jerome climbed the marble stairs toward the huge front door of the police station. Spicey could tell Jerome had never been here before. Jerome stopped at the top of the stairs and looked at Spicey, "You know, I ought to tell them you stole sixty dollars from me! I thought now that we're friends and all, you would give it back."

Spicey looked at him and said, "What does us being friends now have to do with it? Someone steals from you it causes you pain. You learn that from feelin' the pain! Not from me giving it back. A man would consider this a life lesson. Now, if you decided that you should feel the pain, I might consider giving it back to you, so you could donate it to somebody needs it. Not just wants it."

Jerome looked at her, "You want me to miss it, so I don't never do that to someone else. But you give it back to me if I give it away?"

Spicey said, "It don't really belong to me does it?"

Jerome said "No."

Spicey said, "One way or another you are going to learn that in this life, you do something wrong, you are going to pay. This here is a cheap lesson if you choose to learn it."

She was hoping this would be a positive experience for him. John Barry had just arrived and was talking to the desk sergeant when Spicey and Jerome entered the main hall. They walked up to the desk, and Spicey looked at Jerome. Jerome said, "I would like to report that my momma is missin'."

The desk sergeant started to hand the clipboard to Jerome, but John grabbed it. He said, "Let me take this for you." John motioned for Spicey and Jerome to follow him into a small interview room.

John Barry took a very complete statement from Jerome and Spicey. He learned that Jerome's mother's name was Adele Brown, and she had a small tailor shop in the Quarter. Occasionally she delivered her finished work to her customers. Adele's story didn't sound like a mother who would abandon her son. John was worried there might be a sinister element. He couldn't quit thinking about Devon and hoped to God this young man's mother had not met up with him. John had noticed how intently Jerome was staring at him and asked, "Jerome, I imagine you have questions you want to ask me. Go ahead."

Jerome said, "You say you are really going to look for my momma. But you don't know us, and momma said the police don't have time for the likes of us. Spicey says we have to let the police have a chance to do good. I already looked everywhere my momma would go. She's just gone!"

John stood, put his arm on Jerome's shoulder, and said, "You have just defined what it really means to be a law enforcement officer, Jerome. The police have more resources for finding people than you do. Give me a chance to find your mom. After I do, you will understand why we do this job. This is a very proud profession. A lot of us who are policemen now, became policemen because we were helped by one. You might even think about joining the police or the FBI when you get older."

Jerome's eyes got big, "How do I do that?"

John laughed at his expression and said, "Do you want me to start sending you material about these jobs, so you can study the right things?"

Jerome whispered, "Yeah."

John smiled and said, "It's yes, not yeah."

Jerome said "Yes."

Spicey told Jerome they would have to walk a couple of blocks before they could catch a cab. She expected him to give her trouble about going to school today. He didn't. When they got in the cab, she gave directions to the cabby for Jerome's school. She told Jerome to come to her place after school, and hopefully she would have some news for him. He agreed, and when the cab stopped, he leaned over and kissed her cheek.

Spicey giggled, "You be kissin' your momma's cheek pretty soon."

Jerome's eyes glistened, "Until then I'll kiss you."

Spicey said, "Yeah"

Jerome raised his eyebrows, "You mean yes, not yeah."

Spicey slugged him. "You best get to class Mr. POliceman!"

CHAPTER 23

Tourey busily searched his data bases looking for anything connected to Mathew Core. He found two CIA documents that referred to a Core as being an independent contractor. He found another link that Core was used by the FBI a few months ago in New Orleans to verify the identity of a suspected human trafficking ring. It also looked like he had been contracted to provide intelligence on a weapons bust. Contracts went back ten years on Core. Everything Tourey was reading sounded like Core was one of the good guys. This didn't make sense. Tourey wondered how he hadn't crossed paths with this guy before. Tourey hit print on his computer and watched the pages print out. He went back to the CIA report to see if he could get any other names associated with that assignment. His screen went black.

Tourey walked around his house testing his power and came back to his library. His computer had been shut down, maybe fried. He sat staring at the black screen and decided to try his laptop. As soon as he logged in to the CIA site, he was met with a big black screen that said, Access Denied. Tourey left his house and walked to a payphone down the street. This was the only payphone in the Quarter that worked. It was his. He dialed his supervisor. "You have a reason I can't log in?" He was met with silence.

After a brief pause his supervisor said, "I can't log in right now either. I don't know what is going on."

Roger and Paul found the Mailbox Office and had to threaten a warrant and seizure to get cooperation. Nawlens wasn't used to law enforcement. Unfortunately the clerk on duty had the same level of computer skills as the bank manager, and it was thirty minutes after arriving before Roger had an address. Ray called to tell Roger to look at the GPS map in his car. Ray had found one of the phones. Ray could get them within a two block area with a ping booster, but then they were on their own. Roger had to tie the girl's phone to Devon's alias, Parker, before he could get a warrant for that address.

Paul said, "How are we going to find a cell phone in a two block area?"

Roger said, "We can at least try." They followed the map and ended up in a business district of sorts with a couple of office strip malls.

Paul said, "This is impossible."

Just then Roger said, "Look at the corner of that building there."

Paul saw a black cat standing on its hind legs waving. "You've got to be kidding me." Roger pulled their car to where Ellen had been and followed her around the back of the mall. She was sitting on a dumpster licking her paws.

Roger and Paul jumped out of the car and ran for the dumpster. They knew they had to read the messages before the batteries went dead, or they would have to wait for Ray to restore everything. Roger jumped in the dumpster and started digging. Paul was ready to get in but Roger said, "Wait, I see a couple of purses." Roger used a piece of two by four that was in the dumpster to raise the purses out. They put on their gloves and carefully opened the purses. They only found one phone. Rebecca's. Paul was much more tech savvy than Roger, so he looked back through the messages.

Paul said, "Here! Rebecca sent this to Amy: Can't shop with you...ran into Mike...Atty. Parker...he is taking me shopping and to dinner!" Paul kept reading, "A bunch of nothing after that."

Roger said, "Let's get this phone to Ray before the batteries die and coordinate the raid of Devon's place. I'll order the warrant through the field office. Why don't you call John Barry and see how many guys Frank Mass can lend us. While you do that, I will take a quick shower at the Star Ship."

Paul said, "Good idea there buddy. You stink."

Devon woke with a headache. He thought he heard noises. He turned on the security screen and couldn't see the girls in the room. Maybe they're in the bathroom, he thought. He sat there a minute or so longer. Man, he was tired. He couldn't believe the clock said 11:00 am. He glanced out the bedroom window. It looks like a storm coming. His room was hot. He walked over to the thermostat and saw the air conditioning had been turned off. When did he do that?

He glanced at the security screen again. Still no girls. He threw some sweat pants on and grabbed the key to his secured room. He sure didn't feel like sex, but he wouldn't mind looking at them. He turned the corner to the basement staircase and saw the door was open! "What the Hell?" He stormed down the stairs and started screaming. He looked in the bathroom and in his garage. He ran to the end of his driveway and looked down the alley. HOLY SHIT! He didn't know what to do. He ran back in the house, ran upstairs, and found his phone. He saw Patterson had tried to call him seven times. He couldn't imagine what was going on. Patterson almost never called him!

Devon dialed Patterson. "Where in the *hell* have you been? I have been trying to reach you all morning!" Patterson sounded exasperated.

Devon answered, "I haven't left home. I have a problem."

Patterson screamed, "You sure as hell do! And now I have one too! I took care of your two girls. I found them staggering around in your alley! In broad daylight! Do you know it's your fault the FBI has a whole team here, in Nawlens? Just for us?"

"What?"

Patterson said, "You better figure out some place we can talk."

Devon said, "I'll come to your place."

Patterson screamed, "You will *not*! Meet me at that stupid little place over by Jackson Square. No wait! Let's go to that place called Mickey's. A lot of tourists go there, not many locals. Meet you in thirty minutes." Patterson hung up and shook his head. Devon was going to get them killed.

Devon looked around his room. His head was throbbing. How did they escape? They both knew his alias. Oh no, his money! He called the bank and had them wire all but one thousand to his off-shore account. Thank god he had thought of that. How much cash did he have on him? He looked in his wallet. About a thousand. After he met with Patterson he would take those earrings back and get those nine hundred dollars back. Devon grabbed a towel and went in to shower. This day already sucked.

✳ ✳ ✳

Amy and Rebecca had fallen asleep in Patterson's SUV. The drugs and the air conditioning lured them under again. They were awakened by Patterson yelling at them and pointing a gun at their heads. He had fired the gun in the air and screamed, "Do you want to die now? Move it!"

Amy was trying to focus. What had happened? Wasn't this the man who had saved them? Why was he pointing a gun at them? She reached over and shook Rebecca. "Becca! Wake up!" Patterson told them to get out of the truck and start walking. The wind gusts were up to about fifty miles per hour now, the storm was nearly there. Rebecca was hanging on to Amy as they staggered down the dirt path toward the edge of the swamp. Amy yelled back to Patterson who was following them, "We can't walk any farther because of the swamp!"

Patterson yelled back at her, "Your choice. You walk into that swamp and keep going, maybe you hit the island or the other side. Or you just stand still, and I shoot you here."

Amy whipped around nearly dropping Rebecca, "Why are you doing this?"

Patterson smiled, "It's you or me little girl, and I have the gun. Now move it! I don't have all day. If it takes you too long to get out of my sight, I might just shoot you anyway! And I have binoculars. I can see you far longer than you can see me!"

Amy and Rebecca were both crying. Amy could feel the soft sludge at the bottom of the marsh envelope her legs and creep up toward her waist. The bottom wasn't even, and they kept tripping and falling and sinking. Rebecca saw an alligator in the distance and began screaming uncontrollably. Amy grabbed her shoulders and said, "This asshole isn't going to win this. Alligators will not hurt you unless you threaten them." Amy was thinking, usually. Rebecca quieted down some. They walked for some distance, and Amy turned around. She couldn't see Patterson anymore and decided they should try to just walk back. Just then two shots rang out from the shore, and she thought she heard him yell something. They quickly turned and continued walking into the deep waters of the swamp.

Rebecca was getting some strength back and told Amy she could walk on her own. They saw an area where the land mass looked higher. There was a clump of giant cypress trees in the center. Rebecca pointed and said, "Let's get out of the water over there for a while." Amy thought that sounded good, and they crawled up the bank to the center of the tree trunks. One beam of sunlight had escaped through the black clouds. Probably the last one.

Amy said, "We have a bad storm coming."

Rebecca sighed, "Of course."

* * *

Dusty had been blasted awake by the cell phone lying on his neck. His head pounded from last night's drinks with his friendly bartender, Scotty. The caller was Agent Frank Mass requesting that Dusty borrow his brother's boat to take two FBI Agents to Mambo's place. Dusty told Frank to go screw himself. Frank told him there was a thousand dollars waiting at the end of the trip.

Dusty tried to blink his vision into focus, "What time does this tour boat leave?"

Frank answered "Now. I'm having them delivered to you as we speak."

When agents Nelson and Manigat arrived at the boat landing, Pablo asked, "Aren't you the artist who did the sketches last night?"

Dusty yawned, "That would be me. Artist by night, Mambo tours by day. You guys know we have a bad storm almost here?" Just then a large branch crashed from a nearby tree to the ground. Dusty jumped. The gusts were bending some of the trees and the marsh grasses were wildly swirling. The sky was an ugly black blue. Lightning could be seen in the distance.

Todd said, "Let's get this show on the road. Where's the motor?"

Dusty laughed, "Got me a city slicker. No motor on this type of swamp boat. You got yourself a long pole. One."

Pablo raised his voice, "Then we are going to marathon this puppy. We have agents in trouble. Get two more poles! Let's go! Now!" Dusty couldn't help wonder why these damn Yankees were always in such a rush. It wasn't even mornin' yet to him. The young agent who drove them, gave Todd a card, and told him to call when they were on their way back.

Like synchronized sailors they staggered their strokes and were speeding through the marshes and into the deep waters of the swamp. Dusty guided them past dozens of water paths that cut through the swamp at various angles. They had maneuvered their way through a maze of tiny islands. Large cypress trees, nearly fallen, arched and covered in long strands of moss nearly hid most of the places where Dusty carefully steered them forward. Green eyes watched them from every shadow. After about twenty minutes Dusty proclaimed he thought Mambo's hut was right around the next little peninsula.

"What do you mean you think Mambo is there?"

Dusty said, "Don't get your shorts in a bunch. I'm pretty sure. I only came here when I was high and lookin' for forgiveness from the Saints." Todd rolled his eyes as he took his shirt off and threw it on the bottom of the boat. The air was heavy with humidity and downright hot. Pablo did the same. They were both wearing muscle t-shirts, soaked in sweat, with their shoulder harnesses for their weapons. Dusty straightened up, "Damn. Feel like I'm giving a tour to a couple of Rambo's." Just then they heard a gunshot, then another, and another. The sound of gunfire was getting louder and faster. They could hear people shouting.

Pablo yelled, "Move it! Push! Push!**"**

Dusty screamed, *"TOWARD* the gunshots?"

Fifty feet from Mambo's hut, Jeremiah's boat was stopped in the water. The boat was surrounded by water moccasins, big ones. The storm had the snakes spooked. Their thrashing caused the water to look like rapids.

Our little angel group had just arrived, and started throwing the snakes back into the water as they came on shore. As fast as we threw the snakes in the air, Jeanne and Thor were shooting at them.

Teresa screamed, "Can we talk to snakes?" as she tossed one off to her left back into the water. They were heavy and huge! They were in the trees! I was pretty sure we had disturbed a huge nest because there were skinny little baby ones too. We were trying to create a clear landing spot for everyone on the boat.

Mary yelled back at Teresa, "Say something! Tell them to go away!"

I jumped out to the center of Mambo's little yard and yelled, "All snakes need to leave, now!" That did nothing. So much for angel powers.

Linda yelled, "Don't alligators *eat* snakes? Maybe we should call for the alligators to come."

Teresa yelled, "NO! These guys will shoot them by accident and the alligators might actually start harming people too. Remember, Jeremiah said they attack if they feel threatened."

Linda screamed, "There is a snake on the boat! They don't see it!" She flew over, grabbed the snake and tossed it in the water. "Dang! They are heavy."

I was standing in the middle of the yard still trying to think what we could do when Mary yelled, "Get SNAKES!" I realized she was brilliant. Of course! I manifested myself a big broad leaf rake and started swooshing the snakes from the edge of the bank back into the water.

Teresa yelled at me, "What are you doing?"

I answered, "Mary said to get rakes. It's working!"

Teresa screamed, "She said get snakes, not rakes! Mortals can see your stupid rake!" She tossed another snake into the air. I looked around. Thankfully everyone was so busy shooting, I don't think they saw. Except maybe Jeremiah. He had that one eye turned at me.

We saw the second boat come around the corner of the peninsula. Thor yelled to them, "These are water moccasins! Highly poisonous! I think we hit a nest. I'm almost out of ammo." The guys in the second boat were pushing forward with everything they had. They let their boat glide up next to Jeremiah's, and Todd tossed an ammo clip to both Jeanne and Thor.

Pablo yelled, "Holy Shit! They are coming on your boat!" Jeanne whipped around and threw her knife at one, cutting it in half about six inches from Thor's foot.

Thor heard the thunk of the knife, looked at the snake, and said, "Remind me, you owe me some shorts."

We kept tossing snakes in the air as they got close to the boats, and everyone kept shooting them. Jeanne yelled, "The trees!" Dusty, Alan, and Jeremiah all squatted down as low as they could to stay out of the line of fire. They had their hands over their ears, and their eyes kept alternating from wide open to pressed shut. It looked as if it were raining dead snakes.

Alan screamed at Jeremiah, "Have you ever seen snakes try to fly?"

Jeremiah screamed back, "Nope," and ducked down even lower. Suddenly Mambo was standing in her doorway, her arms raised high and chanting.

The water instantly calmed, and the snakes slithered away from the boats. It was like they had never been there. Thor was panting as his head darted from side to side. "Where'd they go?"

Jeanne laughed as she yanked her knife from the boat. "Mambo sent them away." Thor slowly turned his head toward the hut and saw the bent old woman waving her arms above her head. Then she slowly put a Popsicle in her mouth and disappeared into her hut.

Jeremiah looked at Jeanne, "Told ya she'd like 'em."

Thor looked at Nelson and Manigat and said, "Good idea taking your shirts off except the mosquitos here can carry off a dog." He shook his head, "This would be one hell of a training exercise wouldn't it?"

Jeanne said, "That storm is not going to wait for us, and we don't need rain pounding our boat from the top." She looked at Dusty who was spellbound by her, "Aren't you the artist?"

Dusty slowly nodded his head.

"How much weight can you hold on that boat?" His boat definitely had a better deck and sat at least four inches farther off the water than Jeremiah's.

Dusty raised an eyebrow and looked around. He shrugged his shoulders and said, "I have no idea. Not my boat."

Thor sighed, "Great. Now we have two boats to sink."

Jeanne and Jeremiah left the boat for shore to get Adele Brown from Mambo's and to explain to Mambo what was happening. Thor moved to Dusty's boat and noticed the dozens of little skulls and clumps of feathers hanging from the trees and bushes. "Lady could use a new landscaper," he mumbled as he swatted a mosquito. He picked it off his arm and held it up, "Look at the size of this thing! It could be a small bird. Miserable place. Why would someone live here?"

Teresa had taken off when the snakes went away and was now flying back to us at warp speed. "Guys, guys! Rebecca and Amy are in the swamp!"

Mary asked, "What?"

Teresa took off again and yelled, "Follow me!" We followed her, I missed grabbing Linda's shirt and had to fly on my own. Other than getting tangled in that stupid moss, I did okay. We saw the girls huddled at the base of the cypress tree, crying.

I said, "Oh no! How are we going to get everyone to come way over here?" It seemed like we had gone a long distance from the group, and I know we had passed where you would turn off to go to Jeremiah's house.

Linda said, "Mambo can see us. Can we tell her to send Jeanne out here?"

Mary said, "Good idea!" We flew back to Mambo's. This time I grabbed Linda. Jeanne was just leaving. We burst through the wall shouting at Mambo to stop her. Mambo touched Jeanne's arm, and Jeanne stopped. Mambo was staring at us. Mary said, "Tell Jeanne to go back to where Jeremiah found her! Please? There are two more women there!"

Mambo was tilting her head and staring. I started trying to do a pantomime of what we wanted, and Teresa asked, "What are you doing?"

I realized it wasn't working anyway and said, "Swatting mosquitos."

Mambo pulled Jeanne to the center of the room and said, "Spirits are trying to tell you something."

Jeanne looked at her and said, "Am I supposed to do something?" We all nodded our heads yes.

Mambo said, "Yes."

Jeanne asked, "In the city or the swamp?"

Mambo looked at us and I held up two fingers. Mambo got it. "In the swamp." Mambo looked at me. I held up two fingers again and then cupped my boobs and lifted them a couple of times.

Mary's mouth flew open, and she yelled, "What is wrong with you?"

Mambo nodded and told Jeanne, "There are two women in the swamp." I stuck my tongue out at Mary.

Linda was shaking her head as she said, "Unbelievable."

Jeanne gave Mambo a hug and told her she would bring more goodies for the fridge. Holding a Popsicle, Mambo asked, "More?"

Jeanne laughed, "Yes." Mambo told Jeanne the snakes had become a problem for her visitors. She was grateful they had killed so many.

Jeanne ran to Jeremiah's boat. Adele was already on board with Todd and Pablo. Thor had moved to that boat too. That put five people on that boat, but it was holding the weight better than Jeremiah's would have. Jeanne announced they had two more women to pick up. Everyone looked at each other. That would put five people back on Jeremiah's boat.

Pablo looked at Thor and said, "Let's get 'em."

Jeremiah's nephew Alan said, "I wish some-one would tell me what the hell is going on. We got five dead people in a box, and we're pickin' ladies out of the swamp like mushrooms!" Nobody answered him.

Thor frowned at Jeanne, "How do you know there are two more women out here?"

Jeanne answered, "Mambo."

Thor looked exasperated and asked, "How does she know?"

Jeanne tilted her head and smiled, "She's Mambo."

Just then there was a deafening violent crack of lightning. Rain dumped from the clouds with the force of a waterfall. Thor yelled, *"Jesus!"* He was grabbing for anything to gain balance on the slippery wooden deck. The force of the downpour was practically sinking Jeremiah's boat. Mary yelled, "AL! We need you!"

Sure enough, our angel Al Roker was standing next to Mambo's door eating a Popsicle. "Oh, this isn't going to work for you guys is it?" He snapped his fingers and said, "Let's say we have another hour before the storm really hits. And now for the weather in your neck of the woods..." And he was gone. The rain stopped. The thunder and lightning stopped. The swamp was silent.

Thor was looking up at the clear sky with his soaked hair plastered against his head, "The snakes disappear. The storm disappears. What kind of nightmare place is this?" He was wringing the water from his shirt.

Pablo answered, "You should come out here at night." Thor shuddered.

Jeanne had helped push the boat off for Jeremiah and said to Thor, "When Patterson made me walk into the swamp, I was pretty drugged.

I think I probably was bitten by a cypress spider. Better than a black widow, they're out here too. Still, I was too sick to go back into the water. I spent two nights and three days on the trunk of a tree. Jeremiah thought I was dead." Pablo looked at her. He wondered what comfy bed he had been in while she was in a swamp. He owed her so much. The look wasn't lost on Thor.

Thor yelled from his boat over to Jeremiah and said, "I want to get paramedics to your place for these women. What is your address?" Jeremiah and Jeanne both started laughing. Thor looked puzzled and then said, "Of course. You don't have one." Thor's phone rang. It was Roger. Thor answered, "Yeah?" Thor listened awhile then spoke, "We have been told there are two more women out here. Maybe they're your missing tellers. I am going to need paramedics sent out here, but Jeremiah doesn't have an address." Thor listened a bit then said, "I'll call when we're heading back." He snapped his phone shut. Thor looked at Jeanne, "Roger will have paramedics at Dusty's place. He has an address on Devon and is assembling the assault team now."

Jeanne asked, "He found him already?"

Thor nodded. "Population over three hundred-fifty thousand, and he found him before lunch!" Thor thought Jeanne looked disappointed. He understood why. She probably would have liked to be in on his arrest, Pablo too. This actually worked out for Roger. Stick his two problems out in the swamp while he caught the bad guy. Roger really had the golden touch.

CHAPTER 24

Paul and Roger were at Star Ship. Ray was working on saving the phone data from Rebecca's phone. Roger had taken a quick shower and put on some of Simon's clothes. Roger had seen a pile of clothes on the floor behind the door. They looked like the clothes Simon had been wearing after shopping with the cabby. Roger chuckled to himself. He was sure Simon wouldn't mind him taking his clothes, but his own stinky mess made him realize they needed some sort of laundry service. They had some swamp clothes coming in soon. Roger asked if Ray wouldn't arrange laundry service through the field office. Hopefully, they knew a trusted laundry.

Paul had the field office prepare the warrant. Everyone was set to move in on Devon's house at 11:30 exactly. John Barry had agreed to join them. They were to assemble at the field office and go from there. Ray wished them luck and went back to the basement to finish what he was working on. Roger had Paul, Simon, John, and four agents from the field office. Devon didn't stand a chance.

A caravan of black SUV's silently crawled through the streets and surrounded Devon's block. State troopers blocked all traffic. Roger and Paul followed the assault team through the front door. They moved swiftly and silently. Roger entered Devon's bedroom first. He saw the mirror in the bathroom was still steamed over. They had missed him by minutes. Roger used his radio to announce to the team, "Don't disturb anything. We just missed him. He may come back." The team carefully left everything as they found it. Roger and Paul collected several documents and personal items they didn't think would be readily missed. Roger and Paul walked around the basement room Devon obviously used as his prison.

Paul said, "I can't figure how those girls got out." Then he studied the door jam. "Hydraulic lock, one of those girls knew how to depressurize it." Roger tried to imagine the terror those girls felt while trying to escape. Where were they? Roger called the New Orleans Police Department and was told no one matching the girls' descriptions had been there. Roger put out an APB on Devon's car and added the alert that there might be passengers in danger.

He snapped his phone shut and looked at Paul, "I bet he is disposing of them, or they did escape and are hiding from him. I'll have units sent to their homes just in case. Thor says two more women are in the swamp they are going to rescue. It could be Rebecca and Amy were taken there."

A surveillance unit was assigned to Devon's house in case he returned. The FBI occupied the vacant house across the alley, and the caravan retreated. In fifteen minutes the neighborhood looked normal again. Roger and Paul had ridden together and were sitting in the car wondering what they should do next. Roger's phone rang. It was Kim. Roger answered, "Hi there. You have already missed an interesting morning."

Kim said, "I think it is about to get even more interesting." Roger knew when *Kim* said something like that, it was the understatement of the century.

He moaned "Oh brother. Should I go to speaker? Paul is here."

Kim answered, "Oh yeah."

Roger looked at Paul and mouthed, "Not good," as he put the phone on speaker. "Okay, we're ready."

Paul sat up straighter in the car and leaned forward. Kim started, "Ellen has a boss too, you know. They call her Granny. I guess she's like the Grand Poopah or something." Roger and Paul gave each other puzzled looks. Roger feared the decision had been made that Ellen and the gals couldn't help them anymore. Kim continued, "Ellen said this case is going to mushroom into much more than either of you can imagine. Since mom and everyone are already so involved, Granny said just get the whole mess done."

Roger said, "I don't think I'm following, Kim."

"Ellen wants you to bring John Barry into your confidence and explain Ellen, Mom, Linda, Mary and Teresa, you know."

Both Paul and Roger said, "What?"

Kim continued, "Ellen says John is going to be instrumental in going forward, and he needs their help. More than you do really. He just doesn't know it yet."

Roger said, "How can we convince him we aren't crazy?"

Kim laughed, "*HA!* Welcome to my world! Ellen will help you convince him. She is also going to point you all toward another problem, but I don't know what that is. Ellen is hoping you can do this fast, at you hotel room, so she can have some privacy with all of you."

Roger said, "I'll call him now and have him meet us there. I am assuming Ellen is going to use *you* to help us explain, right?"

Kim was laughing, "Are you saying you hope I don't decide to go shopping or take a nap?"

Roger laughed, "I will *get* you if you do! You owe me!" Kim and Roger knew they could tease each other.

Kim said, "I owe you? Where do you get that Mr. FBI dude? If I were you, I would be a little nicer to me about now." Kim was laughing. "I guess we'll just see what happens." She hung up without saying goodbye. Roger's trick.

Roger and Paul sat in silence. Paul couldn't control his laughter any longer. The look on

Roger's face was a combination of fear, disbelief, and amusement.

Paul tried to compose himself and said, "Oh brother...*Oh shit...*" He gave up on composure, and his mind raced with visions of John's reaction when they told him about Ellen.

Roger put his forehead on the steering wheel, "What are we going to say? Hi, like you to meet our angels."

Roger looked at Paul, "You call him."

"Hell no!"

Roger started driving to the hotel. He cleared his throat and dialed John. After a minute or so Roger said, "John, could you meet with Paul and me at my hotel room? As soon as you can get there, yes. Thanks." Roger snapped his phone shut and said, "John will never be the same."

Paul paced the hotel room while Roger changed into his own clothes in the bathroom. John knocked on the door, and Paul let him in. John asked, "What's up?" Paul froze. He had no idea how to start any of this.

Roger walked into the room. "Hi John. Thanks for getting here so fast. Let's sit down for a minute. Paul and I have a little story to tell you, and I guess we will see how it goes from there."

John looked suspicious as he took a seat. He asked, "Should I take notes?" Paul and Roger both chuckled. Roger composed himself first and started by asking John to please hear them out before he came to any conclusions. They took turns telling John the story about Ellen and the gals from the beginning. John was being polite, but they knew exactly what he was thinking. Ellen popped into the room, and John jumped. Roger said, "John, meet Ellen. When she is around mortals, she takes on the image of a black cat. She and I have a system of communicating. When she means 'yes', she winks at me. A 'no', she closes both eyes. Let me show you." John looked at Roger like he had lost his mind.

Roger looked at Ellen, "Do you know where Devon is right now?" Ellen winked. "Will we find him soon?" Ellen winked. Roger asked, "Is this case almost over?" Ellen shut both eyes. Roger looked at John, "Ask her something"

John looked at Paul, "This is a joke right? You guys are punkin' me."

Paul said, "John, ask a question we wouldn't know."

John shook his shoulders and looked at Ellen, "Am I expecting an important phone call?" Ellen winked, and John's phone rang. He nearly dropped it. He walked over to the corner, took the call, and returned to the table. He looked at Ellen, "Did I just get good news?" Ellen closed both eyes. John looked at Roger just as Roger's phone rang. Roger answered. It was Kim. Kim told him to give the phone to John.

Kim said, "John, tell Roger and Paul to leave the room for exactly ten minutes and then come back." Roger and Paul left the room.

Paul and Roger were in the hall waiting. Paul said, "What do you think is happening?"

Roger answered, "I think John is being convinced at a very personal level we don't need to know about."

Paul rolled his neck and smiled, "I have never laughed this much in my whole life, and we are on the worst case in FBI history!"

Roger was chuckling too. "I know, it's crazy! We may be going mad. How would we know?"

After a couple more minutes Paul looked at Roger, "What time is it now?"

Roger took a deep breath and answered, "Time to go back in."

They opened the door. John was on one bent knee and praying. He turned to them and stood. It looked like he might have been crying. Roger remembered how he felt when he first realized Ellen and the Gals were truly angels. Roger had been surprised by the power of the revelation. Roger asked, "Do you need some more time John?"

John swallowed and said, "No. I think they need us to do something." John looked at Roger, "I feel so small, so privileged. I don't want to do anything wrong and mess this up."

Paul said, "That was the exact thing Roger said!"

Roger added, "Paul and I have found it somewhat challenging to explain how we know things. You have to be very careful."

John piped up, "Especially with people like Thor around!" John chuckled, "Ellen did a good job convincing me this is really happening. I am a little worried they feel I need their help. I know they know things we don't. What are we getting into?"

Ellen appeared on the table and winked at Roger. Suddenly the TV came on. Roger looked at John, "*This* happens too. This is something from Ellen." They watched a man sitting at a desk marking papers. It looked like a very important office. The view was as if they were watching through a camera. Roger asked, "Does anyone know who this is?"

John answered, "That is your Director. You've never met him?" Roger answered no. Another man came into the picture and asked the Director something. The Director pointed to a pitcher of ice water on a credenza. The other man walked over to the pitcher. It was like the camera followed him.

Roger asked, "Who is that?"

John answered, "Your Deputy Director, William C. Thornton." They watched Thornton pour a clear substance into the glass, add ice, and add some bottled water. The camera had zoomed in for all of it. The director took a big gulp and continued writing. Thornton was looking right at the camera with a sneer.

Suddenly the Director grabbed his chest and fell from his chair. Thornton sat on the corner of the desk and made a phone call. People started rushing into the room, and Thornton was acting like he was very concerned. Numerous times the camera caught him sneering. Paramedics arrived, hooked up IV's, and took the Director out of the room. Thornton made everyone leave the office, and he locked the door behind him. He sat in the Director's chair and picked up the phone.

Roger's phone rang, he looked at the caller ID, and said, "It says Director." Paul and John were alternately looking at the TV and Roger. Roger answered, "Yes Director." They could see Thornton talking on the TV screen. Roger listened a few moments, and then answered, "I would like to tell you we are close to wrapping this up, but that isn't the situation." Roger listened while he watched Thornton smiling and talking on the screen. Roger said, "I don't understand why this case wouldn't be a priority any longer. My designation on this case can only be granted or revoked by the Director. I respectfully reject your analysis, and I intend to continue as the Director assigned." Roger snapped his phone shut, and they saw Thornton wipe a pile of folders to the floor with his forearm and bang his fist on the desk. The screen went black.

Roger, Paul, and John just stared at each other. John asked, "What the hell did we just witness?"

Roger said, "Hopefully not the murder of the Director." Roger made a call, "Find out what hospital the Director was just taken to and alert the hospital staff he has been given some kind of drug. **Absolutely no visitors**. I'll explain later."

Paul said, "Shit! How do you explain knowing that?"

Just then a glass appeared on the table in a plastic bag.

John said, "You don't think…"

Roger said, "John, I don't know who I can trust right now. Can you get this tested, fast?"

John said, "Yes."

He was starting to leave when the TV came on again. They all stared. Now they had sound. They didn't know who was speaking, but there was a man on the phone yelling, "Who authorized this? Well find out!" The man placed another call, "Did you know we were letting this Jason Sims go? He's gone! I was told he was a protected witness. Witness for whom? Nobody is claiming responsibility. CIA won't take my calls. I can't even log in!"

John walked over to Roger's laptop and hit a few keystrokes. Only to be met with a big black screen that said, Access Denied. John turned around, "It will be interesting to hear the explanation for this."

Roger was pacing. Finally he said, "The explanation for that is Jason Sims. He has taken down CIA computers to do something. What do we have here John? William Thornton definitely wants me to get out of town."

John said, "William **C.** Thornton. He's anal that his middle initial be used."

Paul asked, "What does the 'C' stand for?"

John said, "Carl." Roger and Paul looked at each other. Roger's mind raced. Could it be possible that the Deputy Director of the FBI was Mathew Core's contact?

Roger explained to John, "We have some notes from Ellen's mind reading of Mathew Core. His main contact went by the name Carl. William C. Thornton may be Mathew Core's contact. I don't know, but I'm not inclined to check this off as a coincidence." Roger had walked over to the window and was speaking to no one in particular. "If he is the 'Carl' who is connected to Mathew Core, he would know I know who Core is and that he is in New Orleans."

John said, "What are you saying? I guess you lost me."

Roger turned back to look at Paul and John, "We need to go over a lot of paperwork from Ellen with you."

John was shaking his head, "I am trying to absorb all of this, but I have to admit I think I am getting lost. This doesn't seem real."

Paul laughed, "Oh trust us, we understand. Remember last night when you were laughing because everyone thought we were spooky?"

John's eyes opened wide, "Oh no. Now I am one of you!" Just then Ellen appeared on his lap. John jumped, then asked her, "Are we going to figure this out eventually?" Ellen winked. John said, "Thank God." Then he looked at Roger and Paul, "I'm talking to a cat."

Roger said, "That's how I found out I could trust you, John. I asked Ellen. Before you assume anything, you may want to check with her."

John was nodding and asked, "Why did you name her Ellen?"

Roger laughed and said, "I didn't name her. Let's leave that story for later." Roger gave John Kim's number and said, "This is another way to reach Ellen if you need her."

Roger's phone rang, it was Agent Nelson. They were all back at the Star Ship showering off the swamp. Pablo and Jeanne went to her house. The three women were taken to the hospital and should be available to interview in an hour or so. Nelson asked if Roger wanted to join all of them across the street for lunch before they started the second half of the day. Roger knew most of the bars stayed pretty empty well into the afternoon because they were open late at night. He also wanted to touch base with the team before he dealt with the situation with the Director. He asked Paul and John if they wanted to go and told Nelson they would meet them there shortly.

John made arrangements for the delivery of the glass for testing and was in the corner with Ellen giving her names to see who he could trust. Paul saw him cross off two names on his list and rub his temples. Ellen wasn't making him happy.

Simon and Pablo reached the door of Mickey's Bar at about the same time and went in together. This place was perfect for lunch. Other than one small woman at the bar and one guy in a booth, the place was empty. They walked the length of the bar and took over a large table in the back. Pablo laid his gun on the table while he adjusted his shoulder harness. The man in the booth saw the gun. He quickly left his booth and headed for the door. He placed a bill near the register and waved goodbye to the bartender.

Pablo commented, "We probably aren't very good for business."

Simon responded, "Like I give a shit right now."

The rest of the team filtered in. They had to pull over another table to have enough seats. The bartender told them to do anything they wanted. There wouldn't be any real customers for hours. Dusty and Alan joined them too. Dusty had hitched a ride back into town with Pablo and Nelson. Agent Frank Mass had told Dusty he would pay him as soon as he got to town. Pablo invited Dusty to join everyone at Mickey's for lunch, and after lunch Pablo would drive him to the field office to get his check. Alan had hitched a ride into town also, so Jeremiah didn't have to drive him home. Alan figured Jeremiah would sleep all afternoon. Alan had a friend who could drive him back home to Slidell after lunch.

Jeanne, Roger, Paul, and John were the last to arrive. Roger looked at them all and said, "Doesn't look like you guys spent the morning in a swamp." Thor glanced up at the ceiling. Pablo introduced Dusty and Alan to everyone who hadn't met them yet and explained why they were there. The bartender took their food order and brought their drinks. He placed full pitchers of cola and ice tea on their table which they were emptying as fast as he could bring them. At least four weapons were lying on the table.

Roger glanced at the weapons and the guilty parties holstered them. Roger said, "I am looking forward to the report on your morning." He was looking at Thor. Thor looked at Jeanne, and she smiled. Roger chuckled, "Seems like you two bonded during this trip."

Thor exclaimed, "She owes me a pair of shorts. And hey! We all learned a new sport, snake skeet shooting!" The whole table laughed.

Roger noticed Jeanne suddenly tense. She was staring at a man who had walked in and was looking down the long row of booths. As he got closer to them, his eyes drifted to their table and locked on Jeanne. He looked like he had seen a ghost. Jeanne *hissed*, "Devon!" She stood and her chair crashed back all in one motion. She did not draw her gun. Her jaw set. Her eyes were backlit blue lasers. Devon couldn't look away from her. Every agent was up with their weapons aimed. Dusty and Alan dove under the table.

The bartender vaporized behind the bar and quickly crawled to the kitchen.

The little woman sitting at the bar just kind of slowly looked around. She was obviously drunk. Devon grabbed her beer bottle, broke it against the bar and pulled her off the bar stool. His forearm pinned her back against his chest. Devon held the broken bottle to her throat and screamed, ***"Stay Back!"*** Devon sneered as he pulled the woman backwards and inched his way closer to the door. His eyes were still locked on Jeanne. In Roger's peripheral vision he could see Jeanne's hand flexing next to her gun. She glanced at Roger. He gave a small nod. In one smooth motion she raised her arm and shot Devon between the eyes.

Devon was dead.

The woman staggered into a booth, looked at Jeanne, and said, "You go girl."

Agent Frank Mass walked through the door with Dusty's check just as Devon fell to the floor. Frank drew his gun; saw the table full of agents and realized whatever had happened was over. He stepped over Devon giving him a quick glance and holstered his gun. Damn good shot. Frank walked to the back, reached under the table, and handed Dusty his check.

Dusty sputtered, "Not enough man!"

Agent Mass looked at Roger. "Want me to clean that up?"

Roger answered, "Please."

Pablo walked over to where Devon's body was lying and spit on him. He was clenching his fists. Jeanne had her eyes closed and her head tilted back. She crossed herself and rubbed her amulet. Thor watched a single tear stream from the corner of her eye.

Agent Mass got a quick update from Paul and assured him his agents would do the paperwork. He made a phone call and said, "I have an agent with your swamp gals at the hospital. Is this guy responsible for them?"

Roger nodded, "He's one of the guys."

Frank smiled, "More fun to come then. I will call off the surveillance team and get CSI over to

Devon's house. Doesn't look like he will be going back there. Anything else you need right now?"

Roger shook his head, "I appreciate everything you've been doing for us. This team is good, but we seem to cause some paperwork."

Agent Mass chuckled, "That you do. I sent the Medical Examiner and one of our forensic guys out to your swamp man. The Medical Examiner called a few minutes ago to tell me they had the box of bones. They are going to the actual site where the bones were found now. There is at least one child." Agent Mass shook his head and walked over to get a better look at Devon. The coroner arrived, and Devon's body was removed. The janitor cleaned up the floor. The juke box started playing, "Feels like Rain," by Buddy Guy. Back to normal in Nawlens.

The bartender meekly walked over and asked, "The cook wants to know if you guys are still eating?"

Everyone laughed, and Thor yelled, "**Hell yes**! *What is taking so long?*" The bartender looked like he had wet his pants, went running to the kitchen.

Jeanne frowned at Thor and said, "Why do you pretend to be an ass?"

Thor looked at her, "Why do you pretend to be human?" They both started laughing. Pablo looked at Simon with one eyebrow raised. Dusty and Alan had surfaced again and were sitting in their seats, very quietly.

Dusty said, "I hope you guys are paid a whole lot of money."

Nelson answered, "Yeah, we do this for all the money." There was a round of laughter.

Roger leaned over and asked Jeanne, "Are you okay?"

Jeanne smiled, "Yeah. Thank you for that." Roger nodded. John was looking toward the door. A man had come in to sit at the far end of the bar.

John whispered to Roger, "That's Tourey." Jeanne glanced up and raised her glass. Tourey did the same.

Roger asked, "No one is here, should I introduce myself?"

John said, "Nope. There are still employees, and someone could come in. He will pick the place to talk. He must just want to see what everyone looks like." John called Ashley. After giving her the good news he passed the phone to Paul.

The bartender and cook both started delivering their food. Nelson made the comment he might have to move to New Orleans, as he shoved a huge spoon of jambalaya in his mouth. John Barry asked the bartender to bring him a bourbon. Thor said, "If anyone deserves a drink it's me! You know what *this* guy tells me when I called to tell him I'm on a sinking boat in the middle of a snake infested swamp? *Keep me posted!*" Roger shook his head and chuckled. He had completely forgotten that conversation. Thor continued, "I just want to point out that we are having a dead body with every meal." Alan and Dusty looked at each other.

Simon asked them, "You guys want to meet us for dinner?"

They both put their hands up and said, "NO!"

Thor asked Roger, "So how did you find Devon anyway?"

"We just got lucky, a couple of lucky breaks in a row."

Thor looked at John, "What did I say? Damn *spooky*." John spit out some of his bourbon, wiped his chin and glanced at Roger. Paul pushed his chin forward in his nervous twitch. Yup, this was going to be interesting.

Roger asked the group, "Who were the first ones here?" Simon and Pablo raised their hands. Roger asked, "Was anyone here that left?"

Pablo pointed across the room and said, "Yeah. Some guy that was sitting in that booth."

Roger nodded, "Devon came here to meet someone. I bet you just saw Patterson."

CHAPTER 25

Mathew Core was at the bookstore watching the activities across the street. He saw the saxophone man walk in and sit by the door. The door was all glass, and Mathew could tell he wasn't talking to anyone. Mathew surmised he probably wasn't a cop, but he was *somebody*. He had a knack for being where the action was. Mathew couldn't tell who came out on a stretcher. He thought he would wait until the cops left, meet saxophone man, and get the gossip.

* * *

John told Roger and Paul he was going to go to the hospital to drive Adele Brown home to see her son. Roger suggested John meet up with them as soon as he was finished to go over some paperwork and maybe take a quick jet trip to see the Director. John nodded. He knew that trip was going to be very interesting.

Simon said he and Ray could use Jeanne's help with the money transactions if she was up to it. Nelson and Pablo said they would try again to use the FBI center's computers to find out something about Mathew Core.

Thor looked at Roger and said, "I know I will regret this, but what do you want me to do?"

Roger smiled and said, "I'll probably have something in a few hours. Take some free time if you want, or you can tag along with Paul and me."

Thor looked surprised. "No offense, but I'm not up to tagging along with you! Just call me when the fun starts."

Mathew Core walked over to Mickey's. Tourey had seen him in the bookstore window watching. He looked a lot like the sketch of the guy who had been at the Crab Shack. This should be interesting. Mathew took a stool about four seats away from Tourey and nodded to him as he sat down. Scotty, the bartender, came over and got his beer order. The TV over the bar was showing *Breaking News*

about a shooting at Mickey's Bar in the Quarter. News journalists had long ago stopped sending camera crews for events like this. They were just too common.

Mathew looked at Tourey and asked, "You here for that?"

Tourey put his street voice on and answered, "Nothin' new for Nawlens. Missed the fun, got here for the clean up's all." Tourey started to push his stool out. If this was Mathew Core, and Mathew really wanted to talk to him, he would offer to buy him a beer.

Mathew said, "You're not going to make me drink alone are you? Let me get you a beer." He raised his mug to the bartender and made a circular motion in the air.

Tourey pulled his stool back to the bar. "Thanks man. It's a hot one today. Don't feel much like going back out in that." Mathew was nodding. The news was still on.

Mathew said, "Looks like there was a serious cop presence in here when that came down."

Tourey said, "Yeah, I've been comin' here for years. Never seen *that* many in here. Place still stinks."

Mathew chuckled. Tourey still couldn't figure out who this guy was. Mathew asked him, "There's a good lookin' broad left here. Wonder if she's a cop too?"

Tourey made his move, "That bitch is no cop. She's FBI and let me know it, yesterday! She slammed my head on the bar just because I was on the sidewalk too long to please her."

Mathew shook his head and asked, "So why *were* you on the sidewalk too long?"

"What, you FBI too?"

Mathew's eyebrow went up, "Let's just say they interest me."

Tourey smiled, "Well, there you have it. They interest me too." Tourey laid a ten on the bar and pushed his stool out.

Mathew said, "You going to make me drink alone?"

Tourey smiled, "I 'spect you have friends you could call if you wanted."

Mathew Core smiled. "That I do." Tourey left. He had made the connection. This guy might not be Mathew Core, but he was *somebody*.

After Tourey left, Mathew called Scotty over and held up a hundred dollar bill. Scotty wiped the bar, took the bill, and asked, "What do you want to know?"

"Tell me about that guy."

❋ ❋ ❋

Simon, Ray, and Jeanne were in the basement computer room of the Star Ship reviewing the data from the Securities and Exchange Commission. Ray was eating the lunch they had brought him and listening to Jeanne tell about Devon just walking in. Jeanne said she couldn't believe Devon and Patterson were so stupid as to meet in a public place for lunch.

Ray swallowed and said, "Actually a bar in the Quarter, in the middle of the day, is pretty safe. If a crook looks fairly normal, they just blend in with the tourists. The tourism in the Quarter supports the whole city." Simon was nodding agreement even though he was concentrating on the print-outs from the computer.

Simon looked up at Ray, "Didn't you specify you wanted non-swift code transactions too?"

"Say what?"

Simon frowned, "Non-Swift Codes. A swift code is a bank's nickname by code. Many international transfers won't allow for swift code especially if the currency is something other than US Dollars. You haven't even been given the IBAN transactions and the ABA numbers from the Treasury for half of this."

Jeanne looked at Ray. "Slacker."

Ray frowned at her, "You know what he is talking about?"

Jeanne laughed, "Not a clue."

Simon started rolling up his sleeves and said, "Where's a notebook? I'm going to write down what you are going to tell the *TREASURY* Department we need, get their filter ID's, and make the Security and Exchange geeks flip the correct flags. They just sent you trash to shut you up."

Ray spouted, "Those bastards. Let's make them work and tell them it is FBI Level one."

Simon said, "It is."

✳ ✳ ✳

John Barry headed toward the hospital to get Adele Brown and take her to Spicey's. He had called Spicey and told her they had found Adele. He knew she had Jerome. John wasn't sure what would work out the best for the reunion. Spicey told John, Jerome would be home from school around three. Spicey thought she would fix them a nice supper, and let them decide what to do from there.

John walked into the small examination room at the hospital where Adele was waiting for him. The doctor had said too much time had gone by for a rape kit, and John had told him they really didn't need one anymore. John told the doctor he was worried about Adele's emotional state. Based on an earlier report, she wasn't speaking to anyone. The doctor flipped through his papers and twirled his pen. "You know, I don't think she spoke to me either. She just nodded and shook her head." John said he wanted to talk to her before they released her from care, and the Doctor pointed him to her room.

Adele was sitting on the edge of the small bed. She had huge brown eyes and was beautiful. She looked to be about thirty- four years old, had caramel colored skin, and held herself with perfect posture. John introduced himself and said, "I met Jerome this morning at the police station. He had come with his new friend Spicey to report you missing. She is a very nice woman who reminds me a little of you. She has been helping Jerome since you went missing."

John saw tears rolling down Adele's cheeks. "The other women Devon took all said they were threatened. If they came back, their loved ones would be killed. Were you told that too?" Adele's eyes were wide open, and she nodded. John continued, "The FBI shot Devon about two hours ago Adele. He is dead. We are on the hunt for the man who took you to that swamp. He has bigger problems than looking for you. You and Jerome are safe. I promise you."

Adele started sobbing. She slid off the exam table and cried on John's shoulder. "I want to see Jerome," she said as she pulled back and looked in John's eyes.

John smiled and said, "I'll drive you to him and let you meet his new angel." After he had said that, it reminded him he had a new angel too. Evidently a group of them. He wanted to get Adele and Jerome settled and get back to Roger.

John and Adele parked as close as they could to Spicey's place and walked the remaining two blocks. When John stopped at the Voodoo shop, Adele looked at him, "Here?"

John smiled and nodded, "Yes, here. Let's go in. Spicey is expecting us." John and Adele entered the shop and the tinkling bells announced their arrival. There was a delicious aroma in the air, and Spicey appeared from behind the colorful cloth door.

Spicey squealed and came running at the sight of John with Adele, "You're Jerome's momma? Oh praise the Lord! Praise the Lord!"

Spicey's friend Sasha walked through the door to start her shift, and Spicey yelled at her, "Sasha! This is Adele, Jerome's Momma!" Sasha squealed, started crying, and gave Adele a big hug.

Adele was crying, "Mr. Barry told me you have been lookin' out for Jerome. How can I ever repay your kindness?"

Spicey swatted her hand like she was shooing flies and said, "You don't owe me nothin' ma'am. You have yourself a real good young man. We've been just fine."

Jerome walked through the door with his school bag and saw John. Then he saw his mom. He dropped his bag, and he ran into her arms sobbing. Sasha just started pulling tissues from a box by the handfuls and handing them to Spicey saving some for herself. Jerome wiped his eyes, straightened his posture, and walked over to John. "You told me you would look for my Momma, and you did." Jerome hugged John's waist.

John looked at Spicey, "Is there a private place where Adele, Jerome, and I can talk for about ten minutes?" Spicey told him to go to the kitchen and stir the Jambalaya every now and then.

They made their way to Spicey's kitchen. John was glad that Adele assigned herself to the stove. John and Jerome sat at the small dinette table and John said, "Jerome, this is going to be a test of your character now more than ever before." Jerome looked puzzled. John continued, "Over time your mom is going to say things that make you realize what hell she has gone through over these two weeks. She didn't just leave you. She was stolen. What is the first natural reaction for you?"

Jerome didn't even pause, "To go get the son of a bitch that hurt my momma!" John held his hand up to stop Adele who was ready to slap Jerome for cursing.

John said, "That is the natural reaction, but a man of character is going to look at the whole picture and see another way."

Jerome had fire in his eyes but asked, "What is that?"

John said, "The main man that hurt your mom has already been caught by the FBI. He is dead. The other guy is scared and trying to hide. Do you believe me when I tell you we will find him?"

Jerome nodded his head and said, "I believe you Agent Barry."

John smiled, "You can call me John, Jerome. I think we are friends now." Jerome smiled. John said, "A man of character is going to realize that revenge on scum brings you down to their level. That turns you into scum by your own hand. Do you see that?"

Jerome nodded, "That is what Ms. Spicey been tellin' me about stealin'."

Adele asked, "Stealin'? Who been stealin'?"

John put his hand up to Adele again. John looked at Jerome, "I remember my dad telling me that whenever I thought I had a choice in life, the right decision was usually the one that sounded the hardest to do."

Jerome answered, "You want me to leave the policin' to the police and go about making good decisions for me."

Adele was ready to explode with pride. John rubbed the top of Jerome's head and said, "I think you have yourself a man of character, Adele."

Adele smiled and said, "Yeah, I do."

Jerome turned to her and said, "It's yes, not yeah."

Adele smiled and said, "You are correct Jerome. I am too intelligent not to speak properly." Adele looked at John with a questioning look on her face.

John stood and said, "I'm going to leave to join my team now. I wouldn't have missed this reunion for the world." He rubbed Jerome's head again as he stood.

Jerome stood and put his hand out for John to shake. "You gave me your card today. Can I still call you sometime? And you said you were sending me that class stuff."

John corrected him, "Class material, yes, I am sending it, and yes, I want you to call."

Jerome looked at his mom, "I'm going to be an FBI Agent."

Adele's eyes got big, "Well, we'll talk about that! Sounds dangerous to me."

John walked out to the front to say goodbye to Spicey and Sasha. They were on their second box of tissue and taking turns honking their noses. Customers were leaving as soon as they came in. John guessed it didn't look good for someone who professed to talk to Spirits to be sobbing in the middle of the store.

CHAPTER 26

Milliam Patterson sat in a club chair sipping a brandy, fixated on Mathew Core's card. Mathew's proposal would only leave him with about thirty million dollars. His hobby was costing him about five million a year. That would only be six more years of fun? And then what? There had to be another way out of this.

"You're going to give me how much money?" Rolland replaced a leather bound book on the mahogany shelf behind his desk. The sunlight was making stripes around the room as it fought with the slats of the blinds for prominence.

William Patterson leaned forward and had his elbows on the massive desk. "Will you just sit down and listen? Christ. You have people who will tidy up for you. This is important."

Rolland sat heavily on his overstuffed desk chair and offered up a small sneer, "I am sure I heard ten million dollars. Now, what in the world kind of mess are you in that costs that kind of money?" Rolland was one of the founding members of the club. There were several members locally who shared the same appetite for children and numerous chapters of the club nationally. William Patterson had been the newest member, and Rolland actually liked William. Even though he only knew him by his alias, Bernard Jacobs.

William whispered, "We only have time for the short version."

When William had finished, Rolland looked at him like he was from an alien planet. "What the hell are you telling me this for? Why do I want to know all this? What do you think I can do for you? Damn, I'm a retired U.S. Senator! You have FBI and this crazy spook type guy looking for you? I just now found out your real name? William f—— Patterson? Are you kidding me? You are legendary!" Rolland began pacing and flexing his fists.

William had his head resting in his hands, he didn't know where else to go. He whispered, "You have to help me….. or kill me. I know too much. About all of you. If you help me, you will be ten million dollars richer."

Rolland glared at him, "If I have you killed, at least I can sleep at night."

Teresa had found Senator Rolland Kenny's name in Patterson's black book. She had been listening to him talk to the man she now knew was

Patterson. Teresa signaled for us to meet her. *NOW.* I was the last to get there, but at least I found them. Teresa brought us up to date on what the conversation had been before we got there. Linda decided to record and film the conversation while we floated near the ceiling.

Mary didn't look happy. "That is Patterson? We weren't supposed to find him were we?"

Teresa shrugged, "Too late now." Oh brother.

Rolland glared at Patterson, "You realize we are supposed to meet at the country house tomorrow night to review the contestant video? We have been waiting months for this. The whole damn bunch of us sitting there with the likes of you?"

William said, "How different is my situation from the rest of you? None of us can be found out. Our lives would be ruined. We've always known that! I have money Rolland. Lots of it. I just need to lay low until I get rid of some of this heat. Why don't I stay at the country house? After we pick our winners someone is going to have to keep an eye on them anyway? This might actually work out."

Rolland asked, "How do I get my ten million without showing it came from you?"

William smiled, "I can have that covered with one phone call. I use offshore accounts Rolland. Deal?"

Rolland looked up. "Deal. Make the call now. Then go home and grab whatever you need. In one hour I will send a car for you. If you don't come out, I will assume you have been caught. We are going to have your house torched. Who knows what kind of evidence could be there."

William winced, his beautiful home. Oh well, he'd buy another. William opened his phone and began to punch in a number.

Linda marked the time stamp and alerted Ellen we needed a phone call traced. Ellen answered, "Done."

✳ ✳ ✳

Todd and Pablo arrived at the New Orleans FBI field office and settled in for what promised to be a grueling search for any information they could find on Mathew Core. Todd called Ray at the Star Ship and asked him which data bases they should use.

Ray suggested a few and then said, "You know, you might have more luck in the military data bases for some of the background stuff. Roger said Core was used as a private contractor by us and the CIA. I'm kind of tied up chasing money right now, but if you log in with my ID number you can avoid a lot of password blocks."

"Good point. What's your code?" Todd hung up and looked at Pablo, "Log out. We are going to use Ray's ID for this stuff."

Pablo looked around and saw an agent heading their direction. "Right." He logged out, leaned back, and snickered at the local agent, "You should have come with us to the swamp. Missed a real good time."

The agent he was speaking to looked about ten years older than he or Todd but had a big smile and said, "I don't think I want to be anywhere near that Dance guy you work with." He was laughing now, "We don't normally pack that much fun in one day. I'm the asshole stuck doing all of your reports for you. I know what a good time you've had today."

Todd was busy scanning data bases while Pablo made small talk with the agent. Todd looked up and asked, "Were you in the raid yesterday on Mathew Core's place?"

The agent looked at him and walked over. He held his hand out to shake. "Phil Mathews, we only have four agents out of this office, so we all have to do everything. Yeah, I was there. Too bad we missed him."

Pablo asked, "How did you get a full assault team together so fast then? Were there more people here yesterday than normal?" Todd pretended to be engrossed in his computer.

Agent Mathews answered, "Yeah, you called at the best time possible. We had three guys here from Virginia helping us on a weapons case. Some kind of planning meeting. I think that case will be blowing up Friday. Nasty mess from what I hear. I try to stay close to the office and as far away from field work as I can."

Todd shot a quick e-mail to Roger about the three Virginia agents who were in New Orleans yesterday for the raid on Core. They were in New Orleans because of some big weapons bust going to take place on Friday. He would follow with names ASAP.

Pablo pushed the agent for more, "Roger will want the names of everyone in that raid for his report. Can you bring those to me? Get their jacket numbers too." Agent Mathews said no problem and left the room.

Todd looked at Pablo, "Nice work. I already sent Roger an e-mail. Our local problem may not be local after all."

Roger and Paul were in Roger's room at the Marriott working on Ellen papers and waiting for John Barry to finish with Adele Brown. Roger said, "I am going to reprint the e-mail from this Voodoo lady so you have your own copy. This has been gnawing at me all morning, but I haven't had two minutes to get back to it."

Paul was busy highlighting any comments from Jason or Mathew that referred to Carl. He knew as soon as John arrived they were leaving to see the Director. Neither Paul nor Roger had ever met the Director, and Paul had never even spoken to him on the phone. Paul looked at Roger, "When you get a mental moment, I want it."

Roger looked up, "I'm all yours."

Paul said, "Would you rather I stay here and just you and John go to see the Director? I don't think I'm bringing anything to the table on this."

Roger looked thoughtful but said, "I want the Director to see the level of trust I have in you. If something were to happen to me, I want you taking over." Roger looked back to his paperwork.

Paul was staring at him. "What makes you think something might happen to you?"

Roger chuckled, "Nothing, bad choice of words. Relax."

"Neither one of us is going anywhere until we talk this out more." Paul had leaned back in his chair and fixed his gaze on Roger's eyes.

Roger exhaled, "I have a feeling is all. Watching Thornton's level of frustration when he was on the phone to me was very telling. He's in some kind of situation he is losing control of, and he is making some desperate decisions. He wants this case to go away and me with it. And I don't know why. If he is the 'Carl' Mathew Core gets orders from, then he is willing to kill federal agents without blinking an eye."

"Have you asked Ellen?"

Roger said, "No."

Paul pushed his arm out and said, "Hand me those Voodoo pages. If we are going to do this the hard way, I might as well be prepared."

Roger chuckled. He appreciated that Paul didn't push it. Roger noticed two new e-mails from Todd and opened them. He read them out loud to Paul and said, "I guess now I could use Ellen."

He no sooner said it than Ellen was on Paul's lap. Paul jumped, "I will never get used to this!"

Roger read off the names of the FBI staff that went on the raid at Mathew Core's building and got an all clear from Ellen on all but the last name he gave her. SSA Jim Spelling out of the Virginia office. Roger asked Ellen if Agent Spelling made the call to Mathew Core. Ellen winked. Roger asked if the weapons case the field office was working on was connected to Core also. Ellen winked. Roger asked if the weapons case was going to be compromised by Agent Spelling. Ellen did nothing. Roger said he didn't understand. He asked Ellen if Agent Spelling was working with Mathew Core. Ellen did nothing. Roger's phone rang. It was Kim.

"I bet Ellen told you to call. I'm putting you on speaker for Paul."

Kim answered, "Okay. Ellen said you were asking questions she couldn't answer with a yes or no. Here is your answer, but keep in mind I don't know the question. Spelling called the Deputy Director when you ordered the raid on Core's building. Spelling had been told that the Deputy Director had based the entire weapons case on information from Core. The Deputy Director told Spelling to call Core and warn him you were coming. The Deputy Director told Spelling you were not in the loop and were messing things up for everyone. He told Spelling Core was too important to the weapons case to risk you getting in their way."

Roger said, "Really." Kim thought Roger sounded angry.

Kim said, "That's it. End of answer. Ellen asked if you could get to the Director ASAP and take John and Paul. She is going to prepare the Director for your visit."

"What does that mean, prepare the Director?"

Kim laughed, "I don't have a clue. I don't understand anything I have said to you. Hopefully, some of this makes sense to you?"

"Unfortunately it does. Thanks Kim, I'll call later when I get a minute." Roger turned to Paul, "What do you say we get involved in this weapons case?"

Paul shook his head and said, "Might as well, I mean, we probably have an hour or two tonight we haven't booked yet."

Ellen jumped over to Roger's computer and touched the space bar. A full screen of notes made by Agent Frank Mass detailed the case like a journal, from assignment to where they were now. He even had updated the file yesterday after the planning meeting on the weapons deal. Roger printed it out and gave a copy to Paul.

Paul stopped reading after about five minutes and said, "If they really have the amount of weapons Mass says they do, thirty tons, this would be one of the biggest busts in FBI history. Why are they waiting until Friday to do this? Mass thinks it is already here at the port. Friday is two days away."

Roger said, "Did you notice that Agent Spelling was the one who suggested they would have more manpower if they waited until Friday? He's also the one who has said all along he didn't trust Frank

Mass's information on this. He doesn't think it will prove out. Let's see if the Director will flip this to us since we are here."

Paul looked more somber. "If we are right about Core's *Carl* being our Thornton, taking this weapons bust won't make Thornton very happy."

Roger smiled and started putting his folders into his briefcase.

CHAPTER 27

Ellen decided we should meet in Paul's room at the hotel, so we could move papers around and not be seen. Paul was in Roger's room, and we would have privacy. We were all sitting on Paul's bed with the papers spread out in front of us. We told Ellen what we had found from following people in Patterson's address book. Linda showed her our video of Patterson talking to Senator Kenny.

Ellen looked thoughtful and said, "Patterson may have to go on the back burner for today. I think Roger and Paul might end up in a big weapons deal. There is only so much our mortal friends can do in a day."

Teresa asked, "A weapons bust? YES! Now we are talkin' some real fun!"

What is wrong with her?

Linda started humming that song again.

"What is with you and that song? Last year when we were chasing down Devon and Patterson, you started humming that, and now here you go again. *What is it?*" I couldn't stand not knowing. It was one of those melodies you wanted to join in as it got louder and faster. I had heard Mary sing with her a couple of times as we were flying. I caught myself humming it too.

Ellen answered for Linda, "She is humming "Hall of the Mountain King" by Edvard Grieg. Very exciting little three minute melody that starts out playful and ends up in chaos." Ellen laughed, "I think it is very fitting to this assignment actually. It's kind of motivational too."

Ellen announced she needed us to go to the port, locate the ship the weapons were on, and locate the building some of the weapons were being moved to. Little cameras attached to straps appeared on our foreheads. It looked like we were wearing miner caps. Ellen wanted us to record everything we saw and get good surveillance pictures for Roger to use to plan the raid. We were also supposed to read as many minds as we could to figure out what the bad guys were planning. She said she was leaving to see the Director of the FBI and would need our videos in about an hour.

Geesh! Not a heck of a lot of lead time here. I looked around and everyone was gone. You're kidding. They just left me to find the port on my own? I caught myself humming Linda's little song while I flew around New Orleans looking for the port. There was water and ships everywhere. This was going to take a minute or two.

* * *

Tourey had flipped through the papers he had gotten from Spicey. Nothing really jumped out until he looked at the very small pages of what was probably an address book. Several names had the word club next to them. Tourey recognized the name of the gallery owner where George worked, Theodore Chain. Other names with club written next to them were Rolland Kenny, a retired U.S. Senator, Andre Baton, a wealthy benefactor of Loyola University, and Harold Williams, a Mississippi judge.

Tourey wondered what kind of club Bernard Jacobs had been able to infiltrate in less than a year living in town. The judge's name actually caught his attention first. Judge Harold Williams had almost been named in a child trafficking bust last year, but they could never get any hard evidence.

Tourey did a web search on the Gallery owner's name and saw an announcement that he was a member of a National philanthropy group that sponsored young artists. The group bragged they had chapters in nearly every state. Tourey saw there was currently a local contest with the winner being announced by the end of the week. A picture on the philanthropy group website showed the group presenting the oversized check to a child in last year's contest. Tourey recognized four of the five men in the picture. He assumed the last man was Bernard Jacobs.

In itself the picture meant nothing. The club names in Bernard Jacob's book could be the one decent thing the guy did in his life. Tourey leaned his chair back and stared at the picture. Something in his mind was trying to crawl forward. He clicked his pen and waited. Then he felt a wash of dread. He had a faint memory from last year connecting a murdered child to an art contest in Mississippi. He selected the key words for more info and found a tab that said "Last Year's Winners, Mississippi Chapter". There it was, just as he remembered it. A picture of Daniel Morris.

Tourey searched Daniel's name and found the newspaper article describing the missing five year old boy, the plight of the parents, and the eventual discovery of the boy's body six months later in California. The case had never been solved, and there were no suspects. Daniel had vanished from his family's front yard a week after winning an art contest. The FBI still carried it as an open case.

Tourey did a search on every contestant name from last year's contests from each chapter of the group across the United States. He ran the names through law enforcement data bases for the entire country. From the contestant lists of last year, there were ten missing children. Three had later been found dead. The dates of the abductions were about six months apart and from different states. The pictures of the missing children filled his computer screen. He bet the connection had never been made.

Tourey called Spicey. "You got any friends who work at the Senator's place in Uptown? Good. I need someone at Judge William's place too. I'll call you later." Tourey hung up and started pacing in his small library, occasionally glancing at the menacing images on his computer monitor. He had also seen the name of Attorney Michael Parker in Bernard Jacob's book. Tourey knew from John that was the alias for Devon. Tourey couldn't think of any good reason Bernard Jacobs would have Devon's phone number in this private little book. Tourey exhaled. This felt bad. It was time to pay a visit to Bernard Jacobs.

Alan had hitched a ride home to Slidell after his lunch with the FBI. What a day. He couldn't believe Uncle Jeremiah was caught in the middle of so much drama. Nobody ever did explain to him what was going on. He guessed the guy Jeanne shot at lunch had something to do with the kidnapped women who were showing up in the swamps. There hadn't been anything in the newspapers about any of it. Uncle Jeremiah had a whole box of people bones? What was *that* all about? Alan popped open a beer and sat at the picnic table in his backyard. The first phase of the storm had passed and he watched the clouds rolling in for phase two.

He couldn't stop thinking about Mambo. How did she survive out there? How old was she? Was that even human? He saw her stop the snakes and the storm with his own eyes. What was that? How did she know about the other two girls in the swamp? What did it all mean? Had he lived his whole life ignorant of the true Spirits around him? He felt like a child who had nothing but questions. When Uncle Jeremiah had picked him up this morning, he was full of nothing but answers.

Alan had worked hard building his electrical business and trying to provide a positive role model for his two sons. His wife was a teacher in the Slidell school system, and his boys were just now entering high school. He decided it would be a good idea to have his boys meet Mambo after this mess was cleared up. A little respect for the Spirits is a healthy thing. A lot of respect might save your life.

Alan flipped open his appointment book. He decided to head into the city and purchase the supplies he would need for tomorrow's jobs. Maybe he would pick up some staples to drop off at Jeremiah's. He had realized today how alone and vulnerable his uncle was out there. He felt guilty he hadn't given him more thought over the years. Uncle Jeremiah was a good man, and a wise one.

He could help Uncle Jeremiah in a lot of ways. It was time.

* * *

Dusty had set up his easel is Jackson Square and tried to forget the morning. At least he was able to find a spot in the shade. It was over a hundred degrees. He wouldn't draw for long; he just felt the need to do something normal. He had a check for a thousand dollars in his pocket. That wasn't normal. No part of this morning had been normal. Normal would be he was just now waking up!

Crap! He still couldn't hear right. All that damn gun firin' and people screamin'. Mostly him doing the screamin'. He shivered. Snakes! Mambo! Women sittin' in the middle of the swamp! Dead people with every meal, and he was with the good guys. What was Nawlens comin' to?

He finished a portrait for a tourist couple and then Thor sat down. "Mind if I sit a minute? This heat is brutal."

Dusty looked up, recognized Thor, and moaned, "Long as you don't want to take me nowhere."

Thor chuckled and then got a very serious look on his face. "You recognized one of those drawings from last night. We need any information you have. I think you know we mean business." Dusty swallowed hard. Thor continued. "Anything you can think of might help."

Dusty said, "The man who used to have that building you're in, across from Mickey's? That *was* the man at the Crab Shack. Same dude, no doubt. He used to hang out at Mickey's some, and I have seen him over at Colby's by the port. He hangs with some brute who wears a ponytail and some big black dude from Uptown. That's all I know man. I got no names."

Thor said, "Need to ask a favor Dusty."

Dusty could feel the dread spreading through his body. Damn it. *"What?"*

"Ride with me to this Colby place. We won't go in. Just let me get a feel."

Dusty said, "That place is hard core man! Almost as bad daytime, as night. Dock workers, local brutes, whores. I saw ponytail guy take on two big dudes in the parkin' lot about a month ago. Just banged their skulls together and walked away. He is bad ass."

Thor raised an eyebrow.

Dusty snapped his easel shut, grabbed his pad and box of pencils, "Fine. My own government tryin' to get me killed."

They walked the long block to the corner, and Dusty hailed a cab. When they got in, Thor said, "Well, if it isn't my ol' buddy Albert!"

The cabby looked in the rear view mirror with a puzzled expression then his eyes opened wide, "Oh shit!"

✳ ✳ ✳

John Barry notified Roger he was ready to leave. Roger told him they would meet him in the hotel lobby and leave immediately. Roger arranged for a car to pick them up and drive them right onto the tarmac where an FBI jet was waiting. It would be almost a two hour trip. On the way they planned to go over the Ellen papers about the mind-reading and the Voodoo papers from Spicey.

Once they were seated and were airborne John said, "Tourey called and said he is following up a lead on a Bernard Jacobs. This Jacobs had Devon's alias in his address book. Tourey said it might not be anything, but this guy's name has come up before as a pedophile. Bernard Jacobs is affiliated in some way to an art group Tourey thinks may have a sinister connection to some dead kids."

Roger sifted through the papers from Spicey and showed John they had that name too. Roger called Ray and asked him to run the name Bernard Jacobs in their transaction data. Then Roger called Nelson who was at the field office with Pablo and asked them to run the name Bernard Jacobs also. Nelson told Roger he remembered that name from a plaque at the police department. Bernard Jacobs gave the police a check for one hundred thousand dollars. Nelson told Roger he had actually joked with Simon that the guy looked like a skinny Patterson with a beard.

Roger waited until John had finished reviewing the Ellen papers, and he said, "Before you start feeling like you know what is going on, we have a new twist." Roger and Paul filled John in on the weapons sting, and the connection between William C. Thornton, SSA Spelling, and Core.

John was silent. He was looking out the airplane window as he said, "I have to admit this case is intimidating. Seems to be leaping toward the top of a pretty bad shit pile." He looked right at Roger. "You will find Patterson soon. He may be this Bernard Jacobs guy. You could go home. Call it done. You don't have to get deeper into this Core mess."

"I think for whatever reason I am meant to stay with this until the end which in my mind includes Core, Thornton, and anyone else we find in this."

Paul nodded and said, "I feel the same way Roger does, John."

John smiled, "Heaven help us."

George was preparing the gallery for an exhibit on a new featured artist when he received the call from Tourey. Tourey wanted to meet with George in two hours. He wanted any information George could get him on his boss, Theodore Chain. George had protested he wasn't comfortable with the request. Tourey had said, "Trust me Georgie. You said you wanted to make a difference. Here's your chance. Two hours, Jackson Park."

Was Tourey suggesting Theodore was a pedophile too? Was Theodore connected to Bernard? George knew if he got caught snooping into Theodore's private business, he would be banned from working anywhere in the Quarter. Theodore knew everybody. George was tempted to just tell Tourey he couldn't find anything.

It was as if the heavens planned it, because the next song that came over the piped in radio was "Man in the Mirror." Wasn't that what the bartender Jill had said? If you want the world to change, you start with the man in the mirror.

George took a deep breath and walked down the long narrow hall toward Theodore's office. He had no idea what time he might show up today if at all. When he got to the door and opened it, Theodore was sitting at his desk. He looked up when George entered.

George stammered, "I wasn't sure if you were here or not. I will need a few more spotlights for the exhibit. Some of these pieces are sixty by eighty, and our lighting won't work on the north wall. We are getting glare from the oils." George's mind was racing. What he had said was actually true. He was surprised he had been able to improvise that fast. Maybe he was better at this spy stuff than he thought.

Theodore looked up and smiled, "Whatever you need George. Do you have the videos from the kiddy art contest for me? I am going to need them for tomorrow night, and I would like to preview them today."

George answered, "I picked them up from the library yesterday as soon as John finished producing them. They are on my desk. Do you want me to get them for you?"

Theodore was still smiling when he said, "How much trouble would it be to make another copy of them? I think I may start a private library of these contests."

George felt a shiver creep up his spine. Could Tourey really be on to something? George answered, "Give me a couple of hours, and I can be done."

Theodore stood and said, "Great. You do that, and I am going to do some shopping. I'll stop back before we close and pick them up."

The two men walked back to the main gallery showroom together. George showed him the problem wall and the artist's pieces he had to display there. Theodore was barely paying attention and waved his hand for George to do whatever he wanted. George watched him leave the building, and he quickly went into his own office and set his computer to download the video of the contest. He made two copies. One for Theodore, and one for Tourey. George's mind was messing with him as he watched the film in fast speed. These kids all looked so cute and proud of their pictures. Surely these contests were not a part of some sordid plot?

When the videos had been copied to disks, George placed one in his briefcase and walked back to Theodore's office. Once inside he closed the door and sat at the desk. His heart was racing. He didn't belong in here. He surveyed the papers on top of the desk. Nothing appeared out of the ordinary. He slowly opened each of the desk drawers. In the center drawer was an address book. He cupped it in his hand and left for his own office to make copies. This would have to do for Tourey. George felt like he was going to be sick.

When the copies were all made, he placed them in his briefcase and returned Theodore's book to the desk drawer. George sat in his own office chair and watched the clock unable to think of anything other than his meeting with Tourey in ninety minutes. What had he started?

Jeanne came down the stairs carrying three bottles of water from the upstairs fridge. She handed Ray and Simon each one. Simon asked, "How hot is it out there now anyway? This air conditioner isn't even trying to keep up anymore."

Jeanne answered, "The bank clock on the corner says a hundred and two. With the storm this morning, the humidity is probably seventy percent. At least we aren't outside this afternoon."

Simon took a big gulp, "Yet."

Jeanne looked at Simon, "I am stuck. I feel like I am going in circles. The account Devon received the money from is the same account he sent five million back to. Unless I am going nuts."

Simon answered, "This will drive you nuts. That's because this is only a clearing account. I actually have six million coming in and then being split up in Devon's account. I have been working on sourcing the six mill deposit to the clearing account."

Jeanne said, "I have been trying to follow the five million from Devon's account to the payee. I am getting stopped at a clearing account. What transaction identifier are you working with?" Simon showed her. "Why is your number coming in the same as mine going out only with a different sub text number? Wouldn't that just be a wash?"

Simon answered, "I think what we are seeing is whoever paid the six mill went through the clearing account. Devon kept one mill and sent the five mill on using the same clearing account he received it from. So we have three parties using this clearing account. Whoever paid the six mill to Devon, Devon, and whoever is the owner of this clearing account. That is what I am trying to identify now. It is definitely not an individual. It has a corporate sub text."

Simon looked at Ray, "Can you access any data from the computer lab that was blown up and search for these two sub-text numbers?"

Ray wasn't sure he could search anything without sending up alarms that they were looking. Ray answered, "I think I am going to want to enter that cloud through what looks like a hole. "

Jeanne's interest was piqued. "How did you find a hole?"

Ray answered, "I wish I knew. It seems to be tied to my ID somehow. I think I can enter the data like a snooper." Ray hoped he hadn't said too much. He knew Roger was worried about who knew about the cloud. He had to assume his own team was okay. Ray asked, "Should I go in? Roger is beyond anal that nobody finds out about this. Nobody."

Simon thought back to Roger's comments in Indy about there being a problem in the New Orleans office. Also, someone had obviously leaked Intel from that computer lab and alarmed someone enough to blow it up. Whatever was in this data cloud was dangerous enough to risk killing two CIA agents.

Simon said, "Roger has good reason to worry about this. Let's try an amateur hack approach and see if we get booted out. No harm no foul." Ray and Jeanne nodded, and they watched Ray hit a few keystrokes and quickly get booted out.

Ray shrugged and said, "Well, that was fun."

Simon thought a minute and said, "We need to know if we can move securely or not. Ray, go in with your ID and see what happens. I'm SSA, this will be on me. We won't search for anything yet. Let's just review some log history."

Jeanne asked Ray, "You want me to do it? I'm already going to be on the Bureau's shit list for staying in this case and then shooting Devon."

Simon laughed. "You obviously don't realize who you are working for. Roger Dance is the

Golden Boy of the entire Bureau right now. You're fine."

Ray keyed in his ID and logged into the website. Suddenly his screen started scrolling log history from about two hours ago up until real time right now. He was shown the activity path and entries of someone who was in the data cloud making programing changes to CIA programs. Ray pushed his chair back and turned the screen for Jeanne and Simon to see.

Simon watched a minute and said, "Jeanne, follow Ray with a snooper. Make sure we aren't leaving a path."

Jeanne hit some keys and watched her screen. "I'm not sure what just happened. Ray's ID is being split, like network. I'm being identified as him too. No path. No trace. You want me to join our visitor and get screen views on what he's doing?"

Simon was taking his suit jacket off, "Just a minute, I want to log into the CIA computer and get my own status." After a minute Simon said, "Can't log in. System being restored." They all looked at each other.

Ray pushed away from his screen, narrowed his eyes and asked, "Restored to what? How long has this been down?" Jeanne went to log histories and found a time stamp of when the CIA super-frame had been shut down. The exact time stamp, to the second, of when this snooper history started on Ray's printout.

Ray stood and pointed to Jeanne's screen, "Whoever we are watching, took down the CIA super-frame and is making changes the CIA won't see if he restores from this data base. This is way beyond the three of us."

Simon whispered, "Shit! Ray, start looking for him! Follow him home and hurry." He pointed at Jeanne. "You start printing this activity log. Let's pray this hole stays open long enough to fix this. Ray is right. This is way beyond us. I'm calling Roger."

CHAPTER 28

Thor had Albert park the cab in the far corner of Colby's parking lot in the shade of a tree. Albert kept the cab running because they needed the air conditioning. The thermostat in the cab said the outside temperature was a hundred and three degrees. Quite a few trucks were parked in the lot for mid-afternoon, and several men walked from the neighboring loading docks into the bar.

Dusty said, "See? I told you it was a dive."

Thor asked Albert, "You get many fares for this place?"

Albert laughed, "You kidding me? Nobody comes to the port unless they have to. 'Cept the folks looking to board a cruise, and if they are this far down, they are pretty lost."

Thor looked at Albert and said, "Based on our history, I want to remind you that you are answering questions to a Federal Agent who expects honesty. You lie to me, you go to jail. That simple."

Dusty spoke, "I watched these guys kill one dude already today. Don't mess with 'em man."

Albert pulled his head back and opened his eyes wide, "You got the whole truth, anything you ask."

Just then Dusty shouted, "There's that ponytail dude! Goin' in the bar right now!"

Thor asked Albert, "Any chance you know who this guy is?" Albert squinted and then shook his head. They were still watching the door when a black Ford Explorer pulled into the parking lot and stopped. There was something about it that captured their attention. First of all, it was new and polished. Not exactly the typical vehicle in this lot. It slowly rolled directly towards them. Thor considered the possibility it was Mathew Core coming to meet with ponytail. "This could be our man."

Albert held up a newspaper like he was reading, "You better think of something fast. Whoever this is, comin' to check out this cab and what we doin' parked back here."

Dusty screamed at Thor, "He's comin' this way man. You better think of some reason we're parked back here in the corner!'

Albert yelled, "He's pullin' up next to us man! Get to kissin', do somethin' *fast*." They could hear the gravel crunch under the Explorer's tires as it crept closer.

Thor looked at Dusty, "Pucker up," grabbed the back of his head and planted a big kiss on him. Dusty tried to act normal as he watched the Explorer out of the corner of his eye. He was sure the driver was Mathew Core.

Dusty pulled away enough to talk, "That's your guy, man! The one in my picture!" Thor was wiping his mouth and swearing. Albert was desperately trying to keep from laughing. They must have passed the test because Core drove slowly on by, parked by the door to the bar, and walked in. Thor told Albert to get close enough they could write the plate number down and then get the hell out of there.

Once they were a safe distance from the bar, Thor told Albert to pull over. Thor called Nelson and had him run the plates. The Explorer was registered to a company named Global Corporation. Thor told Nelson to bring Pablo, get street clothes, a cover car, and a couple of GPS locators. Thor called Simon and asked if he could find out anything about Global Corporation and get back with him.

Thor looked at Albert, "I'll make sure you earn plenty to cover all of this. Do you need me to talk to your boss? We aren't going anywhere until my guys get here."

Albert said they could wait and call his boss when they were done. If they called him with a fare, he would just pass. "I guess I owe you that."

"Damn right!" Thor answered.

Dusty looked at Thor, "You know that kiss you planted on me?" It made Thor cringe to hear those words spoken out loud. "Sad thing is, that's the most activity I've had in six months!"

Thor watched out the window of his door. He didn't want to miss Core leave. He shook his head and smiled. Damn. *Just had to kiss a dude.* It was only about fifteen minutes before Pablo and Nelson pulled next to them in an old Impala. Thor told Albert to step out of the car and say hi to the guys again. Albert looked like he was going to wet himself.

Pablo walked over to him and said, "Funny man. Huh." He started circling Albert and nodding his head. Nelson smiled, stuck his head in the window, said hi to Dusty, and asked him what he was doing with Thor.

Dusty answered, "I've been kidnapped! And molested! Save me, man!" Pablo just shook his head, smiled, and walked away.

Thor asked Albert, "Can these guys go in that bar without getting made?"

Dusty stuck his head out the window and frowned, "You look mighty clean." Nelson bent down and grabbed a handful of dirt from the road and smeared it on his sweaty arms, face and shirt. Pablo did too, and they both waited for the verdict.

Albert looked at Dusty, "I think they look okay. Maybe part-time dock workers?" Dusty nodded. Thor told them Mathew Core and one of his men, ponytail, were in the bar. He asked them if they felt okay to go in and get a beer after planting the GPS. They both nodded. Thor asked if they were armed. Both men pulled up their pant legs to expose ankle holsters.

Thor cautioned them. "Core might remember you guys from the Crab Shack. Even if he makes you, he knows we are in town for some reason. Not necessarily him. I don't see him starting trouble." Nelson and Pablo nodded and drove off.

Thor watched as they pulled the Impala next to the Explorer. Pablo casually got out, placed the GPS, and kept walking. Never even broke his stride. Thor watched them walk in. He hoped to hell he hadn't made a big mistake.

They waited about twenty minutes when Thor saw ponytail guy leave the building and walk around the back. Thor asked Dusty, "Where is he going?"

Dusty answered, "Nothin' but storage barns and hangers back there. Cargo holders, you know."

Then Thor saw Core come out of the building, get into the Explorer, and drive off. Thor told Albert to drive down as far as he could into the storage area to see where ponytail might have gone. They couldn't see him anywhere. Thor's phone rang. It was Pablo. "I don't think they made us. We started a pool game with a couple of guys. They talked at the end of the bar and left." Thor told Pablo not to ask any direct questions because these guys were regulars there. Just see if anyone volunteers anything. Thor said he would have the field office send the GPS signal to both Nelson's phone and his own. They should leave and take up the tail when they could.

Thor checked his phone and saw the GPS transmission was ready. He showed the phone to Albert and asked, "Where's this guy headed?"

Albert studied the tiny map and said, "I think he's headin' toward the Quarter or Uptown. Give it one minute here, and we'll see what he does at Highway 10. Yup, he's going to Uptown. Good residential over there."

Dusty piped up, "I think we're at the end of our date, don't ya think? I got my kiss an' everythin'. How 'bout you just dump my ass somewhere in the Quarter 'fore you start the rest of this field trip?"

Thor laughed and told Albert to let Dusty out as close to Jackson Park as he could.

Dusty said, "Actually, I think I want to visit my favorite bartender back at Mickey's. Just drop me at Bourbon and St. Peter if you can." Dusty looked at Thor, "If anyone knows something about this Core dude, it's Scotty. I might be able to find out something for ya. Scotty already saw me there with you guys at lunch. I want to explain I was tricked into givin' you a boat ride is all. I sure as hell don't want people thinkin' I spend time with FBI for fun!"

Thor laughed, "I'm hurt. You haven't had fun today?" Thor passed Dusty his card.

Dusty said, "I still got the one you gave me last night." He shook his head, "Shit, I can't believe I've only known you less than a day! How many times I almost got killed with snakes and guns and shit?"

Thor laughed, "Yes, but you did get a kiss."

✳ ✳ ✳

Wilma walked into the Voodoo shop crying and holding a fistful of tissues. Sasha came from behind the counter to give her a hug. "Wilma, Hun, what's wrong?"

Wilma choked out, "I just got fired! Mr. Jacobs is closin' the house an' movin' away." No notice or nothin'. Just called me and told me not to come there no more." She plopped down heavily on Sasha's chair behind the counter. "I need the Spirits tell me what to do. I can't *live* with no job!"

Sasha hit the buzzer to summon Spicey to the front of the shop. Spicey entered the room, and saw Wilma sobbing into her elbow sitting on Sasha's chair. Spicey looked at Sasha and pointed to Wilma.

Sasha shrugged her shoulders, "Wilma got a call from that Bernard Jacobs man sayin' he's gonna leave town, close up his house. Wilma got no job no more."

Spicey patted Wilma's back, and Wilma looked up with tears in her eyes and pleaded, "I'm needin' the Spirits find me a job."

Spicey straightened her shoulders, "Wilma, what page in the *Bible* tells you the Spirits are runnin' an employment agency?" Spicey was twirling her long beaded necklace and frowning. She couldn't help but think sometimes people just expected the world to do for them. Take no gumption on them own selves. Spicey added, "Don't you know anybody thinkin' bout retirin' or something? Maybe you could get their job. Hurry 'em along maybe."

Wilma perked right up. "I got a lady friend at the church told me she not working after the end of this month. She gonna go live with her boy in Texas. I guess I could talk to her."

Spicey took Wilma's hand and said, "I got me a courage disc I gonna give to ya. You don't wait 'til Sunday church to talk to this lady. You find her phone number and call her today. You explain how bad you need her job and proud you will make her cuz you so good. You just wait right here, and I'll be back." Wilma was smiling.

Spicey went into her kitchen and carefully placed four gum drops on a small piece of wax paper. She put them into her microwave and watched them melt into perfect circles. Once they were melted she removed them and put them into her freezer for a minute. She normally sold her courage discs for five dollars each, but she would give these to Wilma for free. While she waited for them to cool, she called Tourey. He picked up on the first ring.

"Yeah Spicey, what you need?" He was down the street from Bernard's house and had watched Bernard's car pull in the driveway and Bernard enter the house.

Spicey told him about Bernard firing Wilma and closing up the house. Tourey said thanks and hung up. If Bernard Jacobs was William Patterson, he may have heard about Devon being shot earlier. Tourey decided there was only one way to find out. He walked down the block and knocked loudly on the brass plate on the front door.

After a minute Bernard opened the door and looked at Tourey. "What the hell? You aren't supposed to be here for an hour. I just got here! I haven't even had time to pack!" He looked angry. Bernard looked past him, "Where the hell is the car? Aren't you my driver?"

Tourey thought fast, "I'm your security for the trip. Your driver will be here a little later."

Bernard appeared to like Tourey's response. "My security, huh? That is probably a good idea. You work for Rolland?"

Tourey answered, "You might say I am independent."

Bernard answered, "Whatever, I'm in a rush. You want to be inside or out?"

Tourey answered, "I'll be both. You just go about your business, and I'll do mine."

Bernard nodded his head and said, "Keep an eye out for the arsonist. I don't want him torching this place 'til we're gone!"

Tourey nodded and watched Bernard shuffle his way up the stairs. Tourey walked around to the side yard and placed a call to John Barry.

CHAPTER 29

John, Paul, and Roger had just entered the hospital receiving lobby after being cleared in the security room. This part of the hospital was a secured government facility. The security clearance process had been quite lengthy, especially, if your intentions were to visit a patient as important as the Director of the FBI.

They had just stepped into the elevator when all three of their cell phones went off. Paul was taking a call from Thor, Roger was talking to Simon, and John was talking to Tourey. They all finished at the same time, and stared at each other.

Paul asked, "Who goes first?"

Roger replied, "Why don't you start."

Paul nodded, pushed his chin out in his twitch, "Thor says he located Mathew Core at some bar by the port. Core is with one of his guys. He had Nelson and Pablo go there, snoop a little, and secure a GPS to Mathew's truck. Thor is now following Core. Pablo and Nelson will be taking over the surveillance because Thor is in a cab. He wants to know if we have learned anything else on Core he needs to know. I told him I would call back."

Roger looked at John, "Next?"

John said, "Tourey is at Bernard Jacobs' house right now. Bernard thinks Tourey is hired security. They're waiting for a driver to arrive to take Bernard somewhere, and also for an arsonist to come torch the house. Tourey thinks retired Senator Rolland Kenny is helping Patterson hide, and that Bernard *is* William Patterson." Roger's eyebrows went up. John continued, "That's not the bad part. Tourey says these guys are part of a club with chapters all over the United States. They hold art contests for children. There is some evidence this club selects winners that are kidnapped, moved across the country, abused, and murdered." They were all silent.

Roger swallowed hard, "My call was from Simon Frost. He says the data cloud Ray established before the bombing is showing evidence of someone making programming changes to CIA programs. That same individual shut down the CIA super-frame temporarily. We assume the intention is to restore the super-frame from the infected cloud database. Simon says they have discovered some kind of access hole that is allowing them to watch what is happening, and record it all. I am sure that part has something to do with Ellen. He wants to share access to the hole with CIA super techs. He says we aren't capable of handling this."

John looked at Roger, "Your call wins the top spot. I have to bring in OSI and CIA, and they will probably bring in the President and the Security Council."

Roger looked at Paul. "Could you tell Thor not to move on Core. Surveillance only. We'll brief the team when we get back." Paul nodded. Roger called Simon and told him to expect a call from CIA. Roger looked at John, "I think you need to check with Ellen on names before you make your call. Someone has been a step ahead of us all along on this computer mess."

An earpiece appeared on John Barry's head. He looked like he had been shot with a stun gun. Kim started talking to him. John took out a notepad and wrote down two names and said goodbye. The earpiece disappeared.

John looked at Roger and Paul, "How have you worked like this?" Roger and Paul just shrugged. John looked at his phone, "I have to make this call."

The elevator door opened, and the three men stepped out. John walked about ten feet away and made a series of phone calls. When he had finished, he looked at Paul and Roger.

"I don't know how I can explain knowing this stuff. Right now we are covered. I blamed you." John smiled at Roger.

Roger smiled back, "That means next time I can blame you."

Paul chuckled, "This might work. Everyone knows there are secrets in both agencies."

The three men looked down the hall toward the Director's room. They didn't have much time.

***

By the time I found the right building Teresa, Mary and Linda were already on the cargo ship taking pictures with their video cameras. Linda laughed, "You made it! See? You can do this."

"How do we know we are on the right boat?" They all looked the same to me. I had just seen Teresa flying around this one taking pictures.

Teresa answered me, "Go look in that long box over there." She was pointing to a part of the cargo hold that was stacked almost to the ceiling in long wooden boxes. I flew over and concentrated on lifting the lid. I'm getting much better at controlling mass.

"Whoa!" There were big guns in that box! Really big guns! Yikes. I looked at Teresa, "Have you looked in all of the boxes already?" She answered no, they were hiding from the guards. They didn't want them to see things moving.

I looked around, "What guards?" Mary pointed to my left, and I saw three guys playing cards at a small table. Eeek. Oh them. They did not look like your everyday, bring a lunch box to work, dock workers. Forget about the fact they all had guns strapped to them. The one I was looking at had biceps the size of my thighs!

Linda said, "There are guys up on the main deck of this ship moving boxes with a crane to that building on the dock. We were just getting ready to go there and see what is happening." I flew over and grabbed Linda's shirt. She looked at my hand on her shirt and said, "You know you don't need that anymore. You used to do just fine. Then you started obsessing that things might hurt you. Just remember we control mass with our minds. If you don't think about it, you can fly through it. If you need it to be there, just think about it. Why don't we just fly next to each other and see how it goes?"

I knew this day was coming. I said okay, but I didn't mean it. We didn't even make it out of the cargo hold, and I ran into a wall. Full speed. I remember thinking, *that sure looks like a wall.* How do you not think about a wall that you can see?

Linda had her hands on her hips. "Why don't you imagine your mind can make tunnels through anything?" Hey, that sounded like it might work. I went back and flew through the wall full speed.

"That works! You're a genius!" Now I won't have to pretend that things I *see* won't hurt me when my mortal is screaming *"This might hurt!"*

We spent at least a half hour looking into every box we could find and snooping around people trying to read their minds. So far we hadn't heard anything we wanted to record. We went into the storage building on the shore, and Ellen popped in.

"Okay you guys, I am ready to show your little videos pretty soon. Just keep up the good work and try to show us everything you can okay?" We all nodded. Ellen looked at me, "You are doing good. Keep it up!" Then she was gone. That was nice of her to say.

* * *

The Director's room was the one with two armed guards flanking the door. Roger stopped at the nurses' station and identified himself as the man who had called earlier to arrange for the meeting. A pleasant looking nurse held her index finger up, smiled, and buzzed an intercom. "Your appointment is here Director." She looked up and smiled at Roger, "You gentlemen can go in. He is expecting you." She winked at Paul.

Roger smiled, said thank you, and glanced at Paul and John. Kim had said Ellen was going to prepare the Director for their visit, but he had no idea what that meant. When they entered the room, the Director was in pajamas and slippers with the headrest of the bed fully elevated, so he was in a sitting position.

Roger spoke first, "Director, Roger Dance. It is a pleasure to meet you sir."

The Director extended his hand to Roger and clasped his other hand on top of Roger's. "It is an honor to finally meet you Roger."

The Director smiled and said, "John, nice to see you. This must be Paul." He stretched his hand out to shake both of their hands. "Now that the formalities are over with, it seems we have some important business to attend to." The Director had moved his legs over so they were hanging over the side of his hospital bed. He was staring at Roger with a very serious look on his face. Roger didn't know what the Director had been told.

The Director continued, "I have been visiting with Ellen for quite a while. I understand she will be returning while you are all here."

Roger nervously glanced at both Paul and John before he said, "Director, could you please elaborate on the visit you are referring to? I want to be sure I don't make inappropriate assumptions."

Roger was startled when the Director threw his head back and started laughing. Paul was nervously shifting his weight, and John had turned to face Roger. The Director composed himself and invited them all to take a seat.

He looked at them all and said, "I don't mean what I am about to say to sound pretentious or self-serving. I believe we have been chosen to change the planned events of those who do not care about consequences. We are being given extraordinary advantages to obtain these goals. Any of our life's accomplishments will pale in importance to the challenges we will face now." The Director cleared his throat, "I admit Ellen had a job convincing me. I am not going to share with you how she finally did."

He was shaking his head slowly and was extremely serious. "I will never be the same after today. I expect you can all say that." No one spoke, he was clearly not done. "Roger, Paul, what can I say? You have lived with this for over a year now. I can't imagine how challenging this has been. John, I understand you are almost as new to this as I am?" John nodded. The Director continued, "Ellen has brought me up to the shooting of Devon today. She told me she wanted to present some videos for us to review. Roger, do you know how to signal Ellen we are ready for her?"

Roger nodded and said, "I believe we can just ask for her to appear, sir."

Ellen was suddenly sitting on the bed next to the Director. She looked *very* human and looked exactly like Ellen DeGeneres. She had on a blazer, blue jeans, and tennis shoes. She was kicking her feet and smiling. "Hi, guys. I got permission to show myself as a human image. It is much easier to talk, and we have a *lot* of talkin' to do." Roger quickly looked around. He felt short of breath and fearful Ellen would be seen. Through the glass walls of the hospital room he could see people outside of the room were frozen in their positions. Ellen had stopped time everywhere but in this room.

Paul and John were looking around too. The Director laughed, "She did this the first time she was here. Very eerie isn't it?"

Roger cleared his throat and looked at Ellen, "It is such an honor to see and talk to you. I want to thank you for all you have done. I'm struggling to find the right words." Roger spoke to the Director, "Up until now, Ellen has always appeared as a black cat, and we communicated with winks."

The Director laughed, "I heard you had a thing about some cat. This is starting to make sense."

Ellen said, "I am not actually in a human form. What you are seeing could best be described as a three dimensional hologram. Here, hold my hand." She had held her hand out to Roger. When he went to grasp it, his own hand went through the image, and he felt no mass. Ellen laughed. "Kim will always be the human we communicate through for this assignment, but I did get special permission to meet with you today in this form. We have much work to do."

"I have information gathered that may assist you in developing conclusions. I can only provide you information mortals would have eventually discovered anyway. If I can find you information, I will get it to you. I do not have a way to monitor how ready your mortal minds are for additional information. So it is important you ask for my help when you need it."

With that she produced two large screens on the glass walls and was holding what looked like a remote control. She looked at the Director, "First, it is important to re-evaluate some relationships. Director, this will be difficult for you to watch, but you need to make mortal decisions based on factual information." Ellen played the video of the Director being given a drug by William C. Thornton.

The Director sat silently as he watched the screen. When the video was over, he looked at Ellen and asked if he could watch it again. Ellen replayed it for him. Roger could see the Director was very disturbed. Ellen told him she wanted him to watch the next video before discussion. This was the video of the phone call from William C. Thornton to Roger. With this video they heard both sides of the phone conversation. The Director watched William C. Thornton push the files from the desk and slam his fist. The Director was shaking his head.

The Director looked at Roger. "Is this when you called the hospital?" Roger answered yes. The Director said, "I was told the drug they would normally administer to someone in my condition, would have killed me. You calling and telling them to look at tox screens saved my life. Again, thank you." The Director looked at Ellen, "What should we do?"

Ellen answered, "I can only bring factual information to you sooner than you would have normally found it. I cannot offer advice. These are mortal issues. I can tell you the drug you were given by the Deputy Director was not meant to kill you. Only to make you feel very sick. I cleansed you of toxins on my first visit. You should feel only a slight effect from some of the hospital medications now. Mr. Thornton was unaware of the dangers subsequent medications posed. Also, I can only stop mortal time for very short intervals. I am leaving all of you to discuss business. I will return very shortly. I have images of the weapons delivery to show you." Ellen was gone and the people outside the room were moving and acting naturally.

Roger asked the Director, "We have several other issues to bring to your attention if you are feeling up to it sir."

The Director asked, "Did Ellen say weapons delivery? I have a feeling I haven't heard the worst of this."

John spoke, "Actually sir, we have an item of National Security we need to discuss with you that takes priority to the weapons."

Todd and Pablo had taken over the surveillance of Mathew Core and were parked in a nice residential area in Uptown. Mathew Core had parked in the driveway of a home and entered through a side door fifteen minutes ago. Todd and Pablo had parked more than a block away but had a visual on the house.

Pablo looked at Todd, "So where do you live? What's the Todd Nelson story?"

Todd chuckled, "Got a condo rented in St. Joseph, Michigan, on the lake. Nice. Lots of chicks in the summer."

Pablo smiled, "Except you're never there right?"

"Right. Just lost my girlfriend yesterday for that reason." Todd looked at Pablo and raised his eyebrows like "Oh well." Then he said, "Story is, third generation FBI, and I want to be the best. That gets in the way of personal stuff, but I guess I'm okay with that for now. You?"

Pablo answered, "I let my lease in New York expire, and Simon talked me into coming here. I guess I'm homeless for the moment." He chuckled, "Not the first time for that either. Started out a blues singer, like my mom." Pablo looked out the window when he said, "I'm not driven to be the best, but I want to be damn good. Hell, I'll never be half as good as my sister! Now there is someone driven." Pablo looked at Todd, "It's hard to know where you fit in the world with this job."

Todd pointed to the house Mathew went in, "Let's have Simon or Ray check out who owns this house. Core might be at home now, and Thor might want us doing something else." Pablo agreed. Todd called Simon then he asked Pablo, "What do you think makes Roger tick?"

Pablo rubbed his chin, "He's a tough one. I heard he lost a girlfriend to cancer a few years back and has been all business since then. Simon claims Roger is one of the best the Bureau has ever had. Turns down every promotion they offer him, wants the field. It's funny he hangs with Paul. They seem like opposites. Roger is so controlled, and Paul is pretty laid back. Paul just *drips* women. I guess he is the bureau poster boy, has his picture in our recruiting brochures. He has a damn good rep, too. Simon says they are practically a team after this many years." Pablo looked serious, "I know the Bureau doesn't really encourage teams, but I wouldn't mind hangin' with Simon a while. He's a smart dude. I can learn a lot from him."

Todd asked, "So you sing huh?"

* * *

Mathew Core walked into his living room to find three huge boxes filled with vibrant colored clothes. He looked at Lisa smiling, "You guys aren't movin' out on me are you?"

Lisa chuckled, "Tonight is Jamie's play, remember? We're taking costumes over to the school so the prop people can get them ready." She placed her hands on Mathew's cheeks and gave him a big kiss. "You didn't forget about tonight did you?" Mathew shook his head.

Jamie walked in the room and ran over to hug Mathew's waist. "Just in time Daddy. We need help moving these boxes."

Mathew smiled at Jamie and said, "You get the door, I'll move 'em now." Jamie skipped to the door and held it open. Lisa told him they would be back within the hour.

Pablo had his binoculars up, "Got a woman and a kid getting into an SUV, and Core loading boxes in the back. Core is waving goodbye to them. He's back inside the house. Shut the door. Now what?"

Todd said, "We have GPS on him. Let's follow the woman and tag her car too if we can. This might be a girlfriend or something."

✳ ✳ ✳

Thor had Albert drop him off at the Star Ship. He was good on his word and paid Albert a bonus for his trouble. When he was leaving the cab, Albert said, "I'm sorry I messed with you guys. Nawlens needs all the help we can get."

Thor nodded, "I appreciate the apology. We haven't left town yet, so I might be seein' you again." With that he walked up to the door and entered his pass code. The air conditioning felt great, and he could hear Ray, Simon, and Jeanne talking in the basement. Thor grabbed a bottle of water from the refrigerator and walked down.

Thor sat in a chair near Ray and asked, "Anyone know where Roger and Paul are?"

Simon answered without looking at him, "They are somewhere meeting with the Director. John Barry, too."

Thor asked, "Director of what?"

Simon gave Thor a sideways glance, "FBI Director. I think they are at some hospital." Just then Simon's phone rang; he checked the caller ID and looked at Ray, "Here we go...this is CIA geek king. I'm going to pass this to you." Thor's eyes opened wide, and he pushed his chair back.

Ray said, "Just put it on speaker. They are going to be screaming at all of us."

Simon answered and told the caller he was on speaker. Thor could tell from everything being said they were in the middle of some kind of huge geek emergency. The caller was getting instructions from Ray about some cloud hole, and Jeanne was typing so fast Thor couldn't believe it. Simon was shouting for someone else to call on the second line because he had to explain what they had found so far. When that line rang, Thor heard Simon explaining Ray had stored all of the hard drives from the bombed computer lab in a data cloud, just before the bombing. Simon told the caller Ray had re-entered the data cloud to find someone making changes to CIA programming.

The caller yelled from the speaker, "How did you make this pass through hole?" Ray screamed back that he had no idea. Maybe something happened electronically when the bomb went off.

Based on the facial expressions of everyone, and the phrases being yelled from the phone, Thor felt like he was watching some kind of computer geek horror film. At one point Thor heard the caller exclaim,

"Jesus! If this gets restored to the super-frame, we *have* no more security! WHO IS THIS ASSHOLE?"

＊ ＊ ＊

Tourey sat in the front seat with the driver. Bernard Jacobs sat in the back seat reading the daily news from the Picayune. Tourey knew better than to engage in conversation and tried instead to memorize the trip. After half an hour, the car pulled into a drive that twisted and turned for at least five minutes, exposing a beautiful brick mansion.

The driver pulled up to the front stairs and turned the car off. He looked to the back seat and handed Bernard some keys. "You will find a car in the back garage and the house has been stocked for your needs. The Senator requested you be available for his call to you later this afternoon. He also said to remind you that your company will be arriving at eight."

Bernard said thank you and opened his car door. The driver removed Bernard's bags from the trunk and asked Tourey, "Are you staying here or am I taking you back?"

Tourey looked at Bernard, "I am expected back in the city for now."

Bernard nodded his head and said, "I think I am perfectly safe for the time being. Am I supposed to pay you or what? I don't know how this works."

Tourey said, "Give me your phone number, and I will contact you regarding further services and payment. What's happening tonight? Do you want me here?"

Bernard checked a piece of paper from his wallet and copied a number to the back of a business card he handed Tourey. "I just got this number, so I don't know it yet. There you go. Thank you. Tonight? No, tonight should be fine. Just a club meeting, you know, bunch of guys watching videos. Nothing dangerous." If Tourey hadn't known what slime Bernard was, he would have thought he was one of the most perfect gentlemen he had ever met.

Tourey thanked Bernard for the number and told the driver to take him back to the city. On the ride back Tourey thought about George. He should be right on time for their meeting.

Dusty walked into Mickey's bar, took a stool at the far end, and smiled at Scotty who walked down to him. Scotty pulled the bar rag from his shoulder and wiped the area in front of Dusty. "Thought I'd seen the last of you today. Loved that move of yours, divin' under the table when the shootin' started." Scotty was laughing so hard he nearly lost his balance.

Dusty shook his head, "You know how I got messed up with them? After boozin' with you half the night, I got a call from the FBI wanting me to use my brother's boat and take two FBI agents to see Mambo, of all things!"

Scotty straightened up, "Mambo? What the hell?"

Dusty said, "No shit! And guess what Mambo had? Some woman had been left in the swamp to die! Then we found two more!"

Scotty asked, "Two more *what*?"

"Women!"

"Is that why they shot that dude in here?"

Dusty nodded, "Yeah, I think so. Damn. You wouldn't believe all the shootin' when we were at Mambo's. Huge snakes everywhere tryin' to get in the boats. It was hell man." Dusty took a swig of his beer. "Those guys can shoot though. And you should see that FBI chick throw a knife! Cut a snake clean in half right next to this dude's foot."

Scotty's eyes were wide open, "She's the one shot that guy in here right between the eyes, and he was moving. I'm thinkin' best not mess with that broad. You know she slammed Tourey's head flat on the bar yesterday? Fact, after she left Tourey went over to the juke box there and played "What kind of Woman is This," Buddy Guy. Cracked me up. He even said he bet Buddy Guy met that broad before he sang that song! Tourey laughed but I think he was pissed when it happened."

Dusty was hoping the conversation would move to Tourey or Mathew Core. "Tourey Waknem?" Scotty nodded. Dusty continued, "What the hell would she be pissed at Tourey for? He don't ever bother nobody."

Scotty leaned in closer and said, "I heard her ask him what he was doin' sittin' on the sidewalk for so long."

Dusty chuckled, "He's studies people ya know? Told me he's gonna write a book someday. Bet that pissed him off."

"Yeah, I heard him tell one of my regulars she pissed him off good. Fact, that guy paid me a hundred bucks to tell him what I know about Tourey. Poor Tourey, seems he's drawin' all kinds of attention he don't need."

Dusty took a swig of his beer, "I don't get it. What could you possibly say about Tourey that's worth a hundred bucks?"

Scotty laughed, "This dude is paranoid man. He's owns this building, one across the street, probably a bunch more. Always nosin' around. Hell, I don't care. I'll take his money. I told him Tourey is plenty smart but ain't no cop. Some retired egghead that's just flippin' off society."

Dusty laughed, "That's a good description of Tourey. Just flippin' it all off."

CHAPTER 30

Roger decided the Director needed at least a brief outline of the events of the last two days for the computer problem to even make sense. Roger explained how Mathew Core had selected the doubles to take the place of Devon and Patterson and the associated murders resulting from that plan. He also showed the mind reading pages to the Director where Jason and Mathew kept referring to a Carl as their contact. The location and subsequent bombing of the computer lab, Ray's memory of someone removing the flash drives from his car, and Jason Sims subsequent release from custody all pointed to some very powerful inside strings being pulled.

Roger looked at the Director and said, "I believe Ellen protected the information Ray had stored in the data cloud by creating what we are calling a hole for Ray to re-enter. I also believe Jason Sims has resumed his activity in those programs since his release from custody. All of the data and the programs at Jason's computer lab had direct access to our highest technology and security programs. The time stamp of the CIA super-frame being shut down and the new activity in the cloud are exactly the same. *To the second.* I am being told whatever changes are being made right now if restored to the mainframe will undoubtedly contain program alterations."

The Director was standing now. Roger put out his hand to help steady him, and the Director shooed him away. "I'm fine…just a little druggy…. *what the hell!* Are you saying that someone, maybe Sims, has shut down CIA super-frame in order to download changes? What are we doing about this?"

John answered, "I have called the CIA and OSI and notified them of the hole Ray has been using and what we believe is happening. The CIA super techs are working with your tech team now to take this over and follow through. Nobody knows what kind of time frame we are on. All Jason has to do is finish and program a new restore."

The Director was pacing. Roger knew he needed a minute to think it through, so he refrained from adding more. The Director looked at Roger, "We don't know who this Carl is for sure. Do we know where this Jason Sims is?"

Roger shook his head, "We just found out someone let him go. His release was happening about the same time you got sick a couple of hours ago, sir."

The Director scowled, "Let's call it what it is shall we? You mean when that bastard poisoned me. The CIA tech guys will do whatever needs to be done. John, can you assign OSI people to help locate Sims in case we have a *CIA* problem person getting in our way? I will call the Director of OSI and have everything available put on Thornton." The Director looked at Roger, "How do you know who you can trust?"

Roger answered, "Ellen. Just ask her. Director, can we discuss another matter quickly before we move on to the weapons?"

The Director frowned and sat on the edge of the bed, "There's more?"

Roger began, "We believe we have identified a man in New Orleans, using the name of Bernard Jacobs, as William Patterson. We have evidence he has joined a pedophile club with branches around the United States. This club masquerades as a philanthropy group to support the arts and holds contests for children. We have been able, through an agent of John's, to link this group to ten missing children and three child murders. I think John should bring you up to date with his most recent information."

John straightened his shoulders and said, "Other members of the New Orleans branch of this club include retired Senator Rolland Kenny, and a federal judge, Harold Williams. My man is posing as a security agent for Patterson and is actually riding with him now to what we believe to be his hiding spot in the countryside. There is going to be a meeting of this group tonight at this country house. We believe there will be planned abductions of more children shortly."

Everyone stopped talking and waited for the Director to indicate he was ready for more. The Director wiped his brow and looked at Paul, "I don't hear you saying much. What are you thinking?"

Paul pushed his chin forward in his nervous twitch and said, "I'm thinking you haven't heard the worst of it yet and neither have we. Mathew Core believes he is *untouchable*. That worries me. Both Core and the Deputy Director want Roger off this case and out of New Orleans. That worries me. A sophisticated, well-funded pedophile group with national reach worries me. Your safety worries me. Ellen is giving us a lot of information in a short period of time, which worries me." The Director nodded slowly.

Roger stated, "At the risk of moving through all of this too fast, I want you to review the notes SSA Frank Mass of the New Orleans field office prepared on this weapons case. SSA Spelling, out of the Virginia office, was told by Deputy Director Thornton to warn Mathew Core we were going to arrest him. Core has been identified as the FBI's broker in this weapons sting. Thornton told Mass I was not in the loop on the weapons case, and was getting in the way."

The Director's eyebrows went up, "You didn't know about the weapons case, did you? Hell, *I* didn't know about it!" The Director put his reading glasses on and reviewed the notes. He shook his head and said, "Dear Lord what is going on? Have our guys even prepared for this sting to go bad? Why hasn't Thornton called ATF or at least arranged for more of our guys to be there?"

Just then Ellen was back sitting next to the Director on his bed. "Hi guys. Sorry to rush everyone, but we have some more videos."

They all nodded. Ellen froze everyone outside of the room and screens appeared on the wall. Ellen narrated as they watched, "Roger, Kim's mom and her friends have cameras they are taking these shots with, so if you want to see something closer, just ask me. I am going to divide this screen into four sections, one for each angel camera. You will see them opening box lids, so you can see inside. You can stop this at any time." Just then the bottom quarter of the screen showed a view of the camera running into a wall and sliding down past a light switch. Ellen cleared her throat, "Uh, that was Kim's mom. She's still having a few flying issues." Paul and John glanced at each other. Roger let out a short chuckle. The Director was looking at Ellen with a questioning expression. Ellen said, "Angels have to learn how to fly."

They watched as they were shown an aerial view of the docks with close ups on the surrounding buildings and the ship in question. Then they started seeing views of weapons and ammunition. Ellen stopped the screen and said, "I will furnish you copies of these videos and a full manifest of items. I believe you will find thirty tons of weapons on the ship and sixty tons of weapons being moved to the building on the dock."

Ellen continued, "You will find these items on your manifests. Kytusha rockets, medium range 107 millimeter rockets, artillery shells, grenades, mortars. M4 Carbine with grenade launcher, Beta C-mag double drum magazines, A3 Tactical Carbines, 20 and 30 round magazines. Fully automatic and semi-automatic assault rifles, AR 15's, M16's, AK47's, all new and boxed. You have tonnage of high capacity magazines and a variety of ammunition. In total, you are looking at slightly over ninety tons."

The room was deadly silent. The Director flipped through Frank Mass's notes on the weapons. "I show that we expect there to be thirty tons, total. Which is huge."

Ellen said, "Ninety."

The Director was pointing to the paper, "It says thirty."

Ellen exhaled, "Ninety." Roger cleared his throat. The Director looked at him and realized he was arguing with an angel.

The Director asked Ellen, "How did they manage to get ninety tons of weapons into a harbor with the Coast Guard, Port Authority, and Navy located at the same port?"

Ellen answered, "The entire operation has been an FBI protected mission, as far as anyone else with authority has been told. The weapons are being divided between the ship and the shore. Two deals will be happening, Mathew Core is involved in both. One is Friday, thirty tons of weapons in that deal. One is sooner. The Friday buyer is a representative of a Mexican drug cartel, trading cocaine for guns, and the other deal I don't have any information on yet. I have to go now, but I will stay in touch. Director, you may prepare a list of names for me so I can assist you in determining who you can trust. Whenever you need me, just ask." Ellen smiled at them all, "Bye for now."

Just that fast she was gone, the screens were gone, and the people outside the window were moving naturally. Roger stood, stretched his back, and rolled his neck. He couldn't stop thinking that any one of these problems would be considered urgent. He knew they had to deal with them all. Paul was tapping his pen on his knee. John was staring at the Director who had started pacing across the room again.

The Director moved to the edge of the bed, and a nurse stuck her head in the door, "Sir, I am very sorry to interrupt you. I need to get a blood sample, these are being timed. You also have another visitor waiting, a Mr. Thornton?"

The Director stuck his arm out. "Do it now, fast. Please tell Mr. Thornton I will see him in about fifteen minutes."

The nurse quickly drew the vile of blood, pressed a cotton ball to the Director's wound, and left. They were all silent. No one wanted to rush the Director's thinking. Finally the Director looked at John and said, "How much of this does OSI know?"

John answered, "Nothing. My supervisor knows I hooked up with Roger's team yesterday, to locate Devon. I have actually been otherwise assigned. I will tell you I believe my current OSI assignment and this case would have eventually merged."

The Director nodded and looked at Roger, "I plan to contact the Director of OSI and have them investigate and monitor Thornton. I think we need him to believe he is free to continue his manipulations if we are going to nail him." Roger nodded. The Director looked at John, "Can we borrow your guy to help Roger and Paul with this club of pedophiles? He seems to already be in the loop, but this is more FBI than CIA or OSI." John nodded his agreement. Then the Director looked at Roger, "You are the Behavioral Specialist here. What am I facing with Thornton?"

Roger said, "Based strictly on the video, I would say a very dangerous man in a highly charged situation. His smiling when you were taken away on the stretcher, suggests he feels his goals justify any means." The Director nodded. Roger continued, "I need to find out what kind of deals are going down on these weapons, and it doesn't sound like we have much time. I'm also not comfortable there are only four local FBI and three agents from Virginia in on the sting. This is a cartel and tons of weapons. It sounds to me like our guys are exposed, or have a false sense of security. With your permission sir, I would like you to expand the authority you have given me on the Devon/ Patterson case to include Mathew

Core and any activities or associates I can trace to him."

The Director was nodding, "Of course, but how do I give you that kind of authority without putting a target on your back? You are not making friends lately. We have an arrest warrant on Core now. How do you ignore that and proceed to use him as an FBI broker?"

Roger answered, "I have a good team sir. I prefer to proceed with the safety of our agents as the priority. A bent nose or two does not concern me. I will get Core eventually. " Roger smiled.

The Director shook his head and said, "I suspect I will learn to pay attention when you smile. Look where I am right now. A hospital. You call that a bent nose?" The Director was smiling. Roger sensed the Director was comfortable with his suggestion and trying to frame how he would present this to Thornton.

Roger leaned forward in his chair, "May I offer a suggestion? Perhaps you could tell the Deputy Director I found out about the weapons sting and asked to take it over. This is true. You decided the additional manpower couldn't hurt anything. I think Mr. Thornton will have a hard time objecting to that argument without looking suspicious."

The Director asked, "Any of you guys have a laptop? I'll amend my authority to you right now, before I meet with Thornton. That way I can honestly say it is done." John produced his laptop, and they watched the Director make some changes and place a security call to his staff. He informed them he felt fine and would be back in the office in the morning. He stated he wanted the authorization change he had just made posted immediately. The Director stood, shook all of their hands, and said, "I guess this is where I audition for my Oscar with Thornton. I actually thought this ass was my friend. When you leave, send the bastard in. I want to hear how worried he is about my health."

Roger, Paul, and John left the Director and walked down the hall toward the waiting room. Roger walked in the waiting room where William C. Thornton looked up, threw a magazine against the wall, and stood. Roger noticed Thornton's veins were throbbing in his neck, and his eyes were san paku, meaning showing three sides of white. First alarm of a troubled mind. Thornton's nostrils were flared, and he practically spat the words, *"I've* been waiting while *you* were with the Director? How the hell did you even know he was here?"

Roger said nothing and waited for the next outburst. He knew a calm demeanor would annoy Thornton more than anger.

Thornton's face was beet red. He thrust his finger towards Roger's face, "You and I are going to talk." He pushed his way past Roger, did not acknowledge the presence of Paul or John, and stormed down the hall.

Paul winked at Roger and said, "See, you still know how to spread the love."

Roger chuckled, looked at his watch, and said, "We need to get on that jet."

They were walking to the cab when John said, "Well, now I know why you call her Ellen."

✳ ✳ ✳

Spicey and Sasha watched Wilma leave, all smiling, sucking on her courage disc. Spicey looked at Sasha and said, "You know last night I had a visit from Spirits that would have turned even you into a true believer! I had furniture moving around, my purse flying from room to room, little pieces of paper stickin' on my nose and vanishin'...." Sasha started to protest and Spicey waved her off. "You think I don't know you don't really believe? Now listen, like it or not, the Spirits are involved in something Tourey is snoopin' in. I need to check out some people of importance in a very sneaky way, so I'm goin' to need help from the Spirits. Will you go to Mambo's with me?"

Sasha started crying, "Mambo's? In the swamp? Can't you talk to the Spirits through that ball of yours?"

Spicey frowned, "Girl, why you cryin'? Mambo is a protector. I think we are both needin' protection is all. Go put on your Sunday best, and I'll find us a boat ride."

✳ ✳ ✳

George had his elbows on the back of the park bench and his legs crossed. He was trying to look casual. He uncrossed his legs and rearranged his briefcase on his lap. The stifling heat was making him perspire. He hated that. He looked at his watch and his phone rang. It was Tourey. "Where are you? I am cooking in this heat."

Tourey chuckled, "Look in the window of the restaurant on the corner. See me wavin'? Come on over for an iced tea. Nice 'n cool in here."

While Tourey waited for George to get there, he called Spicey and told her Bernard Jacobs was going to torch his house. If she had seen anything there she wanted, she should go get it, fast. Spicey said thanks, and asked Tourey if he knew anyone who could take her to see Mambo. Tourey gave her Dusty's number and snapped his phone shut. That ought to just about send Dusty over the edge to get that call. Tourey was still chuckling to himself when George slipped into the other side of the booth.

* * *

Spicey hung up from talking to Tourey and called Willie. She gave him Bernard's address and told him to bring his biggest covered truck and one of his boys. She had some fast furniture moving to do and would pay him right. Sasha came through

380

the door all gussied up and crying. Spicey yelled, "Girl, you cry more 'n a newborn babe. Now let's lock this place up and get to walkin'. We got us a little side job to do first." Sasha was wiping her eyes with tissue. She wanted to speak her piece but saw Spicey was in no mood for conversation. She already had the door open and her keys in her hand. "Got your gun?"

Sasha stopped crying mid sob, "What kind a *job* we goin' to?"

Spicey walked down the block so fast, Sasha could hardly keep up in her heels. They turned the corner on Burgundy Street, and Sasha saw the big truck in front of Bernard's place. All she could say was, "Dang, *dang*. What we doin' here?"

Spicey nodded hello to Willie and his son and walked up the wide front staircase where she picked the lock in under a minute. She opened the door wide and declared they should start with the parlor furniture. Sasha had her head tilted and asked overly sweetly, "What we doin' Spicey?"

Spicey answered, "Gettin' us some free furniture before this place gets torched." Spicey saw a long gold Chevy Impala turn the corner and slow down. She walked to the street and knocked on the passenger window as the car pulled to a stop. The man inside grinned and said, "Ms. Spicey, what's you doin' over here?"

Spicey put her hands on her hips, "Get your ass out of that car Abram and help us move some furniture. Don't matter what I doing. What matter's I know what you about to do. And your momma be none too happy to find out."

Abram looked at her like he was deciding whether or not to argue with her. Unlike Sasha, Abram did believe in Spirits and Voodoo. He believed that somehow Spicey knew exactly what he planned on doing. A few more minutes wouldn't matter. He got out of the car and started helping Willie move things out of the house.

Sasha was carrying two lamps and whined to Spicey she wasn't exactly dressed for a robbery. Spicey frowned at her and told her it was a church donation, not a robbery. Spicey waved her past, gave Willie three hundred dollars, directions, and a key to a storage garage the church had on the west side. There was a big auction comin' up and the church could make some good money on this stuff. After Willie pulled his truck away Spicey looked at Abram and said, "It's all yours now. You best be thinkin' 'bout how you been makin' a livin'." Spicey pointed to the heavens, "Don't be thinkin' you ain't been found out." She frowned at Abram and motioned Sasha to follow her.

Tourey listened to George's questions and decided he really didn't want to answer any of them. His mind was processing what he thought he knew about Bernard Jacobs and what he needed to find out yet from his computer. Tourey noticed George was growing impatient with his silence, "I think there is a chance your boss is in some deep shit, but I don't know this for fact. Just a whisper in the wind. This address book and CD will probably help." George had told him the CD was of a kids' art contest, and Theodore said he needed it for tonight. It all fit.

George looked at Tourey, "You know what I think? I think you are something more than a retired inventor. I think you are a lot more than that."

Tourey smiled, "We are all more than what people have labeled us, aren't we? I just have some friends in the right places. Years of keepin' my nose clean, and my ears to the ground. I call in favors from time to time. I told you I would help you get Bernard. Unless you've changed your mind?"

George sat up straight, "No, but I never thought about other people being involved."

Tourey shook his head, "There are always other people involved. It's how they hide."

Roger excused himself from the jet's work table where Paul and John were still reviewing the tapes from Ellen. He walked toward the back of the jet, stretched his back, and sat next to a window. The silent passing of their plane through the clouds made him wonder how angels felt while flying. Having seen Ellen today made him wonder if he would see Sharon in heaven. Roger felt a lump growing in his throat. He closed his eyes and forced his mind to return to the problems at hand.

His gut told him Thornton didn't plan this weapons sting. Probably didn't want it. There was no upside for Thornton in this. Roger didn't see anger in Thornton; he saw fear. Someone is using Thornton. The thirty ton sting is a diversion. Who is expecting the other sixty tons? Roger knew that kind of tonnage severely limited the players. Procuring FBI protection for the ship also required weight. Thornton. He had to flush out the real players. Roger's mind kept refining the questions.

John looked at Paul and asked, "You think Roger is okay?"

Paul turned his head and saw Roger looking out the airplane window. He turned back to look at John, "He's putting together his orchestra." John raised an eyebrow. "Roger told me once if he can form an image of a problem he can begin to solve it. He is a fan of classical music, orchestras in particular. He told me he can see players in a deal like instruments in a music score." Paul smiled at John's expression. "I know it sounds strange, but I bet he is building his score. That will eventually tell him what kind of song we are playing."

John nodded. "I hope it doesn't take him very long."

CHAPTER 31

Todd and Pablo followed the woman and child to a school about three miles away. They watched as the woman and girl moved to the back of the SUV and opened the hatch. Pablo looked at Todd and said, "I'm going to place the GPS. Why don't you park a little closer, and I'll see if I can't help them with those boxes."

Todd nodded his head and said, "Good idea there buddy. You look like a bright young man lookin' for a teachin' job." Pablo laughed.

Todd parked behind the SUV, and Pablo got out and yelled back at him, "I should only be a minute or so." Lisa looked at him as he started to walk by and smiled. She reached in and started pulling the first box to the edge of the door. Jamie was holding both of their purses and said, "Wait Mommy, I can help." She had both of her little arms out and was waiting.

Pablo stopped walking and stepped back, "Ma'am? Could you use a hand with that?"

Lisa looked him over and said, "That would be wonderful. We have the costumes for tonight's school play in here. Are you sure you don't mind?"

Pablo smiled and said, "Not only do I not mind, but my brother can help too." Pablo looked over his should and said, "Hey, bro…give us a hand with these boxes." Pablo looked at Jamie and whispered, "He's lazy."

Jamie laughed, "He's gonna be mad you called him *lazy*."

Pablo smiled at her, "He is lazy. Won't hurt him to help us will it?" Jamie shook her head.

Todd walked over and said to Lisa, "Hi. At your service ma'am." He looked at Jamie, "All these clothes yours?"

Lisa answered for her, "These are for tonight's school play. We just need to take them in that side door and leave them by the stage."

While Lisa and Jamie talked to Todd, Pablo placed the GPS and grabbed the first big box. Todd and Lisa each grabbed a box, and Jamie skipped ahead to open the door for them. Jamie raced down the hall and opened the stage door, to call for someone to come get the costumes. Lisa yelled after her, "Jamie, slow down. Just wait for me." Jamie disappeared through the stage door, and Lisa dropped her box and took off after her. She yelled apologies to Pablo and Todd as she ran past them. "That child does not wait for anyone!" Lisa disappeared behind the door too.

Pablo turned to face Todd. "She is wearing a wedding ring, and there is set of golf clubs in the back that say "Core" on a tag." They had reached the stage door. Pablo held it open for Todd and went back to get the box Lisa had dropped in the hall. Pablo carried the boxes in and placed them next to the one Todd had set on the stage. Todd was saying goodbye to Lisa, and Jamie yelled after him, "Tell your brother you are not lazy!" She giggled and ran onto the stage. Lisa said thank you. Todd and Pablo walked back to their car.

Todd looked at the GPS tracker screen for Core's car and said "He's moving. Lazy, huh?"

They followed Core's signal for ten minutes when Pablo said, "Looks like he's going back to Colby's." They watched Core's SUV pass the parking lot entrance to Colby's and drive down the service road behind the dock storage buildings. They lost sight of his vehicle. The GPS indicated he had stopped. They went back, parked at Colby's, and walked down the service road. Todd said if anyone stopped them they could say they were just looking for jobs. Pablo thought that sounded lame but couldn't offer anything better.

At the end of the service road was a drive that went to a loading zone for the rail cars. Miles and miles of rail cars. There was a small building by a gate that said Port Authority Escort office. Pablo said, "Let's ask in there if anyone is hiring. At least we can establish a cover. Let's say we are only here for a few months. Don't want anything permanent." Todd nodded, and they walked into the small office.

A chubby man sat at a filthy desk talking on the phone. He motioned them to sit. The man finished his conversation, looked at Todd, and pushed his hand out, "Give me your TWIC."

Todd shrugged, "Don't know what you're talkin' about man."

The man scowled, "Transportation Worker Identification Credential, you have to have that before I can get you an escort into the yard." The man looked at their blank faces and shook his head. "What are you doing here?"

Pablo answered, "We were thinking we could get a temporary job on the docks for a couple of months."

"Not without a TWIC. You get that at the Port Authority Office, or Harbor Patrol back there. Then someone has to hire your ass. Once you've done that, I can escort you to your job." He was pointing back in the direction they had come. Todd saw Mathew Core's SUV drive past the window heading back out of the dock area.

Todd looked at Pablo, "Guess we got to do some paperwork first." He looked at the port officer and said, "Hope to see you later." They walked out of the small building and started around the corner only to walk straight into the chest of ponytail man, Mathew Core's buddy.

Ponytail smiled big and whispered, "I know who you are, act casual, I'm ATF."

The Port Officer had stepped outside of the building. He had a menacing scowl on his face, "Everything okay out here?"

Ponytail smiled, "Just gunna show these boys the way back to safety is all."

The Port Officer shook his head, "Just don't go breakin' nobody. I don't need any shit around here today, you hear me?"

Ponytail yelled, "Yeah, I hear ya." He put his arms on both of their shoulders and said, "Walk out of here and don't come back. I need to meet Dance later tonight. I will contact him. Let him know."

Todd and Pablo kept walking after Ponytail stopped. They heard him yell, "Ya 'all come back heeah' sometime."

✳ ✳ ✳

Ellen joined us on the boat and helped us get some better pictures for Roger and Paul. While we were taking pictures, she caught us up on the Director and John now knowing about us. It seemed to me we were becoming a fairly well known secret among fellas with three letters in their job title. Ellen was looking at me.

I said, "What? I just wonder how this many mortals are going to be able to keep us secret. Mortals and secrets don't really go together well. You know that don't you?"

Ellen had a puzzled expression on her face. "I don't understand what you are saying."

Mary, Teresa, and Linda had been listening to my little exchange with Ellen and now had stopped in their tracks and stared at us. I thought maybe I needed to ask this another way. "Ellen, do you trust mortals will keep secrets when you ask them to?"

Ellen looked shocked, "Of course. Why wouldn't they?"

We all started talking at the same time. Teresa looked like she was going to stroke out. She was talking fast and her face was getting red. Linda was trying to talk louder than Teresa. I was just wondering how bad this was going to get if we were depending on mortals. *Ugh.*

Ellen started laughing at us, and we realized she had worked us into a lather again over nothing. Ellen said, "I'm sorry, but you guys are just so much fun to mess with. Your mortal minds keep you thinking you have all the answers to everything. It is really quite amazing. What I find fascinating is that from that delusion, mortals make a remarkable number of discoveries of truths. It is truly amazing." So glad our mortal minds provide her entertainment.

Ellen sat down on a deck chair she had conjured up and invited us to join her. The docks were really a very noisy place. While the deck hands on our boat seemed bored, all around us were trucks and heavy equipment moving cargo to and from ships. The sea gulls were squawking overhead. Ellen said, "Roger has a lot of information to sort through. I don't think I should burden him with any more for the moment. I do think I need to visit the computer techs at the CIA and help Ray with some work. I need you gals to help monitor Thornton. John has ordered extreme surveillance on him, and people are getting in place to monitor everything he does. I will provide a pink aura to the good guys, so you will know when it's safe to leave Thornton alone. You will see the monitoring people in place."

Ellen continued, "There is a skill I wish we had thought to teach you, but we didn't. I don't know if you guys can learn this on your own or not."

Teresa asked, "What is it?"

Ellen said, "There are entities that could help you if you could communicate with them."

We all asked at the same time, "Entities?"

In my mind, an entity is like in economics, the analytical study of the relationships that exist between entities that are numerically measurable. Or an entity is a privately or publically held business, *or* like the Post Office, a congressionally chartered entity for a specific purpose. I started laughing in my head, we are not the only group that can't communicate with Congress!

Ellen was shaking her head, "One example of what I am talking about is what mortals call ghosts."

Mary freaked out! "You want us to learn how to talk to *ghosts*?"

Teresa said, "Cool."

Linda and I just looked at each other. I can't speak for her, but I would rather learn Chinese. I don't even have a good handle on English.

Ellen answered, "In a way, yes, and in a way, no. I think Mambo can help us, but we have a communication problem. I am sure she is willing to try. She can see you, but she isn't hearing you. You can speak to animals, and so can she. I'm just not sure of the link."

I had a thought, "Maybe we could talk *through* an animal. You know, take a squirrel with us, tell it what we want, and have it tell Mambo." I thought that sounded pretty logical.

Mary asked again, "What's *wrong* with you? A squirrel? What's with you and squirrels? Are you going to carry it around like a cell phone to Mambo?"

Oh, that's a thought!

Teresa asked if Mambo really communicated with Spirits.

Ellen answered, "I believe she does. It's not in the way angels communicate, but Mambo is a protector of mortals and has the gift of drawing strengths from her Saints through prayer. You might say Saints work at a closer level to mortals than we do."

Ellen looked thoughtful, "Well, let me think about this while you gals are with Thornton. Try to keep him from accomplishing anything until John's people are in place. You will see pink auras around people and objects that have been secured by John's people. Maybe after that we can work on the Mambo thing."

Ellen left. We decided to try to locate Thornton by his aura. Linda was humming her song, "Hall of the Mountain King." We all joined in as we flew. We passed a group of geese that really gave us some funny looks. Guess they don't appreciate classical music.

* * *

Simon, Thor, Ray, and Jeanne sat in silence just looking at the blank computer screens in front of them. The CIA had taken over the problem. They had been thanked and dismissed in one sentence prior to the caller hanging up. Jeanne had been sitting in what Thor thought looked like a Yoga position. She untwisted her legs, stood and stretched. Thor and Simon both looked away as her top rose exposing her belly. Thor lost every single thought in his mind. Simon announced he was going upstairs to get something to drink. He asked if anyone else needed anything.

Thor hardly heard him. Ray kicked Thor's foot from his chair, "You want some water?" Ray had a smirk on his face. Thor answered no and said he had to go upstairs to make some calls. He followed Simon.

When they were both gone, Ray looked at Jeanne, "You know Thor can't even *think* around you, don't you?"

Jeanne waved him off and started searching the money transactions again. She felt Ray looking at her waiting for an answer. Without looking at him she said, "Get back to work, or I'll have to shoot you."

Tourey had gone home to review the copies of Theodore's address book George had given him and to watch the video. The professionally prepared video provided fifty separate interviews with the children. Each child told a little bit about themselves and their art entry. They ranged in age from six to ten both boys and girls. At the end of the video, like credits, were the names and addresses of each child. The names and phone numbers of club members in New Orleans along with a few out of state members matched the names and addresses Tourey had seen in Bernard Jacobs' book. Tourey placed a call to John.

John answered on the first ring and told Tourey he should be back in New Orleans in about twenty minutes. He asked Tourey to get the video and the papers to Roger's team before then. Tourey answered, "Ok. Will you have time to stop by the library later?"

John answered, "I'm not sure, but I do need to talk to you. Can I call later?"

Tourey said, "I have to talk to you by seven tonight. You might want me to go to a meeting of the sicko club."

Tourey hung up, grabbed his saxophone, and headed towards Mickey's bar. He laughed to himself as he checked to make sure he had a reed in his mouthpiece. It was over a hundred degrees outdoors and the tourists were pounding the sidewalks escaping into the air conditioning at each store front. Tourey cursed himself for not getting Jeanne's cell number from her.

He dropped his hat on the sidewalk, leaned against the corner of Mickey's and played to the building across the street. It was the sexiest, most beautiful rendition of 'Girl from Ipanema' he could play. Tourists stopped in their tracks and threw money into his hat. He was developing quite a crowd.

Halfway through the song Thor looked out the window at Tourey. Cute. Roger had told them at the bar when Devon was shot to get a good look at Tourey. It was John Barry's undercover CIA guy. Thor walked to the top of the basement stairs and yelled down to Jeanne, "Oh senorita, I think you are being serenaded from across the street."

Jeanne bolted upstairs, walked to the window, and laughed at Tourey. She could tell he saw her. She cracked the window open and shook her head at the beauty of his playing. Then she reached into her pocket for the cell number she had gotten from him yesterday.

Jeanne watched as he stopped playing and answered his phone. "Got something for ya. It's under the new welcome mat at your door."

Jeanne chuckled and left the room for the stair-well. Thor watched Tourey play another song to the crowd, take a bow, then go into Mickey's. Thor nodded his head, the guy was good. He turned away from the window and went back downstairs.

Jeanne arrived a minute later and announced they had a video to watch. She put the CD in her player and began thumbing through the papers. She passed the papers to Simon and Thor and asked, "What are these?"

Ray turned up the volume on the CD player, and they listened to the sweet voices of the chil-dren eagerly showing off their artwork. Jeanne dialed Tourey and asked what they were looking at. Tourey couldn't talk so he said, "You got the wrong number sweetheart. Ain't no John at this here number." And he hung up.

Jeanne repeated what Tourey had said and Thor commented, "I think he's telling us to call John Barry." Thor called John and asked about Tourey's gift. John explained the club, the art con-test, the web site, and the probability of what was going to happen to at least one child they were watching on the CD. John told Thor he assumed the names on the pages were suspected members of the club. At least the New Orleans branch. It was national. He told Thor he was going to get more information later tonight from Tourey but would appreciate if they could start gathering information and alert the appropriate field offices. John also confirmed Patterson was probably using the name Bernard Jacobs.

Thor repeated what John had said to the group and they all returned their stares to the screen. Just then a perky little six year old girl announced, "My name is Jamie Core, and I am six years old…" The little girl continued to talk and Simon reached over and hit stop and replay. "My name is Jamie Core, and I am six years old."

Simon stood, "What are the odds?"

Thor had opened his phone and called Todd. "Didn't you say you were tailing a woman and a kid from Core's place?"

Todd answered, "Yeah, we got GPS on that car too. Followed them to a school and helped them carry in some boxes of costumes for a school play tonight."

Thor asked, "Did you get the kid's name?"

"Yeah. Girl, about five or six I think. Name is Jamie."

CHAPTER 32

Dusty had walked about half way home, lugging his box of pencils and pad, and dragging his easel. The heat was oppressive. When a truck blew its horn at him, he nearly had a heart attack. Dusty jumped and leaned forward to see the driver.

"Sorry man, didn't mean to startle ya. You want a ride somewhere?" It was Alan, Jeremiah's nephew.

Dusty answered, "Yeah!" Dusty put his load in the back of the truck and crawled into the passenger seat. He leaned back to let every pore of his skin soak in the air conditioning. He looked at Alan, "Looks like you got a shithouse full of supplies back there. They for your work tomorrow?"

Alan nodded and said, "Yeah, it's a lot cheaper buyin' materials this side of the bridge, save about thirty percent."

Dusty thought about it, "Why would that be? Seems there would be a bigger demand for electrical stuff in the big city compared to Slidell."

Alan shrugged and said, "I guess somebody wants to get paid for driving shit across the bridge. I don't know."

Dusty laughed, "Speakin' of gettin' paid, I haven't even had a chance to cash my damn check from the Feds. You know one of them kidnapped me this afternoon and made me go on a stakeout? I don't think these guys ever stop. Not exactly normal law enforcement for Nawlens." They both laughed.

Alan asked, "Where am I takin' ya?"

Dusty's phone rang. "Just a sec, man," as he looked at the caller ID. Dusty looked at Alan, "I got House of Voodoo callin' me? What the *hell*." Dusty answered, "Yeah?" Alan watched Dusty's facial expression go from quizzical to fear in one minute. Dusty was yelling into the phone, "How'd you get my number? What the hell? Hang on a minute." Dusty cupped his hand over his phone and told Alan, "This Voodoo lady wants me to take her and a friend to Mambo's place. NOW! Says she'll pay me a thousand bucks! I ain't gonna live to spend all this damn money."

Alan started laughing, "Why don't I go too, and we split it? We can take Jeremiah's boat, I'm going there now anyway. Tell her she has to get to Jeremiah's now, and we won't stay long 'cause we don't want to be on that swamp at night."

Dusty looked at Alan like he had lost his mind, "Are you crazy? Did you forget the snakes?"

Alan answered, "Jeremiah said the snakes were bad because of the storm rolling in. The storm is gone now. Heat of the day we should be fine. I gotta tell you man, I think there is somethin' to this Spirit stuff. If this lady is a Voodoo somethin', I'm not wantin' to piss her off."

Dusty rolled his eyes and went back to his phone, "You still there Voodoo lady? You got a gun? You best bring it. Lots of snakes out there. You bring lots of ammo too!" Dusty spent another ten minutes giving Spicey directions and finally snapped his phone shut. "Why you smilin' man? You're goin' too." Alan turned his truck to head for the bridge to Slidell. Dusty looked out the window, "I can't believe I'm doin' this again."

Roger placed a call to the Director and explained his plan. The plan was bold and unconventional and it would require extraordinary cooperation of agencies. It would also require authorization from the National Security Council. With the computer threat facing the CIA right now, Roger felt the climate was perfect for obtaining approval.

The Director agreed and stated, "You were correct about your expanded authority leaving

Thornton no room to protest. He didn't say a word, but I can tell you he is not happy." Roger asked the Director to pave the way for the technology and manpower he was going to need. Roger wanted to put his plan in place tonight at nine o'clock. The Director agreed to make the arrangements and call back with an update.

Roger rejoined Paul and John at the work table on the jet. According to the pilot they would be landing in ten minutes. Paul said, "I just got an update from Thor. They are working on notifying our field offices about this club and opening those investigations. Also, Thor has been getting some surveillance information on Core. I called Agent Spelling in Virginia and told him you needed him in New Orleans by seven o'clock this evening. Frank Mass will have his guys there. Our team is still in the dark."

Roger gave a short nod and looked at John, "Do we know if this computer issue is under control?"

John shook his head and said, "No word yet. I imagine there is a lot going on. I did get a call from the Director of OSI. Evidently we are on a first name basis now. Never met the man. I have been given some expanded authority myself for this mess. Seems he and your Director are BFF's now."

Roger chuckled, "It certainly narrows down who gets blamed if any of this goes bad."

Paul smiled, "I told John about your problem solving technique of building an orchestra. Did you make any progress with that?"

Roger answered, "As a matter of fact I did. I think we are going to host a dress rehearsal and see who shows up."

John asked, "At what point do you know what you are dealing with?"

Roger laughed, "When I see the percussion section show up, I get a feel for it."

John and Paul looked at each other and John moaned, "I sense a somewhat unconventional plan coming."

Roger emphatically nodded his head, "Exactly." He proceeded to tell them his plan for the weapons deal. When Roger finished, Paul and John were silent.

Paul pushed his chin out in his nervous twitch, "One thing really worries me. I like it."

John said, "I don't think this has ever been done before."

Paul asked, "And that surprises you?"

The three men laughed, and Roger asked them to help him make the appropriate calls to prepare for the plan. They had about five hours to prepare. Roger called Thor and told him they should be at the Star Ship within the hour. Roger wanted Thor to have the entire team there if possible.

✳ ✳ ✳

Spicey was knocking on the bathroom door. "You can't stay in there forever. Come on! I told that man we be there directly." Spicey listened at the door and heard sniffling. "You in there cryin' again? Girl! You make me miss my Mambo boat, and you be finding plenty more to cry about!"

The door slowly opened, and Sasha stuck her head out. She frowned at Spicey and said, "Somethin' real wrong 'bout havin' to threaten your best friend to go see Spirits!"

Spicey straightened her shoulders and said, "I agree with that. You should be grateful I'm making sure you get protection too. Costin' me a thousand dollars, plus this here basket of food for Mambo. Willie's out front waitin' to drive us there. Hurry up." Spicey had walked to the door and was holding it open for Sasha to leave. Spicey had the keys to lock up ready in her hand. "You got your gun?"

Sasha's eyes got big, "Why we need a gun to go to Mambo's?" Spicey thought better 'en tellin' Sasha about the snakes.

"Case we get mugged somewhere. We in Nawlens girl. You should take your gun like you take your lip gloss!"

The name on the brass plate over the door said William C. Thornton. Teresa pointed and we all went through the wall and floated across the room from him to get a good look. Thornton was looking at his computer screen with a scowl on his face. He pulled on his tie to loosen it some and answered his ringing phone. "How long will it be? This is ridiculous! I haven't been able to email or log into anything." After a minute of silence he barked, "What was your name? You ask your supervisor how patient I need to be. I want this up and running. While we are on topic, my cell phone still has static. How hard is it to get a decent cell phone?" Thornton slammed his office phone down and started pacing the office.

Thornton quickly turned around and hit an intercom button, "Sam, come in here. Bring your cell phone."

Mary said, "I bet he wants to make a call. We'd better stop him!"

Linda asked, "How?"

Teresa had moved by the door. I was worried she was going to attack this Sam guy. Sam gave a quick knock on the door as he opened it. He had a bright pink aura. Thank god! He handed Thornton a phone and said, "Here you go. I got you a brand new phone and transferred your sim card for you. You have a secure frequency and should be okay." Sam nodded and left the office. Obviously Sam was a good guy and had been brought into Ellen's security loop.

Thornton walked to his door and looked down the hall. An electrical contractor was working on something and a janitor was wiping down the elevator. We could see pink auras around them both. Thornton walked over to the window at the end of the hall and looked down into the parking lot. He opened his cell phone and dialed Mathew Core.

"Everything okay on your end for tomorrow?.... Good....Keep me posted." He placed a call to Thomas. "Everything is set."

✳ ✳ ✳

The Director had his driver waiting outside his hospital room to take him home. Security guards flanked the door, and the Director could see a motorcade waiting outside near the Government exit. The Director had been on hold for five minutes already. Finally his contact answered the phone.

"Okay, sorry about the wait but it isn't easy getting the Security Council to agree to anything these days. The CIA computer issue your people discovered went a long way in making people feel the need to cooperate. Frankly, scared the crap out of them. That could have been a real mess. I understand it is under some control now.

"I have the Naval Satellites ready for 8:45 tonight, all cell towers and land lines in a fifty mile radius are on tap order. All radio frequencies, including government are to be monitored and recorded. That wasn't easy, by the way. I have a no fly zone for non-military, and we have Coast Guard, National Guard and Navy personnel at ready for nine o'clock tonight. We are in the process of adding the triggers you provided to the communication filter. We have over a thousand communication and computer staff, between four agencies, ready to go online at 8:45. What am I forgetting?"

The Director chuckled, "What's left?"

* * *

It looked to us like Thornton had pretty tight security. We called Ellen to see if she had found some way for us to communicate with Mambo. Ellen told us to go to Mambo's. Ellen had invited a Saint she knew to meet us there to try to help us. Ellen said, "In this Saint's mortal life she had been a teacher. Maybe that will help. Take your sticky notes with you. They may help too."

Mary said, "I was a teacher in mortal life too. That doesn't mean I can teach someone how to talk to ghosts!"

Linda said, "You aren't a Saint either. Maybe Saints have an easier time talking to the Mambos of the world."

I started giggling. I couldn't stop. Mary looked at Teresa, "Don't even ask her what she's laughing at. We probably don't want to know." Hey.

I couldn't help it, "Can you imagine any circumstance in mortal life, where Linda would have made the statement that maybe Saints have an easier time talking to the Mambos of the world than we do? Don't you see how bizarre that sounds?"

Teresa pointed out, "Name something that has happened since we died, including dying, that hasn't been bizarre." Hmmmm. Good Point.

We flew to Mambos and entered through the wall. I knocked. It looked like the Statue of Liberty standing in the middle of the room. It was Ellen's Saint friend. I was worried her dress was going to catch fire she was standing so close to the open pit. Mambo rolled her eyes. I wonder if anyone told her she was getting company tonight? She didn't look real excited to see us again. She doesn't have a TV or anything. What does she do? Mary elbowed me. I think to stop me from thinking. Nice try.

The Saint said something, but it was all mumbled and sounded like she was in a tunnel. Was that even English? I looked at Linda who put her finger over her lips to signal me to be quiet. I didn't say anything!

The Spirit walked over to Teresa and held her hand. She mumbled something. Teresa tried to imitate what the Spirit had mumbled. I couldn't stop giggling. This was going to take a while. Mary frowned at me and told me to do something with my mouth. What? I started humming Linda's song, Hall of the Mountain King. I figured it would give my mouth something to do besides giggle. The Saint turned and smiled at me. She started humming it too. I couldn't believe she knew that song!

Pretty soon even Mambo was humming it, and at the end Linda yelled "Yeah!" The Spirit yelled

"Yeah." We all yelled, "Yeah." What just happened? The Spirit looked at Mary, "I think we have made a spiritual connection through music. Can you understand me now?"

Mary answered, "Perfectly!"

Wow, that was like the space ship in Close Encounters!

Mambo asked, "What is happening to mortals in this swamp?" We all started talking at once to answer her question. I looked around. The Spirit was gone. Huh. Mambo had us all sit around the fire pit with her and tell her about Devon and Patterson, the pedophile club, the weapons bust, the computer mess, and how I finally learned to fly right. Then she let us ask her questions about her life. How she lived in the swamp, what she could do to help people, how she dealt with black magic voodoo.

Suddenly there was a quiet knock on the door, and Spicey walked in with Sasha hanging onto the back of her skirt and following. Mambo gestured for them to sit, and she started chanting. Spicey told Mambo about Spirits visiting with her the night before and how they had her send an email to some government email address. Spicey wanted to know what was going on and wanted Mambo to confirm in front of Sasha that it was true.

Mambo looked at us and Teresa said, "It's true. We needed her to send information she obtained for Tourey to Agent Roger Dance."

Mambo looked at Spicey and said, "The Spirits needed you to get information to an FBI agent named Roger Dance in order to help some children. The man you spied on is a murderer and intends to harm more people. Your friend Tourey is helping too." Sasha went pale. Mambo continued, "Tourey needs to be very careful. Some very powerful men will want to stop him from finding out too much." Mambo lifted an amulet from around her neck and handed it to Spicey. "Give this to Tourey and warn him that Lucy is alive." Mambo gave Sasha and Spicey each a small sack of potions. Mambo looked at Spicey, "These did not begin as gum drops."

Sasha started to slide over in a faint. Spicey grabbed her shirt and held her up. I looked at Linda, "What gumdrops?" Mambo looked at me and winked. Huh?

Mambo pinched some powder and threw it into the flames. It briefly ignited and a sweet smell filled the air. Mambo began chanting and then stopped, "You may leave." She resumed chanting. Spicey and Sasha backed out of the hut, bowing and waving to Mambo.

We decided to follow the boat back to the mainland to make sure the snakes or alligators didn't bother anyone. Spicey had her gun out ready to shoot anything that moved, and Sasha had her head in her hands moaning. Mary was laughing at Sasha, "She cracks me up! Can you imagine if she had been on one of the boats before the storm? Oh brother!"

✳ ✳ ✳

Roger, Paul, and John arrived at the Star Ship. Roger was glad to see Thor managed to get the whole team there in time. Thor updated everyone on what had happened in the surveillance of Mathew Core. He left out the part where he kissed Dusty. Simon and Ray brought the team up to speed on the computer crisis that was still in progress.

Ellen had provided a video disc that was ready to view. Ray handed Paul the control knowing Roger was challenged with technology. Roger had obtained permission from the Director to show his team everything Ellen had provided, including the video of the Director being poisoned. Roger wanted the team to have all of the information available. He wanted them to feel invested in his plan.

"In Indy this team discussed a problem in the New Orleans field office. Also, a larger, unknown danger responsible for the bombing of Core's computer lab, and the subsequent deaths of four federal agents. The first two films I am going to show you are courtesy of OSI and took place this morning, shortly before lunch." Roger nodded to Paul to begin the video. Paul stopped at different points and explained who they were looking at. When they got to the part of the video with the Director clutched his chest, there was a gasp in the room. Paul stopped the film.

Roger said, "The Director was given a drug that would make him sick, not kill him. What Thornton didn't realize is the drug most likely administered to the Director at the hospital, would have reacted violently and caused the Director's death. We notified the hospital to run tox screens before treatment. The Director is fine and is an active part of the plan we will be discussing shortly."

No one in the room asked questions or commented. Roger could tell they were processing the seriousness of what they had seen. Paul played the video, with audio, of Thornton calling Roger. Again, everyone was silent.

"There is a weapons sting planned for this Friday here in New Orleans. Our field office here was told Mathew Core is brokering the deal as an FBI sting. When we called the field office for the arrest of Mathew Core and the seizure of his building, SSA Spelling contacted Thornton for instructions. Spelling knew Core was the FBI broker in the weapons deal. Thornton gave Spelling Core's phone number to warn him of the raid and told Spelling we were outside of the loop and risking the sting. Our field office and Spelling have been told thirty tons of weapons will be sold to the Zelez Cartel in exchange for cocaine this Friday."

Now there were comments. Thor shouted, "Thirty friggin' tons?"

Simon asked, "How many agents were going to do this sting?"

Paul answered, "Seven. Four local and three out of Virginia."

Pablo asked, "Isn't that a little light? Do we know how many cartel people will show up?" Paul answered no.

Nelson asked, "Where are the weapons now?"

Roger answered, "On the dock. They were transported on a ship from Algiers to the U.S."

Simon asked, "Why wasn't this ship stopped before port?"

Paul answered, "It has been protected."

Everyone asked, "By whom?"

John answered, "FBI."

Roger watched their facial expressions and their interactions with each other. He listened to them discuss what they had seen so far among themselves. This was a very good team. Probably the best he had ever assembled. Roger was quite sure the heavens had played a part in all of that.

Roger cleared his throat and everyone stopped talking. "That description of the sting is what the seven agents assigned to the sting have been told. With the assistance of OSI and some clever surveillance, this is what the truth is." Roger nodded to Paul, and Paul started showing the videos of the ship, its cargo, and the dock holding building. Roger looked at Paul, and Paul stopped the film.

"You are looking at *ninety* tons of weapons and ammunition divided into thirty tons of cargo on the ship, and sixty tons loaded into the holding building. Paul is passing out lists of exactly what we have determined is here." Roger let everyone study the lists. When everyone had finished, he asked them for their questions.

Thor raised his hand, "Okay. We were told about the ship and the thirty tons, right? That is supposed to happen Friday with the Zelez Cartel.

Do we have any idea who the rest of this is for? If Core knows we are coming Friday for the sting, isn't he afraid we'll find this too?"

Roger looked at Simon who also had raised his hand, "You are saying that sting was a cover to bring in weapons for another purpose and another buyer using FBI protection? That deal must be scheduled for tomorrow."

Jeanne had her hand up, "What is Mathew Core to the FBI? We have a murder warrant on him, and we are using him to broker weapons deals?"

Roger looked at Ray, "Tell the team who has been trying to reprogram the CIA super- frame all afternoon."

Ray looked at the group, "Jason Sims, Mathew Core's guy."

Simon looked at Ray, "*That* is who we were watching all afternoon? How could that be? He's in custody." Roger looked at Paul. Paul played video of the telephone conversation of the man trying to find out who authorized the release of Jason Sims.

Simon asked, "When did that happen?"

Paul answered, "About the same time the Director was being poisoned. Around eleven this morning."

Roger resumed talking, "You have all asked good questions. I have devised a plan I believe minimizes the risks to our agents and increases our opportunities to identify the real players. My plan is a cyber-communication sting. We are going to take all of the weapons tonight and have them moved to the secured naval yard down the dock.

Instead of guessing who might be involved, we'll see who screams.

"We are capturing all communications within a fifty mile radius of New Orleans from 8:45 this evening, Wednesday, until late Friday. We have Navy satellite support. All cell communications, land lines, government bands, and bank wire activity are being filtered with our list of trigger words and names. Over a thousand computer staff will be monitoring communications and reporting to us and the Security Council. We will have the Coast Guard, Navy, and National Guard at our disposal. Any comments?"

Everyone was stunned. John had been quietly listening and now stood. "We suspect the information we get from this will uncover some very nasty players in some very high positions of authority. This operation required the authority of the National Security Council to designate this plan a Martial Law operation."

Thor stood up, "HOLY CRAP! You got this all done this afternoon?" Roger, Paul, and John just started laughing. John answered, "Obviously some very important people are investing faith and their reputations in the success of this operation."

Roger continued, "We are going to meet at eight this evening at the field office and show the weapons film only to those agents. I will outline the plan, and we will suit up to arrive at the docks at 8:45. It should be fully dark by then. I need you all rested. If you can at least get in a good nap sometime between now and eight, it would be a good idea."

Simon raised his hand, "I am thinking there may be some resistance to this change of strategy since this sting belongs to the local boys?"

Roger nodded, "I don't expect they are going to fully understand. I have been given authority by the Director today to expand my designation to include Mathew Core and anything he is involved in."

Thor looked at Simon and said, "Roger just put a very big target on his back. Core and anyone he is doing business with? That includes our Deputy Director." Simon nodded.

Jeanne looked worried. "I agree with Thor. I think one of us should be assigned as your personal security."

Roger smiled and said, "I think I'm safe for now. Let's worry about getting this done tonight. I am not minimizing your concerns." Roger smiled. "I appreciate them. Make no mistake, we are *all* staring down the devil. Maybe now we find out what he really looks like."

* * *

Simon gestured to Thor he wanted to talk to him. Thor came over and Simon said, "You want to get a quick bite before we all take our naps?" Thor answered yes and suggested they invite Pablo, Jeanne and Nelson too. Thor overheard Roger tell Ray to keep working on the money transfers and do whatever he wanted tonight. It was geek's day off.

Everyone agreed to meet at a little place over by Jackson Square. Dusty had told Thor the place had good food, just looked like a dive. Simon and Thor hailed a cab and the rest said they were going to walk. When Simon and Thor arrived, they sat at a large table in the back of the room facing the door and ordered soft drinks. When they were alone, Simon said, "This is a brilliant plan. I am worried it is going to work."

Thor was nodding, "Makes you wonder why it hasn't been done before doesn't it?"

The waiter asked if they were eating, and Thor told him to come back when the rest of the group arrived. Thor whispered to Simon, "Ninety tons? What the hell? It takes some balls to do that and get an FBI protected ship."

Simon answered, "Roger knows he is up against the Deputy Director of the FBI, at least one drug cartel, and Core, so far. Whoever is supposed to get these weapons will certainly start making calls when they find out it's all gone."

Thor lowered his voice to a whisper, "Didn't he say the National Security Council has declared this a Martial Law operation? What the hell? That sounds like overkill, even for ninety tons of weapons."

Simon answered, "I don't think the weapons are the reason this is going down. I also think the excessive manpower is to discourage retaliation.

Roger did that for us. I think Roger was able to pull this off because this bunch breached the security programs of the CIA." Simon rubbed his chin, "Sims must have left himself a lot of back doors to the super-frame when he was their top geek. I don't know how you protect from that. Ultimately a human is going to have an opportunity for access if they are determined. If you are the top geek, who is going to find your dirty deed?"

Jeanne, Pablo, and Todd walked in and came over to sit down. The waiter brought their drinks and everyone ordered. Jeanne was the first to speak, "I'm still worried about all of this being done on Roger's name. I think we need a plan to keep him covered."

Simon answered, "I agree with you, but we don't know what he is doing half of the time."

Thor shook his head, "I'm telling you this guy is spooky. How did he figure this out in one day? How did John get a camera into the Director's office and CIA holding where Sims was being held?"

Pablo added, "Or the film of the weapons and the guards. Did you guys see the guards over in the corner? Not kids."

Todd leaned forward, "Ground to air missiles? High velocity ammo? Is there a war in the States I haven't heard about?" He was whispering, but Simon waved for him to lower his voice even more.

The glass doors to the street opened and Spicey, Sasha, Dusty, and Alan came in and sat at a table. Dusty was casually looking around the room when he saw Thor. Thor smiled and blew him a kiss. Dusty held a menu up to cover his face. "*Damn!* You see who's here?" he hissed at Alan.

Alan said, "Oh shit! This is dinner time!"

Spicey and Sasha looked at each other. Spicey looked at Dusty, "What's got your shorts in a bunch boy? They're obviously cops over there."

Dusty lowered his menu, looked at Spicey, and whispered, "They're having a dead body with every meal today!" Spicey scrunched her face and shook her head. She figured Dusty was doing some bad drugs.

Sasha's mouth fell open, and she looked at Dusty, "I don't have to eat no dinner. We just figured it be nice to get you guys food for takin' us to Mambo. Fact is, I ain't hungry at all no more." She laid her menu on the table and pushed her chair back.

Alan said, "I don't need anything. My wife will be fixin' stuff at home."

Dusty quickly stood up and said, "Let's go then. No sense hangin' out if nobody's hungry."

Spicey asked Dusty, "Are those guys FBI?" Dusty nodded. Spicey said, "You give me one minute then I'll be ready to go." She walked over to the table of agents and asked, "You be FBI?" They all nodded. Spicey asked, "Any of you named Roger Dance?"

Thor frowned, "No, but we know him. Why?"

Spicey shoved her hand in her purse and the entire table tensed and reached for their weapons. Spicey froze. She very slowly said, "Let's not get excited. I want to give you a business card to give to Mr. Dance." Spicey took a deep breath and scowled when she exhaled, "No wonder you guys are havin' a dead body with every meal! Pretty *touchy* about your feedin' time, aren't ya?" Spicey handed the card to Thor. She turned around and walked out to meet the others at the sidewalk.

Thor looked at the card and handed it to Simon. "Now you tell me that's not spooky." The card said: House of Voodoo, Let the Spirits Protect You. Spicey's phone number was on the bottom of the card.

Jeanne was only five blocks from home. Pablo said he would be there later. It was already starting to get dark. The noise from the city was growing distant. This part of town was seeing the signs of crime moving in. Broken street lights, a few boarded up homes. The beautiful music from the clubs in the Quarter replaced with the steady bass sounds from cruising car stereos.

Jeanne felt his presence before she ever heard anything. Behind her, ninety feet. She kept walking at her normal pace. Behind her, fifty feet. She reached the porch of her home, unlocked the door, and walked in. She turned on a light near the door, then ran to the back of the house and outside again. She could see his form in the shadows leaning against the neighbor's house.

She circled the neighbor's house, kicked off her boots, and silently ran through the grass. With the stealth prowess of a panther she leaped behind him and put her knife to his throat. "Freeze. FBI."

"Not again." It was Tourey.

Jeanne started laughing, "What are you doing Mr. Waknem?"

Tourey answered, "Trying to protect your ass." A truck turned the corner down the street and Tourey motioned for her to take cover. He whispered, "Dude in that truck took an interest in you when you left Star Ship. Followed you to dinner and now here."

The truck was rolling very slowly toward them and pulled to the curb about five houses down. Jeanne could hear the truck door open and barely close again. Tourey motioned for her to back up. Jeanne frowned at him and shook her head. Tourey pulled a gun from his waistband and looked at her knife. He raised an eyebrow. She knew he was asking "Is that all you got?" Jeanne frowned.

They watched him walk up to Jeanne's front door, pick the lock and enter. Jeanne noted how fast he had entered her home. Tourey whispered, "Do you have an alarm system?" Jeanne shook her head. They worked their way back to Jeanne's house and caught glimpses of the man inside. He looked very military except for his long ponytail. He was obviously fit and did a quick search of the house. Satisfied he was alone, he turned on the television and sat in Jeanne's chair. He had placed a gun on the armrest and checked his watch.

Tourey motioned for Jeanne to walk away with him. "You better call your brother and warn him you have company at home." Jeanne nodded. When she reached Pablo, he was just getting ready to leave. He told Jeanne to stay outside. He was pretty sure the guy was ATF and wanted Roger. Jeanne relayed what Pablo had said to Tourey.

Tourey told her he would stay until Pablo arrived. Jeanne frowned at him, "I can take care of myself." Tourey shrugged and walked away.

Pablo called Roger and told him about Ponytail meeting them at the dock. Roger picked Pablo up on the corner, and they drove together to Jeanne's house. When the car pulled up, Jeanne walked to the curb and greeted them. "He's in my chair."

Roger chuckled, "Let's see what he wants." They walked up to the house and walked in guns drawn. Ponytail had his hands in the air.

"Name's Zack, code 46 ab5. ATF. Check me out." Roger dialed and received confirmation. Jeanne and Pablo stood flanking Ponytail and holstered their guns.

Roger asked, "I assume you are undercover. How long have you been with Mathew Core?"

Zack answered, "Not quite a year. Look, I'm way out of my element with this guy and I haven't been able to reach my contact for five days. I don't know what is going on. The ATF has no clue what this guy is capable of. Mathew has been keeping close tabs on me since you guys got to town. I can't stay now either. I don't know if my cover is blown or he's just jumpy. He calls me when he wants something. Otherwise I have no idea what he's doing." Zack handed a card to Roger, "I need you to contact this man and tell him they need to get a handle on this fast."

Roger asked, "Why didn't you contact our field office?"

Zack answered, "I don't know who I can trust in New Orleans. I hope I can trust you." Zack put his gun back in his waistband and said, "Watch your back man. This dude is on the edge about something." They watched him leave, and Roger said, "You guys try to get some rest. I'll see you later."

* * *

Tourey had to speed to get to the country house before eight. He had spent too much time in town. Damn. She had gotten him again. Was he going soft, or was she just that good? Why was ATF undercover working with Mathew Core? Pablo had said the guy wanted to talk to Roger. John had said it was going to be a big night. Maybe at some point this would make sense. Tourey brought his thoughts back to the task at hand. He was right about Patterson. He could *feel* it.

Tourey wanted to get cameras and bugs installed before the club had their meeting. He hoped Patterson hadn't mentioned his new security man to anyone. Patterson answered the door and looked annoyed. "Can you believe a manor as beautiful as this with no caviar in the kitchen? I don't dare go shopping do I? Well, there really isn't time now anyway. It's just humiliating is all." Patterson walked away and fussed with some drapes.

Tourey walked in and shut the door behind him. "What room do you have your meeting in? I want to check out the windows and exits for you." Patterson looked puzzled but pointed to a large drawing room on the left.

Patterson asked, "You don't think the FBI knows I'm here do you?"

Tourey answered, "I would bet not. It doesn't hurt to be sure though. I'm going to check around and make sure there aren't any listening devices or anything."

Patterson said fine and asked if he was going to stay for the meeting could he stay outdoors. Tourey answered he would be gone before the guests arrived. Patterson seemed happy with that answer and left the room humming.

CHAPTER 33

Seven p.m. at the New Orleans FBI field office, Roger introduced himself to SSA Spelling and asked if they could speak privately for a minute. Roger found a small office and shut the door. He told Spelling about their concerns about Thornton, and the attack on the Director. Roger told Spelling that as a result of new information, the Director had expanded Roger's designation to include Mathew Core and any criminal associates.

Roger also explained that Mathew Core had an associate who ran a computer lab for him. The FBI had seized it yesterday. He also explained the lab had been bombed just hours later and two CIA agents had been killed. Roger explained Core's computer guy had been mysteriously released today and had begun an attack on the CIA super-frame.

Spelling just said, "Damn."

Roger nodded. "I am taking over this weapons case. I believed the Friday sting is a cover for a larger deal. I think we have devised a plan to identify the real players in this through a communication sting." Spelling had a puzzled expression on his face and Roger continued, "We have verified there are actually ninety tons of weapons sitting at the dock, since yesterday.

Spelling was in shock, "Ninety tons? What are we doing tonight?"

Roger smiled, "We're going to steal some guns and see who gets upset."

After the videos of the weapons had been shown to everyone, they all suited up in their assault gear and piled in two large panel trucks. Roger reminded them that all communications were going to be monitored from 8:45 on. At 8:40 the trucks sat just outside the dock area and idled. It was already pitch black outside. The air was still thick and sticky with humidity. Roger could taste the stench of the docks. He didn't want a single warning call to go out before they were ready. At 8:46 he gave the order to drive to the target holding building.

Roger motioned for his team to surround the building. When the team was in place, Roger spoke into his shoulder radio, "Light 'em up."

The loud metallic click of mega lamps blared light over the entire area. Four Navy helicopters with spotlights flew in to section off the corners of the dock yard. Coast Guard ships were shinning spotlights on the ships at dock and at least three

hundred fully armed National Guard officers surrounded the loading zone and the docked ship.

The scene was surreal, like a movie set. Roger
hoped the excessive display of force would discourage any retaliation. He lifted the electronic megaphone, "This is the FBI. You are surrounded. By
the authority of the President of the United States,
Martial Law is now declared. Come out of the
building with your hands up. Any resistance will
be met with deadly force. I repeat, do not resist.
You will not survive."

The service door to the target holding building opened, and a man centered himself with
an AK47 leveled in front of him. He had thirty
rounds in him before he cleared the threshold of
the door.

Roger spoke again, "I repeat. Come out with
your hands up. Resistance will be met with deadly
force." Two men, with their hands up, slowly walked
out of the doorway screaming, "Don't shoot!"

Roger heard Paul shout from behind the building, "Hands up! Freeze!"

Jeanne and Thor were guarding the side door
of the target building when Jeanne yelled, "Three
o'clock!" Thor spun around to look behind him
and the doors to the building next to them opened
and five men were walking out with their hands in
the air, shouting, "Don't shoot!"

Thor leveled his gun on them, "What the
hell?" Jeanne had moved up to flank Thor and
was smiling. Thor shook his head and yelled, "On
the ground! Arms out. Legs spread." The men

complied and four Guardsmen ran over to secure the prisoners.

Thor and Jeanne worked their way to the back of the building to assist Paul. Paul had cuffed what looked like a hobo, who claimed he had been at the side of one of the rail cars relieving himself. Roger's megaphone demanded he freeze and put his hands up. By the stains on his pants, he had not finished his business.

Paul chuckled, "I let him put the family jewels back before I cuffed him. I'm sure he will be released to tell his story a few hundred times."

Jeanne could hear Pablo yelling, "Get on the ground!" a couple of buildings down the line.

Nelson yelled, "Rail cars!" Simon and Roger spun around to see two red rail car doors sliding open and three men with their hands up jumping down to the ground.

As the team secured the buildings and rail cars the Harbor Police and National Guard rounded up the prisoners. Jeanne chuckled and pointed for Thor to look at the ships. The Coast Guard had three ships where the crew was standing with their hands up waiting to be boarded.

Roger walked over to Paul and John, "Can you believe this?"

John said, "I wasn't sure what was happening when every building out here had guys walking out with their hands up. Even the friggin' train cars. I guess we call that a bonus."

The Coast Guard Commander asked Roger to show him the weapons that needed to be moved to secure storage. Roger told him some were in the cargo hold of the ship, so Roger told him to just take the whole ship. Then he walked him into the building. Pablo and Todd had already taken the lids off a dozen boxes and were shaking their heads.

The Coast Guard Commander was stunned. "I was told there would be a lot. This is tons!"

"Ninety tons to be exact," Roger said. "Do you have your equipment ready?" The Commander nodded, "That we do." He said something into his radio, three fork lifts came around the corner and entered the building, and two large semi tractors were waiting outside the loading door.

Roger said, "I know there is more here than you expected. We don't even know yet about these other buildings. How much time is it going to take you to have all of this broom clean?"

The Commander smiled, "Two hours. Including making the ship disappear. I am glad you got us the navy boys." The Commander's facial expression turned serious, "What the hell has been going on? Right under our noses. Do you know who is responsible for this?"

Roger said, "I'm hopeful we're going to find out. At least it's a beginning. We can't fix a problem we can't identify." Roger pointed to the rail cars and the other buildings, "We didn't know about these. There is a problem at the docks that appears systemic."

The Commander nodded agreement and said, "You're right. We can't fix a problem that isn't identified. Seems this is an opportunity to shine a light on some people."

Roger had the team split up and document what else had been seized. Paul and Roger went into the rail cars.

Paul whistled, "Guess how much?"

Roger asked, "Can I guess a range?" John had joined them and was listening.

Roger said, "I guess between thirty and forty tons."

Paul said, "I think more like forty- five."

John smiled and said, "Fifty- two tons of Yosemite weed. And someone by the name of Juan is having a fit on the phones already. So far your plan is working."

SSA Frank Mass walked over, "Please tell me my guys don't have to do the paperwork on this." They all started laughing. Frank said, "You guys are something else. I have never heard of a weapons sting where we steal the weapons."

Roger smiled, "Let's just hope it works. I don't see any reason our guys need to be here anymore. Coast Guard and Navy promise this whole area will be broom clean in two hours. Our people need rest. Tomorrow may be interesting. I will pass on any information I can to you as I get it Frank."

Roger told Paul and John he was going to let everyone know they were done for the night. John looked down the long row of buildings. It looked like broad daylight with an entire army at work.

Paul laughed, "He can sure get people movin'."

* * *

Mathew Core turned his phone on to take a picture of Jamie and her classmates taking their final bow in their play. She was beaming and Mathew and Lisa both felt she had stolen the show. They had no idea Jamie could sing as well as she did. The audience gave a standing ovation when Jamie bowed on her own. Lisa moaned to Mathew, "You think she's been hard to live with up until now?" They both laughed.

Mathew noticed he had missed a call. He told Lisa he would meet them outside at the car. When he was clear of the crowd around the building, he listened to his message. "Carter is DEAD. FBI raid. I'm turnin' myself in man." The message ended.

* * *

Jeremiah sat at his little table and wiped a tear from his wrinkled cheek. He looked around his home and saw a television, an air conditioner, and at least twenty bags of staples. Alan had told him he realized today what a treasure Jeremiah was. A treasure. Jeremiah wiped another tear. Alan was a good boy. His dad would be very proud of him. Jeremiah was proud. He stood and began sorting through the food Alan had brought. In the morning he would take some of it to Mambo. He held up a box that said, Fruit Loops. Jeremiah frowned and tried to imagine what a fruit loop could be. He put that in the bag for Mambo. Let her figure it out.

Roger took a hot shower, put on the hotel robe, and looked at his e-mails. He only opened the one from Kim. "Call me when you get home. Anytime." Roger smiled, microwaved himself a cup of soup, and carried it over to the bedside table. He turned the TV on low and dialed Kim. They talked for over an hour. When Roger finally snapped his phone shut, he felt as if finally he'd had a few moments of normal life.

Kim's sense of humor was exactly the mental teasing that kept Roger entertained. He chuckled a couple of times later, remembering parts of their conversation. Kim always knew how to make him laugh by making mother-in-law jokes. Roger turned off the bedside light and stared at the darkness. His heart felt warm and full. He had promised Sharon he would love again. Roger smiled as he laid his head on his pillow.

* * *

Jeanne walked into the living room in her PJ's. "How am I supposed to sleep with this racket?"

Pablo had a drill and was on the floor installing an alarm system contact at every door and window in the house. He looked up, "I'm too worked up to sleep. I have to do something! I'll be at the back of the house soon, it shouldn't be as loud." He started drilling again, and Jeanne came over and placed her hand on his shoulder.

"It's nice you worry about me, but I can take care of myself."

Pablo put the drill down and stood up, "We don't know what kind of nest we kicked tonight. We'll probably start finding out tomorrow." Pablo had a very serious expression on his face, and Jeanne could tell he was troubled. "I keep thinking you have a good point about Roger. He'll have more than one target on him now." Pablo picked his drill back up and looked at Jeanne, "Did you see Roger shoot that guy tonight? I think you have competition. He had the first shot, and it was right between the eyes."

Jeanne started walking back to her bedroom, "Don't forget eight o'clock breakfast. You better set an alarm it's already one."

Mathew Core made his way past the fences and barricades of the dock staying in the shadows. He was looking for a guard about his size. He found one, easily over took him, and pulled him to the tall weeds in the dark shadows. He wasn't dead, but he would be out for a while. Mathew put the guard's uniform on and took his weapon. He walked to the side of the building and inched his way forward until he could see the dock below. The ship was gone. He blinked his eyes and looked down the dock. Maybe it had been moved. He couldn't see it anywhere.

He leaned against the building back into the shadows. The docks were crawling with National Guard, Coast Guard and Navy personnel. The FBI sting was set for Friday, and that ship had FBI protection. Mathew looked out at the dock again. The ships he could see looked nothing like the one that held his cargo. He retreated back into the shadows. What now?

He would have to improvise and hold back thirty tons from tomorrow's deal. He couldn't risk the Friday sting not going down. Not with the FBI involved. He couldn't imagine where the ship had gone. Who screwed up? Mathew knew his name was all over this thing, with people you didn't want to piss off. Last week he had decided this was his last deal.

Mathew forced himself to focus and take a few deep breaths. Thirty tons of weapons don't vaporize. He would find out what happened and get them back. Somebody screwed up was all. Worse things had happened, and he had fixed them. He would have to find some way to explain the shortage for tomorrow's deal, and replace thirty tons of weapons fast. He inched his way to the service door of his building and unlocked it. He slipped in the building, closed the door, and turned on his flashlight. He couldn't believe his eyes. The building was empty.

Mathew closed his eyes and leaned against the wall. His mind was racing back to his phone message, *Carter's dead. FBI raid.* Mathew made his way back to the tall weeds in the shadows and saw the soldier he had punched was stirring. Mathew punched the soldier again. He put his own clothes back on and made his way to his SUV. He took out his phone and dialed Carl.

Thornton answered on the second ring, "Do you know what time it is?" Carl spat.

Mathew spoke very slowly through clenched teeth, "Tell me about the FBI raid tonight at the dock."

Carl sounded genuinely surprised, "What dock? What raid?"

✳ ✳ ✳

Paul was in the Marriott restaurant reading the Times-Picayune account of last night when Roger joined him. The waitress came over, poured them coffee, and asked if they were ready to order. Paul told her they might have a few joiners, and they would wait. Paul gave the front page to Roger. The headline read, "Extreme Heat Warning" with a subtitle that read: *and we're not talkin' Nawlens weather.*

Roger looked at Paul's facial expression and laughed. "How many factual errors?"

Paul answered, "Well, to start, according to an unnamed source we killed over fifty people."

"What?" Roger started scanning the article. He looked up, "I don't know whether to laugh or get mad. We don't need the added pressure of an entire city out to get us."

Thor sat down. He was carrying a paper. He looked at Paul, "Did I go to the wrong raid?" Roger started laughing.

Ray joined them moments later, and everyone remarked they couldn't believe he was out of the dungeon. Ray told Roger the front of their building was getting a face lift because someone had painted 'Pig House' all over it along with a target symbol.

Roger looked at Paul and said, "That's what I mean. Now we have these cracked out punks on us too."

Paul said, "Local PD is getting caught with their shorts down on this. Is there any way we can help them out? We have this Martial Law window until

Friday, and the retaliation to last night might go on for a while. A lot of people are not gettin' their coke or weed today."

Roger looked at Paul, "I know you are right, I just hate the idea of adding any more to our plate. Maybe I can get the field office to do this."

Roger placed a call to SSA Frank Mass, "The local paper here has a few facts wrong about last night. We have already seen some retaliation this morning. Four hundred Guardsmen are deployed here that we can keep until late Friday. Should we offer them to local PD? Might be a way to turn this into lemonade for them. You would have to supervise this. I'm going to have my hands full today." Roger listened a while, laughed a couple of times, and ended by saying thanks.

Roger told the group, "The field office got a face lift too along with a couple of their cars. Frank likes your idea Paul. He is going to have John help him set it up."

Jeanne, Pablo, and Simon all came at the same time and found seats at the table. Jeanne sat next to Thor again.

Thor frowned at her, "When you yelled **three o'clock** last night I almost did my shorts again. You have to find a less intense way of screaming at people."

Jeanne chuckled, reached over, and patted Thor's cheek. "Why don't I just pick up a good supply of shorts for you, so you can quit bitchin'." Thor eyes opened wide, and he was actually speechless. Ray was smiling ear to ear.

Pablo looked at Ray, "What's so funny?"

Ray shook his head and buried his nose in his menu. He peeked over it to look at Jeanne, and she winked at him. He was right!

CHAPTER 34

Roger and Paul were looking over the banking data Ray, Simon, and Jeanne had been working on. Simon reported the five million dollar payment Devon had made was going through a clearing account owned by a corporation. Simon was having trouble identifying the account from any other sources. Roger remembered the mind reading papers on Jason Sims had mentioned a Global Corporation.

Roger said, "Try the name Global Corporation."
Simon keyed it in, "That's it!"
Ray asked, "Isn't that the name of the company that owns the car Core was driving yesterday? I know Pablo said something like that. We were in the middle of the CIA mess." Ray was sorting through a stack of notes, "Yeah, right here.... Global Corporation."

Simon said, "Now that I have the company name, I can get a Fed ID number and trace the original deposit back." He looked at Roger's puzzled face. "I can see where the money came from to get into Global Corp's account. Once I'm in Global Corp's account, and I see everything they have done with money, this will be our proof line." Simon was now sporting a very big smile, "I have a very good feeling about this."

Roger chuckled and looked at Jeanne, "We think Patterson and this club are positioned to start another round of kidnapping if Tourey's information is correct. Can you compile background on each of the kid's families on that video? We need to alert the parents about the risk without harming the investigation. Then find out what the other field offices are doing. I want lists from every single club contest the entries came from. We have a chance to stop this bunch right now."

Paul walked down the stairs and gestured to Roger. Roger followed him back upstairs. Thor, Pablo, and Todd were waiting. Roger could tell from Paul's expression that he was going to say something he wasn't going to like.

Paul started, "John just called from the local PD. He is helping Mass organize a Martial Law type sweep of some of New Olean's really bad areas since they have the Guard to help. The local PD is begging. The Governor is begging. They claim it is the least we can do for them after last night. Frank says the Guard is well trained in this and wondered if we could spare any manpower to captain these teams."

Roger sat down and looked at all of them, "Street gangs are kids with AK47's. They are going to react with the mentality of drugged out scared kids. This is a potential blood bath. I don't like risking you guys in an environment this unstable. A Martial Law sweep was not what I had in mind when we offered military support for retaliation security."

Thor could tell Roger was angry. He cleared his throat and said, "I would guess the local PD sees this as their one chance to clean out a large part of that element from this city. I am only speaking for myself, but I don't have a problem helping out." Todd and Pablo nodded agreement.

Roger said, "Then let's get over there and plan strategy. We have an hour at best to plan. Thank God we're dealing with military." Roger looked at Thor, "I imagine the local PD feels exactly like you said. They are right. This kind of power would never be made available to them under normal circumstances. All we can do is our best. You guys will captain assault teams. Stay back and let the Guard do their job. I won't give the go unless it looks solid."

Roger motioned for Paul to step away from the group. "You are not going to be a part of this. I need you here." Roger looked at his watch, "The Director plans to come to this area at two o'clock this afternoon, so we can trade notes on what has been happening. I need you to take this meeting if I get hung up somehow."

Paul frowned and kept his voice low, "I don't disagree with you often, do I?" Paul raised one eyebrow and stared at Roger. "This time you're wrong. You stay here, and I'll go." Paul started to check his weapon.

Roger's voice was firm, "That was not a debatable statement. I need you here. Figure out what the hell we can do to protect these kids." Roger opened the door to the stairwell outside and motioned for the others to follow him. He did not look back at Paul.

Paul watched Roger leave. Roger had no business going into a street war in the middle of all of this. Paul cursed, called John, and told him to keep Roger out of harm's way.

John was livid, "What the hell is he doing? I don't want him here!"

"Don't ask Roger for his team and expect to get them without him." Paul snapped his phone shut.

John moaned, "What have I done?"

In the car Roger called the number Zack had given him. "Jesus! You could have given me a heads up last night!"

Roger answered, "No, I couldn't Zack. Are you safe? I made the call you asked me to, but I think your people are underwater right now. You may be on your own."

Zack answered, "Then I'm comin' over to you. There is no reason for me to stay under now."

Roger answered, "The more the merrier. I'm on my way to the local PD. Meet me there. We're going to throw a couple of block parties and could use your Intel."

"Great."

* * *

Jeanne looked at Simon and Ray, "Awful quiet up there. Where did everyone go?"

Paul had been coming down the stairs and answered her question, "They went to help the locals play cops and robbers in the hood."

Jeanne asked, "Pablo?"

Paul answered, "Everyone but me. I guess I'm grounded."

Simon could tell Paul wasn't very happy about the turn of events, "You know Roger wouldn't trust this mess to just anyone. You should be flattered."

Paul smiled, "You know how it is. We've been partners a long time. I think my job is to watch his back. He thinks my job is to carry on with this case.

Bring me up to speed on the sicko club. At least we can try to save these kids."

Jeanne got a determined look on her face and asked Paul, "Did you know Mathew Core's daughter is on this video?"

"No. I did not know that." Paul pushed his chin out, "That is some kind of sick irony. Daddy sets the bad man free to harm his own kid."

They decided first to get the background info finished on the New Orleans art contest kids. Then start directing the field offices around the country to send their investigation results to them in real time. Simon said Tourey thought they held their contests about the same time but staggered the abductions. Ray decided to compile a grid on last year's pattern, so they could identify likely scenarios.

Simon asked Paul if he could continue to follow Global Corp bank accounts. Paul felt at a loss of what to do. He wanted to be busy. Simon asked him, "I need help with this unless you have something else. I could go twice as fast if you got on that laptop." Paul nodded. Simon showed him what needed to be done.

Paul was only half listening.

✳ ✳ ✳

Teresa looked at Linda and asked, "Did you hear that? I just heard Ellen tell us to go to the New Orleans Police Department."

Linda said, "I didn't hear anything."

Mary looked at me, "Did you hear anything?"

"Nope."

Teresa said, "I think we better go. She just said she is in some kind of communication web and super busy. She can't leave."

Sometimes this stuff is really fun. Sometimes, not so much. I am a law abiding citizen, well angel, but police stations would not be on my short list for tourist stops. We went inside the police station, and there was hardly a place to stand. It was packed with all kinds of men and women in uniforms.

Mary whispered, "I think something important is going to happen."

Teresa pointed across the room, "Roger is with John and some other guy."

Roger walked to the front of the room. He used a speaker and asked for quiet. He asked for a show of hands of police officers who had not yet completed their weapons designation. The majority of the New Orleans officers raised their hands. Turnover was so high that more than half of the city troops were new at all times. Roger said, "Those of you who have not been certified will not be participating in the assault operation. You will be needed to assist Navy and National Guard personnel for transport of prisoners and securing contraband. You are not to leave the zones we have marked as 'C' zones. Are there any questions from this group?"

One young officer raised his hand, "I've been waiting two years for this kind of opportunity to clean up this city. I think it's our city, and we should all be involved."

Roger looked at him and asked the room, "Who else feels this way?" About twenty officers raised their hands. Roger said, "Keep your hands up. John, take note. You men will not be allowed to leave this building. That is precisely the attitude that is going to get someone killed." There was a mumble, but no one raised their hands with a question.

Roger continued, "Martial Law does not mean there are no rules. Any officer here that doesn't respect the orders of his team Captain will face a swift and harsh court martial. This is a military operation. Obey orders. We represent the United States of America. It has been determined there is a deadly threat to our civilians, on our soil. Unfortunately this threat will involve persons who are not even adults yet. They will not make good choices. Try not to kill them, but do not risk your own safety.

"This is morning. We may catch them off guard. A perimeter will be established by Navy around these four neighborhoods. Four National Guard assault teams will be doing a house to house sweep. Each search team will have an FBI Captain and an arrest unit to clean up for them. Each arrest team will have a contraband team to identify and remove any items seized. Search, identify, and move on. Be safe. We will be broadcasting our purpose and intentions to calm the fears of the law abiding citizens in these neighborhoods.

We will be asking them to open their doors and allow a peaceful search of their property. If a house does not have the doors open, we will make one additional request. We will then make a forceful entry.

"We've been given three hot spots to check based on ATF information. Those spots will be hit first. If gunfire is exchanged, the captains will use megaphones to alert the neighborhood of our purpose and to keep the good citizens that live here calm. Any questions?"

A young officer in the middle of the room had raised his hand. Roger pointed for him to speak. "Sir, I don't know if there was a mistake made or not, but one of these hot spots is a neighborhood church. I know the address from when I was a kid and went there."

Roger nodded and said, "I am told there is close to one thousand kilos of cocaine in the basement." Roger could hear the gasp in the room. "Any more questions?" No one raised their hands, so Roger told them to check the list they were given and find their assigned Captain for orders. Roger instructed the National Guard Commander to get his people and vehicles in place and secure the target neighborhoods perimeters immediately.

John and Roger stood off to the side of the room and were joined by Zack. Zack said hot spot one and three should be hit at the same time. The church would be heavily guarded by neighboring buildings. It was the same gang. Roger left to pass the information on to the commander in charge.

Zack whispered to John, "He sounds like a son of a bitch. Pretty hard ass."

John looked at him, "He's not. He wants these guys scared and careful. He didn't want this today."

Zack smiled, "I read the paper. Did Roger tell you I defected?"

John nodded, "Yeah, and I'm going to find out why you were left out to dry."

Zack asked, "Who are you?"

John answered, "OSI."

Zack looked surprised and said, "This is a friggin' alphabet soup. How do you know who's in charge?" John pointed to Roger. Zack asked, "For all of it?"

John nodded, "Oh, this hasn't even *begun*." And he walked away.

We were all talking a mile a minute. We weren't sure what we should do. Teresa said, "Look. Roger has four teams going into four neighborhoods right?" Uh oh. I think I see where this is going. Teresa continued, "I think we should each take a neighborhood, and just move mass or mortals or whatever we can to help the good guys. Maybe we can go into the houses before the good guys and actually stop the bad guys. We could push their guns, so their aim is off!" Teresa was so excited she was wiggling while she floated above us.

I looked up, "Will you settle down a little? My gosh you are about to come unglued. I vote we do what Teresa says."

Mary and Linda looked at each other, and Linda asked, "Did you really listen? She wants you to fly around bad dudes and actually *do* something."

"I know. I guess Roger's speech kind of got to me. There are good people trapped in these neighborhoods who we will be helping. I like that."

Linda just said, "Huh. Who would have thought Vicki would turn into a Ninja angel?" Mary was laughing so hard she started choking. I guess I have to prove myself. The neighborhood Roger selected for himself and John was already surrounded by National Guardsmen, trucks, and jeeps. It looked like a military operation in some third world country. This was the United States. How sad.

Todd and Pablo were riding in open jeeps and crossed into the center of their subject neighborhood. Todd waited for the assault team to assemble near them and then picked up the megaphone. "This is the FBI. Martial Law has been declared. Every home will be searched. Please open your doors for the search team. Any home not made available will be entered by force."

Pablo heard the first bullet flash past his face. The ground in front of the jeep was pelleted with bullets from an automatic weapon. One of the National Guard team members yelled second story, second house. The shooter exposed himself in the window just enough that they got off a kill shot. Another shooter replaced the fallen shooter and was also killed. Moments later the front door opened. Seven men, and one woman carrying a baby exited the home through the front door.

One of the men grabbed the baby from the woman and pulled out a hand gun. "Get back! I'll shoot the kid!" Todd motioned for the assault team to back up. They slowly moved back as a Navy assault team advanced from the back. The man was screaming and turning in circles, his gun pointed at the screaming baby's head.

Three armed men came from a house two doors down. They began shouting and firing at the assault teams. Pablo cursed at the total disregard for the lives at stake. Roger was right. These were punk kids. All three were shot immediately. The man holding the baby was still wielding his gun and screaming.

Todd walked toward him. "Put the baby down, gently. You will not survive an encounter with us. Take your chances with the courts. Don't die in the street. Don't kill an innocent baby."

The man pivoted his head and saw the staggering number of troops around him. He dropped the gun and lowered the baby, who sat in the street crying. Todd had the arrest team take the man away and a guardsman get the child. It was a vision Pablo knew he would never forget. That baby sitting in the filthy street, rubbing its eyes and crying, surrounded by chaos.

Pablo went into a house and found a little old lady crying. She was in a wheelchair and had struggled to get her door open. He started to comfort her because he thought she was scared, but she shooed him away and said she had prayed for them to come.

Eventually the entire neighborhood had been searched. The National Guard had stopped numerous vehicles and several persons trying to leave the area. There was nowhere for them to go. The net was tight, and it was efficient. Their block was clean.

Todd called Thor to see if he needed help. Thor answered that his block was clean.

Thor called Roger. No answer. Thor called Pablo back and told them to meet him by the church with their assault teams. That was where Roger was supposed to be. Thor told his assault team to take him to the church. That was probably the hot spot since the cocaine was there.

Thor's team arrived in hell. Gunfights were in almost every building surrounding the church. These thugs would die trying to save their cocaine. Pablo and Todd's jeep pulled up next to Thor. Pablo yelled, "Any idea where Roger is?"

Thor yelled back, "As close to the coke as he can get." Thor's assault team positioned itself to enter the church. Thor had the other team take the house next door. He could see flashes of gunfire through the windows and hear screaming. An old woman had stepped out on her porch.

She waved her cane at Thor, "Bad men are in my house."

Thor yelled, "Shit!" He motioned for two assault team members to come with him. Thor ran up the front steps, tackled the old woman as gently as he could to get her down. A gunman came from her foyer hall with an AK47. Thor was staring down the barrel. A second later the man fell, a gunshot wound on his forehead. Thor turned around, and Pablo was standing behind him.

Thor tried to comfort the old woman some and told her to please just stay low and in the corner of her porch. She nodded, scared out of her mind. Thor went into the building. He heard short spats of gunfire from the back. Then silence. He made his way to the back of the house. Pablo was standing over a dead kid hugging a gun. Pablo looked at him and said, "This is sick man." They both left to head for the church.

The shooting had stopped. Thor saw Roger and John exit the back door of the house next to the church. Roger was shaking his head and holding his arm. John turned and yelled to Thor, "You brought back up just in time. We were outgunned on this one."

One of the clean-up crew came out to report to Roger. "I don't think people really lived in these houses. There were a couple of bunk rooms, but I think they were just here to guard the dope. The walls were lined with weapons, loaded and ready at every window. They would never have run out of ammo. I think our count at this place is over ten, anyway. I'll check the place next door." He walked away. Roger said, "I think the average age here is twenty. How stupid."

Thor asked Roger, "What's wrong with your arm?"

John answered, "He got nicked. I'm taking him to the hospital as soon as we check out the basement of the church."

Roger frowned, "We've got EMT's at the perimeter line. This is just a flesh wound."

John said, "Whatever."

Zack came from inside the house next door holding a blood soaked cloth to his neck, "I want to see this basement for myself. I've only heard about it."

John said, "Then you can ride with Roger and me to the hospital. Let me see your wound."

Zack pulled the cloth away, and John could see it was just a flesh wound. John shook his head, "I don't want to hear the body count from this."

They made their way down the church stairwell to the basement floor. At the bottom of the stairs were two doors leading from the landing. One had kid artwork taped on the door and a sign that said Bible School. The other door had a large lock. One of the guardsmen brought some large cutters down and snapped through the lock.

Roger swung the door open to view floor to ceiling shelves all stacked high with shrink wrapped blocks of cocaine. John whistled. Zack pointed to the far wall where the shelves looked virtually empty, "They were expecting a shipment of weed today. The Manio cartel grows in our National Parks and sells in our big cities. No worries about the borders anymore."

Roger said, "I think we got their shipment last night. Does the name Juan Diez mean anything?"

Zack shook his head, "No, but I'm sure word has gotten to his people by now. That should have been a big shipment. They distribute from here all the way up the coast."

John said, "Fifty-two tons."

Zack shook his head, "Someone is going to pay big for that being gone. This cartel has a presence in almost every major city in the U.S." Zack looked at Roger, "At what point do we admit we lost this drug war? They are growing this shit in our National Parks, using our legal guns to protect themselves, and selling to our kids in our cities."

Roger answered, "I don't know the answer to that Zack. I am assuming Core has a relationship with this cartel or you wouldn't know about this church."

Zack answered, "Where do you think they get their guns?"

We decided we would stay with the National Guard troops a while longer. Roger had told them to patrol the entire area in two jeep teams and enter any dwelling that looked suspicious after giving the Martial Law notice. The word must have already been out on the street because every neighborhood they slowly cruised through, people opened their doors and waved at them. Some had made up little flags they were waving. One lady on her porch pointed to the house next door. After checking, two men were arrested and a variety of guns and dope were confiscated. I felt really good seeing the faces of so many people who were happy this was happening. One house had a stereo blaring Etta James singing "Oh Happy Day." Three people were on the porch dancing.

Teresa said, "Some of the officers I was around earlier said now the city could enforce some new landlord regulation. He said if there is criminal activity in a house, the city can seize it, and the landlord loses his permit to rent. The landlord can either convert the property to single family occupancy, and sell it, or forfeit ownership to the city. After Katrina a group of famous movie stars pledged to take seized properties, fix them up and give zero interest mortgages to deserving families. The program has been in place, and somewhat working, but the city has had trouble getting rid of landlords."

Mary said, "How cool."

Linda asked Teresa, "Have you heard anything else from Ellen?"

Teresa answered, "She checked in to make sure we were okay and tell us we did a good job." Teresa looked at Linda, "Ellen said you pushed a gun right out of a bad guy's hand!"

Linda smiled, "Yup. By the time he picked it up again, the good guys were in the room."

We decided we would be the most help if we split up and each took a jeep of guys to protect. I sat on the hood like an ornament and pretended I was the general of some army of good guys saving the people of the world from evil. What a blast!

CHAPTER 35

Mathew sat on his porch sipping sweet tea and staring at his laptop. Jason wasn't answering. This morning's Times-Picayune was folded so just the headline stared at him. Extreme Heat Warning. *No shit.* Mathew tried to stay calm. Carl should call back soon. This was just as bad for Carl as it was for him. Thomas would have to get involved.

Mathew could hear sirens in the distance. He heard the National Guard had seized entire blocks of the city. Well, wasn't that what the citizens had been asking for? The crime page posters in the paper would have a field day today. He keyed in the Picayune website and started reading the comments on the article about the dock raid. They were certainly polarized. Some people praised the action, and some people said it was proof our government had taken away all of our rights.

He heard a noise behind him and saw Lisa coming.

"I'm going to do some errands and get groceries. Anything special you're hungry for?" She sat on his lap and gave him a hug.

He gave her a tender kiss and said, "I have everything I could ever want with you and Jamie." Mathew smiled, and Lisa got up to leave.

She mussed his hair and said, "We kind of like you too." And left.

She had barely shut the door when the phone rang. It was Carl.

Mathew answered, "Yeah."

Carl said, "We need to restructure all of this for a later date. I don't know what happened yet, but Dance is behind it. Look, Thomas thinks it will go easier if we don't have to worry about Dance or Casey."

Mathew replied, "Are you ordering a job? I want to hear specifics from Thomas. Who is explaining this postponement to our customers?"

Carl answered, "You're the *fixer*. Fix it. I'll have Thomas call if you insist. He won't be happy." Carl hung up. Mathew watched Lisa pull from the driveway and wave goodbye. He waved back. This was as good a time as any to finally stop.

Mathew dialed the FBI field office. "Give me the number for Roger Dance."

✳ ✳ ✳

Tourey called Jeanne and told her John wanted the surveillance info from last night's meeting at the country house streamed to her computer. Jeanne gave him the id info and asked, "How sick is it?"

Tourey answered, "See for yourself. I have identified everyone who was there last night. I'll email you that too. You guys have been busy! I see the whole city has patrol jeeps snailin' through. How'd the good guys do?"

Jeanne answered, "Haven't heard yet. We did hear there have been a lot of arrests, some dead and injured. Fingers crossed."

Tourey said goodbye and thought about John in the middle of all that. He knew John was hoping to just get his time done, retire, and get his family back. He sure hoped nothing had happened.

Tourey's phone rang, it was Spicey. "Hey beautiful. What you need?"

Spicey answered, "I know you're a busy man, but I need you to come to my place quick. I went and saw Mambo yesterday, and she brought your name up. All on her own. Can you come now?" Tourey answered yes, sent the data to Jeanne, and grabbed his keys. How would Mambo know his name?

✳ ✳ ✳

Dusty was blasted awake by a megaphone blaring through his bedroom wall demanding he open his front door or face an assault team. *Will this horror ever stop? What the hell?* Dusty opened his door to what looked like six swat team dudes. They walked through his house, looked in his closets, said thank you, and left. Dusty scratched the back of his hip as he watched them go to his neighbor's place. They definitely weren't selling cookies. He stepped outside and retrieved his morning newspaper from the bush. He unfolded it and read the big bold letter headline, **'Extreme Heat Warning'**. He sat on his front step in his tee shirt and boxer shorts and read the article. *Holy Crap!*

"Senior Manio you have a call." The older man held the phone out in front of him as far as he could. He was bowing and noticeably nervous. Jesse Manio answered, "Yes?....Thank you." He put the phone down and keyed in the web address for the Times-Picayune. He read the article. He had already been notified of the development last night. He had people in place. He placed an international call, "What has been done to correct your problem? I am not a patient man. I expect delivery."

Jesse dialed his operative in New Orleans and listened to his reports of what was happening on the streets. He decided to obtain some additional insurance.

"I have it!" Simon's raised voice startled everyone. "The six million dollars originated in a Cayman account under the name of Bernard Jacobs. It went to Global Corp's clearing account where Devon kept one million. He then sent the other five million through Global's clearing account, directly into Global Corporations Cayman account. I have Global's account number and all I have to do now is print off the activity." Simon looked at Paul, "How far back should I go?"

Paul wasn't sure. "I know we want proof the escape was paid from this account, go back at least to the December arrest date. Can you do that?"

Simon answered, "I'll try. I'm not sure how long this bank keeps records on line." A few minutes later Simon's printer was printing away. Simon said, "I am going to try to print all of last year. Where's our extra paper?" Ray pointed to an open shelf unit at the far side of room. Simon walked over, grabbed a ream of paper and said, "This guy had some weird termites down here. They only ate in the cracks of the paneling."

Jeanne laughed and told him to move aside. She pulled a knife from her boot, flicked it from her wrist, and stuck it in the wall next to Simon. Directly in the crack. She looked at Paul, "He's a blade man."

Ray pushed out his bottom lip and said, "Dang girl. Good throw."

Simon yanked the knife from the wall, brought it back to her, and chuckled, "Do you have trouble getting dates?"

Jeanne laughed, "Actually I do. I never even went to a school prom."

Ray was stunned, "Look at you! You're kidding, right? My god woman, you are gorgeous."

Paul said, "I saw a gal for a while who was gorgeous. She told me the same thing. She said men were afraid to ask her out. Afraid they couldn't keep her."

Jeanne asked Paul, "Why did you stop seeing her?"

Paul answered, "I think I was afraid she was way out of my league." Jeanne raised her eyebrows. Paul said, "Huh."

They heard the guys coming in upstairs. Jeanne ran up the stairs. Paul heard her ask if anyone had been hurt. Simon said, "I want to hear this." Paul and Ray followed him upstairs. It didn't take long to find out Roger and some guy named Zack were the only injuries for the good guys. Roger was the last in the room. He grinned at Paul and simply said, "Just a scratch."

Roger waited for everyone to find a seat or a place to stand, and then he asked if he could have their attention for just a minute. The room grew quiet. Roger said, "I wasn't a fan of this neighborhood sweep idea, but I think it went very well. In hind sight, this was a good decision and probably the only opportunity for this city to have something like this." He looked at John, "Thank you for putting this together so well." John shrugged. Roger continued, "Paul, John, and I will meet with the Director at two o'clock this afternoon to go over the communications from last night and this morning. I have no idea what he may have to say since we need to speak face to face. It is already eleven-thirty, so I plan on going back to my hotel, and take a shower, and just get a sandwich after. Probably across the street. If anyone cares to join me the bureau will pick up the tab. I want our focus now to be nailing Patterson's club. I also would like everyone to meet Zack. He is currently ATF and has been undercover with Mathew Core for almost a year. He will be helping us from here forward and probably working out of the field office."

Paul asked, "Do we know what the numbers are on this sweep?"

Roger answered, "John and Frank are compiling them now at the field office. We should hear later."

Roger excused everyone to do whatever they wanted, and he would try to have assignments before two o'clock for them. Paul and Roger left together and started walking to the hotel. It was the first day the heat wasn't over a hundred degrees. Roger asked, "You mad at me?"

Paul answered, "A little."

They walked a few more steps, and Roger asked, "You going to get over it?"

They walked a little further, and Paul smiled, "Probably."

Roger's phone rang, "Dance." Roger stopped and cupped his hand over his other ear. The caller was Mathew Core.

"I have just received an order to get rid of both you and Paul Casey. I can stall, but I'm not the only contractor out here. I want to trade information for my family's safety. I'm looking for a way out."

Roger signaled to Paul he needed something to write on. Paul searched his pockets and found a small slip of paper. Roger asked, "What is a number where I can reach you?" Roger was writing. "Who ordered the hit?"

Mathew answered, "I got the call from William C. Thornton. He gets his marching orders from someone else. I have that information too."

Roger looked at Paul, "Will you share that information?"

Mathew answered, "I will share that and a lot more, but I want my family safe. Soon." He hung up.

Roger looked at Paul, "That was Mathew Core. Thornton put a hit on both of us."

Paul smiled, "Oh, now you're going to include me?"

✳ ✳ ✳

John spent twenty minutes on the phone with his director. One call was intercepted from William C. Thornton ordering what sounded like a hit on Roger and Paul. OSI didn't know the identity of who Thornton had called, yet. OSI was sharing the information they were getting with the FBI Director, and John was told he would get quite a bit more at the two o'clock meeting.

John called Roger to warn him. John's phone rang again. It was Tourey. Tourey said it was important and could he meet him ASAP at their regular spot. John agreed, grabbed his keys, and headed for Loyola University Law Library.

Tourey was waiting at the entrance and signaled for John to join him over in the park area. They found a secluded bench, and Tourey said, "Do you know what a Mambo is?"

John looked surprised, "In the last couple of days I've heard the name a lot."

Tourey said, "I have a friend who went to see Mambo yesterday. Mambo gave her this amulet for me. By name. Mambo told my friend to tell me Lucy is alive."

John's eyes opened wide, and he said, "Tell me this again, slower."

John and Tourey just sat looking at each other. They both knew what it meant. John stood to leave. "All we have right now is the words of a Mambo, but it fits with some things I have heard." John shook his head. "I'll try to dig around."

Tourey asked, "I know this isn't my deal, but I gather the FBI seized guns last night at the dock, and somehow obtained a Martial Law status. Can you enlighten me on how that came about?" John laughed and told Tourey everything except about Ellen and the Gals.

Tourey asked, "How the hell did you guys find out all of this, and then get the cooperation of every agency in the soup, so fast? This is a communication sting? What is secure?"

John answered, "Nothing. No cell phones, no government lines, nothing. We think our problem is us. Some of us. That's what I mean about Lucy. We may find out something soon anyway."

Tourey shook his head, "Gonna try to kill me again, aren't ya?"

John chuckled, "I told you Roger's team would turn this into the Wild West if they had to." John scratched his head and looked at Tourey, "I kind of promised the Director of the FBI, Roger could borrow you."

"You did what? You borrowed me from CIA. Now you are lending me out to the FBI?"

John laughed, "Just for this Patterson crap."

Roger and Paul went over to the Star Ship after lunch and helped Jeanne compose a script to use with the parents of the children in the art contest. Jeanne offered to post the script language on the FBI site for other offices to use. Roger asked her to post a request that personal notifications be made today. Roger had a feeling the New Orleans contest was one of the last ones, and decisions were probably being made.

Jeanne said, "Tourey gave us an address of a country house where he says Patterson is hiding. A club meeting was held there last night. He had the video and sound from that meeting streamed here, but we haven't had a chance to watch it yet. He also gave us names of everyone who was there."

Simon volunteered, "I watched it. I got back from lunch before the rest of you. It will make you sick."

Paul said, "Let's see what you've got." When it was over, nobody spoke for a few minutes.

Roger finally said, "Did you catch the reference to a Monday delivery from Los Angeles?"

Simon answered, "I looked it up. They have a club branch there and had thirty contestants. Their contest was two weeks ago. They mentioned at the beginning of this meeting that their video had been sent to their other branches. I think their rule is you can't pick one from your area."

Roger looked at his watch and shook his head, "Let's divide ours up and get to these parents. Paul and I have to leave to meet the director. Thor is in charge. We should be back fairly soon. Simon, if you could keep following up on Global Corporation, it may prove to be our only proof material on Mathew Core."

✳ ✳ ✳

Mathew Core was sure Tourey was something. He had spotted Tourey, followed him to Loyola and watched him talking to John Berry on the bench. Mathew pointed his listening monitor at them. He wasn't getting feedback. They were too far away to read lips. He knew John was working with Roger's team. Tourey had to be undercover for someone.

Mathew decided to use the opportunity to search Tourey's home. Find out what might be there. Somehow he had to find out where his guns were and what the plan was. In Tourey's library he found several notes scratched out about Bernard Jacobs. Mathew didn't care if they found Patterson, he had bigger worries.

He hacked into Tourey's computer and checked his web browser history. CIA. That made sense. He saw Tourey had spent a great deal of time on an art website and read about some children's art contest. Mathew started to get a bad feeling. He followed each site Tourey had been in. Last year three murders, previous winners. The same names were on one of Tourey's notes. Senator Rolland Kenny. One of Tourey's notes said, "Bernard stashed by Rolland".

Mathew was starting to think Tourey was only interested in what Patterson was involved in. Maybe as soon as the FBI got Patterson they would leave. That would certainly solve a few problems.

Mathew saw a download called, "Meeting of the sicko club," had been downloaded late last night. He clicked on the download and watched it play. He saw Jamie describing her art piece. He couldn't believe his eyes. When had this happened? He saw the men in the room laughing and talking about how she was going to be a winner for sure. At the end of the video Tourey had pasted a message. Property owned by Senator Rolland Kenny, with an address. Mathew's blood was running cold. He wrote down the address.

Mathew heard a car door. He quickly made his way to the back of the house and opened the back door when he heard the key in the front. He was gone. Mathew called Lisa when he got back into his SUV.

She answered, "Hi handsome."

Mathew knew from her voice everything was still okay. His mind was racing on how to protect Jamie without alarming Lisa. God why was this happening now? He would send them on a vacation somewhere.

He asked, "You and Jamie available for lunch?"

Lisa answered, "We are just leaving the grocery store and have to drop off books at the Library. Is this a date?"

Mathew answered, "Yeah, I'll meet you at the house in about an hour."

Mathew headed toward the dock area. There was a chance Carl had figured things out. Maybe the rest of the weapons were on trucks and in safe keeping. Maybe the ship was back. Something had to make sense. Ninety tons of weapons couldn't vanish into thin air.

Tourey stood in his foyer, something had his hairs up. He walked into his library and saw his computer was on. He walked through the house knowing whoever had been there was gone. He had a pretty good hunch.

CHAPTER 36

Jeanne made sure her list of kids included Mathew Core's daughter. She went to the work places of the parents on her list and discussed the FBI's concern that their child had been exposed to a pedophile group that was under investigation. She gave the web address for the FBI and explained to them there were numerous safety booklets they could download and other helpful information. She assured each of them they were a priority. She gave them hotline numbers and a promise someone would keep them posted on the investigation.

Jeanne sat in the SUV provided by the field office and collected her thoughts. The FBI didn't know if Mathew's wife Lisa was aware of his occupation or not. Jeanne also knew this visit could be dangerous if Core was at home or came home while she was there. It struck her that Mathew Core's home was only two blocks from where Devon had lived. She shuddered at her memories of him. It was only yesterday she had shot him.

Jeanne found the house and parked at the street. It was a pleasant looking two story with flowers and landscaping that showed pride of ownership. An SUV was parked in the driveway. From her notes of Pablo's surveillance report, she knew the car in the drive was Lisa's. She could hear the commotion a mile down the street from the National Guard vehicles, and she could see the flashing lights. Traffic had been terrible getting across Canal Street.

As she walked to the front door, she noted that this house, like so many others, also had an alley running along the back of the property. Core's driveway connected the street in front to the alley with a two car garage built off to the side. Jeanne admired the layout. Core must have purchased the lot next door at some point and tore down the house to build the garage.

She knocked on the front door and a very perky, smiling Jamie answered. Jeanne said, "Hi. Is your mommy home?"

Jamie answered, "Yes, I will have to shut and lock the door and go get her though. That's the rule."

Jeanne smiled, "That is a very good rule. I'll wait." After a brief wait Jeanne heard the door unlock, and Lisa met her with a smile.

"Can I help you?"

Jeanne kept her voice low and showed Lisa her badge. "Hi Lisa, I am with the FBI, and I need to speak with you about a matter of great importance. May I come in?"

Lisa's eyes opened wide, and she asked, "Is Mathew okay?"

Jeanne answered, "Yes, this has to do with Jamie."

Lisa stood back to let Jeanne in, "Jamie?" Lisa directed Jeanne to take a seat in the living room, and she asked Jamie to go to her room until she was called. Jamie didn't look very happy, but she quickly minded. Jeanne could tell she was a well behaved child. The house looked comfortable but not pretentious, and Lisa looked like the typical soccer mom.

Jeanne started, "Lisa, do you remember Jamie entering an art contest recently through the library?"

"Of course, I helped her frame her picture and take it there."

Jeanne continued, "I can only give you limited information because this case is under investigation. We are investigating a pedophile group that is using these contests to actually select which children to abduct."

The look of horror on Lisa's face was unmistakable. She was choking back tears, and her voice was barely audible, "If you know this, can't you stop them?" Little spurts of sobs were catching in Lisa's throat and breaking through. She put her hand to her mouth.

Jeanne reached out and touched her other hand, "This is why I am here now, to ask you to be extra alert. We are working on the investigation. This is very new. We are trying to find a balance between protecting the children and ensuring we do not alert the bad guys. Do you understand?"

Lisa was nodding and dabbing her eyes with a tissue. "Can I call my husband to come home and talk to you too?"

Jeanne sat up straight. "I would rather you did not do that Lisa."

Lisa looked in Jeanne's eyes, she was searching for what Jeanne wasn't telling her. Lisa didn't know if it was because she was scared, or because Jeanne eyes truly looked almost other-worldly. "You have remarkable eyes. You are scaring me. Please tell me why you don't want me to call Mathew."

Jeanne tried to relax her focus on Lisa and said, "We have a felony arrest warrant on your husband. If he comes home now, I will have to arrest him. I don't want that happening around Jamie."

Lisa drew back and was unable to hide her shock. "There must be some mistake. Mathew is a wonderful person. A wonderful father. What do you think he did?" She was standing now. She looked angry and afraid.

Jeanne stood too. "He will be arrested for several murders."

Lisa started to sway and her eyelids were fluttering. Jeanne knew she was going to faint. She guided Lisa back to the couch and waited. Lisa stared at her, "That can't be the Mathew I know." Jeanne said nothing.

Jeanne saw a copy of the newspaper on the coffee table and asked, "Did you read that?"

Lisa looked at the paper and then back at Jeanne, "Mathew has something to do with that?" Jeanne hoped she hadn't said too much. She knew Core was in so deep, Roger would understand her telling Lisa this much.

Out of the corner of her eye Jeanne saw an SUV pull up behind her vehicle. Three men were inside, and they were looking at the house. Jeanne saw the back door open and the man exiting pull a gun against his leg for cover. Jeanne looked at Lisa, "You have to trust me. I don't know who is coming here right now, but they are armed. Go to Jamie's room. Do not leave until I get you."

Lisa looked out the window. She saw two men going toward the back of the house and one man walking up the walk toward the front. "What are you going to do?"

Jeanne pushed her, "Go. Stay quiet, no matter what."

Lisa ran down the hall. Jeanne checked her weapon and moved her extra clip from her boot to her waistband. She ran to the kitchen and put every knife she could find in a row on the island counter top. She positioned herself in the center hall where she had a view of the front door through a foyer mirror and a view of the back door directly to her left side. The knob on the back door was turning. The knob on the front door was turning. She was within reach of the knives.

The back door opened, and Jeanne shot. The front door opened. Jeanne shot. Two shots, two kills. She heard a noise to her left, and a second man was coming through the back door. He fired and missed. Jeanne fired and killed him. Another SUV was pulling up front. Jeanne went to the living room window and shot them both before they got to the house. Her car was totally blocked.

Jeanne screamed to Lisa, "Lisa! You and Jamie come here now. Hurry!" They both ran out of the bedroom, and Jeanne said, "Lisa, we have to get out of here. We need to take your car. Where are the keys?" Lisa was shaking so badly she could hardly point. Jeanne saw them on the counter, "These?" Lisa nodded. Jeanne said, "Cover Jamie's eyes and follow me." Jeanne pulled the body of the man out of the back doorway and ushered Lisa and Jamie to their SUV. She pulled into the alley and saw a black SUV at the far end idling. The SUV started to head toward them. Jeanne blasted through the alley scattering gravel and fueling a growing dust cloud. She turned onto the main street. The SUV was closing in on them.

Jeanne told Lisa and Jamie to put on their seat belts. They were going to see what the car could do. Jeanne was fairly familiar with the side streets and knew she had to avoid the congestion of town. She had to make a decision fast. She didn't want them trapped in traffic. That could endanger even more people. She decided to make a run for Jeremiah's and take them to Mambos.

Jeanne temporarily lost the SUV in her maneuverings and headed for the bridge to Slidell. The SUV had a full tank of gas, and Jeanne was pushing eighty miles per hour. Where the hell were the cops? They should be pulling her over. Jeanne kept watching her rear view mirror. A high spot on the bridge coming up would let her see farther behind her. They would be exposed too. When she reached that point on the bridge, she could see the SUV weaving through traffic behind her. She knew they must have seen her too. She knew she had at least two advantages. Someone had souped up Lisa's SUV; Jeanne could feel the unused power and Jeanne knew the area well. They had a chance.

Traffic on the bridge was light, and Jeanne was sure she remembered a back way Jeremiah had shown her to where Patterson had taken her to the swamp. By land it was only a few blocks from Jeremiah. She really didn't want to lead these guys to his house. Jeanne floored it and yelled to Lisa, "Do you have your phone? Mine is in my vehicle."

Lisa was crying, "Mine is in my purse at the house!"

Jeanne said, "I can't reach over and hold your hand, but I want you to pretend that is what I'm doing. We are going to be fine. I will protect you. These men will not harm you or Jamie on my watch." Jeanne set her jaw and floored it. After about three minutes of over one hundred miles per hour Jeanne yelled, "Brace yourselves, we are going to slow down fast and take a corner up here."

Jamie was in the back seat and made her first comment, "You are breaking several traffic laws that even I know of."

Lisa said, "Jamie! She is saving us from bad men!"

Jamie scrunched her mouth, "Just sayin'."

The SUV took the turn pushing the vehicle's limits. For a brief moment Jeanne was afraid they would flip. She sped down the dirt road and yelled. "We're turning again, hang on."

Lisa yelled, "There's no road!" As soon as she said that she saw a barely visible dirt lane on the left. Jeanne turned into it, drove for about two minutes, and came to a dead stop at the edge of the swamp.

Jeanne said, "Quick! Get out of the car and run to those tall weeds on the right. I'll be there in one minute." Jeanne watched as Lisa and Jamie began to run for the weeds. She gunned the SUV and drove it into the swamp. She crawled out of the driver's window and joined Lisa and Jamie in the weeds. She hugged each of them and said, "They will follow those tracks, we have to hurry, follow me." Jeanne walked carefully on the soggy marsh ground. As they made their way through she explained that their tracks would be harder to follow because the water in the soil would soon wash over their prints.

Jeanne heard their motor a distance behind them. She figured they would waste a few minutes looking at the sinking SUV. She whispered, "We are almost there, hurry." They reached the edge of Jeremiah's property, and Jeanne could see the boat was gone. Her heart sank, and then she remembered the tunnel. She motioned for Lisa and Jamie to follow her to the shed. When they were in the shed, Jeanne could see through the small window, the heads of three men, walking toward them still in the marsh grasses. They were much closer than she thought.

Jeanne looked at Lisa and put her hand on Lisa's arm. "There is a tunnel through that door that is safe. There are lanterns you can turn on when you get to the bottom of the stairs. Stay there until I come for you. Do you understand?" Lisa nodded and opened the door. Jeanne watched them descend the stairs and turn the lantern on. She closed the door and ran into the marsh grasses toward her prey.

＊ ＊ ＊

Everyone had returned to the Star Ship except Jeanne. After about thirty minutes Thor looked at his watch and looked at Simon, "What names did Jeanne take? Did she take Core's kid?" Pablo turned from the computer screen to hear the answer.

Simon said, "I don't know. I turned around, and she was gone."

Pablo dialed Jeanne's phone. No answer. Todd had entered the room, and Pablo asked him, "Was

Core's kid on your list?" Todd shook his head and grabbed an apple from the counter.

Thor looked at Simon, "Give me Core's address. I'm going over there."

Pablo stood, "I'm going with you."

They made their way past the National Guard barricades by showing their ID's and Thor's screaming. When they finally crossed Canal Street Thor said, "We have really screwed up this city." Ordinarily Pablo would find Thor's temperament abrasive and excessive. Right now he was grateful. Pablo was consulting his map and giving directions. They turned on Core's street and were met with flashing blue lights and NOPD officers. An officer attempted to stop their SUV, and Thor yelled, "FBI, Can't you read a badge? Get out of my way!" Pablo had jumped out of the vehicle and was running to the house. He held his badge up and yelled "FBI" to everyone he passed. He saw two dead men in the front yard, shot. He pushed his way through the front door to find another body. He yelled for PD to exit the building. He went toward the kitchen and saw two more men, shot.

Thor was standing next to him, his chest heaving, his eyes darting about the scene. His gaze landed on the row of knives on the island counter. Jeanne's car was out front. Pablo said, "Either they took her, or she has the mom and the kid in another vehicle."

Thor pointed to the row of knives, "She saw them coming. And she still has ammo or these wouldn't be here. If she still has ammo, there was nobody left to shoot. I'm betting she's got the wife and kid."

Pablo stared at Thor, "You're right." He ran out the back door and yelled back, "Lisa's SUV is gone! We have a tracker on it!"

Pablo pulled up the GPS and saw that Lisa's car was out by Jeremiah's. He looked at Thor, "I bet she is taking them to Mambo's."

Thor shook his head, "Why the hell would she do that? Take them to a swamp when half the city is crawling with law enforcement?"

Pablo's mind was racing, "She had to have a reason. Maybe someone was chasing her? The traffic? She feels safe there."

Thor called Simon and told him to bring Nelson to Core's house and secure the sight. "Local PD is walking all over everything. We have to leave. There are five dead men here. The wife and kid are missing. So is Jeanne. We think Jeanne has them and is heading to that Voodoo lady's place." Thor snapped his phone shut.

Simon stared at his phone, "What? Why would she do that?" The line was dead. Simon looked at Todd, "We're off to Core's house. Been a shooting and maybe abduction."

"Did someone take Jeanne?"

"We don't know what has happened. Jeanne, the wife, and the kid are gone. Five men shot. You drive. I'll bring Roger up to date."

Roger closed his eyes for a brief moment and said a prayer for Jeanne's safety. Thor and Pablo were on their way to help. Jeanne was good. It was out of his hands.

Mathew had promised lunch to Lisa and Jamie. He wanted to spend time with them and find some way to alert Lisa to be extra vigilant about Jamie. Maybe he could just tell her he heard about a pedophile club in New Orleans. He'd think of something. What he *needed* to be doing was finding out where his guns were. He only had five hours before Manio's men expected delivery. He was sure they had heard the news about the raid. He was also sure they didn't care. They wanted their guns. They had paid for them. Mathew had to figure this out.

He abruptly stopped his car at the end of the block. What was happening at his house? Mathew felt fear for the first time in years. His mind was racing, he thought he would puke. He slowly rolled his SUV past the house. He could see the bodies of two men lying on his front lawn and one up by the door. He slowed to almost a stop and saw Lisa's car was gone. Maybe they were okay? Maybe the cops had actually saved them? He rolled a little farther down the street and stopped where a young officer was leaning against his patrol car.

Mathew asked, "I live in this neighborhood. What happened back there?"

The young officer said, "All I heard was some lady and her kid were abducted. FBI guy said some pedophile bunch or something." Mathew's jaw set. He pulled away and headed toward the country house address he had from Tourey's desk. Patterson. The irony wasn't lost on Mathew. His mind kept repeating, it's my fault. It's my fault.

When he reached the country house, he parked right in front. He didn't see Lisa's car anywhere. He walked up to the door and picked the lock. Inside he heard a television and saw the feet of someone in a recliner. Their back was to him. He walked up quietly and saw Patterson was sleeping. Mathew lifted the remote and shut off the television. He walked around the chair, stood directly in front of Patterson, and shot his left arm.

Patterson screamed, saw Mathew, and started crying. He grabbed his arm and with terror etched on his face asked, "What the hell did you shoot me for?"

Mathew answered very quietly, "Where's my daughter? Where's my wife?"

Patterson shook his head like he was shaking water from his ears. "What? I have no idea where your daughter is."

Mathew shot his right knee. Patterson screamed like he was on fire. "I don't know. I swear. We don't take kids from our own cities. It's a *rule*." Blood was covering Patterson's clothes and hands. He held his hand up like he couldn't believe he was looking at his own blood.

Mathew shot Patterson's left ear. Patterson screamed and began grabbing his body everywhere.

Mathew whispered, "I can shoot about seven more body parts before you bleed out. So far none of these is life threatening. Who has my address? Where did that sick video go?"

Patterson sobbed so hard he could hardly be understood. "All over the country. I don't know who picked her. That's one of the *rules*."

Mathew's phone rang. It was Roger. Mathew answered, "Yeah." He was holding his gun on Patterson and trying to decide where to shoot him next.

Roger said, "I believe one of my agents has your wife and daughter. I think there was a cartel abduction attempt. I want you to know I do not have them in my custody yet. My agent has removed them from the danger sight, but we have not had contact with her. I will keep you posted."

Mathew snapped his phone shut. Roger had said 'her'. Mathew guessed she would have taken them to the tunnel by the swamp if they were not in the city. He looked at Patterson, "Well, I have some good news and some bad news."

Patterson stared at him, shaking so violently his glasses had fallen off from his face.

Mathew said, "The good news is I believe you. The bad news is it doesn't matter. That's *my rule*."

Mathew shot him in the groin. He watched him double over in agony and shot the back of his head at the base of his spinal cord. He wasn't dead yet. It would take about twenty minutes. It would be an excruciating death. Mathew left the mansion without closing the door and headed toward Jeremiah's.

CHAPTER 37

Thor and Pablo saw the deep tire tracks in the turn before Jeremiah's. Thor twisted the wheel at the last minute and said, "She was movin'. Look how deep these tracks are. She didn't want whoever was chasing her to find Jeremiah's place."

Pablo was nearly out of his mind when they reached the end of the drive and saw Lisa's SUV in the swamp. Another SUV was parked at the marsh edge and was empty. Thor saw trampled grasses heading toward Jeremiah's. "Stay in the car, we're movin'."

They raced back down the drive and nearly collided with a truck when they reached the road. Thor stood on the throttle until they saw Jeremiah's drive. They nearly flipped the vehicle turning in. Pablo yelled, "I don't see anyone."

Thor yelled, "The boat is gone." They heard a gunshot from the six foot tall marsh grasses.

Pablo jumped from their vehicle and yelled, "FBI. Cease firing!" He was shot in the shoulder. Another bullet passed his face and plowed through the gravel next to him.

Thor yelled, "Get down," as he tackled Pablo. "Get in those grasses. How bad are you hurt?"

Pablo answered, "I feel it."

Roger, Paul, and John climbed up the boarding steps to the jet. They had decided a meeting on the jet was the most secure place for the Director. When they entered the cabin, Roger thought the Director looked ten years older than the day before. They all shook hands and the Director motioned them to take a seat.

The Director handed them each a stack of about twenty pages. "Ellen has boiled down our problems to these transmissions, for now. You can't imagine the number of communications being scrutinized already." He was shaking his head. "We couldn't possibly do this without her help. She just told me she is heading to some swamp to help Jeanne. Does that make sense to you?" The Director was talking to Roger.

Roger told him about the abduction attempt of Mathew Core's wife and daughter. He told the Director they believed the woman and child were with Jeanne. Roger expressed his concern about the amount of force the abductors were willing to use. The Director shuffled his pages. "Item seventeen on page twenty." They all flipped to that page. Roger whistled. "*The Manio Cartel?* We already have the involvement of the Zelez Cartel for Friday. "

The Director said, "Read the entire conversation."

When they were through reading, Roger asked, "Do I understand this right? Lisa and Jamie Core were kidnapped for insurance to get this deal done? He sent eight guys? Talk about overkill. Jesse Manio was promised safe delivery to twenty-six U.S. cities, and he expects the weapons available to him by five o'clock today? How can Core do that? Manio is threatening blood baths in fifteen major U.S. cities tonight if he doesn't get his guns? He obviously was one side of the deal for today."

The Director rubbed his neck, "It gets worse. Look who made the first set of calls at the time of the raid."

John said, "We have the prisoner from the target building at the port calling Core. Core calling Thornton. Thornton calling *Thomas Fenley*. Shit."

The Director said, "Keep going."

John continued, "Fenley called *Manio?* Manio called someone in Algiers, who called someone in London, who called someone in Yemen."

Paul couldn't keep silent any longer. "What is happening?"

John answered, "Algiers is diamonds, drugs and oil. London is oil and diamonds, Yemen is weapons and manpower. It appears old enemies are now strange bedfellows."

The Director nodded and focused on Roger, "The call Mathew Core received from Thornton followed a call Thornton had received from Thomas Fenley."

John asked, "What call are we talking about now?"

The Director answered, "A hit was placed on Roger and Paul this afternoon. It was contracted to Core. Core called and warned Roger."

John stood and paced, "I knew about the hit call. I am starting to confuse the good guys and the bad guys. Why would Core warn Roger?"

Roger answered, "Core says he wants to trade information for his and his family's safety." Roger looked at John, "Who is Thomas Fenley?"

John answered, "Oil and diamonds. OSI thinks he's the fixer for the top one percent of the top one percent. Never been able to nail him. He's like a ghost. If oil needs a government dismantled, they call Fenley. CIA has him in their crosshairs on a regular basis, and he vaporizes away. I am working on him with OSI."

The Director said, "Ellen is keeping me updated. When I have something important, I will fly here again. I think it is important we keep our communications as private as possible. I'm sorry I've been hogging all of Ellen's time. She told me the other angels helped with the community sweep this morning. My reports indicate several cities are asking for authority to copy you on this."

Roger asked the obvious question, "How do we handle this threat of Manio's. Blood baths in fifteen cities?"

The Director looked at Roger, "I have no idea. We have four hours before his delivery deadline. A little good news, we have Jason Sims again. He's doing a little explaining to CIA right now." That was probably the understatement of the day.

Roger looked at the Director, "I think we can assume that our communication sting cover will be blown any time now. Too many people had to be involved for people like Fenley and Thornton not to get wind. I may want to use that to our advantage. We will want them to think they are in the clear. If I can put something together I am going to call you directly and I am assuming you will pass what I say on to Thornton. He may find out about the call anyway based on his sources. We need this to look legit."

The Director nodded slowly, "If I get a call like that from you I think I will ask Ellen to find a way for us to communicate easier than me flying here. Just to make sure I am following your plan."

Roger said, "Perfect. We may be able to spin this our way without Thornton and Fenley realizing it."

* * *

Roger, Paul, and John were in the SUV driving back to the city. There wasn't a lot of talking. Paul and John were reading the papers the Director had given them. Roger was driving and looked in the mirror to the back seat at John, "You have a pensive look on your face."

"Pensive? What kind of word is that? If I look like I'm scared shitless, that I would understand. How is your *orchestra* rehearsal coming, by the way?"

Roger answered, "The percussion section showed up."

Mathew Core pulled up in front of Jeremiah's house. His SUV was hidden from view of anyone in the back. He heard a gunshot and saw Pablo was running toward the marsh grasses holding his shoulder. He could see Thor heading into the grasses from the other direction. The boat was gone. He knew Jeanne thought highly of Mambo. She might have taken Lisa and Jamie there. He saw a man coming up behind Pablo in the tall grass. Mathew took aim and fired. The man fell. He saw Pablo look around, but he didn't change the direction of his assault.

Jeanne had waited silently in the tall grass as one of her attackers crept forward. She stabbed him in the chest, retrieved her knife and stepped over his body. Like a lioness she crouched for her next attacker. She saw him through the reeds aiming his weapon. Jeanne made a noise to draw his attention and landed her kill shot as he turned to face her.

Mathew went into Jeremiah's house, moved the kitchen chairs, and lifted the trap door to the tunnel. He could see there was a light on. When he got to the bottom step he yelled, "Lisa? It's okay it's me." Mathew heard the sound of someone running toward him. He aimed his gun in the darkness, and then saw Jamie's face.

"Daddy!" Jamie was hugging Mathew's hips and crying. "Daddy, we are so scared." Mathew could feel her little body shaking. Hiding in a dirty stone tunnel. Jamie pulled away, her big eyes searching his face, "Daddy, why are you holding a gun?"

Lisa had run up behind Jamie, and wrapped her arms around Jamie's chest. Lisa pulled her back against her body. Mathew and Lisa just stared at each other. Lisa could barely speak, her throat felt closed, and she could hardly breathe. She swallowed, "It's all true isn't it?" Tears streamed down her cheeks.

Mathew took a deep breath, "Lisa, I'll explain everything someday. Right now you need to stay with the FBI. I have to make some things right." Mathew looked at Jamie and touched her hair. She turned and buried her head deep in Lisa's waist. Mathew said, "I love you both."

Mathew and Lisa heard Jeanne yell from the other side of the tunnel, "All clear, Lisa."

Lisa shoved Mathew's hand from Jamie. Her eyes kept searching his, "Who are you?"

"I don't know anymore." Mathew turned and left.

The Shallow End Gals...Book 2
List of Characters
FBI

Supervisory Special Agent Roger Dance, Senior FBI "lead" on case

Supervisory Special Agent Paul Casey, number 2 FBI Agent on case

Supervisory Special Agent Dan Thor, Indy Senior Agent...involved with Patterson arrest

Special Agent Ray Davis, FBI Computer tech

Special Agent Todd Nelson, arresting officer of William Patterson in Book One, team member Book Two

Supervisory Special Agent Simon Frost, Senior agent transfer from NY Fraud Division

Special Agent Pablo Manigat, New agent transfer from New York, brother of Jeanne

Supervisory Special Agent Frank Mass, Senior Agent in New Orleans office

Special Agent Jeanne Manigat, sister of Pablo and victim of Devon and Patterson in New Orleans

Supervisory Special Agent Jim Spelling, based out of Virginia

List of friends *not* approved by Mom

Attorney James Devon, serial rapist and murderer convicted and jailed, escaped...alias Attorney Michael Parker

William Patterson, convicted embezzler, child molester, escaped…alias Bernard Jacobs

Mathew Core, the Fixer, does work for CIA and DOD, started own side business

Jason Sims, Ex CIA computer genius, in business with Mathew Core

Daniel Warren, "double" that replaced Devon in jail

Guy Johnson, "Double" that replaced Patterson in jail

Mark Mills, sniper that works for Mathew Core

Thomas Fenley, works within DC inner circles is known world wide

William "Carl" Thornton, Deputy Director FBI

Senator Rolland Kenny (Retired), friend of Patterson

Theodore Chain, Gallery Owner

Interesting characters

Tourey Waknem, CIA Undercover, native N.O.

Judge Ashley Tait, had been a victim of Devon in Book 1

Mambo, Voodoo Queen that lives by Honey Island, NOLA

Jeremiah Dumaine, old swamp man

Alan Dumaine, Jeremiah's nephew

Adele Brown, "Other woman", found in swamp by Jeremiah

Jerome Brown, Adele Brown's son

Lisa Core, Mathew Core's wife

Jamie Core, Mathew Core's daughter

"Spicey", Sadie Corbin, self-proclaimed psychic in New Orleans
Sasha, Spicey's friend and co-worker
Wilma Abrams, cleaning lady for Patterson
George Fetter, William Patterson's gay encounter, works at Gallery
John Barry, retired CIA, now OSI (Office of Special Investigations)
Detective Johnson, NOPD Homicide
Officer Demiere NOPD
Dusty, portrait Artist
Scotty, Bartender at Mickey's
Rebecca and Amy, bank tellers captured by Devon
Ponytail, a person of interest
Kim, Angel Vicki's daughter

Angels

Al, Angel that looks like Al Roker, in charge of Weather
Ellen, Angel Trainer that looks like Ellen DeGeneres
Betty, Angel Trainer that looks like Betty White
Granny, Top Angel
Linda, Mary, Teresa, Vicki…Angels in training

The Shallow End Gals

Teresa Duncan
Mary Hale
Linda McGregor
Vicki Graybosch
Kimberly Troutman